Outpost

Before writing *Outpost*, Adam Baker worked as a gravedigger and a film projectionist.

ADAM BAKER

Outpost

HODDER &
STOUGHTON

First published in Great Britain in 2011 by Hodder & Stoughton
An Hachette UK company

First published in paperback in 2011

3

Copyright © Adam Baker 2011

B Format ISBN 978 1 444 70904 9
ebook ISBN 978 1 444 70905 6

Typeset in Plantin Light by Palimpsest Book Production Limited,
Falkirk, Stirlingshire

Printed and bound by Clays Ltd, St Ives plc

Hodder & Stoughton policy is to use papers that are natural, renewable and recyclable products and made from wood grown in sustainable forests. The logging and manufacturing processes are expected to conform to the environmental regulations of the country of origin.

Hodder & Stoughton Ltd
338 Euston Road
London NW1 3BH

www.hodder.co.uk

For Helen

THE ARCTIC

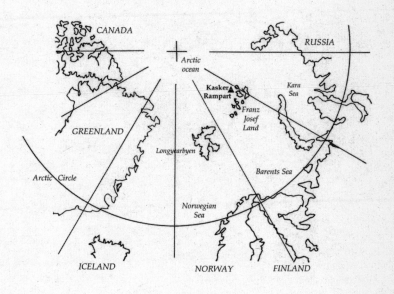

Rampart

The Barents Sea is so cold that if it were still for a day, if it were no longer churned by Arctic winds and ocean currents, it would freeze solid. You could walk across it. Shine a searchlight downward and illuminate the ice-locked dreamscape of the ocean floor. Ridges and canyons, silted wrecks, eyeless organisms that live and die in perpetual darkness.

The Con Amalgam refinery Kasker Rampart is anchored a kilometre from the clustered islands of Franz Josef Land. A skeleton crew of fifteen haunt corridors and accommodation blocks that used to be home to a thousand men. Each day they perform desultory system checks then get stoned, watch TV, or stare out of a porthole at the bleak sun. They retreat into memory, navigate a landscape of nostalgia and loss, kill time until the day Con Amalgam reboot the platform and set the seabed pipeline pumping again.

Part One

Survival

Fat Girl

Jane woke, stretched, and decided to kill herself. If she hadn't found a reason to live by the end of the day she would jump from the rig. It felt good to have a plan.

Jane jogged down service tunnels on C deck. Part of her morning routine. The walls and deck plates were autumnal shades of rust. The pipework throbbed like a heartbeat. Heating, sewage, desalination.

Jane was fat. It often hurt to walk. She struggled to wipe each time she used the bathroom. It was the main reason she took a job on the rig. The gargantuan refinery would be her health farm. Six months sequestered from supermarkets and junk food restaurants. She would return to the world transformed.

Each morning she put on her super-ironic, super-self-hating, *PORN STAR* shirt and shuffled a kilometre-long circuit through the metal labyrinth. She wore Lycra cycle shorts so her thighs didn't chafe. She wore a towel wadded down the back of her shorts to stop perspiration trickling into the crack of her buttocks. Her tracksuit hung wet and heavy.

Jane used fire point fifty-nine as her finish line. A red locker full of breathing apparatus and extinguishers. Lung-bursting effort. The final stretch. She fell against the locker whooping for breath and fumbled for the Stop button of her watch with sweat-slick fingers. Fourteen minutes. She was getting slower. Barely faster than a walking pace. The first time she ran the route she flew fast and strong, but now her knees stung with each heavy footfall. She should rest for a few days, give her body a chance to recuperate, but she knew that if she broke her routine she might not run again.

She usually followed her daily run with calisthenics, punished her disgusting body with a round of sit-ups and squat-thrusts, but this morning she was overcome by a strength-sapping wave of what's-the-point. She returned to her room and stripped out of her wet clothes. She showered. She soaped her barrel belly, kneaded fistfuls of dough-flesh. Her skin, usually mottled pink and white like the inside of a pork pie, blushed red under the heat of the shower jet.

She towelled herself dry. She dusted the creases and folds of her body with talc and sprayed herself head-to-toe with deodorant. She avoided her reflection. She hated mirrors. Sagging breasts. Rolls of blubber as if her flesh were poured from a jug in gloops and folds like thick custard.

She dressed. She clipped her dog-collar in place and headed for the chapel.

The chapel was last in a row of retail units. Three years ago, when the refinery ran at full capacity, Con Amalgam provided a hairdresser, a general store and movie rental. Now the mall units were shuttered and padlocked. The remaining crew still called it Main Street.

Jane unlocked the chapel and hit the lights. The chapel was a white room filled with metal chairs. Coloured wall lamps projected the illusion of stained glass.

She took her cassock from a cupboard and wrestled it on.

She began the service. She blessed empty chairs. She sang along to 'Classic Hymns of Worship'.

She stood at the lectern and read her sermon. She read the same sermon every week. Sometimes she read it in a silly voice. Sometimes she read it backwards. Today she gave up halfway through. She folded each page into a paper plane and flew them

6

across the room. She experimented with different wing designs to see if she could reach the back wall.

'It's a tough job,' the bishop had said, as they sipped sherry in his study. 'You'll be away from home a long time. You'll be mother to a thousand men. Deckhands. Brawlers. A tough crowd.'

'My dad used to be a sailor,' said Jane. 'I can handle rough-necks.' But she couldn't handle irrelevance.

Rampart used to be a busy town. Installation lights burned through the Arctic night as if a chunk of Manhattan broke loose and floated away. There was a cinema, a gym and a Starbucks. There was even a radio station. Three marshals kept order. There was no booze on the rig but tempers ran high. Long shifts and nowhere to go when they were done. Sometimes fights got out of hand. Marshals zapped the participants with a Taser and let them cool off in a holding cell.

A deckhand job on an Arctic rig was like joining the Foreign Legion. Guys fled bereavement, addiction, all kinds of personal failure. Jane expected to nurse tough men through those midnight hours of heartbreak and loss. Let them talk it out in the privacy of the chapel. Send them home fixed and whole. Instead she found twilight and dereliction.

'I can't understand why they sent you here,' shouted Punch, as he helped Jane lift her kit-bag from the supply chopper.

Gareth Punch. Ginger goatee. Short and slight. Mid-twenties.

'I suppose your Church didn't hear the place got moth-balled.' They ran from a typhoon of rotor-wash as the Sikorsky took off. 'Rampart hasn't been pumping for a year. The Kasker field is running dry. All the easy oil got sucked. Sooner or later the rig will get redeployed someplace like the Gulf of Mexico or sold to India for scrap. Dumb bureaucracy. Same wherever you go. Anyway. Hello.' He shook Jane's hand. 'Gary Punch. I'm the chef.'

He showed Jane to the accommodation block. 'This is your

room,' he said, 'but there are plenty of others if you want to switch. You have this entire block to yourself. Most of the crewmen meet for dinner in the canteen at seven. Other than that, people keep to themselves. Better get used to your own company, because this place is a ghost town.'

Jane threw her cassock over a chair. She took a chocolate bar from a stash hidden behind a big Bible in the vestry cupboard. She perched on the altar and ate. She was useless, alone and unloved.

She headed back to her room. It was a long journey down white corridors that receded to vanishing point. The refinery was so big some guys used bicycles to get around. The infirmary had a stretcher-car like a golf buggy. It was kept chained to stop the crew taking joyrides.

She walked the route out of habit, but stopped by an exterior door when it occurred to her there was no reason to return to her room. Earlier that morning she had resolved to jump from the rig. Why wait until nightfall?

She spun the hatch wheel and stepped into a quilted airlock.

WARNING

EXTREME COLD

SAFETY CLOTHING AND TWO-MAN PROTOCOL

AT ALL TIMES

She heaved open the exterior door and the sudden shock of cold sucked breath from her body. Vicious wind-chill. Minus thirty and no coat. Her skin burned.

Jane stepped out on to a walkway. Boot clang. Bleak daylight. A vast machine-scape. Massive storage tanks. Gantries, cross-beams and pipework dripped ice. A steel archipelago. One of the largest floating structures on earth.

She leaned over a railing. She touched the iced metal for a moment then snatched her hand away like it had been scorched on a stove. She looked down. Far below, hidden by mist, was the sea. She could hear water lapping between the great floatation legs of the refinery. If she climbed the railing and allowed herself to topple forward it would be over in an instant. A hundred-metre drop through white vapour. The impact would smash her bones as if she hit concrete. Quick extinction, like an Off switch.

She put one foot on the railing and willed herself to jump. She had been outside less than a minute, but was shivering as if in an epileptic seizure. Her vision blurred. She wanted to jump but couldn't do it. Muscle lock. Too scared of falling. Too scared of pain. She went back inside and stood beneath a corridor heat vent. She cursed her cowardice. She plucked a frozen tear from her cheek and watched the little jewel liquefy between her fingers.

Plan B: retreat to her room and swallow a fatal overdose of painkillers.

Jane had been collecting painkillers for the past couple of months. Each time she bought deodorant or gum from the table in the canteen she took a packet of paracetamol. The pills were in a bag beneath her bed.

She stopped at the canteen kitchen to collect a tub of ice cream. The steel door of the refrigerator rippled her face like a funhouse mirror.

Accommodation Block Three. Long passageways. Empty stairwells.

Each crew member was assigned a small cell with a bed and a chair. They got a clothes locker, a washstand cubicle and a metal toilet. A scratched Perspex porthole allowed Jane a view of the basalt cliffs and jagged crags of Franz Josef Land. Desolate, lunar terrain. Volcanic crags dusted with snow. In a few weeks the sun would set and the long Arctic night would begin.

'Hi, honey. I'm home.'

She stripped, sat on the bed and popped pills from their foil strips. She piled the tablets on the blanket until they formed a little white mound. She mashed the pills into a tub of Cookie Dough. She wanted to write a note but couldn't think what to say.

She opened her laptop. She wanted to hear a familiar voice. She selected an old message from home. A cam clip. Jane's sister, sitting in a sunlit room. Jane clicked the Play arrow.

'Hi, Janey. How are things at the top of the world? Just wanted to say hello and tell you how proud we are of what you are doing. Can't imagine what it must be like up there. It must be tough looking after all those guys. Or maybe you are enjoying a bit of male attention. Fighting them off with a chair. Anyway, Mum sends her love . . .'

If she were home, she might pick up the phone and reach out for help. But the only contact with the mainland was the microwave link in the installation manager's office. An open line with a stilted, two-second delay.

Jane scooped pills and ice cream, and sucked the spoon clean. Bitter. She grimaced. She scooped more painkillers. She didn't want to lose consciousness before she ate enough pills to kill herself outright. She didn't want to wake. For once in her life, she would do the job right.

Ice cream. A sweet kiss goodnight. It would be a meek, apologetic death. She consoled herself with the thought that, in these final moments, she would be communing with countless life-long losers who extinguished the world with a glass of Chablis and a bellyful of painkillers.

She was about to swallow a third mouthful of tablets when there was a knock at the door. She quickly shut off her laptop. A second knock. Must be Punch. No one else knew where to find her.

'Hello? Reverend Blanc? Are you in there?'

Jane sat still as she could.

'Reverend?'

Jane wondered if it might be easier to answer the door and get rid of him. Claim she was ill. Tell him to come back later. Much later.

Punch tried to open the door but it was locked from the inside by a plastic dead bolt like a toilet cubicle.

'Reverend? Hello?'

Jane spat pills and ice cream into a tissue. She put on a dressing gown and opened the door.

Punch in a mad, Hawaiian shirt.

'Sorry. Sleeping.'

'Rawlins sent me to get you. He wants to talk to everyone in the canteen right away.'

Jane sagged against the doorframe for support.

'Reverend? Are you okay?'

Jane bent double and vomited over his shoes.

Punch helped Jane to her feet. He saw the pill packets on her bunk.

'Oh, Christ.'

He helped Jane crouch over the toilet bowl. She vomited ice cream, then she vomited chocolate, then she vomited green stuff she didn't recognise. She sat panting on the floor.

Punch counted the tablets to see how many she had swallowed.

'I suppose you'll be all right,' he said. 'We should get you to Medical.'

'Fuck that,' said Jane.

Punch rinsed his shoes under the tap.

'Promise you won't tell anyone,' she said.

'Let's get you up.'

He helped Jane to her feet. He waited in the corridor while she dressed.

'How do I look?' she asked.

'Wipe your eyes.'

'What does Rawlins want?'

'I don't know, but it sounded serious.'

Outbreak

Crewmen sat in a semicircle round the plasma TV in the canteen. Roughnecks. Bearded frontiersmen. Oil trash. They watched BBC News bounced by Norsat in geostationary orbit over Greenland.

Ridgeback armoured cars parked outside hospitals. Gas-masked soldiers manning checkpoints and barricades. Desert-yellow vehicles blocking each high street like an occupying army.

Helicopter footage of gridlocked traffic. Motorways at a standstill. Family cars jammed with suitcases, furniture lashed to the roof.

A food riot. Supply trucks stormed by refugees. Rifle butts. Warning shots. Sky News correspondent in a flak jacket:

'...*approached the tent city and were literally overrun by hundreds of desperate families that haven't eaten for days. The troops are struggling to contain the situation, but as you can see* ...'

'Martial law, of sorts,' explained Rawlins, the installation manager. 'Some kind of outbreak.'

Rawlins was a burly guy with a white Santa Claus beard. His badges of office: a Con Amalgam cap, Con Amalgam insulated mug, and a big bunch of keys clipped to his belt.

'When the fuck did this happen?' asked Nail, a diver with a bald head and bushy lumberjack beard. A huge man. Six-six. Massive biceps.

'It's been building up for a couple of months. You lot were watching the Cartoon Network and blowing your wages on fucking PokerStars.'

'Terrorists?'

'No idea.'

'Did they mention Manchester?'

'I honestly can't tell you what on earth is going on.'

'The supply ship is still coming, yeah?'

'That's why I asked you here. The ship is coming a month early. That's the big news. Seven days, then we are out of here. Total evacuation. Pack our stuff and power down.'

'We still get paid for a full rotation, right?'

'That's the least of your worries. The ship is due on Sunday morning. In the meantime if any of you want to use the ship-to-shore, if you're worried about relatives, then let me know. You can use my office. The signal is shaky but you are welcome to try.'

Punch distributed coffee and sandwiches. The crew watched TV in silence. They wanted to see their home towns. Birmingham. Glasgow. York. Jane wanted to hear about Cheltenham but the news channels were running the same images over and over. Some kind of bloody plague was sweeping through the cities. Was it a bio-weapon? A spontaneous mutation? Nobody knew. Most of the footage was shaky phone clips mailed by viewers. Armed police suppressed supermarket riots. Gangs fortified tower blocks against intruders, declared them a city state. The Prime Minister called for courage, called on God. Studio pundits discussed Ebola, AIDS, haemorrhagic fever.

Jane joined Punch in the canteen kitchen and helped grate cheese. A steel room. Counters, fryers, dishwashers and mixers. Smell of fresh bread.

'How are you feeling?' asked Punch.

'Okay,' said Jane.

'Want to talk about it?'

'Not really.'

'All fucked up.'

'The TV? I've seen snatches these past few days. I've been trying not to think about it.'

'My mother lives in Cardiff,' said Punch.

'The centre?'

'Riverside.'

They had glimpsed images of Cardiff on the news. Part of the town centre was burning. A department store caught alight and the fire spread building to building. Black smoke over the city rooftops. A church spire crumbled in a cascade of rubble dust. There were no fire crews left to respond.

'She'll be fine,' said Jane. 'People know what to do in this kind of situation. Fill the larder, lock the front door and stay out of trouble.'

'I should be there.'

'Three days to Narvik. Four hours to Birmingham International.'

'Then what? Doesn't exactly look like the trains are running.'

'Steal a bike. Hitch a ride. You'll find a way.'

'Do you have a family?' he asked.

'My mother and sister live in Bristol.'

'Do you think they are okay?'

'You saw that riot on TV. Things are getting tooth and claw. My dad is long gone. They have no one to fight for them.'

'Come to Cardiff. We have a spare room.'

'I couldn't.'

'Seriously. We are going to touch down in a war zone. You'll need somewhere to go.'

Punch lived in a storeroom at the back of the kitchen. He dragged a couple of kit-bags from beneath his bunk and began to pack. Jane sat on a chair in the corner and sipped black coffee.

Clothes on the floor. Jeans so narrow Jane wouldn't be able to pull them past her ankles.

'It seems a bit premature,' said Punch. He stripped out of chef's whites and a blue apron. 'I'll probably have to unpack half this stuff during the week. But I just want to be gone.'

'You like comics?' asked Jane. Posters of Batgirl, Ghost Rider, Spawn.

'That's why I'm here. Six months, no distractions. I was going to draw my masterpiece. Blast my way to the big-time. Brought my inks. Brought my board.'

'No joy?'

'I pissed away the time. Thing is, what does a hero look like these days? Muscles and Lycra? Life isn't a contest of strength any more. Jobs, banks, taxes. Boring social reality. You can't solve anything with a fist. Those years are long gone.'

'Don't feel bad. Pretty much everyone on this platform is in a holding pattern.'

'Sure you're okay?'

'I may switch rooms later. All that despair. The smell hangs around like cigarette smoke.'

Jane picked a new room and unpacked her stuff. The room was identical to the last but it still felt like a change. She flushed her remaining painkillers. She had psyched herself for suicide, but the moment for action had passed.

She sat on the bed. Her life was one lonely room after another.

A double beep from the wall speaker in the corridor outside. A Tannoy announcement broadcast throughout the refinery, echoing down empty passageways, gently stirring motes of dust in distant rooms.

'Reverend Blanc, please come to the manager's office right away.'

Rawlins's office was at the top of the administration block. A wide, Plexiglas window gave him a view of the upper deck of the refinery. A vast scaffold city of gantries, girders and distillation tanks lit by a low Arctic sun.

Rawlins ran the installation from his desk. A wall panel showed a plan of the rig dotted with green System OK lights.

Submerged cameras monitored the seabed pipeline, a concrete manifold anchored to the ocean bed.

He sat by the radio. Speakers relayed the hiss and whistle of atmospheric interference.

Jane pulled up a chair.

'Nothing from the mainland?'

'Comes and goes,' said Rawlins. 'I get snatches of music. The occasional ghost voice. Hear that?'

A man, faint and desperate: '*Gelieve te helpen ons. Daar iedereen is? Kan iedereen me horen? Gelieve te helpen ons.*'

'What's that?' asked Jane. 'Swedish? Norwegian?'

'God knows. Some poor bastard. He's out there, somewhere, calling for help. I can hear him, but he can't hear us.'

'This is starting to scare the crap out of me.'

'Look at this,' said Rawlins. He re-angled his desk screen. 'I managed to pull this from the BBC News site a couple of weeks ago.'

He clicked Play.

Police marksmen creeping through a supermarket. Footage shot low to the ground. A reporter crouched behind a checkout.

'. . . *suddenly attacked paramedics and fled the scene. She seems to have taken refuge at the back of the store. Police have cleared the building and are moving in . . .*'

Something glimpsed between the aisles. A figure, creeping, feral.

'*There she is . . .*'

Sudden close-up. A woman's snarling face masked in blood.

Police: '*Put your hands up. Keep your hands where we can see them . . .*'

She lunges. Gunfire. Her chest is ripped open and she is hurled backward into a shelf of coffee jars.

She's still moving. A marksman plants a boot on her chest, cocks his pistol and shoots her in the face.

Rewind. Freeze frame. That bloody, snarling face.

'What the fuck?' said Jane.

'That's what I wanted to talk to you about,' said Rawlins. 'Not here, though. Outside.' He threw Jane an XXXL parka. 'Let's take a walk.'

They descended metal steps that spiralled round one of the rig's four great floatation legs.

Winter was coming. Ice had begun to collect around the refinery legs. Soon Rampart would be sitting on a solid raft of ice. As the days drew short and the temperature dropped further, the sea would freeze and the rig would be joined to the island by an ice-bridge.

Rawlins walked out on to the ice. Jane stayed on the steps. She inspected the vast underbelly of the rig. Acres of frosted pipework and joists.

'So what do you want from me?' asked Jane. She had been aboard the refinery for five months. This was the first time Rawlins had asked to speak to her.

'The microwave link to shore. I was hoping you could draw up a schedule, help the lads book phone time.'

'Reckon they can reach anyone?'

'That's what I'm saying. Navtex is down. Our sat phone is a fucking paperweight. The guys will demand to ring home, and when they do they will probably get no reply. They'll need a sympathetic ear.'

'Use my counselling skills?'

'Yeah. And there's an issue with the ship. Only fair to warn you. I managed to raise London yesterday. The connection lasted about thirty seconds. They told me the *Oslo Star* was on its way. They were picking up a drilling team from Trenkt then heading south for us.'

'Okay.'

'But I tried talking to London. I got nothing. The Con Amalgam office in Hamburg told me Norway is under self-imposed quarantine. All borders closed. Air, land and sea. If that's true, then *Oslo Star* hasn't left the dock.'

'Damn.'

'They've given me executive authority to evacuate.'

'Meaning what?'

'Nice way of saying we are on our own. Get home any way we can.'

'Shit.'

'It'll be fine. There are plenty of other support ships at sea. Hamburg is arranging a substitute vessel. It might take a while, though.'

'When will you tell the men?'

'Must admit I feel a bit of a fool. Telling everyone they are going home. Getting their hopes up.'

'So what did Hamburg say? What's actually happening?'

'Something bad spreading fast. It seems to be global. That's the sum of it. Most radio and TV stations are down. No one knows a thing. It's all just panic and rumour. Marco, our Hamburg contact, says most of the stuff we've seen on the news is recycled footage shot last month. Things have got a lot worse since then. He's says people are leaving the cities for the countryside in case the government firebomb.'

'So what is it? Flu? Smallpox?'

'A virus. That's what he said.'

'What kind?'

'Marco's English is pretty poor. A virus. Some kind of parasite. That's our little secret, okay? The men don't need to know.'

Jane returned to her room. She swapped her sweater for a clerical shirt and dog-collar.

'Get it together,' she told her reflection. 'People need you now.'

Jane headed for the gym.

The gym was monopolised each day by Nail Harper and

his gang of muscle freaks. A redundant dive crew with nothing to do but lift weights and preen in front of the gymnasium wall mirror.

She heard Motörhead as she approached. 'Ace of Spades' echoing down steel corridors.

Nail was sweating his way through a series of barbell curls. He was stripped to the waist. He had a gothic cross tattooed on his back. He stood in front of the wall mirror and watched himself pump. Bull-neck, massive shoulders. Skin stretched taut over veins and tendons. He looked like he was wearing his muscles on the outside.

His gym buddies sat nearby. Gus and Mal. Ivan and Yakov. They took turns to use a leg press.

'How are you lads doing?' shouted Jane.

Nail set the barbell on the floor and turned round. He took his time about it. He looked Jane up and down. He stood over her, towelling sweat from his torso. He glanced at one of his buddies, a signal to turn down the music.

'Come to burn off a few pounds?'

'I'm going to hold a service in the chapel later on.'

'Good for you.'

'I know everyone on this rig tends to stick to their own little group, their own little faction, but maybe we ought to start thinking like a team. You saw the news. We're in this shit together.'

One of his buddies threw him a protein shake. He swigged.

'I've been here all day, every day. If you fuckers want to talk, if you actually give a shit, you can find me any time. We pass in the corridor, you don't even look me in the eye. You think me and my boys are dirt. Get off your high horse, bitch. You contribute zero to this rig. You can't do a damn thing. You can barely tie your shoes. You just sit around all day eating our food. So don't act like I'm the one with my nose in the air.'

He stared down at Jane. There were centrefolds on the walls

around her. Women spreading themselves, women hitching their legs. He was daring her to look. She held his gaze.

'Point taken. Fresh start, all right? The service is at seven. We'd all be glad to see you.'

Jane led prayers.

'Father, protect our loved ones in this hour of darkness. We commit them to your loving grace. Lord, in your mercy, hear our prayer.'

Nail and his gang sat in the back row and watched.

They sang 'Eternal Father Strong to Save', the sailors' hymn.

Jane blessed her small congregation. Rawlins stood and gave the news. The *Oslo Star* hadn't left port but a second ship was on its way. Oil support vessel *Spirit of Endeavour*. It would arrive at nine the following morning but wouldn't stay long. Everyone better be packed and ready to go.

Time to put the rig in hibernation. Rawlins assigned everyone a task.

Jane shut down Main Street. She threw breakers in a wall-mounted fuse box and extinguished the broken neon that blinked and buzzed above each vacant retail unit. Starbucks. Cafe Napoli. Blockbuster. Signage flickered and died.

Jane took a bunch of keys and closed C deck. Punch tagged along.

'Nice prayer,' said Punch. 'I heard a couple of guys say they liked it. Yakov. He's Catholic.'

Each corridor had a series of blast doors set in the ceiling. In the event of an explosion the doors would drop to prevent the spread of fire. Jane twisted a numbered key into the wall at each intersection and a blast door rumbled downward like a portcullis.

'I bet most of them didn't even know we had a chapel.'

'Do you think prayers are ever answered?' asked Punch.

'It helps to voice your fears.'

'It would be nice to think there was a cosmic parent ready to kiss it all better.'

'I wrapped my car round a tree a few years ago,' said Jane. 'They say I was dead for three minutes. I can tell you for sure there is no God, no happy afterworld. In fact that's why I became a priest. It's a short life and people deserve more than work and recreational shopping. They need meaning. A place to belong.'

They stood in the doorway of the stairwell. Jane took a radio from her pocket.

'C deck clear.'

The steady hum of heating fans died away. Somewhere, high above them, Rawlins flicked a bank of isolator switches to Off. The corridor lights were extinguished one by one.

Next morning the crew gathered in the canteen. They brought kit-bags and suitcases. They wore parkas and snowboots. They looked like tourists in a departure lounge.

They watched TV.

Berlin in chaos. Looting. Riot vans and burning cars. The Brandenburg Gate glimpsed through tear gas.

Bilbao docks. Refugees try to climb a mooring rope and board an oil tanker. Sailors blast them with a fire hose.

The White House south lawn. The President ringed by Secret Service armed with assault rifles. '. . . *may God defend us in this dark and difficult hour . . .*' Brief wave from the hatch of Marine One.

Punch found a box of crisps in a kitchen storeroom. He upturned the box and scattered crisp packets across the pool table.

'May as well use them up, folks,' he said. 'A ton of food going to waste.'

Nail and his gang hogged the jukebox.

Rawlins sat by the window.

'They'll be coming from the north-east.'

Time dragged. Punch took a pack of playing cards from his pocket. He shuffled and re-shuffled.

'There it is,' said Rawlins.

They crowded round the window.

'That ship don't look right,' said Nail.

The plastic canteen window was pitted and scratched, scoured by fierce ice storms. The approaching ship was a blur. The crew ran upstairs to the rooftop helipad for a better view. They stood on the big red H and braced their legs against a buffeting wind. A small tug approached from the north.

'*Spirit of Endeavour* my ass,' said one of the men.

'That's a dinghy,' said Punch. 'That's a fucking rubber duck.'

The ship drew close. It looked like a small fishing trawler. The wheelhouse was little bigger than a phone booth. Maybe a couple of bunks below.

'I think some of us might be staying behind,' said Jane.

The List

The tug entered the shadow of the refinery, splintering ice, and docked at the north leg. The tiny vessel bobbed on the swells like a cork. Chugging diesel engine. The crew watched from the helipad railing.

Rawlins met the captain on the docking platform. He caught the mooring rope and helped the captain aboard. They saluted. They shook hands. The captain wore snow gear and carried a shotgun. No one was surprised to see the gun. Most Arctic teams carried protection against polar bears.

Rawlins led the man up steel steps to the habitation levels of the rig. The first mate stayed on the tug. He paced the deck with a shotgun held in the crook of his arm.

The captain was a short man in his fifties. He took off his parka and sat at a canteen table. He kept his gun within reach. Punch put a steaming mug of coffee in front of him.

'Got any food?'

The skipper ate two Snickers bars and started on a third. The Rampart crew stood over him and watched him eat.

'I've got room for four men,' said the captain. 'That's all I can take.'

'Jane. Sian. Upstairs,' said Rawlins.

Sian was the rig administrator. A timid, petite girl in her twenties. She also cut hair.

Rawlins sat the girls in his office and dumped a box of manila personnel files in front of them.

'Work up a shortlist,' he said. 'People we can live without. People who deserve to go. There's a weather front moving in. The captain says he'll stick around for a couple of hours then he wants to be gone.'

'Why me?' asked Jane, daunted suddenly to find herself in a position of responsibility. 'Why do I have to choose?'

'You're a priest. You're impartial. And I better stay downstairs otherwise there'll be a riot.'

Rawlins took his yellow Taser pistol from his desk drawer and checked the charge.

'Let's finish this quickly,' he said. 'The sooner that boat is out of here the better.'

'Christ,' said Sian, when Rawlins was gone. 'We could be deciding if people live or die, you realise that?'

'Let's start a list,' said Jane. 'See if we can narrow it down.'

There was a whiteboard on the wall next to a picture of a tropical beach. Jane bit the cap from a pen and wrote names.

'Okay,' said Jane. 'Who stays for certain? Who can we strike off the list right away?'

She put a cross through FRANK RAWLINS. 'Goes down with the ship. He'd be insulted if we even considered him.'

She put a cross through ELIZABETH RYE. 'The installation needs a doctor. Essential personnel.'

'Says here she has a son,' said Sian.

'Rawlins won't let her go. I guarantee it.'

She crossed out GARETH PUNCH. 'We need a chef.'

'Any fool can flip an egg.'

Jane shook her head. 'Everyone is talking like we will be out of here in a week or two, but truth is we might be stuck a while. We need someone who can manage a kitchen, eke out provisions.'

Jane crossed out three more names. 'Senior ops. Maintenance. Maintenance. We need people who can keep the lights on.'

'Six down.'

'Anything in the files?'

'I can give you two names right away. Rosie Smith and Pete Baxter. Rosie is diabetic. She injects insulin every day. They have a crate of the stuff on ice in medical. We're supposed to feed her sugar or something if she has a fit.'

Jane circled ROSIE SMITH. 'All right. She's on the boat. Pete Baxter?'

'Heart attack four years ago. He takes some kind of blood-thinning medication. I heard he brought his own defibrillator. Keeps it by his bed. I'm astonished they gave him a job.'

Jane circled PETE BAXTER. 'Two more. Maybe we should pull names out of a hat. It might be the easiest way.'

Fox News looped the same footage over and over.

'. . . *may God defend us in this dark and difficult hour . . .*'

The President's sombre wave as he climbs aboard Marine One and flees the White House.

Food riots. Flaming cars. Humvees in the street.

Nail stood, arms folded, in front of the TV. He stood close enough to see the President's face reduced to picture grain and blur.

He turned round.

The captain was sitting in the corner of the canteen. He was hunched over a bowl greedily spooning soup. His shotgun rested on the Formica tabletop easily within reach.

Nail crossed the room and sat next to his gym buddy, Ivan.

'Reckon you could pilot that boat?'

'Little tug like that? Sure,' said Ivan.

'Seriously. You could get it going? Navigate?'

'Yeah. Pretty certain I could.'

'We have to get his gun.'

'He's got his back to the wall. And look at him. He's twitchy. He's watching for someone to make a move.'

'I should go over there,' said Nail. 'Offer him another coffee. I want to see if the safety catch is on.'

26

'We could wait until he's up and walking. Catch him in a stairway, a corridor. It would give us a chance to get close, but we'd have to take his gun.'

'Yeah.'

'What about the first mate?'

'What about him? We'd have a gun.'

'Could you do that? Could you shoot a man?'

'I'd fire a warning shot.'

'But if it came down to it?'

'Then, yeah,' said Nail. 'Him or us, right?'

'Okay. You and me. Gus, Mal, Yakov. You give the signal. We move at once. We do it quick. But we'd have to be on the boat and gone before anyone has a chance to react. Bags and coats ready to go.'

'I'll tell the guys. Go to the kitchen and fix yourself a sandwich. Get some knives while you are in there.'

Rawlins brought the captain to his office. The captain still carried his shotgun like he expected to be jumped any moment. They examined a map of the Arctic.

'They sent us to a pump station in the Kara. The place was deserted. We swung by Severnaya to see how the Russian team were doing but they had cleared out. Norway is closed for business. Don't dare approach. They have a couple of AWACS planes guiding gunboats.'

'Where will you go?'

'We'll catch the current south. Skirt Norway. Skirt Iceland. Western Scotland seems like a good place to ride out doomsday. We'll find an island. Hide ourselves away.'

'So what have you heard?' asked Jane. 'All we have is the television.'

'Dave, my first mate. He saw it for real in Roscoff a month ago. He was sitting in a café eating lunch. Noon. Not much happening. Suddenly people ran in, yelling for the police. There

27

was a woman in the street trying to bite everyone like a rabid dog. She was bleeding.'

'Bleeding?'

'That's what he said. Some soldiers shot her dead. Then they shot everyone she had bitten. They made a big pile and burned the bodies.'

'Oh, my God.'

'Sorry to break it to you folks, but no one is coming to your rescue any time soon. You might have to find your own way home.'

'Christ.'

'Have you picked your men yet?'

'We're working on it.'

'I could do with some food for the trip, and any diesel you can spare.'

'We'll sort you out.'

'I'm going back to the boat,' said the captain. 'The weather is turning. Wind is getting high. Could be force ten when it hits. I'd like to be gone in thirty minutes.'

The captain left.

'Do you have any names for me?' asked Rawlins.

Jane gestured to the board. 'Two names for certain. Bunch more possible.'

Rawlins scanned the list.

'It's an easy choice,' he said. 'You two. Sorry, ladies, but I need skills. You're both surplus to requirements.'

The fuel store. A wide chamber. Punch switched on the lights. He led the captain between racks of fuel cans, oil drums and propane tanks. The captain loaded jerry cans on to a pallet truck. Punch struggled to help.

'So you need food?'

'We're both starved,' said the captain. 'We ate our last tin of beans days ago. We didn't expect to be at sea this long. We need

Nail was holding a diver's serrated knife. He adjusted his grip. Four metres between him and the captain.

'Seriously, guys. The choke on this thing is set for a wide spread. I can put all of you down with a single shot. Drop the fucking knives.'

Yakov inched along the wall like he was getting ready to attack. Shaved head. Cyrillic knuckle tattoos.

Nail shook his head and threw down his knife. They all reluctantly dropped their weapons.

'Kick them over here.'

They kicked their knives into the stairwell.

'Hands on your head. All of you.'

'No hard feelings, all right?' said Nail. 'If you were in our position, you would do the same thing.'

'Grab some cans, fellas. You're going to help me load up.'

They carried fuel cans to the ship and stowed them in the hold. The captain and first mate stood on the transom, shotguns at the ready.

The men reluctantly disembarked and stood on the dock platform.

'Sorry, guys,' said the captain. 'Wish there was room for you all. Now why don't you folks fuck off and let us get going?'

Departure.

Nail and his gang of muscle freaks were nowhere to be seen.

The remaining crew stood on the docking platform and shouted questions to the first mate. Jane watched from the helipad. The mate stood at the prow, shotgun over his shoulder. He kept his answers non-committal, said less than he knew. He watched for any sign the Rampart crew might make another attempt to storm the boat.

The four chosen crewmen climbed aboard. There wasn't room for their luggage so they left it behind. They stood on deck and waved as the tug pulled away. *Spirit of Endeavour.* A little ship

31

on a big ocean. Jane wondered if the boat would reach Scotland. It was a long journey south, but they might make it if they ran ahead of the weather.

The remaining crew retreated to their cabins to unpack.

There was nothing new on TV.

CNN was down.

Sky News was a test card: '*We apologise for the break in transmission. We are currently experiencing technical difficulties. Normal programming will resume shortly.*'

BBC: a haggard newscaster repeated the same advice. Keep calm. Stay off the street. Stay tuned for updates. Jane remembered the young man. He used to present the weather. He used to stand in front of a map and forecast sunny spells and rain. Now he found himself reporting the end of the world.

Punch muted the sound and cued some tunes on the jukebox.

'Hope you feel good,' he told Jane. 'You did something heroic today. You could be on your way home right now.'

'I'm not sure my mother would agree.'

'She'll be all right.'

Jane looked out to sea.

'Check out the cloud bank. There's a weather front moving in. Waves are starting to build.'

'I went aboard with a box of food. It's little more than a rowing-boat. I wouldn't want to be out there right now. Not with six people crammed inside. It'll be touch-and-go. Take a lot of luck for them to reach land.'

'Think we're better off here?'

'How can we know? Did we give our folks a ticket home or send them to die?'

Rawlins led Jane and Sian to an observation bubble on the roof. The bubble was at the edge of the helipad. A circle of windows gave a three-sixty view of the refinery, the sea and the jagged crags of Franz Josef Land.

'Since you two are staying you better make yourselves useful.' He pulled dust sheets from transmission equipment. 'We should have done this days ago.' He pointed to a swivel chair. 'Sit there,' he told Sian. 'Don't touch the sliders.' He powered up a bank of amplifiers. 'A bloke called Wilson used to play DJ after each shift. Had his own little drive-time show. I filled in for a couple of days when he broke his wrist. This kit is designed to broadcast to the rig but if the atmospherics are right we could reach two, three hundred miles.'

'What about the ship-to-shore?'

'Too patchy. I want to try short-wave. Go broad and local. It's a big ocean. We can't be the only people stuck out here.'

'What do I do?' asked Sian, positioning her chair in front of the mike.

'Press to talk. Release to listen.'

'Mayday, mayday. This is Con Amalgam refinery Kasker Rampart hailing any vessel, over.'

No response.

'Mayday, mayday. This is refinery platform Kasker Rampart requesting urgent assistance, over.'

No response.

'Mayday, mayday. This is Kasker Rampart broadcasting to the Arctic rim, is anyone out there, over?'

No sound but the static hiss of a dead channel.

Fragile

The radar in Rawlins's office sounded a collision alarm. Iceberg warning. His desk screen showed a massive object closing in, moving slow.

They watched from the observation bubble. A mountain of ice passing five kilometres distant. A table-berg, a colossal chunk of polar shelf. Ridges and canyons. Blue ice marbled with sediment. A strange hellworld.

'I walked on a berg once,' said Rawlins. 'They fizz and crackle. Trapped air. Sounds like a bonfire.'

'Some big waves down there,' said Jane.

Heavy swells broke against the ice cliffs. Spume and spray.

'Yeah,' said Rawlins. 'Wind speed is way up. There's another storm coming. Line squalls. One cyclone after another until spring.'

'Mayday, mayday. This is Con Amalgam refinery Kasker Rampart hailing any vessel, over.'

Two a.m. Jane's turn at the microphone.

'Mayday, mayday. This is Kasker Rampart broadcasting to the Arctic rim. Do you copy, over?'

Sian unscrewed her Thermos and refilled their cups.

'We're alone out here,' said Sian.

'I don't even want to think about it.'

The upper deck of the rig was floodlit. A storm lashed the refinery. A blizzard wind scoured girders and gantries. The girls watched the swarming ice particles from the eerie silence of their Plexiglas bubble.

Sian put her hand to the window. A thin film of plastic separating her from the lethal hurricane outside. She felt the warm up-draught of the heating vent between her feet and was acutely aware of the refinery's life support systems, the elaborate machinery keeping them alive minute by minute in this implacably hostile environment.

'Mayday, mayday. This is Kasker Rampart. Can anyone hear me, over?'

'How long until the sun sets for good?' asked Sian.

'Three weeks.'

'Jesus.'

'Mayday, mayday. This is Con Amalgam refinery Kasker Rampart requesting urgent assistance, over.'

'*Thank God*, Rampart. *This is research base Apex One. It's wonderful to hear your voice.*'

Rawlins swept his desk clear and unrolled a map of Franz Josef Land. He pegged the map open with a stapler, a hole-punch and a couple of mugs.

'They are here,' said Jane. 'Indigo Bay. Some kind of botanical research project. Not much of a base. Two guys and a girl. A couple of tents. They ran out of food days ago.'

'Poor bastards.'

'Imagine it. Out there in the middle of this storm. Huddled in a fucked-up Jamesway. I'm amazed they are still alive.'

'Indigo Bay,' said Rawlins. 'Nearly fifty kilometres. That's a long way to hike.'

'They've got a rubber dinghy. No outboard. Otherwise they use skis.'

'Then they're truly fucked.'

'We have to help. We can't abandon them.'

'I wanted to raise a rescue ship, not bring extra mouths to feed. So yeah, I must admit, I'm reluctant to risk men and equipment for no real benefit.'

'That cuts both ways. Why should anyone answer our call? Why should anyone pick us up, help us home? We have nothing to offer. We're just a bunch more problems.'

'If anyone is going to fetch these guys it will be Ghost. Rajesh Ghosh. Our resident fixer. It's down to him.'

Rawlins led Jane to the pump hall. The hall was a vast, poorly lit chamber on the lowest level of the rig. The oil-streaked walls were ribbed with girders and studded with pressure valves, stopcocks and instrumentation.

'Is this the pipe?' asked Jane, walking the circumference of a huge steel column that disappeared into the floor. 'The main oil line?'

'Yeah, this is MOLI.' He slapped the metal. 'It's retracted from the seabed right now, but yeah, that's the umbilicus. When this facility is fully on-stream it can suck nearly a million barrels a day of heavy crude out of the ground. The entire Kasker field siphoned into these tanks. Super-grade. Liquid bullion.'

Jane checked her watch. 'It's three in the morning.'

'He doesn't keep office hours.'

They followed the sticky-sweet smell of cannabis to a bivouac in the corner shadows of the pump room. A camp stove. A pile of books. A guitar.

Ghost lay on a bunk, eyes closed. He was Sikh. He had a turban and a heavy beard.

Rawlins kicked the bunk. Ghost sat up and took off his headphones. Jane caught a brief snatch of Sisters of Mercy.

'We have a job for you,' said Rawlins.

They studied the map.

'It's too far.'

'We could use snowmobiles,' said Rawlins. 'We could cover a lot of ground, if the weather breaks.'

'Until you reach your first crevasse and then you have to park and walk. A few weeks ago it wouldn't have been a problem. But we're down to a couple of hours' daylight and it's minus fifty out there. Normal circumstances, I wouldn't consider leaving the rig. Shit. The sea is so rough we couldn't even reach the island right now.'

'We must do something,' said Jane. 'I'm not going to sit by that radio night after night and listen to those poor sods freeze to death.'

'Okay,' said Ghost. 'Here's the deal. We'll meet them halfway. There's a log cabin at Angakut. Built by whalers. Empty, but good wind shelter. If they can make it that far, we'll fetch them home. I'll go out myself, when the storm breaks.'

'Angakut?'

'It's at the base of a mountain. You can see it for miles.'

'All right.'

'And you better tell them to get going, because the weather is going to get worse before it gets better.'

Rawlins summoned the crew to the canteen.

Most channels were dead. BBC News no longer chronicled carnage. They had lost contact with their outside broadcast units. Instead they re-ran communion from Canterbury Cathedral.

'The BBC has gone religious,' said Rawlins. 'Not a good sign, I think you'll agree. We're doing everything we can to get off this platform. The girls are broadcasting night and day. Sooner or later, someone will respond. But it's time to admit we might be stuck here for winter. Maybe that's no bad thing. Looks like all hell has broken loose back home. So if we are going to make it through the next few months we need to get organised. I know you folks like your privacy, but we can't heat and light the whole refinery. Everyone must move into this block by tomorrow night. We'll live in these few rooms. The rest of the rig can freeze.'

'I want a sea view,' said Nail.

'Flip a coin. Arm wrestle. I don't give a damn. Just get it done.'

Jane joined Ghost in the canteen. They sat by the window. They sipped coffee and watched the storm.

'I didn't know we had snowmobiles,' said Jane.

'Two of them. Part of a cache of stuff on the island. There's an old bunker near the shore. Not much in it. Couple of Yamahas. Some fuel.'

'So we must have a boat to get ashore.'

Ghost smiled. 'Clever. Trying to formulate an escape plan, yeah? Well, that's the big question. What if nobody comes for us? Worst-case scenario: how do we make our own way home?'

Jane liked Ghost. She wanted his approval. She knew full well she was emotionally immature, prone to infatuation. She had to guard against it. Avoid making a fool of herself.

'You seem like a practical guy. What are the options?'

'We have a rubber zodiac with a small outboard motor. Twenty-five horsepower. Room for four men and no luggage. Wouldn't take us very far. We've got plenty of hard-shell lifeboats, but no propulsion. The lifeboats are designed to drift free of a burning rig. They float. That's all they do.'

'We could build a big raft and put up a sail,' said Jane. 'An option, come spring.'

'Now you're talking.'

'We could bolt on an engine. A motor, a drive shaft, some kind of propeller.'

'Want to hear my big plan?'

'All right.'

'Any attempt to sail our way out of here is going to involve weeks, maybe months at sea. We would need to carry a shit-load of supplies. So I say we hitch a ride. Jump a passing iceberg.'

'Seriously?'

'The polar ice shelf breaks up each spring and bergs float

south on the current. They pass by, pretty much every hour. We could track incoming debris. Soon as a decent-size berg is in range we use the zodiac to ferry men and supplies. Those things move slow. Inertia. We would have twelve, maybe sixteen hours to make the transfer.'

'Then what?'

'Camp on the berg. Put up tents. Eat. Sleep. We could tow a string of lifeboats behind us. As soon as the berg hits warm water and starts to break up, we take to the boats.'

'What does Rawlins say about it?'

Ghost shrugged. He poured coffee.

'Everyone is pretty snug at the moment. Plenty of heat, plenty of food. But six months from now things will be very different. People will be cold and hungry. They'll be ready to roll the dice.'

Jane joined Sian in the observation bubble.

'Let me take over for a while,' said Jane. 'I'm wired on caffeine. Why don't you get some sleep?'

Jane positioned her chair in front of the microphone.

'Apex Base, this is refinery Kasker Rampart. Do you copy, over?'

'*This is Apex Base. Damn good to hear from you,* Rampart.' The guy sounded tearful and exhausted.

'How are you folks getting on?'

'*Not so great. The storm collapsed one of the tents and we lost a bunch of stuff. Clothes. Bedding. Hope you got some good news for us,* Rampart. *We need it.*'

'We are worried about the distance. Indigo Bay is quite a trek. Winter is closing in and there isn't much daylight left.'

'*You can't leave us out here to die. That's inhuman.*'

'Have you got a map with you? Can you see a map?'

'*We're in no condition to walk. Alan has frostbite. His feet are black. He can barely stand.*'

'Look at your map. Angakut. Can you see it? There's a mountain halfway between us.'

'*Yeah.*'

'There's a cabin, a wood cabin. It's solid. It's good shelter. It's warm and dry. If you can make it that far, you can ride out the storm. Then we can pick you up.'

'*That's a three-day hike. We'd have to cross two inlets by boat.*'

'What's your name?'

'*Simon.*'

'You've got to move, Simon. You have to put on your skis and move. You have to get your team to the main island. We can reach you from there. We can pick you up.'

'*It's too much.*'

'You've got to dig deep, dude. The weather will lift in a few hours, but there's more moving in. You're only getting weaker. It will be sunrise soon. You're the leader. Get your team ready to travel. Whatever you have to do.'

'*I'm so tired.*'

'You're giving in to death. If you stay in that sleeping bag you'll slowly freeze. I'll call again at nine. You better be on your feet and moving. You've got to get on your feet and move if you want to live.'

'*Okay. All right.*'

'God bless, guys.'

'Do they know about the plague?' asked Sian.

'Their relief plane didn't show up. That's all they know. Might as well keep it that way.'

Punch cut himself a cheese sandwich. He scraped the last smears from a big Country Larder jar of mayonnaise. He took a fresh jar from the refrigerator. He saw himself reflected in the steel door, and saw the phantom blur of a man standing behind him.

'Better make that your last snack,' said Rawlins. 'I need a list. An inventory of all the food we have left.'

40

'Already done.'

'You can lock these freezers and fridges, yes?'

'I've got keys somewhere.'

'One set for you, one set for me. Keep them locked at all times.'

'Okay.'

'Everyone is perfectly civil right now. A few months from now food will run short and it will be a different story. Situation could turn ugly.'

'Yeah.'

'People hoarding, fighting.'

'Absolutely.'

'How about dry goods? Cans and stuff?'

'There's a crappy lock on the storeroom.'

'Speak to Ghost. Get a decent padlock and bring me the key. What's for breakfast?'

'The last of the real eggs.'

'Excellent. Well. See you later.'

Rawlins left the kitchen. He scratched his head on the way out of the door. The edge of his leather jacket lifted for a moment and exposed the yellow butt of his Taser slung in a nylon holster. He had a red can of pepper spray in a pouch on his belt. A sheriff ready to lay down the law.

Jane tried to think up a reason to visit Ghost. Maybe she could help him pack for his expedition to the island.

She walked to the pump hall. She found him sitting on his bunk, slotting batteries into a yellow box.

'Need a hand?'

'I'm okay.'

'What's the box?'

'Nautical beacon. Beeps a locator signal. The Apex guys are stumbling around in the dark out there. If we set this thing pinging it will lead them straight to us. And they'll reach that cabin along the route.'

'Sure they have a tracker?'

'Yeah. They were carrying one so they could rendezvous with their relief plane.'

'Cool.'

'It's short range, though. Too many crags between us and them. We need to get it up high.'

'We could use the radio tower. Lash it to the scaffold.'

'Want to give me a hand?'

They dressed in the airlock. Heavy Ventile coats, rubber boots and ski masks. Ghost unwound his turban and tied his hair in a ponytail. Jane zipped her snorkel hood and buckled gauntlets.

'Been outside much?' asked Ghost as he strapped Jane into a full body harness. His voice was muffled by his mask. His eyes were hidden behind black goggles.

'Never in a storm.'

'Soon as we get out on to the walkway, grab the railing. There's a guide wire. Clip yourself to the wire before taking another step, all right? The wind could throw you clean over the side.'

Ghost handed Jane a shockproof spotlight.

'Million candlepower. Don't look into it. I'll climb the mast. Keep the light on me.'

He sealed the internal door. He spun the hatch wheel and pushed the external door. Alarm. Warning strobes. Sudden jet-roar of wind noise as the power-assisted hatch slid back. Jane was blasted by driving ice particles. She rocked on her feet.

'You all right?' shouted Ghost.

'It's hell out there.'

'Yeah. Know what? I reckon some of us won't make it home.'

Mayday

The storm passed.

Sian stood on the deck and sipped coffee. Her mug broiled like a witches' brew. She was standing on a walkway above the fresh water storage tanks. She wanted to enjoy the sun before the long Arctic night began and the rig was left in permanent darkness.

Sian often took refuge outside. She got a lot of male attention. She heard a rumour the crewmen took a bet when she first joined the rig. First to fuck the new girl. Four months later, nobody won the bet. She overheard Nail call her 'the dyke'.

She took the job because she was bored. She was counter staff at Barclays Bank in Portsmouth. She saw an advert:

Coral Recruitment
Overseas Jobs
Oil industry administrator
   Will provide secretarial support to installation manager. Strong organisational skills and a keen eye for detail are important aspects of the role. Good salary, insurance, flights and negotiable bonus.

She took the job. Friends threw a party the night before she flew to Norway.

They said she was brave. They said she would have a big adventure. She would come home with stories.

There used to be planes overhead. Earlier that year the blue and cloudless sky had often been bisected by the contrails of jets patrolling the Russian frontier. Now the sky was empty.

She saw a ship. A dot on the horizon. A tanker funnel. She dropped her coffee and sprinted to an airlock intercom. Rawlins came running followed by the crew. They gathered on the helipad. They waved and shouted. Ghost fired flares. The tanker didn't turn or slow.

Rawlins had binoculars.

'Japanese flag,' he said. 'There are men on deck.'

'Maybe they saw us,' said Sian. 'It takes a while for a tanker to respond.'

The ship kept going.

Sian joined Jane in the observation bubble. They watched the distant ship through the window.

'Japanese tanker, this is Kasker Rampart twenty kilometres east of your position. Requesting urgent assistance, over.'

No reply.

'Japanese tanker, this is Con Amalgam refinery Kasker Rampart twenty kilometres east of your position. We are British crewmen requesting evacuation, over. Japanese tanker, we badly need your help. Please respond.'

The ship sailed out of sight.

'I can't believe they didn't see us,' said Sian.

'They saw us,' said Jane. 'They just didn't want to stop.'

'Rampart, *this is Apex base.*'

'How's it going, Simon?' asked Jane.

'*We made less time than I hoped. We were walking into the wind. We covered less than five kilometres.*'

'The storm has cleared. You have a window of good weather. Make the most of it.'

'*We're weak. We're hungry.*'

'Once you cross that second inlet you can ditch the boat. Should lighten your load.'

'*We're all pretty shattered.*'

44

'Hold it together forty-eight hours and you're home and dry. A little more walking. That's all that stands between you and the rest of your life. What about food? Do you have anything left at all?'

'*We've been eating toothpaste.*'

'Get some sleep. Just make it through tomorrow. That's all you have to think about. One foot in front of the other. That's all it takes. You're so close to home.'

'This is absurd,' said Jane, when Apex signed off. 'You know how much Arctic survival training I've had? I built a snowman once. I'm talking up this cabin like it's the answer to their prayers, but we don't even know if it is still standing.'

'You're doing a fantastic job,' said Sian.

'I'm trying to coax these poor guys to safety, and I'm not even sure it's physically possible.'

'Sometimes people just need to hear an encouraging voice.'

Jane helped Ghost pack his possessions. They dismantled his bivouac. They stacked CDs and books into boxes, and carried them to a room in the main accommodation block.

'I was thinking,' said Jane. 'We're about three time zones away from the nearest chocolate.'

'Crush that thought. It'll drive you nuts. This past week I've been craving beer. It hit me the other day. I might never taste beer again. I get weepy just thinking about it.'

'Some people get high on bereavement. Life is boring, a lot of the time. Then your uncle drops dead and yeah, you're sad, but on the other hand you relish it because it's the first real, solid emotion you have experienced for months. It breaks the torpor. Suddenly you are awake and alive. I'm no different. I'm scared and tired and I want to go home. But a little, childish part of me is enjoying the drama.'

'Yeah. Well. People are complicated. There's no shame in it.'

Ghost had commandeered a disused tool store. He had glued

a High Voltage sign to the door to discourage visitors, and turned the place into a cannabis farm.

The refinery was equipped with UV lamps and sunbeds to help combat winter depression. Ghost hung lamps over a bunch of grow-bags. Convection heaters kept the room subtropical. The plants had grown tall and strong. It looked like a room full of forest bracken.

'Does Rawlins know about this place?'

'Frank is a pragmatist. As long as the refinery runs right, he's happy.'

'So what exactly is it you do on the rig?' asked Jane.

'Critical systems technician. Glorified caretaker.'

Ghost took a tobacco pouch from his pocket. He rolled a joint.

'Do you smoke?'

'Now and again,' lied Jane. She didn't want to admit her sheltered life.

He lit the joint and passed it to Jane.

'Mad Dog blend.'

She inhaled. Giddy headrush. She felt her world implode.

Ghost wriggled on surgical gloves. He stripped leaves and bagged them.

'I'm going to miss you, girls,' he told the plants.

'You have names for them?' croaked Jane.

'This is Beatrice.'

'You're not really a people person, are you?'

'Humans piss me off.'

Jane cleared out the chapel. She boxed the cross, the candles and the communion wafers. Ghost helped.

'I hope you don't mind,' said Jane.

'What?'

'The only religious space on the rig is Christian.'

'I don't give a shit. I worked at a gas plant in Qatar for ten years. Religious police everywhere. I had to apply for a licence to drink beer.'

Rawlins had told her to use one of the rooms in the main accommodation block as a church.

'Take out the bed and the TV,' he said. 'Improvise an altar. The men need a special place to sit and think. Some kind of meditation space.'

'Okay.'

'Make yourself available. The lads will need to talk.'

'Maybe I should say a prayer each morning in the canteen.'

'Good idea. I think everyone would appreciate it.'

Jane felt useful for the first time in a long while. Part of her was glad the Japanese tanker hadn't stopped. If they were rescued and taken to the mainland her new family would disperse and she would be alone again.

The corridors of the main accommodation block were choked with men and bags like a coach party checking in to a hotel. Rawlins suggested they draw numbers from a cup.

Nail and his gang announced they would take the top floor. They played loud music. They threw mats in the corner of the canteen and laid out dumbbells. Nobody argued. Nobody wanted to be near them.

Jane set up her chapel. She dragged furniture into the corridor. She put a table beneath a window and laid out two candlesticks and a cross. She played Gregorian chant. She left it on Repeat.

She took a room on the ground floor. Ghost lived next door. She could hear him through the wall. She heard him cough. She heard him move around.

Rawlins's voice on the PA: '*Reverend Blanc. Dr Rye. Meet me in the observation room right away.*'

Jane took the spiral stairs to the observation bubble. Rawlins was at the microphone. Sian was at his side.

'. . . *eyes are open but we're not getting much sense out of him.*'

'Nothing?' demanded Rawlins. 'Does he know his name? Does he know what year it is?'

'*He can't speak. He's stopped shivering. His eyes are open.*'

'Can you get him warm? His arms and legs?'

'*We've wrapped him in everything we've got.*'

'All right. Hold on a moment.'

'What's the problem?' Dr Rye joined the group. A thin woman in her fifties.

'They didn't want to camp,' said Rawlins. 'They talked it over and decided to keep walking. They reckoned they had enough batteries to keep their flashlights going through the night. They were crossing an inlet by boat. Alan, the guy with frostbite. He fell through the ice.'

'How's he doing?'

'Several shades of fucked. Pretty much comatose. A dead weight. He won't be going anywhere under his own steam. And his buddies are pretty far gone. I can't get much information out of them. They're cold, disoriented and ready to give up. Jane, when you spoke to them before, did they mention where they planned to cross to the island?'

'Darwin something. Darwin Sound? Darwin Point?'

'Stay on the radio. See if you can raise them again. Get a fix on their location. Landmarks. Anything.' Rawlins turned to Rye. 'Punch has been out on the ice, right?'

'Yeah. He's used the bikes. We drove down the coast last summer.'

'Okay. You, him, Ghost. You're the rescue team. Get your gear. You leave in one hour.'

Jane and Rawlins stood on the helipad. It was dark. Rawlins fumbled at his radio with gloved fingers.

'Hit the lights.'

Floodlights slung beneath the rig flared bright. They lit struts and girders. They lit pack ice collecting between the legs of the refinery.

Punch, Ghost and Rye stood on the east leg docking platform. They pushed floating ice aside with a boat hook. They winched the inflatable zodiac down into black waters. Ghost climbed into the boat. They threw him backpacks.

Jane wanted to tag along, but knew she would be a liability.

Punch and Rye climbed into the boat. They wore so much padding they moved slow and clumsy like astronauts. Ghost pull-started the outboard. The zodiac pulled away from the rig, weaved between plates of drifting ice, and was lost in darkness.

Rescue

'I need to talk.'

Gus Raglan. A short, stocky man with a barbed tattoo round his neck. He caught up with Jane in the corridor outside her room. He looked furtive.

'I need to talk things through.'

Jane looked for a room to use as a confessional. She picked the utensil cupboard at the back of the kitchen. A steel room full of pots and pans. It had thick walls and a strong door. People could speak and not be overheard.

Jane put a couple of chairs at the back of the cupboard. She sat with Gus. Frying pans hung overhead.

'So what's on your mind?'

'My brother. His wife. She and I . . .'

'How long?'

'Three, four years. I asked her to leave him. Asked her a million times. It's difficult.'

'Does your brother suspect?'

'I think he chooses not to know.'

'How would he react if he found out?'

'He's a placid guy. But I'd lose him. I'd lose him as a friend.'

'Have you thought about the future?'

'It's great when we're together. But each night she's with him, and I'm alone. Shit, they might both be dead for all I know. I'd like the chance to put things right.'

'What do you think, deep down, you should do?'

'I took this job to get away. I keep thinking: This isn't me. I'm better than this, you know?'

Ghost steered the outboard motor. They cut through chop. Punch sat in the prow of the zodiac. He swept the shoreline with a spotlight. He lit a lunar landscape. Jagged rocks coated in ice.

'There.' He pointed. A concrete jetty. Snow-dusted steps.

Ghost detached the outboard motor and laid it on the jetty. They hauled the boat out of the water.

'I'll come back for the motor,' he said.

They carried the rubber boat up the steps and set it down in front of massive steel doors set into a rock face. Ghost released a padlock and chain.

'Go inside,' he told them. 'I'll fetch the outboard.'

Punch and Rye dragged the zodiac through the doorway into a cavernous silo. Wind noise dropped to silence. Punch took off his goggles and mask. He shone the spotlight on the walls. They were in a wide tunnel that receded downward into bedrock. The walls glistened with moisture. There were rails in the floor. The wall signs were Russian.

'What is this place?' asked Punch. 'I thought the island was uninhabited.'

'You've been ashore, haven't you?'

'Just ashore. Never here.'

'The Soviet Navy used to dump old reactors on the seabed. Each time they decommissioned a nuclear sub they simply cut off the tail section and dropped it in the Barents Sea. There are about twenty of them down there, all rusted and barnacled. This was going to be their new home. Salvage teams were going to bring them up and bury them in salt for a quarter of a million years.'

'That explains the skull on the door.'

'It's the same the deeper you go. Skulls on every wall, every door, etched in cadmium steel. Future generations will get the message. Bad shit. Keep out.'

Rye pulled a dust sheet from a couple of red Yamaha Viking Pro snowmobiles. She checked them over.

'Keep the light on me.'

She opened a long wooden box on the floor and took out two Ithaca pump-action shotguns. She racked the slides a couple of times to check the action. There were wooden shelves propped against the wall. She opened a carton of twelve-gauge ammunition and slotted shells into the breech. She slid the guns into leather sleeves strapped to the bikes.

'For bears,' she explained. 'We keep them here. Rawlins doesn't like weapons on the rig.'

Ghost staggered through the bunker doorway carrying the outboard balanced on his shoulder. Rye helped him lower it to the floor.

Ghost fuelled the bikes from a jerry can. Gasoline spiked with isopropyl alcohol to prevent freezing. He checked the oil. He gunned the engines to check they worked. He took a radio from his backpack.

'Shore team to Rampart, do you copy, over?'

'Rampart *here.*' Jane's voice. '*Glad you're safe.*'

'We're at the bunker. Any word from Apex?'

'*The guy is still transmitting, off and on, but he sounds delirious. I can't get a precise location from him. You'll just have to head for Darwin and see what you can do.*'

'Okay. We'll get our stuff together and head out at sunrise.'

'*There's another storm-front heading this way. A bad one. We can see it on radar. A solid wall of ice coming down on us like an express train. I reckon it will take you seven hours to reach Darwin, three or four to reach the cabin. If you leave now you might make it before the storm hits.*'

'Shit.'

'*It's down to you guys. Rawlins says you should forget it and come back to the rig, but the decision is yours.*'

Ghost turned to his companions.

'Quick vote. I say go.'

'Go,' said Punch.

Rye thought it over.

'No,' she said. 'They're close to dead. We don't actually know where they are and a storm is moving in. I appreciate the sentiment, but it's a bad idea.'

They took Rye's medical kit, half her food and left her behind.

The snowmobiles had a top speed of a hundred and twenty kilometres an hour, but Ghost throttled down to fifteen while they drove in darkness. Punch followed his tail-lights. His boots barely reached the footrest.

Franz Josef Land was a chain of volcanic archipelagos. A series of pumice islands capped with permafrost. There were jagged boulders beneath the ice ready to rip the skids from the snowmobiles.

They should have arranged a signal, thought Punch. If his Yamaha stalled, Ghost would drive on heedless.

The sky began to lighten. The cold, blue light of an Arctic dawn. They cut through drifts sculpted into strange dune shapes by an unrelenting wind.

Ghost accelerated. Punch revved and kept pace.

Jane fixed breakfast for the crew. She made porridge. Punch had left a plastic spoon on the desk of his kitchen office. There was a note taped to the spoon.

Sixteen level scoops of oats. Five and a half litres of water. No sugar or honey. No waste, no second helpings, no alternative food.

She spilled a few oat flakes on the counter. She carefully gathered them up and put them back in the porridge box.

Earlier that morning Jane went to the kitchen to fix a sandwich. She discovered the refrigerators locked and the food store padlocked. She found herself tugging on the refrigerator door like a desperate junkie denied their fix.

The crew ate in silence. Ivan sat with the TV remote and flicked through a series of dead channels. A dozen different flavours of static.

CNN was off air.

Fox showed the stars and stripes fluttering in slow motion, grainy and monochrome.

BBC News showed a union flag. 'God Save the Queen' over and over. The location of refuge centres scrolled across the bottom of the screen.

'One by one the lights go out,' murmured Ivan.

Ghost swerved his snowmobile to a halt. Punch drew alongside. They were at the edge of a wide crevasse. A jagged fissure of blue, translucent ice. It went deep.

They pulled off their ski masks.

'Shit,' said Punch. 'We've blundered into a crevasse field.'

'Yeah.'

'Bike and rider. Nearly quarter of a tonne. We could drop through the ice any time. We should head back.'

Ghost spat. He watched the gobbet of phlegm fall into darkness.

'No. Just as risky to go back as to press on. I'll ride ahead. Anything happens to me, lower the rope.'

'Okay.'

The crevasse stretched to vanishing point either side of them.

'Could be a long detour.'

They pulled on their ski masks and set off.

Jane washed the bowls and spoons. She put the porridge box back on a food store shelf and, on impulse, stole two packets of M&Ms. She wondered how long it would be before fights broke out over food. She locked the kitchen and gave Rawlins the keys.

She returned to her room to get some sleep. She heard paper

crumple as she lowered her head on to her pillow. A note from Punch.

IN CASE I DO NOT COME BACK.

Jane ripped open the letter.

Jane, if you are reading this, either I am dead or you have no self-control. If you have looked in the storeroom lately you may have worked out we don't have enough food to last six months. I've checked and re-checked. We should have been resupplied by now. Two freight containers of edibles. As it is, we have empty shelves and an empty freezer. At the present rate of consumption we will run out of provisions mid-winter. There simply isn't enough food to go around. Keep it secret. I don't want to start a panic.

There is a map in this envelope. Hang on to it. You and Sian might find it useful in weeks to come.

The internal door that connected the heated accommodation block to the rest of the rig was draped with silver, quilted insulation ripped from an airlock. Jane zipped her coat. She pulled the curtain of insulation aside and hit Open. The door slid back. She shone her flashlight into the dark. The corridor walls sparkled with ice. She closed the door behind her and set off, treasure map held in a gloved hand.

Jane's route took her through miles of unlit rooms and passageways. She felt like an ARVIN drone exploring the silted dereliction of the *Titanic*.

Eerie silence. The hiss and hum of climate control, the constant background to life on the rig, was absent. No sound but laboured breathing and the grit-crunch of snowboots on iced deck plates.

Her torch beam lit gym equipment, vending machines and evacuation signs glazed in frost. Once the heating had been shut off, the temperature in the uninhabited sections of the refinery had quickly dropped to minus forty. Any moisture in the air had condensed to fine dew then crystallised. Ceiling pipes dripped ice.

The map led her to a dank storeroom on C deck. A vacant space. Nothing but a row of lockers against a wall. Four of the lockers were empty. The fifth locker had no back, and was the gateway to a hidden room. Punch had obviously positioned the bank of lockers to mask the entrance to an adjacent storage space.

Jane climbed through the locker into the hidden room.

A dome tent. Guy ropes pegged down with heavy turbine cogs.

Survival equipment stacked in the corner. Warm clothes, sleeping bags, a hexamine stove, frozen bottles of drinking water.

An emergency hide-out. The obvious implication: there isn't enough food to feed the entire crew until spring. But three people could make it through winter if they sequestered themselves and let everyone starve.

Jane opened a box. Torch batteries, protein bars, and three vicious kitchen knives. A Post-it note pasted to one of the blades. *IN CASE THINGS GET UGLY.*

Jane returned to her room. She locked the door and took a packet of M&Ms from its hiding place in her running shoe. One M&M per day. She lay on her bunk and crunched the little nugget between her teeth. She let the chocolate melt on her tongue. Then, in a sudden paroxysm of self-disgust, she hurled the bag at the wall. M&Ms skittered across the floor.

'We can do better than this,' she told herself.

Punch and Ghost reached Darwin Sound. They headed for high ground.

They dismounted the bikes. They took off their ski masks. Punch took a long, steaming piss while Ghost scanned the shoreline with binoculars. Miles of rocks and shingle turned blood red by sunset. Ghost took out his radio.

'Shore team to Rampart, over.'

'Rampart *here.*' Sian's voice. '*Good to hear from you.*'

'We're at Darwin. No sign.'

'*Nothing? Nothing at all?*'

'I've got five-, six-kilometre visibility. No sign of them. How's that storm?'

'*Big. Still coming.*'

'You've got fifteen minutes to raise them and get a fix. After that, we're out of here.'

Ghost turned to Punch.

'We gave it our best shot. Nobody can say we didn't try.' He pulled back the cuff of his gauntlet and checked his watch. 'Ten minutes, then we head home.'

They shared a protein bar.

'Personally, I'd do a Captain Oates,' said Punch. 'If it came down to frostbite and starvation, I'd take a long walk in the snow.'

The twilight sky suddenly brightened, like someone flicked a switch and made it noon.

'What the fuck?' said Ghost.

They both looked up. Something bright at high altitude, behind the cloud, moving fast.

'A plane?' said Punch. 'A burning plane?'

'Too white. Too constant.'

Later, when he was back aboard the refinery, Punch tried to describe what he saw to Jane.

'It was like time-lapse footage. The sun zooming across the sky, dawn to dusk. It did crazy things to our shadows. I totally lost balance.'

The fierce glow crossed the sky accompanied by a high whistle. Punch pulled down the hood of his parka so he could hear.

'It's coming down,' said Ghost. 'It's going to hit.'

The white glow sank below the western horizon. Seconds later they heard the impact. Deep, rolling thunder.

'Now what in God's name was that?'

Survival

Simon woke.

He studied the blue polypropylene weave of the tent fabric. Somewhere a voice was calling.

'*Apex, this is* Rampart, *over. Apex, this is* Rampart. *Can you hear me?*'

He had lost a glove. His right hand was bare.

I'm dying, he thought. I'm dying, and I can barely remember who I am.

He looked for the glove.

Simon woke.

He turned his head. Alan lay sheathed in three sleeping bags, unmoving, lips blue. Nikki had wrapped herself around him to impart warmth. Her head rested on his chest. She was unconscious, mouth open, a patch of frost on the sleeping bag where her breath had condensed and frozen.

Simon's fingers were numb. He looked for the glove.

Simon woke.

Semi-darkness. Daylight outside, but the tent was half buried in snow.

'*Apex, this is* Rampart. *We need your location. We must have your position, over. There are men at Darwin, but they can't stay long. This is your only chance, Apex. If you don't respond you will be left behind.*'

Simon picked up his radio but was too disoriented to work the buttons.

'Hello? Hello?'

He turned the frequency dial. Nothing but feedback. His fingers were swollen. He dropped the radio.

He scrabbled at the tent zip and stumbled into the snow. Weak sunlight. Intolerable cold. He fumbled in his pocket without understanding what he was looking for.

Ghost swerved and brought his snowmobile to a skidding halt. Punch copied the move.

'There.' Ghost pointed east. A red flare slowly drifted to earth two miles distant. They gunned their engines and set off at full speed.

They found Simon face down in the snow. They rolled him. Ghost stabbed him in the thigh with a syringe pre-loaded with epinephrine.

Simon's right hand was blue.

'Give me a spare glove,' said Ghost.

Punch took a glove from his backpack and threw it to Ghost.

'He's going to lose fingers for sure.'

Ghost threw the unconscious man over the saddle of his snow-mobile.

Punch slit open the tent with a lock-knife. He injected Nikki and struggled to drag her to the bikes.

They strapped Alan to a sledge still covered in sleeping bags. Ghost hitched the sledge to the back of his snowmobile.

'Think he's dead?' asked Punch.

'Won't know until we get him unwrapped.'

Ghost slapped Simon and Nikki awake.

'You're both riding pillion, got it?' he shouted in their faces. 'All you have to do is hang on.'

Ghost pulled out. Simon sat in the saddle behind him. Alan was towed on the sledge.

Punch pulled away. Nikki clung to his back.

They followed their own tracks. They drove fast, spewing slush. They checked the sky for the coming storm.

Jane sat with Rawlins in his office. They rewound radar footage. Jane pointed at the time code in the corner of the screen.

'Fourteen forty-six. Any second.'

'You didn't see it yourself?'

'Out of the corner of my eye. I was sitting in the bubble. The sky lit up.'

The radar sweep showed miles of empty ocean, the edge of the island, and the haze of the approaching ice storm.

'It fell to earth north-west of their position. That's what they said. It hit land.'

A sudden white flare, just out of frame.

'Jeez,' said Rawlins. He leaned forward. 'The debris plume must be half a kilometre wide. Stuff in the air for twenty, twenty-five seconds.'

'A meteorite?'

'Possibly. It wouldn't be the first up here. There have been a couple of strikes in Ontario and Troms. Chunks of asteroid the size of a football.'

'Yeah?'

'Back in '78 a Soviet reconnaissance satellite re-entered over the Northern Territories. Chunks landed in deep forest. The Canadian Army spent months looking for a plutonium power cell.'

'I'd love to take a look.'

'If things were different, I'd be out there right now with a rock hammer collecting a souvenir. But we only have two Skidoos. We can't risk them for a joyride.'

'I suppose.'

'Still manning the radio?'

'Calling for help at the top of every hour. Rest of the time we broadcast *Queen's Greatest Hits*. Let people know we have an active transmitter.'

'Good idea.'

'Sian thinks she heard a voice a few days back. A man's voice. Brief. Very faint.'

'What did he say?'

'Couldn't make out.'

'Well, keep on it. We can't be the only people stuck out here.'

Three hours in the saddle. Simon let go of Ghost's waist. He toppled backward. He fell from the snowmobile. He lay in the snow. He pulled off his gloves. He tried to take off his coat.

Ghost brought the Yamaha full circle. He dragged Simon to his feet and slapped him around.

'Look at me. Look at me. Come on, man.'

Simon's eyes were rolling. He couldn't focus.

Ghost jammed gauntlets back on to Simon's hands. Simon tried to slide them off again.

'No, dude. You have to wear gloves, you hear me?'

Punch pulled up.

'He's delirious,' said Ghost. 'Give him another shot.'

Punch slammed epinephrine into Simon's thigh. The guy gasped and snapped awake.

'Can you keep it together a couple more hours, Simon? Can you keep it together that long?'

He nodded.

They set off. Headlights at full beam. Fuel needle edging into red. Snow particles feathered Ghost's goggles, blurring his view.

They made poor time. Ghost's snowmobile laboured to haul two passengers and a sledge. The sledge flipped twice, tipping Alan into the snow. They took off Alan's goggles and face-mask. His eyes were closed. They couldn't get a neck pulse. They couldn't tell if he was breathing.

'Give me your knife,' demanded Ghost.

Punch handed over his lock-knife. Ghost snapped open the blade and cut the sledge rope.

'What are you doing?' asked Nikki, shouting to be heard over the gathering wind.

'He's either dead or dying. We have to outrun the storm.' Ghost pushed Nikki and Simon back towards the bikes. 'It's all right. I didn't give you a choice, okay? It's my decision. My guilt.'

They climbed on the snowmobiles and drove away leaving Alan still strapped to the sledge, snow settling on his face, a blue speck abandoned in a vast ice plain.

The sun set. They rode headlong into a blizzard. Rising wind-roar. Their headlamps lit driving snow. Punch wanted to erect the survival shelter but Ghost ignored his signals to stop.

Ghost checked his sat nav and headed for the cabin co-ordinates. The Garmin unit bolted to the handlebars counted down the metres. He was surprised the unit could still find a GPS signal. He guessed remnants of the US military were still active. A bunch of generals in a mile-deep war room trying to mobilise troops that were long dead or had abandoned their post.

YOU HAVE ARRIVED AT YOUR DESTINATION.

They pulled up. Featureless terrain. White nothing.

Ghost dismounted. He shone his flashlight into a locust-swarm of ice particles. He found a snow bank. He and Punch began to excavate, burrow like moles. Punch hacked at the snow with gloved hands. Ghost unfolded a trenching spade and dug. They exposed a window, and then they exposed a door. The door was chocked closed. They tugged the wedges free and pulled the door wide.

The interior of the cabin was bare. They revved the snowmobiles, drove them inside, and wedged the door closed. Wind noise dropped to silence.

Ghost erected a dome tent in the corner of the cabin. He

hammered pegs into the floor with his boot. Punch set up a couple of LED lanterns. He burned a Coleman gas stove to raise the cabin temperature. He melted snow for coffee.

They wrapped Simon and Nikki in foil blankets. Punch cracked self-heating cans of chicken teriyaki. Nikki ate with trembling hands. Ghost spoon-fed Simon.

'They wouldn't tell us on the radio,' said Nikki, wiping food from her chin.

'Tell you what?' asked Ghost.

'Why the plane didn't come.'

'There's been some kind of outbreak back home. A pandemic. Everything shot to shit.'

'How bad?'

'Pretty fucking bad.'

'The whole of Britain?'

'The whole of the world. Take off your gloves a moment. And your boots.'

Ghost checked Nikki for frostbite. 'Your skin is cracked, but you still have circulation. See? If I press your skin it goes white then red. You still have blood flow. We have a doctor on the rig. She'll check you over properly.'

'Maybe we should go back for Alan,' said Nikki. 'When we have our strength. When the weather clears.'

'It's winter. The weather won't clear for six months. It'll be one storm after another from now on. We wouldn't find him, even if we looked. What can I tell you? I guess we aren't the good guys.'

Ghost turned to Simon.

'Let's take a look at you.'

Simon allowed Ghost to unbuckle his gauntlets. He sat back and let Ghost peel off his socks and shoes.

Simon's toes were swollen and peeling. The fingertips of his left hand were blue. His entire right hand was black, cracked and weeping. The smell was foul. Punch covered his mouth and nose.

'Probably looks worse than it is,' lied Ghost. 'Skin will grow back in time.'

He helped Simon dress.

'Take it easy, all right?'

Ghost picked up the trenching spade.

'I'm going outside to dig us out. Don't want to suffocate.'

He stepped outside into the wind and snow. He shouted into his radio.

'Shore team to Rye. Shore team to Rye, do you copy, over?'

Jane knocked on Rawlins's door.

'They reached the cabin,' she said. 'I thought you'd like to know. Couldn't get much out of them. Bad atmospherics. Imagine they will push for the coast at daylight.'

'Everyone all right?'

'Punch and Ghost are okay. But only two members of the Apex team made it.'

'What happened to the third guy?'

'Like I say, bad reception. I could barely make out a word. But there were three of them. Now there are two. Maybe the cold got him.'

'Christ. There will be a bunch of tears when they get back. A bunch of guilt. Well, that's your problem. Pastoral care. Ghost and Punch are okay, yeah?'

'We'll hear more when they reach the bunker.'

'Take a look at this.'

Rawlins had stapled an Arctic map to the wall. The island and surrounding ocean were dotted with red pins.

'These are all the installations in our sector, as best I can remember. Mostly Gazprom. A couple of Occidental. I suppose most have been evacuated. But if they cleared out in a hurry they might have left some useful supplies. Food. Fuel.'

'What's that?' Jane pointed to a pin tacked to the northern shore of the island.

'Kalashnikov. A cluster of cabins built by whalers. Survey teams use it as a stop-over. There might be a cache of food, if we're lucky.'

'There's a town called Kalashnikov?'

'A Hero of Socialist Labour. He got a patch of ice named after him.'

'So we take the snowmobiles and travel up the coast?'

'Yeah.'

'Our route would pass within a couple of kilometres of that impact site,' said Jane. 'A person could walk inland and take a look.'

'Depends on the weather, but yeah.'

'This time I go, all right? If the boat goes out I want to be on it. I need to get off this damn rig.'

Jane sipped coffee. Sian hurried into the canteen.

'It's Rye. You better talk to her.'

She handed Jane a radio.

'Go ahead.'

'*We're at the bunker. We're heading back in the boat. I need you to boot-up Medical.*'

Jane flipped a wall switch. Strip-lights flickered.

The medical bay was a wide, white room with an operating table at the centre.

Sub-zero. Jane's breath fogged the air. She set convection heaters running.

'Okay. What do you need?'

'*The resuscitation trolley. Plug it in. Get it charged.*'

'Done.'

'*An instrument pack from the wall cupboard. It's on a plastic tray, vacuum sealed in plastic.*'

'Got it.'

'*Bottom shelf. There's a blue nylon bag. It's a hypothermia bath.*'

Inflate it. Don't fill it, though. I'll need to adjust water temperature myself.'

Jane unrolled the rubber bath. It was shaped like a coffin. She recognised it from the survival skills training day Con Amalgam insisted she attend before getting shipped north.

She released the valve of a little CO2 cylinder. The bath inflated like a child's paddling pool.

'Done.'

'Go to the refrigerator. Get a bag of saline and a bag of Haemaccel. Unlock the drug store and fetch pethidine.'

'Who's hurt?'

'Simon, one of the Apex team. Big-time frostbite. Oedema. Possible septic shock.'

'Shit.'

'Meet us on the dock. He's fading fast. We've got to get him in a hypothermic bath and raise his core temperature or we are going to lose him.'

Dealing

Jane and Sian waited on the floodlit dock with a stretcher. Jane had binoculars.

'Here they come.'

The zodiac came in fast. Ghost killed the engine and threw Jane a rope. Simon lay on the aluminium floor of the boat. Jane helped drag him from the boat. They laid him on a stretcher, put it on a cargo trolley and wheeled it to the freight elevator.

The stretcher buggy was parked at habitation level. Rye drove Simon to Medical. Jane and Sian jogged behind the little electric car as it hummed down dark corridors.

They moved Simon on to the operating table.

'Cut off his clothes,' said Rye. 'Get him under the shower.'

Jane and Sian hacked through Simon's clothes with trauma shears. His genitals were so shrivelled by cold he looked female. Nothing between his legs but a tuft of pubic hair.

There was a bathroom at the back of the bay. They dragged Simon to the shower and stood him under a jet of hot water.

Rye stripped out of her survival gear and filled the hypothermia bath, tested it to forty-six degrees.

'All right. Let's get him immersed.'

They laid Simon in the bath.

'Keep his hands and feet out of the water.'

She shone a penlight into his eyes.

'Ideally I would like to test rectal temperature, but we'll spare him that indignity for now.'

'His hand is fucked.'

'We'll see how his condition develops as we restore circulation. Of course, that's when the pain will begin.'

Jane jogged a kilometre circuit of C deck. She was joined by Sian.

'Spoken to Ghost?'

'Briefly,' said Jane.

'What did he say about that Apex guy? The one who didn't make it back.'

'He refuses to talk about it.'

They trotted down unheated corridors. Each puffing exhalation was a great plume of steam-breath. They both wore three tracksuits. The metal floor was slick with ice so they ran in snow-boots with thick rubber tread. Their route was lit by weak daylight shafting through the corridor windows.

Jane ran fast and lithe. She had lost four kilos. Her clothes felt loose. Sian struggled to keep pace.

Jane had been fat all her life. Her body had been nothing more than a sweating, aching encumbrance but now she felt an intimation of what it would be like to be supple and strong.

'What's the deal with you and Punch?'

'How do you mean?' asked Sian.

'Both young, both bright. An obvious match.'

'I always thought Nail and Ivan seemed like a happy couple. Pumping. Preening. Oiling each other down.'

'Nice deflection.'

They ran the kilometre circuit then ran it again.

Sian returned to her room to shower.

Jane walked past Medical on her way back to the accommodation block. Dr Rye was packing packets of drugs into a box. Jane felt obliged to offer help.

'Happy pills,' said Rye. 'Seroxat. Triptafen. You've got to expect depression in a place like this. No daylight. Nowhere to go. There will be plenty of demand, now night is closing in.'

'How is Simon?'

Rye gestured to a side room.

'Stable. Sleeping. Infection: that's my chief concern. This is a first aid station. Serious injuries are supposed to get a priority airlift. We don't have enough antibiotics for long-term treatment.'

'Right.'

'I probably shouldn't mention it, but what the hell. You might need to know. Nikki? That girl we pulled off the ice? She was pretty distraught about the man they left behind. She blames herself. *It should have been me, blah, blah.* I dosed her with Anafranil but it takes a few days to kick in. She'll need a shoulder, someone to coax her through the next few days.'

'Okay.'

'The crewmen are smoking weed and hoping for a ship, but once the sun has set for good the mood will quickly head downhill. There are black days ahead. Thank God we don't have guns on board.'

Sian found Simon watching DVDs in his hospital room. *Goodfellas.* He was pale. His hands and feet were bandaged. Sian held a cup so he could sip from a straw.

'Can you help me up a little?'

Sian pressed the Elevate button to raise Simon's head.

'Where's Nikki?' he asked.

'Eating in the canteen. Eating and eating. Can I bring you any food?'

'No thanks.'

BBC News was still showing slow-motion footage of a fluttering Union flag and a list of refuge centres.

'It's been that way for days,' said Sian. 'The refuge list doesn't update. I suppose the studio has been evacuated. We'll be watching that image until the satellite fails.'

'Are there no other channels?'

'North America is totally off air. All the Russian and Euro channels are long gone.'

'Jesus.'

'See that BBC logo in the corner? I like to look at it. It's comforting. A last little piece of home.'

'I killed my best friend to get here,' said Simon. 'And I'm just as stuck as before.'

'We've got heat, we've got light, we've got food for months. Look around you. This rig is one giant construction set. It's packed full of survival equipment. I promise you, one way or another, we will get you home. We'll get everyone home.'

Rye changed Simon's dressings. She unwrapped his right hand. The smell of necrotic flesh made Sian want to retch.

Sian sat on the edge of the bed. She wanted to distract Simon from the sight of his rotted hand.

'So what's the first thing you will do when you get home?'

'Fuck knows. Doesn't sound like there is much waiting for us. And what can I do? I'll probably never use a knife and fork again. I'll have to lap food from a bowl like a dog.'

'You're exhausted, hungry and dehydrated. You get two days' self-pity, all right? That's your allocation. Wallow. Whine all you want. But after those forty-eight hours are up, you are officially a malingering twat.'

'I need a shit.'

'Is that why you haven't been eating? Worried about using the toilet?'

Sian lowered the bed and helped Simon stand. He shuffled to the bathroom. Sian helped tug down his pyjama bottoms.

'Call me when you are done.'

Sian helped Simon wipe, then walked him back to bed. She found Rye checking the drug cupboard.

'What are you giving him for pain?'

'Codeine. He'll get a couple of cycles. After that, he has to tough it out.' Rye gestured to the pill packets and bottles. 'We don't have much of anything. Once his share is used up, he's on his own.'

Jane knocked on Nikki's door.

'Who is it?' Nikki sounded groggy. She was probably dozing on her bunk.

'It's Reverend Blanc. Do you have a moment? I need your help.'

Jane led Nikki to the observation bubble.

'How have you been?' asked Jane, as they climbed the spiral stairs.

'Standing by every heating vent I can find. Just can't seem to get warm.'

Jane showed her the radio console.

'We've been trying to hail any passing ship by short-wave. We man the radio round the clock. We were hoping you could pull a few shifts.'

'What should I do?'

'Sit here. Press to transmit, yeah? Kasker Rampart. That's the name of the platform. So you say something like: "Mayday, mayday. This is refinery platform Kasker Rampart requesting urgent assistance, over." Then you release the switch and listen for a reply.'

'Okay.'

'Do you like Monopoly? We've been holding a tournament.'

Sian walked Simon to the shower. She set the water running, took Simon's dressing gown and helped him into the cubicle. She sat on the bed and waited for him to finish.

'How's Nikki?' he called.

'Seems okay. They've got her helping out in the radio room.'

'Keep an eye on her. Make sure she's all right. She seems tough, but she's not. We left Alan to die. She may act casual, but on some level it will be eating her up.'

'Jane is looking after her. Jane's good with people. She has an instinct.'

'I'm done.'

Sian wrapped Simon in a bath towel and led him from the shower.

Jane took the elevator down to the docking platform. She found Punch in the boathouse. The boathouse was a steel cabin with a wide hole in the floor. The zodiac was suspended above the water by chains. The walls were racked with survival equipment.

'What's this?' asked Jane, inspecting a big plastic pod.

'A weather balloon. Don't mess with it.'

'Maybe we should build a boat. A raft or something. Give everyone a job. For morale, if nothing else.'

Punch had found a golf club. He putted scrunched paper into a mug.

'Do you think Tiger Woods is dead?' he asked.

'He's probably sipping martinis on a private island some-where. Times like this, the rich buy their way out of trouble.'

'But imagine if we were the only people left. The last men on earth. I'd be the best golfer in the world right now. You'd be the only priest. And Ghost would be the only Sikh. Imagine that. A four-hundred-year religion terminating in a dope-head grease monkey.'

'I thought you liked the bloke.'

'I do. But think about it. All the people that made you feel worthless and small down the years. The bullies and bosses. All gone. It's exhilarating, if you think about it. Freedom from other people's expectations. We can finally start living for ourselves.'

'We can't be the only survivors. There must be others like us. We just need to find each other.'

Jane found a yellow Peli case on a shelf: a crush-proof, watertight plastic container about the size of a shoe box. She turned the box over in her hands.

'Do you mind if I take this?' she asked.

The crew ate dinner in the canteen. Mashed potato, a sausage, a spoonful of gravy.

'Eat it slowly,' advised Punch. 'Make it last.'

Rawlins lifted his plate and licked it clean of gravy. The crew copied his lead.

Jane stood on a chair and called for attention. They looked up, wondering if she were about to say grace all over again.

'Okay, folks. Here's the deal. We've got a bunch of helium weather balloons downstairs. A week from today I am going to launch one of the balloons with this box attached. The prevailing wind should carry it south to Europe. If any of you want to write a letter to someone back home, then drop it in the box. Million-to-one shot? Maybe. Even if the box lands in the sea, one day it will wash up and one day someone will find it. You may think it's a stupid idea, but do it anyway. Put it down on paper. Put a message in the bottle. The things you wished you'd said but didn't get a chance. I'm going to leave this box in the corner. It's a good opportunity to unburden yourselves. Make use of it.'

Sian sat in the corner of the canteen, pen poised over a sheet of paper.

She had a stepfather. Leo. A carpet fitter. He was a nice enough guy. He cared for Sian's mother during that last year of ovarian cancer. Sian spent each Christmas Day at his little terraced house, ate a turkey dinner in front of the TV, but they never progressed beyond superficial pleasantries. It had been three years. Sian often wondered if he had a new girlfriend. A divorcee with kids of her own. Maybe he wanted to drop Sian from his life, but didn't know how.

Leo was a fit, capable man. He kept a bayonet beneath the bed in case of burglars. He would be all right.

Sian screwed up the paper. Better this way, she thought. No one to worry about but me.

The coffee urn. She filled a Styrofoam cup. Punch no longer supplied milk powder or sugar. Everyone took it black and bitter.

Jane sat in her room with a pad on her lap. She wrote love-you letters to her mother and sister. Then she wrote on behalf of the crew.

> *My name is Reverend Jane Blanc. I am chaplain of Con Amalgam refinery platform Kasker* Rampart. *We are marooned in the Arctic Circle west of Franz Josef Land. We have supplies to last four months. Winter is coming. By the time you read this we may be dead. We have little hope of rescue and we are so far from inhabited land any attempt to sail to safety in an improvised craft would almost certainly fail. I often promise the men we will all get home, but I have no idea how this can be achieved or what horrors might await us beyond the horizon. So I appeal to anyone who may read this note: please do what you can to ensure that one day these letters reach the people for whom they are intended, so that they can know what became of us.*
>
> *God bless,*
> *Jane Blanc*

Jane sealed the notes in an envelope and took it to the canteen. She slotted the envelope into the Peli case.

Sudden PA announcement: 'Mr Rawlins, Reverend Blanc, please report to Medical right away.'

Sian. By the sound of her voice, something was very wrong.

Simon was curled foetal at the bottom of the shower cubicle. He was dead. He held a scalpel in the swollen, blackened fingers of his left hand. He had slashed his wrist. He lay naked in a puddle of pink blood-water and unravelled bandages.

'Jesus fucking Christ.'

Rawlins shut off the water. Jane helped drag the dead man from the shower.

They carried Simon to the operating table. They watched Sian wash him down. They lifted him into a rubber body bag and zipped it closed.

There was no mortuary on the refinery, so they laid Simon on the floor of the boathouse overnight.

'He was talking to me,' said Sian. 'Reaching out. Screaming for help and I was too stupid to hear.'

'A person's life is their own,' said Jane. 'It's not your job to save them.'

Nikki sat in the observation bubble reading a magazine.

'We'll be holding the funeral at three,' said Jane.

Nikki flipped pages like she hadn't heard.

The crew processed down steel stairs that spiralled round one of the rig's gargantuan legs. An ice shelf had solidified around each leg. They walked across the ice and congregated at the water's edge.

Jane turned the pages of her service book with gloved fingers.

'O God, whose Son Jesus Christ was laid in a tomb: bless, we pray, this grave as the place where the body of Simon your servant may rest in peace, through your Son, who is the resurrection and the life; who died and is alive and reigns with you now and for ever.'

Simon was swaddled in sheets. He lay on a stretcher. Ghost lifted the stretcher and the body slid into the water.

'As they came from their mother's womb, so they shall go again, naked as they came. We brought nothing into the world, and we take nothing out. The Lord gave, and the Lord has taken away; blessed be the name of the Lord.'

The shrouded body floated just beneath the surface. Ghost pushed the corpse away from the ice with a golf club. It drifted away, drawn by the current, a white phantom shape beneath the water.

'Support us, O Lord, all the long day of this troubled life, until the shadows lengthen and the evening comes, the busy world is hushed, the fever of life is over and our work is done. Then, Lord, in your mercy grant us a safe lodging, a holy rest, and peace at the last; through Christ our Lord. Amen.'

The crew walked back to the rig. Nobody spoke.

Jane stood with Punch and looked out to sea.

'I feel like I'm doing more harm than good,' she said.

'Shall we go and find your asteroid?'

'Yeah. Let's get away from this misery for a while.'

The Crater

Jane steered the zodiac. Counter-intuitive: turn the outboard left to steer right.

'Keep us about three hundred metres from shore,' instructed Punch. 'We don't want to rip the bottom out of the boat.'

They followed the coastline. They hugged a ridge of lunar rock and black shingle.

A milky film in the water. Grease ice. The ocean starting to freeze.

Jane looked back. A rare chance to see the totality of the rig.

The refinery was constructed around three great distillation tanks, each the size of a cathedral. The structure was spiked by radio masts and cranes. The platform floated on four buoyant legs. It was tethered to the seabed by cables as thick as a redwood tree trunk. It looked like something out of a nightmare: a squat spider big enough to crush cities. A million tons of steel. Product of twenty different slipways. Assembled in a deep-water fjord and towed north.

'Terrifying,' said Jane.

'What is?'

'It's one thing to sit with our feet up in the canteen, dreaming up plans to sail home. It's another thing to see it for real. The ocean. The ice. We wouldn't last a day.'

'We have time to prepare,' said Punch. 'Plenty of survival gear aboard Rampart. And you wouldn't be out here alone. We would have each other. Ghost is a solid guy. Kind of man you can rely upon in a crisis.'

'Yeah.'

'And we have you.'

'Sure. When we run out of food I'll be first in the pot.'

'I saw a kid on TV a few years back,' said Punch. 'He went hiking in the Rockies. He got hit by a landslide. He woke up with his arm pinned by a boulder. He lay there for a couple of days hoping for rescue. Nobody came, so he used his belt as a tourniquet, then sawed off his arm with a penknife.'

'Good God.'

'Picked up his canteen and walked back to civilisation minus an arm.'

'Damn.'

'This is your moment. You know that, right? I've seen you, since this shit kicked off. It's like watching someone wake from a long sleep.'

'But what good is it?' asked Jane, looking out to sea. 'In the face of this. All our heroism. All our will to live. It's a bad joke.'

Sian cleared Simon's room in Medical. She gathered up his dog-tags, his signet ring, his watch. She found a heavily annotated copy of Marcus Aurelius's *Meditations* in his coat pocket. She put it all in a plastic box and gave it to Nikki.

Nikki was in the observation bubble staring out to sea.

'Thanks,' she said, as Sian handed her the box. She tossed it aside without looking at it.

Nikki spent the afternoon scanning wavebands.

She turned up the volume and put her ear to the speaker.

'Are you sure you heard it?' asked Sian.

'There was a voice. Male. English. It faded in and out. Has done for days.'

She turned the dial.

'There. You hear it?'

'. . . elp . . . ear us?..urgent assis . . .'

'Get your coat. We have to boost the range on this thing.'

Nikki found a coil of steel cable in the boathouse. She carried it to the upper deck.

'What do you have in mind?' asked Sian.

'When I was at university I had a crappy transistor radio on my desk. It had a broken aerial. If I let the stub of the aerial touch my anglepoise lamp I got a signal. Maybe we can lengthen the antenna and pull the same trick.'

'Perhaps we should talk to Ghost. He might be able to help.'

'Girl, you've got to shake off that passive mindset. We're in deep shit. You can't constantly rely on Ghost to kiss it all better. You've got to start taking care of yourself.'

The short-wave antenna was a scaffold spike four metres tall. Nikki climbed the spike and lashed the cable to the top. She climbed down. She tied the other end of the cable to a balloon pod.

'Okay. Stand back.'

She pulled the red rip cord. The plastic case split open. Silver balloon fabric spilled, unravelled and began to inflate. An explosive roar as the helium canister discharged. The foil swelled and rose. The balloon lifted skyward taking the cable with it. A silver teardrop shimmering like a globule of mercury. The cable extended the antenna ten metres.

'Let's see if that does any good.'

They returned to the observation bubble and threw their coats over a chair.

'This is refinery platform Kasker Rampart, can you hear me, over?'

'*Hello? Hello?*'

'This is Rampart. Go ahead.'

'*Thank God. Thank Christ. This is drilling station Kasker Raven. Hope you're in better shape than us, Rampart. We could use your help.*'

*   *   *

Kalashnikov. Four rotting cabins facing the sea. A wooden Orthodox church with an onion dome. Wooden grave markers.

Jane tethered the boat to the jetty. She climbed ashore. Punch passed her backpacks.

The cabins had been built by whalers. They had partially collapsed. Rooms choked with roof beams and snow. The little church was intact. Some of the fittings were a hundred years old. Rotted pews. A rotted altar.

The back room. A blubber stove with a cobwebbed flue. A shelf loaded with antique supplies. Fry's cocoa. Heinz Indian relish. Tins of boiled cabbage.

The floor was littered with modern camping detritus. Empty stove canisters. Food wrappers. A ripped sleeping bag.

Jane found a box. Calorie bars and a couple of cans.

'Eight years old,' said Jane, checking the expiration date. 'Probably still edible.'

'Bit of a wasted trip. The place is good for firewood, I suppose.'

'What's worth more right now, do you think? By weight. Bullion or a packet of peanuts?'

They stood in the doorway and watched sunset. Mid-afternoon. Eighteen hours of night.

'By mid-winter the ocean will be frozen,' said Punch. 'You could walk to the Canadian mainland. A fifteen-hundred-kilometre hike. Pitch dark and minus fifty, but if you, me and Sian took the snowmobiles and a sledge loaded with fuel we could get a hell of a long way before we had to ski.'

'Global warming. The sea freezes less and less each year. No guarantee we would reach Canada.'

'Worth a shot.'

'And leave everyone else behind?'

'Too many of us. An entire football team. I doubt it's possible to get us all home, by land or sea.'

'I read a lot of travel books before I came here. Fantasised what it would be like. I read Scott's journal. Those last entries

80

as they froze to death in that tent. "Had we lived, I should have made a tale to tell of the hardihood, endurance and courage of my companions which would have stirred the heart of every Englishman." I got totally caught up in the romance.'

'Scott was a self-aggrandising dick.'

'That's my point. Shackleton got his men home. Shipwrecked on an ice floe. Couple of lifeboats. Bit of food. He got them home. Every single one.'

They closed the door and used the ripped sleeping bag to plug holes in the frame.

Punch unfolded a map.

'One or two research stations on this side of the island. Marine biologists. Geologists. Most of them like Apex: little more than a couple of tents. Pretty much all of them will have been evacuated for winter.'

'This one?'

'McClure. Seismologists, I think.'

'Walking distance?'

'Yeah, what the fuck.'

Jane unpacked the radio.

'Shore team to Rampart, do you copy, over?'

She waited for a reply, but instead heard a strange tocking sound like the crackle of a Geiger counter.

'Atmospherics?' suggested Punch.

Jane re-tuned.

'Shore team to Rampart.'

'Rampart *here*.' Sian's voice.

'We made it to Kalashnikov, over.'

'*Tell Punch we miss him. Rawlins is brewing some atrocity in the kitchen. Regurgitated egg, I think.*'

'That ticking noise. Can you hear it at your end?'

'*It comes and goes. It's not our equipment.*'

'We'll move on at first light.'

'*Did you find anything?*'

Jane picked up one of the calorie bars and turned it in her hand.

'No. There's nothing here.'

'You could tow us. Rope your boat to a raft and tow us.'

The guy from Raven sounded tired and desperate.

'A zodiac could make it. It would take a couple of days, but it could make the trip.'

Rawlins thought it over. Nikki sat at the back of the observation bubble and watched him deliberate.

'No. Sorry, but no. If you were in my position you'd say the same thing. It would take more than a couple of days. The motor would burn out. And that little boat is the only sea-going vessel we have.'

Raven was a drilling platform seven hundred miles north on the other side of the Kasker oil field. Seven men running out of fuel. They were crowded in a single room, wearing survival suits for warmth.

'We can keep the lights on another couple of weeks. Basic power. After that, we'll freeze for real.'

'I can't do it, Ray. I'm responsible for the men on this rig. I can't risk them, and I can't risk the boat.'

'So you're going to let us die? Is that what you're going to do? Wash your hands?'

'You're not going to die, Ray. Just chill the fuck out. Give me twenty-four hours, okay? I'll talk to some of the lads. We'll put our heads together. We'll thrash out a workable plan, all right? Let us think it through.'

Rawlins signed off. He sat back and rubbed his eyes.

'Must be tough,' said Sian. 'Being boss in a situation like this.'

'I nearly threw myself down the stairs yesterday. Stood at the top of the steps outside my room and leaned forward. Just wanted to break my arm or my ankle or something. Then someone else would have to take charge.'

'I can't speak for anyone else,' said Sian, 'but I'm glad you are at the helm.'

'I haven't got a fucking clue how to help these guys. Better fetch Ghost. Maybe he can come up with something.'

Ghost wasn't in the canteen. He wasn't in his room.

Nikki put on a parka and descended to the pump hall at the bottom of the rig. She found Ghost rolling an empty oil drum across the floor.

'We have a contact. Seven guys on a drilling platform north of here.'

'Raven?'

'Yeah.'

'Jesus. I thought they would be choppered out for winter.'

'Marooned like us. We've been talking to a guy called Ray.'

'I know him. I met him.'

'It doesn't sound good. Very little fuel. They can't hold out much longer. Rawlins wants you to come up with a rescue plan.'

'Why me?'

'Because you've pulled three rotations out here. You understand this environment better than anyone.'

'Seven more mouths to feed.'

Nikki looked around.

'They say you spend a lot of time down here,' she said.

'I'm looking for anything useful.'

Nikki gestured to the oil drum.

'I'll make you a deal. Be honest with me, and I won't tell anyone you are building a boat.'

'I'm just doing a little housekeeping.'

'You think it's time to bail out. And you're right. There are too many of us to ferry across the North Atlantic. But you can't do it on your own either. I could help.'

Nikki was restless. She sat in the canteen sipping tap water from

83

a mug. Nail and his gang had turned the corner of the canteen into a gymnasium. Nail stood alone pumping dumbbells.

'So how about you?' asked Nikki. 'You and your friends. What's going on in your heads these days?'

'Ever found yourself in a jail cell?'

'I take it you have.'

'It's a waiting game. You have to get a little Zen and do your fucking time, otherwise the confinement will drive you batshit. We're not going anywhere until spring, so Rawlins and his buddies better dredge up a little mental fortitude. All their frantic activity and scheming hasn't got us an inch closer to home. It's all just wasted energy.'

'And come spring? What will you do then?'

'Endure. Survive. Prevail.'

'Yeah,' said Nikki. 'I don't doubt you will.'

Jane and Punch walked four miles inland.

McClure. Three weatherboard huts on stilts. Empty fuel drums and a little latrine hut.

There was a Snowcat and trailer parked outside.

'Looks like we caught a ride,' said Punch.

They climbed the steps of the main hut and pounded the door. No reply. The door was unlocked.

'Hello? Anyone?'

They explored, room by room. Nobody home.

A dormitory. A cramped recreation space with a dartboard and TV. A couple of laboratories jammed with rock samples, ice cores and microscopes.

'Looks like they left in a hurry,' said Jane. 'Personal possessions are gone. Wouldn't expect them to abandon all this lab equipment, though.'

'Probably got an airlift at short notice. Jumped in an Otter. Hand luggage only.'

Punch checked cupboards.

'Maybe they left food.'

'And if they did?' asked Jane. 'Share it with everyone or hide it in your secret den?'

'If we were smart we would go back and tell them this place was levelled by a storm and we found nothing. If we bring back a Snowcat, you can bet we will wake up one morning and find it gone.'

'I've been fat all my life, all right? You don't have to tell me people are shit. But I'm not going to sell out at the first tiny provocation, and neither are you. We're better than that.'

They searched the base.

'Toothpaste,' said Jane. 'That's all I found. Plenty of esoteric lab gear but nothing worth hauling back.'

They checked the Snowcat. A yellow van with caterpillar tracks. Jane checked the trailer. Punch tried the ignition. The Cat wouldn't start. He lifted the hood.

'It's fucked. They vandalised the engine. Stop anyone stealing it, I guess.'

'Fixable?' shouted Jane.

'Not without parts.'

'Come and take a look at this.'

Jane had opened the trailer tailgate and pulled a tarpaulin from a stack of wooden crates.

'Seismologists. Tools of the trade, I suppose.'

DANGER
HIGH EXPLOSIVE

Punch levered a lid.

'Whoa. Blasting caps. Thermite grenades. A shit-load of C4. If you want to shift ice in a hurry this stuff is pure gold.'

They found a plastic cargo sled. They stacked the crates and dragged them back to the zodiac. Jane did most of the pulling.

They loaded the boxes into the zodiac. It sank low in the water.

85

'Let's go find that meteor,' said Punch.

They set off. He steered the boat. Jane tried the radio.

'Shore team to Rampart, over.'

She got nothing but the strange tocking signal.

'It could be military, I suppose. Some kind of interference. You can bet there were a bunch of nuclear subs at sea when this shit kicked off. Maybe they are cruising beneath the ice, ignoring our calls.'

Punch headed for the coast. He jumped ashore and slammed an ice axe into the snow. He tethered the boat to the axe.

'There's not much daylight left. Twenty-five minutes from now we turn around and head back to the boat no matter what, all right?'

They trudged inland. Unearthly desolation. The landscape was so featureless it was like walking on a treadmill: each stride seemed to take them nowhere. The ice was so hard Jane's boots barely left an impression. She checked her watch. Ten minutes gone.

'There,' said Punch. A wide mound up ahead like the cinder cone of a volcano. The lip of a crater.

They doubled their pace. They clambered over ice debris, slabs and boulders thrown from the impact site. They struggled upward. Jane paused to catch her breath.

'Can you see anything?' Punch was standing above her, looking down into the crater. 'What can you see?'

He didn't reply.

Jane scrambled up ice rubble and stood at his side.

'Now what the fuck is that thing?'

The Hatch

'Rampart to Raven, over?'

Rawlins talked through the plan.

'You have lifeboats?'

'*Shitty inflatables. Switlik four-man coastals. No rigid hulls. Nothing with propulsion.*'

'We can't pick you up but we can meet you part way. Take to the boats. Lash them together. Ride the current. It will funnel you west towards us. You'd be a few days at sea.'

'*Jesus. It's a big ocean. How would you find us?*'

'The inflatables should have TACOM beacons. They'll squawk your position soon as they hit the water. There's a relay on our microwave tower. We can track you, once you float in range. Then tow you back to Rampart.'

'*I'll have to persuade the men. It'll be a hard sell.*'

'I doubt it. You folks don't have much alternative. Either roll the dice, or sit and freeze. Talk it over, but don't take too long.'

'*The guys will want to hold on until the very last minute. Wait until the lights go out before they climb in the boats. There's a good chance we'll die. Natural to postpone the moment as long as we can.*'

'I know. I understand. But it would be better if we got it done while there is still a little daylight left.'

'*Like I said, we'll talk it through.*'

'God bless, fella. We're all praying for you.'

Nikki clattered up the spiral steps to the observation bubble.

'Punch and Jane are back. They want to see you right away.'

They sat in Rawlins's office still muffled in thermal suits. Their boots dripped melting snow.

Jane plugged her camera into the PC and brought up pictures.

'Damn,' said Rawlins.

First picture: a round capsule, like a scorched cannon ball, sitting at the centre of a wide impact crater.

Second picture: close-up of the capsule. Punch stood next to it for scale. Twice his height, blackened heat tiles, blackened portholes. No visible insignia.

'Looks sort of Russian to me,' said Rawlins. 'Sort of Soyuz. Some kind of re-entry vehicle.'

'Human?'

'Of course it's bloody human.'

Third picture: long shreds of tattered, candy-stripe fabric in the snow.

'Drogue chutes,' said Punch. 'Looks like they didn't deploy. Probably ripped or tangled in the upper atmosphere.'

'Think there's a connection?' asked Jane. 'All this shit kicks off back home. Space junk falls out of the sky.'

'Doubt it. Poor bastards were probably marooned like those guys on Raven. Sitting in their space station watching it all go down on TV. Dropping through the atmosphere without proper telemetry. Just trying to get home.'

Fourth picture: close-up of the capsule. A heavy hatch with a small, dark window. No obvious hinge or handle.

'We have to get the hatch open,' said Jane.

'Nothing could survive that impact,' said Rawlins. 'It's been days. If they were alive they would have climbed out by now.'

'Come on. You're as curious as I am. Besides, it's screwing up our radio. Long-wave is swamped. The beacon is drowning our mayday signal. No one can hear us call for help while that thing is out there. If we get inside we can switch it off.'

'All right, but you two stay home.'

'Fuck that.'

'I'm going. My turn ashore. And I'm taking Ghost. I'll need him to open the hatch. Sorry, but that's the way it is.'

Sian called Raven and ran through a list of questions. Rawlins wanted to hear their preparations in detail.

'There's seven of you, yeah?'

'*Yeah. Seven.*'

'You'll take to the rafts.'

'*We'll lash a couple together.*'

'What kind of survival gear do you have?'

'*We are going to carpet the rafts with NB3 parkas. The rafts have rain covers but no insulation. We are going to rely on hydro-suits to keep warm. Wrap ourselves in garbage bags. Sleep in shifts. Pack a ton of Pro-Plus to keep us going. We've got canned food, we've got flares. Hopefully that should see us through.*'

'Rawlins reckons you'll make it.'

'*Good.*'

'But if anything goes wrong, if we get picked up and you don't, is there a message you would like to pass along?'

'*I hadn't thought about it.*'

'That's something you could do. Your lads could use the radio, one by one, in private. They could each dictate a message. I could write it down.'

'*I'll mention it to the men. They might take you up on it.*'

Rawlins checked through her notes.

'I wish they had a radio they could carry with them.'

'Not much we could do if anything went wrong,' said Sian.

'A few weeks from now we might be in the same position. Climbing in the lifeboats, hoping for a miracle. If these folks don't make it, I'd like to know why. What did they do wrong? What let them down? I hate to use them as lab rats, but that's exactly what they are. The current should bring them right to our door. If it doesn't, if they get carried west into the

North Atlantic, they'll be dead and we'll know our charts are wrong.'

Jane found Ghost in the pump hall. He was checking the gauge of an oxyacetylene tank.

'Are you busy?' he asked.

'No.'

'If you've got a couple of minutes maybe you could give me a hand.'

He took off his turban. He stripped to the waist. Jane tried not to stare. He straddled a metal folding chair in front of a convection heater.

'How long have you been growing it?' asked Jane.

'Pretty much all my life.'

'What about your religion?'

'Seems God isn't answering the phone right now. Besides, I'm in the mood for a big gesture.'

Jane took scissors and hacked away hunks of hair. She gave Ghost a ragged crew cut. He filled a basin with hot water from a flask, foamed his head and shaved himself bald.

He sat in front of a hand mirror. He snipped his beard down to stubble then shaved himself clean.

'Christ,' he said, examining his reflection in a hand mirror. 'A fucking boiled egg. A stranger to myself.'

'What's this stuff?' asked Jane.

There were two kit-bags on the floor. One contained an air compressor. The other contained a large, steel claw.

'Hydraulic spread-cutter. Emergency services use them to extract people from wrecked cars.'

'Use them to open that space capsule?'

'Yeah.'

'After you fish those Raven guys out of the sea.'

'Something like that.'

'You run this rig. You realise that, right? We'd be lost without you.'

'Is that what they say?'

'The guys need a hero.'

'Let me show you something.'

Ghost led Jane down a corridor to a wide storeroom. A winch bolted to girders in the vaulted ceiling. A huge trapdoor in the floor.

'They used this room for hauling equipment aboard. The supply ship sails between the legs of the refinery. The floor opens and you can winch stuff aboard. Cargo containers full of food, fuel, stuff like that.'

There were three rows of oil drums welded to scaffolding poles. Ghost pulled a roll of paper from behind a locker and spread it on a table. Plans for a boat.

'A sloop, like a round-the-world yacht. It's a reliable design.'

'Why oil drums?'

'Ballasted keel. Stable. Unlikely to capsize.'

'It's going to be huge.'

'Even for a two-man vessel you have to build big. You need to carry supplies to last weeks. Fresh water alone could weigh half a tonne.'

'Two-man?'

'I enjoy your company. Is that a problem?'

Nikki went looking for Nail.

'Dive room,' grunted Ivan. 'Man get his head together.'

C deck. Dark, frozen passageways. Nikki was spooked. She paused, now and again, to shine her torch down the passageway behind her. She felt stalked.

She entered the dive store. The walls were hung with tanks, regulators, wetsuits and fins. A Tilley lamp sat on a table.

A knife blurred past her face and slammed into a locker. The titanium blade punched hilt-deep into the door. The door was peppered with slit-holes. Target practice.

'What the fuck do you want?' asked Nail. Metal shrieked as he jerked the serrated blade from the locker door.

'Ghost is building a boat.'

'What kind of boat?'

'Some kind of crude yacht. He's making it out of oil drums. He's making it in secret.'

'Why are you telling me?'

'Everyone on this rig is going to die. They're passive. Cattle. You and I are different. Survivors.'

'One scumbag to another.'

'You know what I'm saying. I'm not going to pretend I like you. But together we can make it home.'

'Want to shake on it?'

'Fuck yourself.'

'How far has he got with his boat?'

'Haven't seen it. At a guess, early stages.'

'I can't picture him sailing away on his own. He's not the type.'

'He's taking a holiday from virtue. He's flirting with the idea of bailing out but, when the moment comes, he'll pull back.'

'Find the boat. Monitor his progress. When the job is done, we'll take it.'

'You and me?'

'They've got you cooking in the kitchen, yeah?'

'When Punch isn't around. Rawlins's last effort was a disaster.'

'Meal bars,' said Nail. 'Punch gives them to shore teams. He has a few boxes at the back of the storeroom. They give you the keys, right? Get a box. Shove the other boxes around so it looks like none are missing.'

'Okay.'

'Now fuck off. I'm busy.'

Nikki headed down an unlit passageway to the stairs. She heard the knife slam into metal.

*   *   *

Ghost and Rawlins got ready to leave. They met at the boat-house. Ghost loaded the spread-cutter into the zodiac.

Jane and Punch came to wave farewell.

Boxes piled on deck.

Rawlins pulled a tarpaulin aside.

'Is this the gear?'

'Yeah,' said Punch. He opened crates. 'Enough plastic explosive to put us on the moon. Blasting caps, det cord, initiators. And these babies.'

He handed Rawlins a red canister.

'M14 thermite grenades. A couple of dozen. Seemed too good to leave behind.'

'These guys were seriously tooled up.'

'Reflection seismology. Make a big bang, then listen to the ground-echo on geophones.'

'I want this shit off the rig, all right? Ghost. Soon as we get back, I want you to take this stuff to the bunker and hide it deep.'

'Okay.'

'Our little secret, yeah? Nobody else need know.'

Sian prepared dinner. She boiled two kilos of pasta in a saucepan. Nikki grated cheese.

'I hope you don't mind me asking,' said Sian. 'Alan and Simon. Your friends from the island. How well did you know them?'

'We were postgrads from Brighton.'

'So are you doing okay? Everyone making you welcome?'

'I've been keeping to myself.'

Nikki didn't want to talk. She didn't care to know anyone on the rig. She didn't want to hear their life story. She didn't want to hear their hopes and dreams.

'We need more sauce. Pass me the storeroom keys.'

Ghost steered the zodiac. The boat rode low in the water, weighed down by equipment. Rawlins sat in the prow.

They dragged the boat ashore, drove stakes into the ground and lashed it down. They shouldered their gear and set off. A rose twilight turned the snow pink as blossom.

It took them twenty minutes to reach the crater. They stood at the lip of the impact site and looked down at the capsule.

'What do you think it is?' asked Rawlins.

'I read somewhere that low-orbit installations are equipped with escape pods. If anything goes wrong the astronauts can eject. Maybe that's what happened. This thing was meant to land in the Russian Steppes and send out a distress signal but the chutes fucked up.'

They descended to the bottom of the crater. Rawlins erected a dome tent. Ghost ringed the capsule with tripod lamps.

The sun set. They worked in the brilliant white illumination of halogen lights. A tight circle of white brilliance surrounded by endless night.

Ghost tried the radio.

'Shore team to Rampart.'

Every waveband swamped by alien pops and whistles.

'We need to shut this thing down. It's killing every channel.'

Ghost hacked at silica heat tiles with the spike end of a fire axe. The tiles were hexagonal. He chipped away tiles and examined the steel skin beneath.

'Take a look at this.'

Rawlins joined him by the capsule. Ghost had exposed a red, T-shaped handle. An inscription in Cyrillic:

Фпасиость
взрывчашые бопмы

A translation beneath:

Danger
Explosive Bolts

'How do you want to do this?' asked Rawlins.

'You take cover. I'll crank the lever.'

Rawlins sheltered behind the capsule.

Ghost stood to the side of the hatch. He shielded his face, twisted the lever and snatched his hand away quick as he could. The rectangular hatch blew like a champagne cork. It flew twenty feet and landed in the snow.

Ghost shone his flashlight into the capsule. Three seats, one occupant. The body of an astronaut strapped in front of winking instrumentation.

'You think that's the transponder?' asked Rawlins, pointing to a bank of switches.

Ghost held out the radio. A shrill feedback shriek.

'I'm not going to fuck around,' said Ghost. 'We'll toss a thermite grenade. Fry the whole thing.'

Rawlins hauled himself into the cramped cabin. He held a metal seat frame for support.

The cosmonaut wore a bulky pressure suit. Grey canvas webbing. The gloves, boots and helmet were attached to the suit by heavy lock rings. Russian insignia on his chest and sleeve. The suit was connected to a wall-mounted oxygen supply by a hose.

'Wait. I want to check him out.'

'Why?'

'Aren't you curious? CCCP. Old Soviet mission badge. Red fist. I'm guessing military. How long has this guy been floating around up there? Decades? You weren't even born when this guy got launched into space. I want to know who he was. I want to know how he died.'

Rawlins fumbled at the five-point harness. He took off his gloves but couldn't release the buckle.

'Pass me your knife.'

He sawed through the straps.

'Leave him,' said Ghost. 'I don't like it. Doesn't feel right. The whole thing.' He took a red, cylindrical grenade from his coat pocket. 'Call it a cremation.'

'Hold on. Someone, somewhere, will want to know what happened to this guy.'

Rawlins tried to twist the helmet free. He couldn't release the lock ring. He gave up. He pushed the lift-tabs at the corner of the visor. The gold face-plate slid back.

A young man's face. Mirror skin, like he was sculpted from chrome.

Eyelids flicked open. Jet-black eyeballs. A silent snarl. Metal lips, metal teeth.

Rawlins screamed.

Contamination

Punch stood in the kitchen storeroom with a clipboard. Stock check. Jane surveyed the shelves.

'Kidney beans: six cans. Rhubarb: three cans. Chopped tomatoes: two cases of twelve.'

They contemplated the dwindling supply of cans and cartons.

'Good job we keep this place locked,' said Punch. 'If the guys glimpsed how little food we have left they would panic for sure.'

'Maybe we should reduce portion size,' said Jane. 'Use rice and pasta for bulk.'

'There must be someone on board who knows how to fish. Remind me at dinner, when everyone is in the canteen. I'll ask around.'

They heard running feet. The squeak of trainers on tiles. Sian stood panting in the doorway, holding the frame for support.

'There's a message from Ghost. Rawlins is hurt. Injured or something. They're on their way back.'

They descended the leg of the refinery and stood on the ice. Jane scanned the horizon with binoculars. The zodiac was a black dot approaching fast.

'Jeez,' said Punch. 'He's pushing it hard.'

Ghost swerved the boat to a halt, kicking up spray. He killed the engine. Rawlins lay at the bottom of the zodiac. His right arm was wrapped in a foil insulation blanket. They dragged him from the boat and laid him on ice surrounding the refinery leg.

'Don't touch him,' said Ghost. 'Don't touch his skin.'

They hauled Rawlins across the ice to the deck of the platform lift. The lift was bolted to the south leg of the refinery. They laid him on the floor plates.

'Where's Dr Rye?' asked Ghost.

'Waiting at the top.'

'Okay. Punch, you had better stay behind and secure the boat.'

Ghost jabbed the Up button. The elevator jolted to life.

Jane leaned over Rawlins. His face was hidden beneath a ski mask and goggles.

'Is he conscious?' she asked.

'He moves now and again. He's not talking.'

'What's wrong with him?'

'Easier if you see.'

Rye met them at an airlock. She helped carry Rawlins inside and lay him on the stretcher buggy.

Convulsions. Rye wriggled on nitrile gloves. She pulled off Rawlins's mask and goggles. His eyes rolled. His lips were blue.

'No skin contact,' warned Ghost. 'No mouth-to-mouth, whatever you do.'

Rye ripped open Rawlins's coat. Twenty chest compressions.

'He's breathing. All right. Let's go.'

The buggy's headbeam lit the way as she steered down dark corridors. Jane, Sian and Ghost jogged behind, keeping pace as best they could.

Medical. Rye restored power. The white room lit up.

They laid Rawlins on the examination table. Rye re-angled the light canopy above him.

'There's a convection heater in my office,' said Rye. 'Get it going.'

She put on a mouth mask and goggles. She wriggled on a pair of surgical gloves.

'Okay. You folks better get in the office and stay there.'

They sat in Rye's office and watched through an observation window.

Rye took scissors and forceps from a drawer. She snipped through the foil blanket that sheathed Rawlins's arm and peeled it back. Blood dribbled on the floor.

'Treat every drop of that shit like AIDS,' advised Ghost, via a wall-mounted intercom. 'Scrub it. Bleach it.'

Rye scattered swabs on the floor to sop the blood.

'And be careful with his arm,' said Ghost. 'Don't touch it, whatever you do.'

Rawlins's hand had turned dark, skin mottled like a bad bruise.

'Frostbite?' asked Jane.

'No.'

'Are you sure? Looks like Simon's hand when we pulled him off the ice.'

'Look closer.'

The flesh bristled with needle-fine splinters of metal.

'My God.'

Rye sliced away Rawlins's clothes with trauma shears. She plucked dog-tags from his neck.

'O neg.'

She wriggled on a double layer of gloves and canulated Rawlins's left hand. She took a bag of O neg from the fridge and set it to feed.

'His heart rate is high,' said Rye. 'His breathing seems unimpaired. So what actually happened?'

'We opened the capsule. Frank crawled inside. There was a body, an astronaut. Frank tried to take off his helmet. Next minute he was screaming and bleeding.'

'An astronaut?'

'Some kind of cosmonaut. He was dead. Way dead. Then he woke up. He grabbed Rawlins. They fought. I hauled Frank out of there and torched the whole thing.'

'His fingers. That looks like a bite mark.'

'Yeah. Frank said something about teeth, metal teeth. I don't know. Frank wasn't making a lot of sense. Like I said, I didn't investigate. I didn't climb inside. I hauled Frank out and threw a grenade.'

Rye took tweezers and tugged at a metal spine.

'These filaments seem to be anchored in bone.'

'It's spreading. It started at his fingertips. Now it's reached his wrist.'

Rawlins woke. He licked his lips.

'How are you feeling, Frank?' asked Rye, leaning close.

'Don't take my arm.'

'You'll be okay,' she soothed. 'We'll fix you up.'

'It tastes funny,' said Rawlins, and passed out.

'Right,' said Rye. 'You three. Get your coats off and scrub up. I need you in here.'

They lathered their hands and forearms in Bioguard scrub.

Rye unlocked a cupboard. She took out a tray of surgical instruments and slit open the vacuum-sealed plastic. She unwrapped a surgical saw and laid it on the surgical trolley.

'What do you have in mind?' asked Sian.

'You're going to help me amputate his arm.'

'Don't you have anything more high-tech than that?' asked Jane, pointing at the saw.

'I've got an electric blade but I don't want to spray blood everywhere.'

They gave Rawlins a shot of morphine and strapped him to the table. Rye intubated his throat. She wheeled a heart monitor to the table. She pasted electrodes to Rawlins's chest and set the machine beeping.

'Watch the screen,' she told Sian. 'If that figure drops below thirty-five, yell.'

She took saline from the refrigerator and hung it from the drip stand.

'Keep an eye on the bags,' she told Jane. 'Let me know when he needs a refill.'

She swabbed Rawlins's arm just below the elbow.

'Ghost. Keep hold of his shoulders, okay? He could buck. Right. Everybody ready?'

Rye sliced into Rawlins's arm with a scalpel and clamped his arteries. Yellow globules of subcutaneous fat glistened like butter.

She sawed his arm. She worked through bone in short rasps like she was sawing through a table leg.

'Think he will be okay?' asked Jane when they had finished.

'I'll give him another shot when he wakes. After that, it's aspirin.'

'So what about you, Doc? What if we need to fix you up?'

'Anything happens, shoot me a spinal and I'll talk you through it.'

Rawlins's face was pale and slack. Jane instinctively moved to wipe sweat from his forehead.

'No,' warned Ghost.

Husky exhalations through an airway tube. Steady beep of the cardiograph.

'Done that before?' asked Ghost. 'Cut off an arm?'

'Snipped plenty of fingers,' said Rye. 'Standard oil-field crush injury.'

'Reckon he'll make it?'

'Normal circumstances I would expect him to recover from the amputation, as long as the wound doesn't become infected. This disease, though. Never seen anything like it.'

Ghost thumbed through Rawlins's medical notes.

'Stress. Depression. Prostate trouble. Poor bastard. Should have cashed out of this game years ago.'

'Put that down,' ordered Rye. 'That stuff is confidential.'

They stuffed Rawlins's shredded clothes into a red body-waste sack. They bagged bloody swabs and dressings. They slopped bleach on the floor.

Ghost picked up the sacks with gloved hands. He held them at arm's length.

'Throw that shit over the side,' ordered Rye.

She used forceps to pick up the severed arm. She dropped it into a plastic box and sealed the lid. She handed the box to Jane.

'And get rid of that fucking thing, will you?'

Jane called Punch on the intercom. She asked him to fetch a can of kerosene and meet her on the ice.

They walked from beneath the shadow of the refinery and stood at the water's edge.

'How is he?'

'Out for the count,' said Jane. 'He might live. He might not.'

'So who is in charge now?'

'Fuck knows.'

'This isn't a democracy. If we vote on every little fucking thing it will be a disaster.'

'Yeah.'

'Somebody better step up. If Nail and his compadres start calling the shots we'll be dead within a week.'

'Yeah.'

'You actually cut off his arm?' asked Punch.

Jane peeled the lid from the box.

'Christ,' he said. 'How did it happen?'

'We won't know for sure until he is awake and talking.'

'Swear to God, I won't let that happen to me.'

They put the box on the ice, doused it in kerosene and set it alight. It burned with a blue flame. The hand slowly clenched as it cooked.

Medical.

Rye checked on Rawlins. He lay on the examination table draped in a sheet. The stump of his arm was bandaged. Steady beep from a monitor.

Rye examined a drop of blood beneath a microscope. Red

platelets. Black, barbed organisms swarmed and replicated. Hard to see detail. She wished she had better magnification.

Movement in the periphery of her vision. Maybe Rawlins stirred in his drugged sleep. Maybe she imagined it. She watched him for a while. She got spooked. She played music to feel less alone. Charlie Parker. *Live at Storyville*. CD fed into the player. Cool jazz echoed down empty corridors.

Jane helped make dinner. Spaghetti greased with a crude pesto made from dried basil, garlic paste and a squirt of tomato purée.

She carried her bowl to the table.

'I can't stop thinking about it,' said Punch. 'I'd rather my mother was dead than walking round with that shit sprouting out of her skin.'

'Don't. It'll drive you nuts.'

'We should take the Skidoos and split for Alaska. Seriously. You, me, Sian. Ghost, if you want. Anyone can see you dig the guy. A few more weeks and the sea will be frozen. We'd have a shot. We'd have a straight run.'

'What about everyone else?'

'Fuck them. Sorry, but fuck them.'

'We're not at that point yet. We've still got options.'

'Then somebody better lay out the Big Plan. Look around you. Morale is down the toilet.'

Rye's voice on the intercom: '*Jane. Punch. We need you in Medical right away.*'

The operating table was empty.

'Where's he gone?' demanded Jane.

'He didn't leave a note,' said Rye.

'You left him alone?'

'I need to eat now and again. And the occasional shit.'

'How long were you gone?'

'Fifteen, twenty minutes.'

The drip stand lay on the floor. The cardiograph was smashed.

Jane kicked at a scrap of surgical dressing with her boot. 'He tore the canula out of his arm,' she said.

'He'll be losing blood.'

'He had his arm chopped off two hours ago. How is he able to walk around?'

'I've no idea.'

Ghost arrived.

'He's gone walkabout?' said Ghost. 'You're kidding me.'

'We'd better find him quickly,' said Jane. 'It's minus twenty in those corridors. The cold will kill him in minutes.'

C deck. Household stores. Sian scanned the shelves by flashlight. She loaded a trolley with toilet roll, liquid soap and paper towels.

She pushed the trolley down unlit passageways, Maglite clenched between her teeth like a cigar.

Movement in shadow up ahead.

'Hello?'

She reached a junction. She shone her flashlight down a side tunnel. A figure. A glimpse of bare flesh.

'Hello?'

Sian stood in a doorway. A dark chamber. Stacked lengths of pipe.

A naked man crouched in shadow. Rawlins.

'What's the deal, Frank?'

She stepped closer. She saw the bloody, bandaged stump where an arm used to be. And she saw the face. One eye was jet black. The other eye looked at her in cold calculation. She felt herself appraised by a keen alien intelligence.

She backed away and ran.

They searched rooms and passageways near Medical. They found the airway tube. Rawlins had pulled it from his throat. It was lying on the deck plate. It was glazed with frozen saliva.

'We better split up,' said Ghost. 'Cover more ground.'

'Hold on a moment,' said Jane. 'This has to be the same shit we saw on TV, right? Drives you nuts like rabies. Maybe Frank is okay. But maybe not. We have to be prepared.'

'What do you have in mind?' asked Punch.

'I think you should go back to the accommodation block. Warn the others and barricade the door.'

'What are you and Ghost going to do?'

'Head to the island and fetch the shotguns.'

The Hunt

Ghost hauled open the bunker door. His flashlight lit shelves and boxes, and the snowmobiles shrouded in tarpaulin.

'Okay. Better be quick.'

Jane unboxed shotguns.

'Give them to me.'

Ghost checked the breech of each weapon and dry-fired to make sure they were safe. He zipped the guns and their cleaning kits into a holdall.

'Get the shells.'

Jane snatched boxes of 12-gauge shells from a shelf and stuffed them into her backpack.

'There's a sell-by on these boxes. I didn't think ammunition expired.'

'Let's get going.'

Rawlins found he could see in the dark. Not clearly. Not well. But he could make out shapes.

He stood naked at the centre of the dive room. He wondered how he got there. Self-awareness came and went. Sometimes he was Frank Rawlins. Sometimes he was something else.

He lit a Tilley lamp so he could see better. Benches. Racks of diving equipment. The white, steel bubble of a hypobaric chamber.

He opened a locker and examined his reflection in the door mirror. One eye was as black as onyx.

Rawlins took a dive belt from a wall hook. He unsheathed the knife and used the tip to prise the eye from its socket. He did it left-handed. He sawed through the optic nerve. The eyeball plopped at his feet.

He stared at his reflection. The empty socket wept blood. He took a scuba tank from a wall rack and pounded the mirror to glass-dust.

Rawlins's office. A sign on the door:

STRICTLY NO UNAUTHORISED PERSONNEL

Punch switched on the lights. It felt like trespass.

'The desk drawer,' said Sian. 'That's where he keeps it.'

Punch levered the latch with a screwdriver. He took the Taser from its case.

'It feels like a toy. Should stop him dead, though.'

'Then what?' said Sian. 'If he has this infection we can't lay a finger on him.'

'Improvise a straitjacket. Tie him up in a sleeping bag or something. Lock him in a freight container. Quarantine, until we see what's what.'

Sian examined the desk screen. A couple of clicks brought up a floor plan of the refinery.

'He's on C deck, right? We can track him.'

Punch leaned over her shoulder. The C deck schematic was speckled with red dots.

'We dropped some of the blast doors when we powered down the rig. The doors show up on the status board. Keep watching. He might betray his location.'

'Don't move from that chair, all right?' Punch gave Sian his radio. 'If you see movement, shout.'

Punch lowered the blast door, sealing himself inside the accommodation module.

He was armed with a pool cue and the Taser.

He slid down the wall and sat on the corridor floor with the Taser cradled in his lap.

'*How's it going?*' Sian's voice.

Punch took out his radio.

'Sentry duty.'

'*Can we lock the hatches? Can we stop him moving around?*'

'The blast doors seal tight in an emergency. Otherwise anyone can raise them. Only the airlocks have keypads. Protection against piracy.'

'*We have to assume he is infected.*'

'What else can we do? We have to treat him as hostile until we know better.'

'*I wish we could be sure. Severe blood loss. He's going to freeze.*'

'I know. I know.'

A thud against the door. Punch jumped to his feet.

'Frank? Is that you?'

Punch trained his Taser at the door. The hatch began to slide upward. He hit Close.

He pressed the intercom.

'Frank? Are you okay?'

'*I'm cold. Very cold.*'

'Are you infected? Your arm. Can you tell me? Did it halt the infection?'

'*So cold.*' Rawlins sounded weak, delirious.

'You've got to tell us, Frank. We have to know.'

'*So tired.*'

'We can't let you in, Frank. Frank? Are you there?'

He waited a full minute. He hit Open. The door slid back.

Nothing beyond but an empty corridor.

Punch called Sian.

'Frank just tried to get in.'

'*Is he still there?*'

'He's gone.'

'*Wait. Someone just entered an airlock near Medical.*'

'Did he go outside?'

'No. He just opened the interior door.'

'Anyone heard from Jane and Ghost?'

'No.'

'We need those shotguns.'

Rawlins ransacked the airlock. He struggled to pull up trousers. He shrugged on a coat. He stepped into boots.

He searched the rig for cigarettes. He dragged himself down dark, frozen passageways. He slid along pipework for support. He hugged the stump of his right arm, sheathed in an empty sleeve, to his chest.

Cigarettes were forbidden. Big red signs in each recreation area. *'No unauthorised sources of ignition.'*

When Rawlins took control of the rig five months ago he smuggled cigarettes aboard. Two a day for the duration of the tour. He used to sneak outside and light up. He knew most of the crew smoked weed but he didn't care. It kept the men occupied. It kept them sedated. But he was the installation manager and couldn't be seen to break the rules. He kept a pack of cigarettes and a Zippo hidden among fire equipment near an airlock. He couldn't remember which airlock. He couldn't remember much at all.

He sat in the gymnasium for a while, one of the few rooms on the refinery with a large window. Weak daylight. It was noon, and the sun was barely above the horizon. Rows of cycles and treadmills glittered with ice. Centrefolds blurred by frost. He pulled up his sleeve and examined his bandaged stump. Metal spines protruded from the gauze. The skin surrounding his elbow had started to blacken.

'So here we are,' he thought. 'My dying day.'

Frank once saw a man clutch his chest and collapse while queuing in a bank. He guessed it was the same for most people. Walking round with a head full of humdrum until a terminal diagnosis or myocardial infarction struck out of the blue. Was it October? November? Hard to think straight. He was pretty sure it was Tuesday.

He lay on a sunbed for a while and woke up shivering. His parka had fallen open. He couldn't work the zip.

He remembered where he hid cigarettes. Airlock 63.

Jane and Ghost arrived back at the rig. They winched the zodiac into the boathouse.

Ghost showed Jane how to operate a shotgun as they rode the freight elevator to habitation level.

'You've seen it on TV a million times. Slot five shells into the receiver. Pump the slide. Pull it all the way back. Nice, firm stroke. Set the safety to Fire. And for God's sake don't put your finger on the trigger until you are ready to shoot.'

'Cool.'

'Press the gun to your shoulder. Brace your legs. Boom.'

They took a shortcut. They crossed the deck and entered an airlock.

Ghost took out his radio.

'We're back.'

'*I'm in Frank's office,*' said Sian. '*I'm watching the doors. Someone just opened airlock 27.*'

'That's us. We just came aboard.'

'*Watch yourselves. You might run into him.*'

They opened the internal door of the airlock. Ghost surveyed the corridor, shotgun at the ready.

'This feels a bit over-dramatic,' said Jane. 'This is Frank we are talking about. He's probably just confused.'

'You saw that shit growing out of his hand. Want that to happen to you?'

'Not particularly.'

'Don't point that thing at me, all right? Point it at the floor.'

*　　*　　*

Rawlins hugged a corridor wall. Dancing flashlight beams. Two figures stepped out of an airlock. Jane and Ghost. They carried shotguns.

He padded behind them as they entered the pipe store. He stayed in shadow while they crouched and examined the floor.

'This is where Sian found him,' said Jane.

'Blood drips. Must have been squatting here a while. Wonder what was going on in his head.' Ghost took yellow spray paint from his pocket, shook the can and circled the blood drips. 'We'll have to clean this level room by room. Bleach the whole fucking place.'

'Sian said his eye was black.'

'Could be a haemorrhage. Not necessarily proof of infection.'

Rawlins stood behind them. He fought rising bloodlust. He wanted to seize them. He wanted to bite. He wanted to rip and tear.

He ducked behind a pillar as they stood and turned.

'Might be worth re-checking Medical,' said Ghost. 'It's been a while. He might go back. He might want something for the pain.'

They made their way to the accommodation block. Ghost pounded the blast door with his fist. He shouted into the intercom.

'It's us. Me and Jane. We're coming in.'

He hit Open. The door slid back.

'Frank tried to get in,' said Punch.

'Is he infected?' asked Jane.

'I heard him. I didn't see him.'

'He's alive at least.'

'Look,' said Ghost. He shone his flashlight at the deck plates. Footprints on frosted metal. 'He left a trail.'

'Where?'

'See that?' he said, pointing at a cluster of prints. 'That's us, coming and going. But look here.' Bare footprints near the wall. 'That's him. Is Rye upstairs?'

'Yeah.'

'Find her. Tell her to load a hypodermic with some kind of sedative.'

'You want me to tag along?'

'No. Just me and Jane. Keep the door shut, okay? We'll be back in a while.'

They tracked footprints to the gym.

'Looks like he took a nap,' said Ghost, examining a sunbed. 'More blood. Here and here.' He took out his spray can and circled the drips. 'He can't give us the run-around much longer. Not in this cold.'

They tracked prints down a C deck corridor.

'Boots,' said Ghost. 'Fresh.'

'Sure it's not us?'

'We haven't been down this way.'

The footprints led to an open doorway.

FUEL STORE

'Put your safety catch on,' instructed Ghost. 'No shooting, all right? Don't want to blow us all to hell.'

Ghost stood in the doorway.

'Frank?' he called. 'Are you okay?' No reply. 'I'm coming in, Frank. Is that all right?'

Ghost shone his flashlight into the storeroom. Stacked oil drums. Jerry cans. Tins of kerosene.

'Frank? You there?'

Ghost went inside. Jane followed.

Rawlins was kneeling in the corner shadows. Jane saw him first. He was soaked in kerosene, an empty fuel can by his side and an unlit cigarette between his lips.

'Hey, Frank,' said Jane. 'How have you been?'

'Fucked-up day.' His fringe dripped like he just stepped from the shower.

'Yeah. It's been a bad year all round.'

Rawlins had taken off his coat. His arm and neck were bruised black and yellow. His empty eye socket wept blood.

'So what do you say, Frank?' asked Ghost. 'How about we take you back to Medical for a while and look after you?'

Rawlins gave a woozy smile and shook his head. He gestured to his mutilated arm, his missing eye.

'I don't think Lemsip is going to help much, do you?'

'Yeah, but I'd rather you didn't light up. You have to show a little consideration for others.'

'There's no way home. We all know it, so why drag it out?' He stroked the black flesh of his throat. 'It wants things. This disease. It has an agenda.' He reached into the pocket of his ragged trousers. 'Sorry, folks.' He flipped open his Zippo. 'I've got to go while I'm still me.' He closed his eyes and struck the lighter. Blue flame washed over him.

Jane and Ghost ran for the door. They slung the shotguns over their shoulders and snatched extinguishers from the wall.

Frank was dead and burning. They trained jets of carbon dioxide at the fire, but the flames spread between oil drums.

A propane tank blew. It ricocheted off three walls and burst a couple of jerry cans, triggering a massive fireball.

'We've lost it,' yelled Ghost. 'Let's get out of here.'

They ran for the door. Jane hit Close. The door dropped like a guillotine, blocking the tide of flame that threatened to flood the corridor and incinerate them.

Ghost touched the door but quickly snatched his hand away. Superhot metal.

'Let it burn. It'll drink all the oxygen soon enough.'

They jogged down the corridor.

'You okay?' asked Ghost.

'Yeah. I'm fine.'

An explosion punched out the fuel store door like a fist. The heavy hatch cart-wheeled down the corridor towards them, propelled by fire.

They ran for the stairwell. Jane hammered the Close button with her fist. The blast door slid down as a juggernaut of flame rushed to meet them. Fire flickered round their boots as the hatch slammed shut.

Fire

Sian sat at Rawlins's desk. The lights flickered. Slight tremor. A pot of pencils toppled from the desk and scattered on the floor.

Sian picked up the radio.

'Guys? Ghost? Do you copy, over?'

The lights flickered again.

'Guys, what's going on?'

A sudden alarm. A red ceiling strobe began to flash. A woman's super-calm voice: '. . . *Emergency stations. Fire warning. Emergency stations. Fire warning . . .*'

Sian checked the floor plan on the desk screen. The fuel store and adjacent corridor flashed red.

'Folks, I've got multiple alerts in D Module. What's going on?'

Punch ran down the corridor towards D Module. He fumbled for his radio.

'. . . *Emergency stations. Fire warning. Emergency stations. Fire warning . . .*'

'What's the deal?' he said, shouting to be heard over the emergency announcement.

'*Fire and monoxide alerts on C deck,*' said Sian. '*Lots of them.*'

'Is this is a system fault or an actual fire?'

'*I'm going up to the roof,*' said Sian. '*I'm going to check.*'

'Close the blast doors. Drop any left open. Close them all.'

'*What about Ghost and Jane?*'

Ghost and Jane ran up the stairs. They reached the top just as a blast door closed, sealing them inside the D Module stairwell. Ghost jabbed Open. The hatch didn't respond.

'There must be an override,' said Jane.

'There is. A key. Punch has it.'

He took out his radio.

'Sian? Sian, do you copy, over?' No response. 'Fucking stairway. It's a refuge point. Thick walls.'

'That's good, right?'

Wisps of smoke from below. They leaned over the railing. The bottom of the stairwell was hazed with smoke. Ghost ripped open a fire locker. He ran down the stairs with an Ansul extinguisher. Jane followed.

'These doors are supposed to hold back thousand-degree heat for twelve hours straight,' coughed Jane.

'It's not the door, it's the conduits. Electrical fires behind the bulkheads.'

Black smoke seeped from a wall-vent. Ghost discharged the extinguisher into the vent. The jet of carbon dioxide roared, sputtered and died.

'Sian? Sian, can you hear me, over? Fuck.'

They ran upstairs. Ghost took breathing apparatus from the fire locker. One air tank. One mask. They buddy-breathed, drew lungfuls of oxygen as they passed the mask back and forth.

'How much air is in this tank?' gasped Jane.

'Thirty minutes, tops.'

Sian vaulted stairs to the helipad. She forgot her coat. She ran outside in her T-shirt.

Smoke wafted from the adjacent accommodation block.

'We have a fire. A big one. C level. Are you getting this, Punch? Can you hear me?'

Sian leaned over the edge of the helipad to get a better view.

She was shivering with cold. Water gushed from beneath the burning habitation block and cascaded into the sea. A ruptured pipe.

'Punch, I'm looking over the side. Heavy damage. We're losing water. There are flames.'

'. . . *Emergency stations. Fire warning. Emergency stations. Fire warning . . .*'

Punch ran down the corridor to D Module. The hatch at the end of the passage had a porthole. Fire on the other side. A passageway clogged with smoke and flame.

Think like Ghost. What would he do?

Punch ran to the fire point. Breathing apparatus. He took out an oxygen cylinder and struggled to release the valve. He strapped it to his back and buckled the harness. So heavy he almost toppled backward. He tugged on the face-mask.

Rawlins drilled the crew once a month. A three-step procedure in the event of fire:

Seal the doors.

Put on a mask.

Find the nearest fire suppression wall box. Smash the glass. Pull the lever. Trigger the deluge system

Punch ran to a wall box. He smashed the glass with his elbow. He yanked the red lever to On. Nothing happened. He tried it twice more. Nothing. The lever should have released the Inergen gas system. Ceiling valves should have flooded the corridors with an inert mix of argon, nitrogen and carbon dioxide, and choked the fire. Punch ripped off his mask.

'Sian, why the fuck haven't the suppressors kicked in?'

Punch unravelled a fire hose. He twisted the stop-cock. The hose swelled. He trained the low-pressure stream at the blast door. Water gulped and sputtered. It splashed against the hatch and fizzled like spit on a hot plate.

'This is fucked,' he muttered. He threw down the hose and

took out his radio. 'I'm coming up top. There's not much I can do down here.'

Punch joined Sian on the helipad. He threw her a coat.

'Nothing from Ghost and Jane?'

'Nothing,' said Sian.

'Ivan knows how to operate the crane. He can lower me on to the roof.'

Punch stood alone on the helipad. He pulled a silver, fire-retardant proximity suit over his survival gear. The suit was comically big. He had to roll up the sleeves.

He buckled a SCBA cylinder to his back. The sun had set. He looked up at a fabulous dusting of stars.

Worse ways to go, he thought. Die fighting. Die for your friends.

There was a heavy freight crane mounted on the deck between the accommodation blocks. Sian and Ivan could swing him from one roof to another.

He could see them in the cab. Ivan at the controls. Sian crouched beside him.

Punch waved. They swung the jib and lowered the hook. There was a cargo pallet hung from the hook, a wooden platform suspended by a chain.

Punch pulled on his face-mask. He stepped on to the platform. He gave a thumbs up. They swung him towards the burning accommodation module.

Jane and Ghost crouched in the stairwell. The air was thick with hydrogen sulphide. Ghost struggled to stay conscious. His eyelids drooped like he wanted to sleep. Jane crouched over him and pressed the mask to his face. She snatched the mask away and took a gulp of oxygen every few seconds.

The blast door raised. A slight figure in an oversized silver suit. Punch, smiling through the polycarbonate visor.

'Let's get out of here, shall we?' His voice was muffled by his mask.

They hurried down the corridor. They supported Ghost between them. He started to revive.

Ivan sat in the crane cab. Sian stood at his shoulder.

'Punch, do you copy, over? Punch?'

The wind changed. The cab was enveloped in black smoke from the burning accommodation block.

'We must go,' said Ivan.

'Wait.'

'I don't want to get caught up here. Nine-eleven. Jump-or-burn. I don't need it.'

'Just wait.'

They ran past Medical.

'Wait,' said Jane. She ran inside. She flapped open a red body-waste bag. 'We have to save as much as we can.'

She swept armfuls of drugs into the bag. Ghost opened a cupboard and filled a bag with dressings and hypodermics.

Punch stood by the door. The floor felt soft and sticky. He lifted his boot. The rubber sole of his shoe had begun to melt. He crouched and held his hand over the deck plate. Fierce heat. The level beneath them must be ablaze.

'Folks, we need to leave this instant.'

'Go,' said Jane. 'I'm right behind you.'

They ran for the roof. Ghost pushed Punch on to the cargo pallet.

'You go,' said Ghost. 'I'm waiting for Jane.'

'. . . *Emergency stations. Fire warning. Emergency stations. Fire warning . . .*'

The crew mustered in the canteen. They kicked off their heavy boots and zipped themselves into survival suits: insulated wetsuits designed to keep a man alive if he fell into the sea and was immersed in heart-stopping cold. Each man checked his buddy's suit seals and life jacket.

Nail zipped a deck of cards into his suit. Essential supplies. He instinctively retreated to the gym equipment in the corner of the canteen. His territory. His kingdom. He was joined by Mal, Gus and Yakov.

'Any idea what's going on?'

'Keep seeing Punch run back and forth,' said Nail. 'Fucker won't look me in the eye.'

He sniffed.

'Smell that? Burning plastic. If we all sit here waiting for someone to kiss it better, we'll choke.'

'Can we kill that fucking announcement, at least?' said Gus. 'It's driving me nuts.'

Nail ran to Rawlins's office. Empty. He sat at the desk. He checked the screen. The adjacent habitation block flashed red. Fire alerts on every level. He switched on the PA and grabbed the mike.

'All stations. All stations. Abandon rig. Abandon rig.'

The cargo platform swung towards the helipad. Punch touched down.

He ran down the stairwell towards the canteen. Thick smoke. Alarms and strobes.

'. . . *All stations. All stations. Abandon rig. Abandon rig . . .*'

We're going to lose the whole fucking refinery.

What would Ghost do?

Punch stood on a chair in the canteen and clapped for attention.

'Okay, folks. We're out of here.'

He led the crew down the smoke-filled stairway. They coughed. Their eyes streamed. He counted them off as he pushed them into an airlock. One man down.

He found Nail lying unconscious on the stairs. He gripped Nail's ankles and dragged him to the airlock.

They sealed themselves inside. They were choking. Three men puked.

Punch shouldered the exterior door. They whooped freezing air.

'We need to get to the boathouse. The elevators are out of action. We'll have to use the ladders.' The evacuation order was relayed to the crane cab.

'We must go,' said Ivan.

'What about Jane and Ghost?' said Sian.

'I am sorry for your friends.'

He climbed down the ladder to the deck. Sian stayed in the cab. She sat in the operator's seat and tried to make sense of the controls.

'Ghost? Jane? Do you copy, over?'

Ghost ran to Medical. Acrid smoke.

Jane was still throwing drugs and equipment into bags.

'What the fuck are you doing, girl?'

'Help me.'

They hurried up the stairs. They dragged bags.

Alarms. Smoke. Warning strobes.

'Who gave the evacuation order?'

'Sounded like Nail,' said Jane.

'I saw people down on the docking platform. They were climbing into the zodiac.'

'We can't abandon the rig. Without it we are fucked.'

'We don't have a choice,' said Ghost. 'There's plenty of octane distillate left in the pipes. Soon as the fire reaches the injection pumps this place will detonate like a fucking H-bomb.'

They reached the roof.

Driving smoke. They couldn't see the crane cab.

'Sian? Ivan? Do you copy?'

Ghost checked his radio. Low battery warning.

He stood at the edge of the roof and yelled.

'Sian. Ivan.'

He looked down. White furnace heat.

Eight men in the zodiac. The boat rode low in the water. Overloaded. The outboard laboured. They weaved between pack ice.

They reached the island. They lifted Nail ashore. They carried him up the jetty steps to the bunker door.

The crew camped in the tunnel mouth. They lit a couple of storm lamps. They huddled round a hexamine stove for heat. Nobody spoke. They were all thinking the same thing. They were dead bodies. The refinery was life-support. Without the supplies aboard the rig they would last less than a day. Once the stoves burned dry, they would all freeze.

Nail was conscious. He lay still, breathing shallow. Punch crouched beside him.

'How you doing, big guy?'

Nail coughed and flipped him off.

'Take it easy, all right? Give your lungs a chance to recover.'

Punch left the bunker. He stood on the jetty and watched the refinery burn.

D Module was ablaze. The fuel store had been on the lowest level. The fire spread upward, floor by floor, until the habitation block was a pillar of fire.

Flame lit the surrounding sea and ice, flickering orange.

'I'm taking the boat,' Punch told the crew. 'I'm going back to help. Any volunteers?'

They looked away.

Punch rode the zodiac back to Rampart.

He could see the underside of the refinery. Liquid, rippling flame washing over pipes and spars. The sight was mesmeric.

White light at the heart of the conflagration. Thousand-degree heat. It was like staring into the sun. He had to look away.

Debris fell into the sea, spitting geysers of steam.

A shriek. An explosion of sparks. A steady groan, like the refinery was in excruciating pain. A major structural collapse under way.

A cascade of girders: fatally weakened chunks of superstructure tumbled into the ocean with a roar like Niagara.

Punch gripped the side of the boat as waves rippled outward from the refinery, bucking the boat, cracking plates of ice.

Jane and Ghost crouched on the D Module roof. They held each other. They felt the roof begin to buckle and torque. The scream of tortured metal was so loud it became a strange, eye-of-storm silence.

Jane looked up. The crane arm. The cargo pallet descending out of smoke.

Brief glimpse of the crane cab. Sian at the controls.

'Come on,' said Jane.

They threw themselves aboard.

Punch docked the zodiac. He watched D Module fall from the refinery into the sea. Support girders beneath the habitation block, fatally weakened by hours of blowtorch heat, buckled and fractured. The blazing structure slowly toppled forward. It hit the ocean, sending a final mushroom-cloud of flame hundreds of metres into the air. Sudden darkness. Sound of on-rushing water. Punch ran for the stairs, anxious to get higher before seawater washed him into the ocean.

Punch crossed the deck. Devastation lit by moonlight. He stood at the edge of the smoking acre where D Module used to sit. Ragged, twisted girders. Broken pipes. Metal glowed red. Spars part-liquefied by heat. Steel hung in petrified drips. The mangled superstructure ticked and creaked as it quickly cooled in sub-zero air.

Plenty of smoke, but no flames.

The cargo pallet stalled four metres above the deck. The crane was dead. No power. Ghost hung from the pallet and let himself drop. He rolled. He lay on the deck. Jane dropped beside him. She helped Ghost to his feet. He coughed and retched.

'You okay?' asked Punch.

'I'll be all right.'

Jane and Punch explored the remaining habitation block.

They stood in the canteen. Moonlight shafted through the windows. Spectral smoke haze hung in the air. The tables and floor were dusted in a fine layer of soot.

Punch tried the lights.

'Everything is dead.'

'We better check the powerhouse.'

The powerhouse. They surveyed the destruction with an old Aldis lamp. Three John Brown generators, each the size of a bus. The generators were still and silent.

They climbed steps to the mezzanine level. The generator controls were fried. Cabling had burned through.

'You know,' said Jane, 'for a while there I thought we would be okay.'

The Long Game

Jane brought Ghost to the powerhouse. He walked with his arm round her shoulder. She helped him climb the steps to mezzanine level.

'Well, there it is,' said Jane.

Ghost examined the scorched ruins of the generator controls by flashlight. He could barely stand. He leaned on a railing for support.

Two of the control stations were burned and warped. Cracked dials. Cracked screens. A side panel had fallen from one of the consoles exposing melted clumps of cable that hung in tangles like jungle vine.

Ghost coughed and cleared his throat.

'One and Two are fried. Generator Three seems pretty intact. I say we get Three running and maybe cannibalise One and Two for spares.'

'You need to rest. You have a bad case of smoke inhalation. It'll get worse before it gets better. You've damaged your lungs. They'll start to fill with fluid over the next couple of days. Rye wants to get you on oxygen, soon as she can. Give you a chance to heal.'

'You seem okay,' said Ghost.

'Buddy breathing. You gave me most of the air.'

'Honestly. I'm fine.'

'Not for long. If you start chasing round trying to fix that generator you could do yourself serious damage. You could keel over with pneumonia, and there isn't much anyone could do to treat you.'

'If we don't get the generators running we will all freeze to death. I can't sit around and convalesce. And if I get pneumonia then all the more reason to tap my expertise while we still can. We have to get to work right now.'

'Christ.'

'Do we have any amphetamines? Anything that can give me a boost?'

'We've got some pre-loaded adrenalin shots in the survival kits. It'll crank you for a couple of hours, but once it's metabolised you'll be a wreck.'

'Go and get them.'

Jane fetched the shots.

She found Ghost sitting on the deck with his back to one of the charred control panels. She sat beside him.

'How you doing, fella?'

'Pretty fucked up,' he croaked.

Jane gestured to the broken instrumentation.

'Reckon you could fix it?'

'I'm not an electrician.'

'Neither is anyone else. You're the best we have.'

'Wish I could stand without coughing my guts out.'

Jane held up a yellow, pre-loaded epinephrine syringe from a survival pack.

'Do it.'

Jane stabbed the hypo into his thigh and pressed the plunger.

The rest of the crewmen returned from the island.

They cleaned the canteen by lamplight. The wiped a fine dusting of ash from tables and chairs. They swept the floor.

Nail slipped out of the canteen. Nikki followed. She trailed him down dark passageways. She followed his flashlight beam through the cavernous shadows of the pump hall. She found him in a storeroom examining Ghost's boat.

Nail circled oil drums welded to a scaffold pole.

'He didn't get very far,' he said.

He examined sketched plans laid out on a trestle table. A crude yacht. Top view. Side view.

'It's a good design, as far as I can tell. Single mast. Mainsail. Jib. I imagine it would be pretty stable.'

'Could you finish it?' asked Nikki. 'Ghost might be out of action for a while. Could you finish what he started?'

'I'm a dive welder. Been doing eight years, off and on. Yeah, I could do it.'

'Perhaps we'll get lucky. Perhaps someone will answer our mayday.'

'I'm tired of waiting. I don't like putting my fate in someone else's hands. It's not my style. You saw those guys up there. Sitting round, slack-jawed, waiting for Blanc to lace their shoes. Contemptible.'

'Morale is pretty low. The guys are feeling shell-shocked. Helpless.'

'Fuck their emotions. Do they actually want to live or what? Brain-freeze. Paralysis. That's what kills most people in a crisis. Well, not me, baby. I'm the survivor type.'

'So what should we do?'

'If Ghost recovers, then great. He can finish the boat for us. If anything happens to him, then we finish it ourselves. Take the food we need, and wave sayonara on our way south.'

Jane helped Ghost inspect the powerhouse controls. She worked under his direction. She levered a side panel. He shone his flashlight inside.

'Generator Three looks healthy enough.' He coughed. 'This console looks fine. So why the hell aren't the lights on?'

'Maybe the fault is further up the line.'

He shone his flashlight at the wall. Cable thick as drainpipe snaked into a duct. Ghost unzipped his coat and fleece.

'You're not seriously going in there?'

'I'd love to send you in my place,' said Ghost. 'But I need to see with my own eyes.'

He coughed and spat.

'If you pass out in there we will have a bitch of a job dragging you out.'

'That adrenalin shot will keep me juiced for a couple of hours. Let's make the most of it.'

Ghost ducked down and crawled into the conduit.

Punch unlocked the canteen storeroom. Colder than a meat locker. Frosted food. Sian joined him.

'Why don't we pass out survival rations?' she asked. 'Those self-heating cans?'

'Last resort. I want to save those in case we need them on a journey. I still think our best plan is to wait until mid-winter, take the Skidoos and head for Canada.'

'Just us?'

'You and me. Maybe Jane and Ghost if they want. It's an old argument. I've already talked it through with Jane. She dismissed the idea, but she'll come round.'

'I'm not sure.'

'To be honest, I don't talk to the other guys any more. They just sit in the canteen staring into space. They aren't going to make it home. It may sound harsh, but the way I look at it, they're already dead.'

Punch took a box from a shelf.

'Give them cornflakes. They'll have to eat them dry. Good carbohydrate. It's the best we can do.'

'We're all dying by degrees, aren't we?' said Sian. 'Every one of us.'

Punch smiled.

'We're not done yet,' he said, and kissed her.

Ghost wormed along the conduit. Tight tunnel walls. He had a flashlight in one hand and a radio in the other. He examined the thick cable running above his head.

'*How's it going?*' Jane's voice.

'Okay. Just stopped for a breather.'

'*Any fire damage?*'

'Nothing so far. There must be a break somewhere along the line, though. Just have to find it.'

'*I feel bad. We're treating you like Kleenex. Using you up for the common good.*'

'Comes with the territory. You chose to clip Rawlins's big bunch of keys to your belt. You have to take the shit that comes with it.'

Ghost suppressed a coughing fit.

'All right. I'm moving on.'

Nail searched for supplies.

'I want to be ready. There's plenty of stuff we will need when we sail south.'

'The boat isn't even built yet,' said Nikki.

'You can never be too prepared. Besides, I'm bored. No point sitting round with those lethargic fucks in the canteen. I want to achieve something.'

There were lifeboat muster points at each corner of the refinery. The lifeboat stations were named after London underground stations. Moorgate, Holborn, Blackfriars and Pimlico. Each lifeboat station had a survival pack. Nail picked through each pack. Flares. Insulation blankets. Calorie bars. First aid. He threw supplies into an empty kit-bag and carried it over his shoulder like Santa.

He led Nikki across the deck. They contemplated the acre of twisted girders where D Module used to be.

A small sliver of D Module remained. Nail's flashlight lit a buckled staircase and a couple of burned-out rooms.

'Come on.'

'You're not going in there, are you?' asked Nikki.

'See that doorway on the second floor?'

'Yeah.'

'That's my old room.'

They climbed through dereliction. The staircase creaked beneath their weight.

The door to Nail's old room was charred and bubbled. He kicked it open.

His room was black with soot. He kicked aside the skeletal frame of a chair. He pulled the melted mattress from his bunk.

'Take a seat.'

Nikki sat on the metal bed frame.

Nail closed the door to trap body heat. He set his flashlight on the washstand.

He unfolded a hexamine stove and lit the fuel block with a Zippo.

He stretched up and prised the grating from an air vent. He reached inside and pulled out a scorched cash box.

He sat on the bed next to Nikki. He took a key from round his neck and opened the box. Money. Notes rolled tight, held by rubber bands. Nail tucked cash into the inner pocket of his coat.

'You could wipe your ass with it, I suppose,' said Nikki. 'Poker winnings?'

'Fruits of entrepreneurial labour.'

Nail tipped the box into his lap. A spoon. Packets of hypodermics. A Ziploc bag of brown powder.

'Didn't know you had a hobby.'

'It's a six-month rotation. A person needs to chill now and again.'

'And you go home with a triple pay cheque.'

'Loose change. People go to Ghost for weed. They come to me if they want something a little stronger.'

Nail scraped frost from the shoulder of his coat and melted

it in the spoon with a pinch of powder. He unwrapped a syringe and siphoned the fizzing liquid.

'Want to forget yourself a while?' asked Nail.

'Yeah, there's plenty I want to put from my mind.'

She took off her coat and rolled up the arm of her fleece. Nail rubbed the crook of her elbow with his thumb to raise a vein. He carefully inserted the needle beneath her skin and pressed the plunger. A wash of snuggling well-being. She smiled and sat back against the wall.

Nail took off his coat and rolled up the sleeve of his sweat-shirt. He tied a shoelace tourniquet round his bicep and pumped his arm. He shot up.

He pulled Nikki close and hung his coat round both their shoulders. He stroked her hair.

They sat in the burned-out room and gazed at the stove, mesmerised by the ethereal blue flame.

Ghost crawled through the conduit. He jackknifed his body to squeeze round a junction. His belt-loop snagged on a bolt. He tried to twist free. Sudden, sweating claustrophobia. He pushed at the duct walls. He heard himself sob.

He stopped thrashing, closed his eyes and tried to compose himself.

'Talk to me, Jane. Let me hear a voice.'

'*Just thinking. Rawlins didn't want to lose himself. That's what he told me. He didn't want the disease to win. I suppose that's what everyone says. That they'd drive off a cliff in a blaze of glory rather than waste away in a hospital bed.*'

'So what do you reckon? This disease.'

'*I read a book about the Manhattan Project. When they tested the first atom bomb in the desert, scientists wondered if the blast might set the atmosphere on fire. Maybe this was the same situation. They, the big, scary They, were toying with some kind of super-technology. Nanobots. Bio-weapon. Something so cutting-*'

edge, so unstable, they put the lab in space to contain it in a vacuum. But something went wrong, something sudden and catastrophic, and chunks of debris dropped to earth like our friend in the capsule.'

'Sure. Why not?'

Ghost squirmed in the narrow space. He unhooked his belt-loop. He crawled forward on his elbows.

'Feel like I've been wriggling around in here for hours.'

'Nothing?'

'Nothing. The cable looks fine.'

'Find a way out and head back to the powerhouse. We'll take another look at the generator.'

Punch sat in the observation bubble. He cocooned himself in a sleeping bag and stared at the stars.

Footsteps from below. Crazy, dancing light approaching up the spiral stairs. Sian with an aluminium trunk under each arm and a Maglite clenched between her teeth.

'One of the men on Raven is an electrician,' said Sian. 'If we can get him here, he can help.'

'We don't have power,' said Punch. 'We don't have radar. If they take to the lifeboats they'll drift right past us.'

Sian flipped the latches on each case.

'A GPS kit and a radio. I found them downstairs. They run on lithium batteries. They're charged.'

'They won't have much range.'

Sian contemplated the silhouettes of the gargantuan distillation towers, three great shadows that eclipsed the stars.

'What if we got them up high?'

Ghost was overcome by a sudden wave of exhaustion. He rolled on to his side.

'I feel like a fucking sewer rat.'

'I spoke to the careers counsellor during my last year at school.

He asked me what I would do if I were the last person alive. If there were no social pressure, no one left to impress.'

'What did you say?'

'I'd mooch. I'd loaf. I'd sit on a riverbank and read books.'

Ghost reached in his pocket. He pulled out a yellow epinephrine hypodermic. He bit the cap off the hypo and injected his bicep.

'You're in charge now. You know that, right? I mean seriously. For real. With Rawlins gone you are the only authority left. The crew are your responsibility. They'll expect you to have the Grand Plan.'

'Is this your valedictory statement? Are you passing the torch?'

'I can feel a breeze. There's something up ahead.'

Ghost wormed his way along the conduit. A section of duct broke open when D Module fell from the refinery. He leaned over a jagged metal lip. Frayed cable swung in the ice wind. Far below him was the sea.

'I think I found our problem.' He coughed up phlegm. He retched. He vomited. 'I'm turning round. I'm coming back.'

Jane helped Ghost limp to his room. She laid him on his bunk. He was pale and breathless. He shivered. She draped three coats over him.

She lay beside him; let his head rest on her shoulder.

'Take it easy for a while,' she said. 'Get your breath back.'

'Just need to rest.'

Liquid in his lungs. Each breath died away in a bubbling rattle.

'Take your time.'

'I can splice a domestic extension lead into that powerhouse console. We can run a couple of heaters. Cook food. It'll keep us alive. Buy some time.'

'After that?'

'Look for an intact length of three-thousand megawatt cable. A few metres. That's all we need. Patch that break in the line

133

and we are back in business. Just need to rip up floor plates until we find some.'

He took an epinephrine syringe from his pocket.

'Sure you want to do this?' she asked.

'Yeah. Final lap.'

Lifeline

Punch stood at the refinery railing and looked east. Ice surrounded the refinery and spread towards the island. The sun no longer rose. Daytime was a brief pink twilight. The Arctic was entering perpetual night.

He took an old Sony radio from his coat pocket. He had found it alongside a drum of paint and a roller. Someone had been redecorating a corridor and quit halfway through the job. The batteries still held a charge.

He extended the aerial and adjusted the dial. Whistling static.

A ghost voice. Male. French accent. Tired, distressed. Punch pulled back the hood of his coat and pressed the radio to his ear.

'. . . *est advice . . . safe place and don't venture . . . can hear me . . . refuge . . . hopeless . . . God help . . .*'

Punch returned to the observation bubble.

'Anything?' asked Sian.

'Nothing. Doesn't seem to work.'

Punch shook batteries from the radio and tossed it aside.

He and Sian had turned the observation bubble into their base camp. They had pushed chairs back from the transmitter console and erected a dome tent. Each night they cooked on a stove. They ate and counted stars. They zipped sleeping bags together and slept skin-to-skin.

'What do you think is waiting for us back in the world?' asked Sian. She was sitting cross-legged by the stove stirring noodles in a mess tin.

'I bet the worst is over. People will have got organised by now.'

'You think?'

'Yeah. When the chips are down, neighbours help each other out.'

Punch wanted to say: 'Promise you'll kill me. If I get infected, if I turn like Rawlins, finish me off. Don't let me become a monster.'

Instead he asked: 'How are the noodles coming along?'

'Soon be done.'

The powerhouse. A steady hum from Generator Three. Massive megawatt output, enough to power a small town. Ghost had run a single domestic extension lead from the control panel. It ran through an air vent into the submarine hangar next door. A single plug socket. A single convection heater. Crewmen took turns to sit in the orange glow.

The crew were camped in front of the submersible. Steel manipulator claws curved above them like a protective embrace. A couple of crew huddled in blankets and played chess. One crewman relentlessly sharpened a knife. Bottles of drinking water were lined up in front of the heater to keep them thawed.

Ghost lay beneath three parkas. Short, bubbling breaths. Jane sat beside him. She stroked his head. Once in a while he opened his eyes. She smiled. She wanted him to see a reassuring face. She didn't want him to feel alone.

He opened his eyes wide and steady.

'How you doing, champ?'

Thumbs up.

'Warm enough?'

Nod.

He stroked her face. Peeling skin.

'Guess I got too close to the fire,' said Jane. 'Sunburn.'

He licked dry lips.

'Drink something.' She put a canteen to his lips. 'Wet your mouth.'

She rearranged the coat beneath his head to give him a better pillow.

'Get as much sleep as you can.'

'Feel like I've been punched in the gut,' whispered Ghost. 'I can barely breathe.'

'Getting worse?'

'Yeah.'

Jane looked for Rye.

'She's in the sub,' said Ivan.

Jane lowered herself through the roof hatch. Her flashlight lit tight banks of instrumentation. Rye sat in the co-pilot seat. She was listening to an iPod.

'Rocking out?' asked Jane.

'About an hour of battery left. My last tunes.'

'What's the prognosis?'

'Ghost? Not so great. I'm dosing him with antibiotics but the pneumonia is caused by chemical damage to his lungs, rather than infection. If his throat closes much further I might have to intubate.'

'What are his chances?'

'Fifty-fifty. His lungs might recover, given enough time. He could be back on his feet in a couple of weeks, if he's lucky, if he doesn't exert himself like he did yesterday. Another shot of speed would kill him stone dead.'

'So there's nothing we can do but wait?'

'Like I say, I've been giving him antibiotics as a preventative measure. It might help, it might not. And plenty of painkillers just to keep him comfortable.'

'Okay.'

'Question is, when do we pull the plug? He's used up his share of meds already.'

'Give him everything he needs.'

137

'I appreciate you two are close.'

'He was a systems technician. He kept the lights on, the water running. He's worth more than most of the crew out there, worth more than me.'

Jane climbed the side of distillation tank A. The tank was a cylindrical tower one hundred and fifty metres high. The ladder was glazed with ice. Her boots slid on slick rungs. She had a coil of red kernmantle rope slung over her shoulder.

She reached the frost-dusted expanse of the roof. She lowered the rope. Punch stood at the foot of the tower. He tied the rope to the radio case and Jane hauled the case skyward.

She set up the tripod dish and switched on the transmitter.

'Rampart to Raven, do you copy, over? Rampart to Raven, do you copy?'

'*Jesus*, Rampart. *We thought you had been picked up and left us behind. We've been calling for days.*'

'There was a fire. We lost power. We've managed to get heat to a single room, but we're still in a bad way. You have an electrician called Thursby, is that right?'

'*Tommy. Yeah.*'

'We desperately need his help. And we need a twenty-metre length of high-voltage cable.'

'*What kind of load?*'

'Our generators put out about three thousand megawatts.'

'*All right.*'

'You have a medic?'

'*Ellington.*'

'We lost our infirmary in the fire. Most of the drugs and equipment got torched. We desperately need whatever you can bring.'

'*Okay.*'

'When can you take to the rafts?'

'*We've been ready for days. We've been waiting to hear from you.*'

'Then get going, soon as you can. We've still got GPS. We'll watch for you round the clock. Good luck, guys. God bless.'

Jane explored the powerhouse.

She crawled inside a conduit. She wrapped a scarf over her mouth and nose to protect against soot particles that swirled around her. She rolled on her side and inspected the high-voltage cable that ran along the duct roof. Burned and twisted. Melted insulation hung in ragged strips.

'Reverend Blanc?' Ivan's voice.

Jane backed out of the duct.

'It's Ghost. You better come quick.'

Ghost panted for air. His chest heaved. He clutched his throat.

Rye ripped open his coat and fleece. She held him down and pressed an ear to his chest.

'Can't you get a tube down his throat?' demanded Jane.

Rye prodded his chest and diaphragm.

'Fluid in the pleural cavity.'

'Can you drain it?'

'I can try. Surgery by flashlight. Outstanding.'

Jane grabbed a SCUBA tank from a wall rack. She opened the valve and forced the regulator mouthpiece between Ghost's teeth.

'Breathe. Suck it down.'

Ghost gasped the rich Heliox mix.

'Just keep breathing.'

Nail sat cross-legged on the storeroom floor. Ghost's boat. He tried to make sense of the plans. The central hull had a cockpit for the skipper and storage space below. No clear explanation of how it was to be built. Plenty of panels designated '*AFC*'.

He thought it over.

Brainwave. AFC. Air Freight Container.

Specialist hydrocarbon pump equipment had been shipped to the refinery in aluminium crates. Two or three crates shunted to the back of each plant room. *Lufthansa. Emirates. Gulf Air.* Each crate could be broken down into sheets. Lightweight. Easy to cut. Easy to shape. Easy to weld.

Nail got to work. He wheeled an oxyacetylene tank through derelict plant halls. Smoked visor. Heavy gloves. Vaulted chambers lit incandescent by crackling flame-light. He piled silver panels on the storeroom floor.

He stripped to his waist despite the cold and pounded scaffold poles until a skeletal ship frame began to take shape.

Sometimes Nikki watched him work. His skin steamed with sweat. She was revolted. She needed Nail. It was a tactical alliance. He was a strong, amoral survivor. But she gagged at the smell of him as she shivered through their brief, brutal fucks on the storeroom floor. Trading sex for a ticket home.

Nikki studied the plans.

'The sail. What's it made from?'

'Guess.'

'*BFx3*. What does that mean?'

'Puzzled me for days.'

'Figured it out?'

'Balloon Fabric times Three. Mylar. Thin. Light. Rip-proof.'

'So how do we get this thing outside?'

Nail took a lamp from the table and held it up.

'See? A winch in the ceiling and a hatch in the floor. They used it for hauling shipping containers aboard. The floor opens like a bomb bay. Hydraulics. Big enough to lower our boat. The winch can take about ninety tonnes.'

'But there is no electricity.'

'That's right. We need the power back on. Two, three minutes. That's all it would take. Get the hatch open and we're out of here.'

*   *   *

They carried Ghost on a stretcher.

'We need to get him somewhere clean,' said Rye. 'Some place that hasn't been used much.'

They took him to the chapel.

'Get some light,' ordered Rye.

Jane positioned a couple of battery lamps.

'Help me get his shirt off.'

'He'll freeze.'

'Fine. It'll reduce bleeding.'

'Want me to get the altar? Lie him down?'

'No. I need him sitting with his back towards me.'

They dragged Ghost to the front of the chapel and positioned him straddling a chair.

'So what's the deal?'

'I reckon there is liquid building up beneath his lungs.'

'Infection?'

'Maybe. Antibiotics tend not to penetrate the pleural cavity. It's kind of a blind spot.'

'What's the plan?'

'Pleural tap. Siphon off the liquid with a big-ass hypodermic. Place is about as sterile as a toilet seat, but it's the best we can do.'

Rye emptied her pockets on to the altar: 20cc hypodermics; gloves; iodine; dressing.

Rye prepped a needle.

'Ghost? Can you hear me?'

Ghost struggled to focus.

'The cable,' he whispered. 'Listen. In case I don't make it. You need fourteen-centimetre, single-core. Easy to splice. Bolt sockets every thirty, forty metres. Should say Con-Ex on the insulation. Look beneath C deck corridors. One length. That's all it takes.'

Rye measured ribs with her fingers. Second intercostal space. Iodine swab.

'Hold his shoulders.'

Ghost lolled semi-conscious until the tip of a big-bore needle pricked his side and punctured his skin. He convulsed. Jane gripped his shoulders.

'Look at me. Look at me, Ghost. We have to do this. We have to get this done.'

Ghost clutched the back of the chair. Rye drew off three syringe-loads of fluid. She patched the wound. She pressed a stethoscope to his chest.

'Better?'

Ghost gave a thumbs up and passed out.

'Let's get him out of here,' said Rye. 'Get him back in front of that fire.'

C deck. Jane lifted floor grates. Fire had spread through the conduits carried by melting insulation. The cables were burned.

Jane glimpsed Nail at the end of a corridor. He was carrying a sheet of aluminium. She quickly shut off her flashlight. She followed him to the pump hall.

Ghost lay with his back to the yellow hull of the submarine. He took occasional Heliox hits from a SCUBA tank.

'You look better,' said Jane.

'A little less dead.'

'Doing okay?'

'Dr Feelgood and her magic pills.'

'Jesus, you are tripping your brains out.'

'Ask for the pink ones. Seriously.'

'Nail is building something next to the pump hall. Know anything about that?'

'A boat. You saw it. I was going to carry you off into the sunset. Sketched a few plans. I suppose Nail and Nikki found them and decided to finish the job.'

'I'm not sure I can be bothered to intervene.'

'Let them go. Nobody will miss them.'

'You're staying?'

'I'm not in much shape to embark on a long voyage,' said Ghost. 'Besides, I can't ditch these lads.'

'No?'

'You and me. We'll get them home.'

'Want to shake on it?'

Ghost held out his hand.

'Last men off?'

'Last men off.'

Jane visited Punch and Sian in the observation bubble. They had invited her for dinner. Mushroom risotto. They ate from mess tins.

'So you cook for yourself now.'

'The men have stoves,' said Punch. 'They've got pasta and sauce. They've got dried figs. They aren't helpless.'

'Cosy little den.'

'All this doom and gloom. You don't resent a few snatched moments of comfort, do you?'

'The guys are jealous. You can't blame them.'

Sian looked over Jane's shoulder out to sea.

'See that?' she said, pointing at the horizon.

'What?'

'Look west. The stars are going out.'

'Christ.' Jane threw her mess tin aside and stood up. 'That's a serious cloud bank.'

'It's coming fast.'

'God just keeps on shitting on us.'

They zipped their coats and ran outside. Sian and Punch carried the radio case between them.

Jane climbed the distillation tower. She hauled up the radio on a rope, hand over hand as quick as she could. She set up the tripod. She crouched on the roof and shouted into the handset.

'Rampart to Raven, over. Rampart to Raven, do you copy, over?'

No reply.

'Rampart to Raven, come in.'

No reply.

'Raven. Come on, guys. Tell me you haven't taken to the rafts yet.'

No response. A fog bank approached from the west propelled by a bitter wind. A moonlit wall of mist. Jane collapsed the tripod and slammed the case, anxious to quit the tower before cloud eclipsed the moon and left her in absolute dark.

Part Two

Ghost Ship

Hyperion

Jane got some sleep then looked for Ghost. He had joined Sian in the observation bubble. They were sipping tea. Sian brewed a mug for Jane.

'Feeling better?'

'Restless,' said Ghost. 'Been lying on my back for days.'

He unzipped his coat and fleece. He lifted his shirt. A surgical dressing taped over bruised skin.

'Feels like she broke most of my ribs.'

'Rye saved your life. Battlefield surgery. She kept calm. I don't know how.'

'She's a tough person to thank.'

'You're not going to get all distant on me, are you?' said Jane.

'Why would I do that?'

'It's happened to me countless times. I help people through their midnight hours. Later on, they won't look me in the eye. They associate my face with hard times.'

Ghost gave her a hug. She tentatively hugged back.

'Mind the ribs.'

Jane took the GPS unit outside. She and Ghost stood on the big red H of the helipad and studied the screen. They were searching for the Raven lifeboats, scanning for a clear TACOM contact.

A winking signal at the top of the screen.

'Damn,' said Ghost. 'The Raven guys. There they are.'

'How long has it been? Four, five days at sea? Poor bastards. Let's bring them home.'

Ghost steered the zodiac. Jane sat in the prow. They had left Rye shivering at the refinery railing, ready with a spotlight to guide them home.

Jane hunched over the GPS screen. An intermittent signal to the north.

'Left. More left.'

She shone her torch into the darkness and fog. The beam of her flashlight lit nothing but broiling vapour.

'We're getting close. They should be around here somewhere.'

Ghost shut off the engine. They rode the swells. Jane scanned black water.

'I don't get it. They should be right here.'

A blinking TACOM signal at the centre of the screen.

Jane shouted into the dark.

'Hello? Is anyone there?'

Nothing.

Jane took a flare from her coat pocket. She popped the cap and pulled the rip-strip. A red star-shell shot skyward.

'How long do you want to wait?' asked Ghost.

'It would be tragic if they are floating out there and we miss them.'

They took turns to shout.

'Two more minutes,' said Jane, 'then we call it a night.'

'There,' said Ghost. 'See that?'

A faint strobe blinking in the fog. It was hard to judge distance. Ghost gunned the engine and headed for the flashing light.

The TACOM beacon was a cylinder the size of a Thermos flask. It floated in the water attached to a ragged strip of red rubber. The remains of a raft.

'So they didn't make it,' said Jane. 'Lonely place to die.'

'We needed that cable. Guess it'll be at the bottom of the ocean.'

'Over there.'

More ripped rubber. Jane unclipped a paddle from the side of the zodiac and dragged the punctured raft closer. A boot. She lifted the edge of the tattered raft. A body in a red hydro-suit. A bearded man, floating face up. Marble-white skin. Open eyes.

'Was that him?' asked Jane. 'Ray. You said you met him once. The guy I've been talking to these past couple of weeks.'

'Maybe. Hard to tell. Want to say a prayer?'

'No.'

They headed back to the rig. Neither of them spoke. Jane switched off the redundant GPS and sealed the case.

Ghost suddenly swerved the boat. He struggled to avoid a sheer white wall that confronted them through the fog. Jane was thrown to the bottom of the boat.

'Jesus,' said Ghost. 'Fucking berg.'

He killed the engine.

'That's no berg,' said Jane. She shone her flashlight across the white cliff face. Rivets. Weld seams. Steel plate. She looked up. An anchor the size of a bus.

HYPERION.

Jane ran up the steps to the observation bubble.

'Punch, wake up.'

She unzipped the tent. Punch and Sian sat up, shielding their eyes from the flashlight glare.

'Fuck's sake,' muttered Punch.

'Get up. Grab your coat. We just got lucky.'

They hurried to fetch rope from the boathouse.

'It's drifting,' said Jane. 'A superliner. Fucking big. Dead in the water. No running lights. We'll have to be quick. It'll pass out of range in a few hours. We have to get aboard and take control. This is our ticket home.'

'We should get the lads together. Ferry everyone across.'

'No time. Ghost is upstairs pulling the legs off a chair to make a grappling hook. Where's Ivan? We'll need him too.'

'Why him?'

'Ghost is running round like he has fully recovered. I need you two to help him out, slow him down. We don't want to provoke a relapse.'

They ran through the canteen kitchen. Jane unlocked a refrigerator. Punch held her torch.

Shotguns laid across a shelf. Jane tugged the weapons from their nylon sleeves. She slotted shells into the receiver. She swept boxes of ammunition into a backpack.

'I'll tell you right now,' said Jane. 'There will be no negotiation. I don't care how many people are hiding on that boat. They are sure as hell going to stop for us.'

They found the ship drifting twenty kilometres south of its previous position.

'The current is pretty strong,' said Jane. 'No time to fetch the boys. Three or four trips in the zodiac. Guys would get left behind.'

'Jesus. Look at the size of it.'

'Bring us round the stern,' said Ghost. He hurled the grappling hook upward and snagged railings.

'Maybe I should go,' said Punch.

Ghost ignored him. He shouldered his backpack and gun, gripped the knotted rope and began to climb. He hauled hand over hand, walking his way up the side of the boat. Punch tried to keep the zodiac beneath him. If Ghost fell in the freezing water the shock would kill him.

Ghost reached the deck. He climbed over the railing. He caught his breath, coughed and spat.

'Looks pretty dead,' he shouted. 'No one around.'

Jane grabbed the rope and hauled herself up the side of the boat. Weeks ago, when she was fat, she couldn't have managed the climb.

She tipped over the railing and fell on to the deck.

The ship was ten storeys high. Six rows of portholes in the main hull, and four stacked decks like the concentric tiers of a wedding cake.

Jane found herself on a teak promenade laid out for an Arctic pleasure cruise. Whale-watching loungers and curling stones.

She looked up and down the walkway. Every cabin window was dark. They un-shouldered their shotguns. Safety to Fire. Ghost chambered a shell.

'Let's find the bridge.'

They walked towards the prow. A couple of cabin doors were open. Scattered possessions. Jane wanted to investigate, but there wasn't time to explore.

Ghost's flashlight lit vacant lifeboat davits, rope swinging in the breeze.

'Couple of lifeboats missing,' he said. He kicked scattered lifebelts. 'Looks like everyone left in a hurry.'

They reached the prow. Jane pointed to windows high above them.

'That must be the bridge.'

They entered the ship. They were in a functional, crew-only zone of the liner. Bare corridors. Linoleum floor. No heat.

Jane was spooked by shadows. Once in a while she swung her torch beam down the passageway behind them to make sure they were not being followed.

Ghost tried a light switch. He pointed at the red, winking LED of a ceiling smoke detector.

'The power is shut off but some basic systems are active. I guess the generators still work. All we have to do is throw the switch.'

Offices, store cupboards, crew quarters. Corridor floors cluttered with toilet supplies and discarded uniforms. Signs of hurried departure.

They climbed narrow stairs and pushed through doors marked *Tillträde Förbjudet*.

They reached the bridge. Ghost tried the light switch. Dead. 'Thought it might be on a separate circuit or something.'

Jane moved to enter the bridge but Ghost put a hand on her shoulder to hold her back. There was someone sitting in the captain's chair.

'Hello? Bonjour?'

A slumped figure in a white cap and greatcoat, collar turned up. Ghost and Jane cautiously approached.

'How you doing?' asked Jane. Her boot crunched on broken glass.

The captain was a big man in his fifties. He had a white moustache. He had been dead a long while, but the sub-zero temperature had preserved his body from decay.

Green glass in his hand. He had cut his throat with a jagged piece of wine bottle. The front of his uniform, a brass-buttoned tunic, was glazed with frozen blood.

'Help me get him out of the way,' said Ghost. 'Watch yourself. The guy doesn't look infected, but you never know.'

They dragged the man from the chair. He was rigor-stiff. Crackle of frozen blood. They hauled him into a side room.

The bridge looked like the flight-deck of a starship. Three padded chairs facing the sea. Banks of switches, dials and screens, powered down and inert. The steering column was a horseshoe control like the joystick of a passenger jet. Acceleration governed by a central thrust lever.

'I was expecting a big wheel,' said Jane.

'Look at this,' said Ghost. 'A keyhole. What do you reckon? An ignition?'

He ran to the side room. He crouched by the captain's body

and searched his pockets. Handkerchief. Coins. Asthma inhaler. No key.

'Search the place. Let's see if we can find some kind of key locker. If we can get this ship to drop anchor we'll have all the time in the world to figure out the rest.'

Jane looked around. Desks at the back of the bridge. Charts and maps. She tugged at the door of a red cupboard.

'*Brandsläckare*. What the hell is that? You'd think the signs would be bilingual. I mean English is the international language of pretty much everything.'

'There must be a spare set of keys somewhere, but we're running out of time.'

'Hey,' called Jane. 'Check this out.'

A door at the back of the bridge led to a stairwell. They leaned over the railings and shone their flashlights downward. A jumble of furniture heaped against a steel hatch. Chairs, tables, a bed frame. A big, red '*X*' had been sprayed on the door.

'Someone was very anxious to keep that door closed,' said Jane.

Jane called Punch and Ivan on the radio.

'Get aboard, folks. Meet us at the prow.'

Ghost showed them to the bridge.

'We need the master key to this thing, okay? We need to get the ship's systems back on-line. Let's fan out and see what we can find.'

Ghost and Ivan checked the officers' quarters.

'This is living,' said Ivan. 'Plasma TV. En suite.' He picked an officer's cap from a sofa and tried it on. He checked his reflection in a mirror. 'Fuck oil rigs. I need a Cunard gig.'

'Imagine sailing south in this palace,' said Ghost. 'The presidential suites. Gym, Jacuzzi, sauna. We've got to make this work for us.'

'I've never been in a Jacuzzi.'

'This ship is a fucking gold mine.'

'The freezers have been shut off a long while,' said Ivan. 'Most of the food will have spoiled. Lobster will be off the menu.'

'Think of the bars down there. Champagne, vintage malts, any cocktail you care to mix. Imagine how much beer they must have stowed below deck. You could fill a bath.'

They descended a flight of stairs. Another barricade. A fire axe slotted through the crank-handles of a door to keep it closed. A big, red '*X*' sprayed on the hatch.

'This is fucking creepy,' said Ivan. He crossed himself.

Ghost examined an exterior door at the end of a passage. Sooty scorch marks and bubbled paint. He pushed open the door. Someone had built a large bonfire on the promenade deck. A pile of charred debris. A mound of scorched lifebelts and bench-slats. The fire had long since burned out. The cinders were dusted with snow.

Ghost knelt by the debris and prodded the ashes with a stick.

'What have you found?' asked Ivan, joining Ghost on deck.

'Bones. A ribcage. At least two skulls.'

He hooked a can with his stick and read the scorched label. Kerosene.

'I wish there were a few more of those guns to go around,' said Ivan.

'Let's find those keys.'

The administration corridor. A row of offices.

A splash of blood on the corridor floor.

'Steer clear,' advised Jane. 'Assume infection.'

Faint white-noise fizz from a side office. Jane nudged the door open with her foot. The radio room. The radio operator had died at his desk. His body was slowly melting into a telex console, upper body completely absorbed like the workstation was eating him head first.

Jane yanked the power cable from the wall. The satellite console sparked and died. The hissing stopped.

They found the purser's office.

'We could be millionaires,' said Punch. 'All those rich old ladies on a Baltic cruise. The deposit boxes must be packed with diamonds and pearls.'

'But where did those rich old ladies go?' said Jane. 'That's the question.'

She found a key cabinet on the wall. She tugged it. She hit it. She shucked the slide of her shotgun.

'Stand back.'

Ghost unclipped his radio from his belt.

'Jane? You guys all right?'

'*We're fine.*'

'We heard a shot.'

'*We've got some keys. We're heading back to the bridge.*'

'We've found some kind of battery room. I'm going to throw a few switches, see what happens.'

'Reckon these batteries still hold charge?' asked Ivan.

'They're supposed to sustain light and heat if an iceberg or something knocks out the engines. They should be good for days.'

Jane took fistfuls of keys from her coat pocket and dumped them on the console. She threw a fire blanket over the captain's chair so she wouldn't have to sit in his blood. She tried to slot the keys, one by one, into the panel above the steering column then threw them aside.

'How long before this ship drifts out of range of the refinery?'

'An hour. Two at the most.'

Punch stood in the side room and looked down at the captain. The man was lying on his side, legs still hitched like he was sitting down. Punch unfolded a map and draped it over the dead man's head so he wouldn't have to see his eyes.

'I'm going out on deck,' he said. 'Think I'll take a look around.'

Punch climbed exterior steps to the upper deck.

The Lido. There was an empty children's swimming pool with scattered life jackets at the bottom.

The Winterland Grill. Smashed plates and an upturned barbecue.

A vast funnel rose into the fog above him.

He found a skylight. He rubbed the glass with a gloved hand, wiping away frost as thick as snow. He shone his flashlight down into the dark.

Ghost must have found a power switch in the battery room because the ship suddenly lit up brilliant white. Stark floodlights illuminated the decks, the balconies, the badminton court, the miniature golf. Strings of bulbs hung between the funnels glowed in the fog like weak sunlight.

Punch crouched over the skylight and looked down into the Grand Ballroom. Art deco wall lights glowed amber for a soirée, but the dance floor appeared to have been turned into a hospital. Row upon row of beds. Bandaged bodies in the beds, some in pyjamas, some in ball gowns and dinner suits. Punch couldn't see clearly through the smeared glass. He could make out bloody dressings, blackened skin, half-eaten faces.

A squeak of feedback from the deck speakers as the sound-system powered back to life. The genteel strings of 'The Blue Danube' waltz were broadcast throughout the ship.

As if waking from a long sleep, the bodies in the ballroom began to stir.

Power

The prow. Ghost lifted a deck hatch and shone his flashlight inside. Metal steps descending into darkness. He climbed down.

'It's okay,' he called.

Jane followed.

Two massive drums each rolled with anchor chain, each link big as a lifebelt.

'There must be a manual release,' said Ghost. 'It must be part of the design. Some way of stopping the ship dead in the water in the event of catastrophic turbine failure.'

The drums were each powered by a motor the size of a van.

'I think this lever might disengage the gears,' said Jane.

'Yeah?'

'Well, there are warning stickers all over it.'

Ghost found a tool locker.

'Better wear these.'

Jane twisted foam plugs into her ears and clamped defenders to her head.

He tugged the lever. It wouldn't shift. He lifted his feet and swung from it. The lever wouldn't move. He fetched a sledge-hammer.

'Stand back,' he mouthed.

He swung the hammer. Two blows and the gears disengaged. The drum spun free. The massive anchor chain played out through the hull with a juddering roar. The air stank of hot metal.

They took off their ear-defenders. They climbed out on to the deck and shone a flashlight over the side of the ship. The anchors had deployed. The chain hung taut.

'High five,' said Jane. They slapped gloved hands. 'About time something went our way.'

They returned to Rampart and mustered the crew.

'It's called *Hyperion*,' said Jane, standing before them like a teacher lecturing a class. 'It's Swedish, I think. All the bridge controls are written in Martian. We've dropped anchor. All we have to do is start the engines and we are on our way home.'

A general murmur of excitement ran through the canteen. Although the canteen was cold it was still the best place to hold a group meeting.

'Yeah,' continued Jane, her breath fogging the air. 'It looks like our luck has finally changed. But there's a catch. Most of the passengers and crew are still aboard. They're infected, but locked below deck.'

'Shotguns,' said Nikki. 'Go room to room. You saw them on TV. Infected move slow. Turkey shoot.'

'They are people. Wives and husbands. Sons and daughters. They're not vermin.'

'Let's cut the sanctimonious crap, shall we? If we sail an infected ship south to Europe not a single country will let us enter their waters. In fact they'll probably order an airstrike and vaporise the boat. And remember what happened to Rawlins. This disease, whatever it is, drove him nuts. He damn near blew us to hell. You want to set sail in a ship full of ravening lunatics? A floating asylum? Anyway, it's not like anyone ever recovered from this contagion. No one gets better. I vote we shoot them all. The kindest thing. Throw the bodies over the side.'

'We don't have enough shells. A ship like that might carry two, three thousand passengers. And a big crew.'

'So gas them. Rev the engines and channel exhaust fumes into the ventilation.'

'I agree,' said Ivan. 'We couldn't sleep with those rabid fucks the other side of the wall.'

'Right now we have them contained,' said Jane. 'Besides, we don't even know if gassing them would work. They should all be dead. No food, water or heat. That ship should be a grave-yard. But somehow they keep going.'

Nikki looked around. Faces lit by lamplight, all of them looking to Jane for guidance.

'You can't trust her,' Nikki wanted to say. 'In a situation like this, you can't trust anyone but yourself.'

Nikki had a boyfriend. Alan. They spent two years together. A holiday in Mumbai, a holiday in Chile. And she left him out on the ice to die.

You can't place your fate in someone else's hands, she thought. When the moment comes you are on your own.

Some of the crew packed their possessions. They hauled suitcases and kit-bags to the submarine hangar. They sat in a semicircle around the convection heater.

Punch and Sian sat on their cases and warmed their hands.

'Just like *Spirit of Endeavour*,' said Sian. 'I was so sure we were going home. I was counting down the minutes.' She pointed to the cases. 'I bet the guys won't need half this stuff.'

'No. There will be heated cabins, fresh clothes every day. More food than we can eat. Judging by the stuff on TV, we might as well stay aboard when we reach Britain. Moor the ship off the coast. Treat the place as our fortress. Send out forage parties as and when.'

'Nice plan.'

'Maybe we were the lucky ones. Safe at the top of the world while the shit went down. We wanted a ride home and God sent a limo.'

'We're not home yet.'

* * *

Nikki descended to the pump hall and inspected the boat. She had cut and stitched three weather balloons to make a spinnaker. The silver sail hung slack from the mast, waiting for a strong wind.

She kicked the aluminium hull. It resonated like a gong.

Days earlier Nail stripped to the waist, masked his face and spray-gunned the vessel with red rig paint. He used bathroom grout to secure the rubber seal surrounding the boat hatch.

She consulted blueprints. The boat was complete and ready to be stocked. She climbed into the cockpit. Could she sail the boat herself? Did she truly need Nail any more? *The Dummies Guide to Sailing.* Nikki found the manual among the neglected book exchange table on Main Street. Creased paperbacks. Plenty of car magazines. She reckoned she could trim and reef a sail. She could tack left and right. She couldn't navigate. She couldn't steer by constellations. But if she headed south-west sooner or later she would sight the Norwegian coast, then she could let it guide her to the North Sea and home. She didn't need Nail. She could do it all alone.

'So what do you think?' Nail was watching from the shadows.

'It seems solid.'

'I reckon it could ride out a storm or two. Stable? Couldn't say. Ghost's design, not mine. It might capsize if it hit the wrong wave. But it won't break up. I built it strong.'

'Not much use for it now, though,' said Nikki. 'We can all hitch a ride on Jane's liner.'

'Jane Blanc? That waddling fuck? You really want to put your fate in her hands? Reckon she is going to get you home?'

'Since you put it like that.'

'I'm tired of promises. If you and I want a ride out of here we will have to organise it ourselves. So let's get this tin can ready to go.'

'What about the floor hatch?'

'Maybe we should find some batteries. Big ones. Hotwire the hydraulics.'

'Think it would work?'

'Few minutes of juice. That's all it would take.'

Nikki broke into a loading bay. Three forklifts parked at the back. She disconnected the batteries and loaded them on to a pallet truck. She dragged the pallet truck to the pump hall.

She stripped insulation from the hatch hydraulics and clipped jump leads. She pressed Open. Burst of sparks. Brief tremor from the hydraulic rams. The hatch didn't open.

'Fuck.'

She found a tennis ball. She sat bouncing the ball against the boat hull.

Alan, her boyfriend, used to tell a joke. 'What's brown and sticky? A stick.' He said it was the perfect joke. Elegantly simple. She remembered him reciting the joke at the dining table. Christmas with her parents. But she couldn't recall his voice. They were together two years, but already the memories were starting to fade like a photograph left in the sun.

He came to her in dreams. She glimpsed him in crowds. He shouted to her across busy streets.

Was Alan dead when she left him out on the ice? Could he have been saved? She would never know.

Scuff marks round a frosted floor plate. Big boot prints. Nikki pried the plate with a screwdriver and lifted it up. Ziploc bags of brown powder lying on the pipework.

She cooked a pinch of powder and siphoned the syrup into a hypodermic. A humourless smile.

'What's brown and sticky?' she murmured, as the needle punctured her skin.

Nail sat with Rye in the sub.

'Don't you ever go out?'

'It's cosy in here,' said Rye. She gestured to the bubble window of the cockpit. The crew sat round the fire. 'Besides, conversation is getting pretty repetitive. The women they will fuck. The drinks they will drink. If Jane and Ghost don't actually deliver this ship there will be a lynching.'

Rye blocked the cockpit window with her coat. She took a couple of hypodermics from her holdall. Nail opened a snuff box. He tapped powder into a spoon and cooked the mix with a Zippo.

'You have your doubts?'

'Jane Blanc. Stands before us and promises a floating Shangri-La. Forgive me if I don't get too excited. First day she arrived on the rig we had to run around looking for super-sized survival clothes just so she could dress properly. She's lost her battle with chocolate. She's been vanquished by doughnuts. Suddenly she's going to take charge and lead us all to safety? I don't think so.'

They returned to *Hyperion*. Jane and Ghost, Punch and Ivan.

'Okay,' said Jane. 'We've got a couple of lights on. So let's power this baby up for real. Let's get it moving.'

They surveyed the ship stern to prow. They met in the bridge.

'We have free access to the bridge and the officers' quarters,' said Jane. 'But from level two downward there are barricades at every door.'

'Plenty of blood around,' said Ghost. 'The crew fought a running battle. Must have been a hell of a fight. They prevailed, I guess. The ship is locked down pretty tight. We're safe, but most of the ship is off limits.'

'So where are the crew?' asked Punch. 'The blokes who built the barricades?'

Ghost shrugged. 'Maybe they spotted land. The ship was drifting. They saw some kind of habitation. They took to the boats and rowed for shore.'

'Habitation? Out here?'

'*Hyperion* has been adrift a long while. No telling where it's been.'

'Imagine the food down below,' said Punch. 'Caviar. Real eggs. Champagne. All out of reach. I'm not going to loll around in a presidential suite and slowly starve. I say we organise raiding parties. We haven't got enough shotgun shells to kill the passengers, but we've got enough to hold them off while we grab food.'

'Explains the Juliet flag,' said Ghost.

'The what?'

'Blue and white flag near the prow. International maritime signal. Dangerous cargo. Keep clear.'

'See this screen?' said Jane, sitting in the captain's chair in front of the Raytheon console. 'Revs. Engine speed. I'm almost certain these switches govern the propellers.'

Ghost leaned past her. He pressed buttons and turned dials.

'Off-line. If we want more than light, we will need to fire up the turbines.'

'I bet they shut down the engine room,' said Jane. 'When they evacuated the lower decks they must have turned everything off. Standard procedure. The kind of thing people do in a fire drill. Someone will have to go down there and switch it all back on.'

'Shit.'

Jane led Punch and Ghost to the chart room. A wall plan. *Hyperion*, floor by floor.

'We have free run of the top-most deck. But the engine room is nine levels beneath us.'

'Three thousand passengers, you reckon?'

'A liner like this? Yeah. If the ship is running at full capacity there must be two or three thousand infected down there.'

'Then we would have to move fast and get lucky.'

Infection

Jane explored the captain's suite. She sat at his desk. She found a passport in a drawer. Dougie Campbell. British citizen. Fifty-eight.

An envelope on the desk blotter. A thick sheaf of handwritten notes. Part letter, part diary. Campbell spent half his life at sea. He got lonely. He wrote to his wife every night.

Ship gossip. Most of the crew were east Europeans working for tips. Romanian and Polish. The Romanians hated the Polish. Officers had to mediate.

Jane thumbed through the pages, scanned trivia, searched for the moment it all went bad.

She sat back in the chair and put booted feet on the desk.

The ship docked at Trondheim two weeks into an Arctic cruise. They brought aboard fresh supplies and a couple of new waiters.

Three days out: an incident in a kitchen. One of the new waiters went berserk. He cut himself with a cleaver, then attacked two pot-washers. Deep cuts. Bite injuries. The waiter was restrained and sedated. He was confined to the medical bay.

Thank God no passengers were hurt.

A couple of nights later a group of passengers gathered to sip hot chocolate on deck and watch the Northern Lights. They saw a distant figure at the end of the promenade climb over a railing and jump into the ocean. The figure was wearing a white galley uniform. The figure appeared to be hugging a heavy fire extinguisher to help himself sink.

Passengers threw lifebelts into the sea and raised the alarm. The ship came to an immediate halt. The crew trained searchlights on the sea. No sign of the man.

Quick headcount. The missing man was a pot-washer treated for bite wounds.

The captain radioed ashore for medical advice. Four staff and two passengers had been admitted to the infirmary for treatment. They were delirious, restrained, and bleeding from their eyes and ears.

Representatives of Baltic Shipping instructed the captain to implement full quarantine procedures. Isolate all infected personnel and head for the nearby port of Murmansk.

The ship was turned back from Murmansk. Their maydays were ignored. They tried to approach the port, despite the harbour master's refusal to let them dock, but were fired upon by Russian soldiers as they threw mooring ropes to the jetty. Instead, they sailed west towards Norway.

Patrick Connor. Bosun for nine years. The captain's closest friend. The men stayed aloof and professional during the working day, but most evenings they sat in the captain's cabin and uncorked a bottle of claret. Neither man was supposed to drink. The seniority of their positions meant they were never truly off duty while the ship was at sea. So they sipped wine in secret and enjoyed their little transgression.

It has been a week since Patrick was bitten. I have had to watch the horrifying progress of this disease. I have had to watch my friend slowly become a monster. It has been the worst experience of my life.

Patrick was bitten on the face. He was bending over Lenuta Grasu, one of the Romanian cabin maids, when she broke her restraint and bit a chunk from his cheek. He immediately washed and disinfected the wound, but both he and the captain knew it would do no good. The disease was transmitted by body fluid like HIV or hepatitis. Once a person became infected they quickly succumbed to dementia. They, in turn, would bite and claw, be driven to transmit the infection any way they could. Rafal, the Trondheim waiter who was the first to show signs of infection, was lashed to a hospital bed. He spat and snarled. He was horribly deformed. There was little chance he would recover.

Dr Walczak, the ship's surgeon, referred to the disease as rabies, for want of a proper diagnosis. By the time they reached Norwegian waters the fourteen-bed medical bay was full to capacity. The staff commandeered a couple of staff cabins for use as treatment rooms. Patrick Connor had volunteered to help Walczak, allowing the doctor to get much needed rest from time to time.

Patrick wrote farewell letters to his wife and children, then allowed himself to be restrained. It took less than twenty-four hours for the disease to take hold. In rare lucid moments he begged for death.

The captain made frequent visits to the medical bay.

This evening Dr Walczak and I had a long conversation in which we discussed the best form of treatment for Pat, the best way to relieve his suffering.

Next diary entry:

We held Patrick's funeral service at noon today, and committed his body to the deep.

The captain liberated a few bottles of Cabernet Sauvignon from the galley. No journal entries for the next three days.

Jane lay on the bed. She scanned the notes. Page after page of carnage. One by one the captain's crew succumbed.

The engines were shut down. *Hyperion* drifted north of Norway.

They lost the lower levels. They hoped that, by dropping the watertight compartment doors, they would seal infected passengers in the lower cabins. But the passengers found the stairwells before the crew had time to finish building barricades.

First Officer Quinn issued his men with Molotov cocktails. If they held their ground in the stairways, if they drove the infected passengers back down to the lower levels, they might retain control of the upper decks.

I don't think those sent mad by this disease intentionally kill. They are compelled to bite and penetrate, to spread the contagion. Nevertheless I have seen eyes gouged and throats ripped out. Survivors lie injured in cabins and corridors crying for help until they too are overtaken by blood-thirst, haul themselves to their feet and attack.

It was hard to estimate casualties. Captain Campbell conducted a head-count. A minority of the passengers and crew, fewer than a thousand, were declared clear of infection. They treated the injured in the Grand Ballroom.

I wish Dr Walczak was still with us. Quinn tells me the doctor was sighted near the sewage treatment plant just before the lower compartments were sealed. He had no shirt. His back was clustered with spines like a porcupine. He often said he would rather die than succumb to this strange affliction. I suppose he didn't have time to take his life before dementia took hold.

There seemed little chance the captain's journal would reach his wife, so instead he left a warning.

Once a person enters the advanced stages of infection they become extremely hard to kill. Quinn saw a girl cut clean in half when we dropped the watertight doors. She lived for fifteen minutes. She dragged herself across the deck, still trying to bite and tear. The entire lower half of her body had been detached and left behind, nevertheless her legs continued to kick and twist.

Many of the crew armed themselves with knives from the kitchen. Word soon spread. Knives didn't work. Stab wounds didn't even slow them down.

The only effective way to deal with the infected is either to destroy them in their entirety with a weapon such as a Molotov cocktail, or inflict a severe blow to the head.

The captain was shocked to find himself listing the most efficient ways of 'dealing' with the infected. In a matter of days his passengers and crew had become lethal predators.

It is a matter of survival. Those of us who remain must act quickly and ruthlessly to ensure the ship does not become totally overrun.

Campbell wondered if there were some way of scuttling the ship, sending the infected passengers and crew to the bottom of the ocean as a mercy.

Campbell gave the order to abandon ship. He and his crew had been shivering in the cold and dark for days. They were drifting. Navigational instrumentation off-line.

They posted lookouts round the clock in the hope of sighting land. One night they saw what they hoped to see: lights in the distance. Steady, electric light. Too dark to make out detail. The captain estimated they were drifting east of Svalbard. They were probably passing the little coastal township that served the Arktikugol coal field. He ordered his men to take to the boats.

Seventy-four souls.

Hard to believe of all the passengers under my care, all the crew under my command, this ragged handful of exhausted and traumatised people are all that remain.

Campbell gave First Officer Quinn the ship's log and told him to lead the survivors to safety. He saluted his men as they rowed away.

He was alone aboard the ship, the last uninfected individual on the vessel. He retreated to his cabin. He uncorked a Bordeaux.

Campbell could have evacuated the ship with his men, but was determined to play the role of captain to the last.

We all need to believe our lives have some ultimate meaning. I have rank and responsibility. It's not foolish to live your ideals.

Jane woke with a jolt. She had dozed off, crumpled papers in her hand.

She stood at the washstand. She rubbed sleep from her eyes and cleaned her teeth. Toothpaste and bottled water.

'*Jane? You there?*' Ghost.

'Yeah.'

'*Punch and I are going to make a run for the engine room.*'

'I'll be right there.'

Jane adjusted her dog-collar. The room reflected in the mirror. A silver-framed photograph on the desk. Captain Campbell and his wife in happy times.

'Okay, Dougie,' said Jane. 'Let's get our boys home.'

The Engine Room

Ghost chose a hatch near the stern. A big, red '*X*' sprayed on the door. They dismantled the barricade. A cabin sofa and a couple of TVs. The hatch was jammed shut by a crowbar.

Ghost checked the breech of his shotgun. A shell in the chamber. Safety set to Fire.

Punch hefted a fire axe.

'Lock the door behind us,' said Ghost.

Jane removed the crowbar and cranked open the door. An empty corridor. Ghost and Punch stepped inside.

'Good luck,' said Jane, and heaved the door closed behind them. They heard a muffled, metallic scrape as she slid the crowbar back in place, sealing them inside the ship.

'All right,' muttered Ghost. 'Quiet as we can.'

Ghost checked a hand-drawn map. He had plotted a circuitous route to the engine room. He wanted to avoid communal areas where infected passengers might congregate. If the diseased passengers were truly mindless they would wander all over the ship. But if they retained faint memories of life aboard the liner they would gravitate towards the bars and restaurants.

They hurried down narrow service corridors. Company slogans interspersed with maritime lithographs.

Excellence is our watchword

'Ridiculous,' said Ghost. 'Everything in English except the stuff that matters.'

They passed the entrance of a health spa. The Neptune Wellness Centre. The poolside lit cold, medicinal blue. Upturned loungers. Signs for steam rooms, massage suites, herbal and Finnish saunas.

They heard a faint rustling, flopping sound. Something was trapped at the bottom of the empty spa pool making clumsy, spastic attempts to get out. The slapping abruptly ceased. The unseen thing had sensed Punch and Ghost standing in the doorway. It listened to them breathe.

Punch took a step like he was going to investigate but Ghost tugged his sleeve and motioned to keep walking.

Ivan checked the chart room.

'There's an oil heater back here.'

'Fire it up.'

He dragged the oil heater on to the bridge and lit it with a match.

'You know, if we are going to heat this place, it might be a good idea to deal with the captain. He could stink the place out.'

'Yeah,' said Jane. 'Let's put him over the side.'

They dragged the dead man by his boots. They hauled him across the deck. They lifted him by his coat and toppled him over the railing. The captain splashed into the sea. He floated face down for a couple of minutes, then his waterlogged coat pulled him under the waves.

'Probably ought to say something,' said Jane. 'Can't think what.'

'I wouldn't feel too bad about it,' said Ivan. 'That's a better send-off than most people get these days.'

The oil heater burned with a blue flame. The bridge began to heat up. Jane sat back in the captain's chair and unzipped her coat. Something smelled bad. She sniffed her armpits. She stank.

She threw Ivan her radio.

'Back in a minute,' she said. 'Keep my seat warm.'

She checked the officers' quarters. Name tags on each door.

She pulled open cupboard drawers. Fresh thermal underwear. T-shirts. Socks.

A bottle of mineral water next to the bed. Jane filled the sink, stripped and washed. Little sachets of conditioner, body scrub and shampoo. The first time she had washed her hair for weeks.

Toiletries and make-up in the washstand cabinet. She caught her reflection as she closed the cabinet door. She hadn't seen herself naked for a while. She was thinner. Her collar bones were more defined. Her breasts had deflated and sagged.

One of the attractions of Arctic life: it was pretty much asexual. Men and women wore the same quilted cold-weather gear. No hierarchies of beauty and glamour on a polar installation.

Jane toyed with cosmetics. She drew gloss across her lips. It made her mouth seem like a bloody wound.

Ghost and Punch headed for a stairwell. Down nine levels.

'Mind your step,' said Ghost. The temperature had dropped even further. The stairs were glazed with ice. They were deep below the waterline.

MASKINRUMMET

The engine room.

They shut themselves inside and jammed the door with a wrench.

They found themselves on a walkway looking down on massive drive machinery. Gas turbines. Alternators. Four great motors mounted on rubber dampers, four great manganese propeller shafts.

Ghost took out his radio.

'We made it. We're at the engine room.'

There was a glass control booth at the end of the walkway.

'Let's flick every switch,' said Ghost. 'See what happens.'

A slow dragging sound from below the walkway.

'I don't think we're alone down here,' said Punch.

The guy must have been an engineer. His badge said *Hilmar Larsen*. He limped from behind one of the huge Wärtsilä Vasa engines. He dragged his leg like his ankle was broken. His right hand was spiked metal like an armoured gauntlet. The fabric of his boiler suit was lumped and stretched by a strange, spinal deformity. His face was bloody and swollen and his eyes were jet black.

'How's it going down there, Hilmar?' asked Punch.

The engineer looked upward and hissed. He slowly stumbled across the engine room and up the steps to the walkway.

Punch and Ghost backed away.

'Dude, it would be great if you could stop right there.'

The engineer reached the top of the steps and limped towards them, sliding along a railing for support.

'Larsen, if you can hear me, if you can understand my words, you need to stop.'

The man continued to advance.

Punch and Ghost backed into the control booth. Ghost shut the door and held it closed with his foot. Punch helped brace the door with his shoulder.

Larsen slammed against the glass. Ghost saw himself reflected in jet-black eyeballs. The engineer hissed and spat. Spittle dribbled down the glass.

'Shoot him,' said Punch.

'We need the ammo. I'll open the door. You hit him with the axe.'

'All right.'

'Ready?'

Ghost opened the door.

Punch stood back. He adjusted his grip on the axe. He held

it above his head like he was about to whack a fairground test-your-strength machine.

'Last chance, Hilmar,' he said. 'Can't let you come any closer.'

The engineer got ready to lunge.

Punch brought down the axe and cleaved the man's head in two. The engineer staggered backward, out of the booth. He toppled on to the walkway, axe buried between the two halves of his head. His legs danced a jig, last signals from a scrambled brain.

They stepped over the dead man and descended from the gantry to the floor of the engine room.

'Flick every switch you find,' said Ghost. 'Turn every light green.'

They cranked dials and isolator breakers to On. Faint hum of current. Ghost took out his radio.

'Raise the anchor,' he told Jane. 'Let's get this thing going.'

Brief warning klaxon. Turbines hummed then roared. The propeller shafts slowly began to turn.

Jane stood at the helm and watched the turbine rev needles rise from zero to full power.

'Feel that?' she called to Ivan. 'We're moving.'

'No shit,' said Ivan. He was standing at the back of the bridge looking down into the stairwell. Heavy impacts against the barricaded door. Jumbled furniture began to shake and shift.

'Hate to say it, but I think we woke the neighbours.'

Breakout

Ghost walked the floor of the engine room. Turbines roared.

He checked an engine panel. He tapped a dial. A drop of blood splashed at his feet. He looked up. The dead engineer was lying on the gantry above him. Blood dripped through the grate.

'Better clean that up,' said Ghost. 'Any fire blankets around?'

They climbed the walkway. Ghost tugged the axe from the engineer's head. He crouched and inspected the wound.

'His brain is full of metal. Look.'

'I'll take your word for it,' said Punch.

'Little wires. Little filaments spread through his body. There's some coming out of his nose.'

'Sure he's dead?'

'Pretty sure. Better bag him up.'

Ghost wiped the axe blade on the engineer's leg.

They wrapped the dead man in a couple of fire blankets and lashed his body with flex. They threw the body from the gantry. The corpse lay by a wall.

'He'll be okay down there for a while,' said Ghost. 'We'll put him over the side when we get a chance.'

Ghost hefted the axe.

'Mind if I take this?' he asked. 'The gun is too loud. If I shoot, it will bring a shipful of freaks down on us.'

Punch found a big power drill. He revved the trigger a couple of times to check the charge.

They stood at the engine room door. Ghost removed the wrench.

'Ready?'

He twisted the handles and pulled the hatch aside. An empty passageway.

'Okay. Let's go.'

Jane sat at the helm. She tried to make sense of the screens. At a guess: engine output, fuel management, course correction.

She turned the joystick. She slowly pushed the thrust levers forward. A ball-compass mounted in the panel beside her rolled like an eye slowly looking left. The Alstrom dynamic positioning system. The ship was turning east towards the rig. It was exhilarating to think she could steer an object the size of a mountain by the touch of her fingers.

Jane dry-swallowed Dexedrine. Amphetamines were a basic Arctic survival tool. Rye kept an extensive stock of stimulants locked in a trunk under her bed. Hoarded them like a connoisseur. Treated them as her personal wine cellar.

Ivan stood guard in the stairwell behind the bridge. He watched the door at the bottom of the stairs. The steel hatch was wedged shut by a stack of chairs. He could hear relentless pounding from the other side like someone was hurling their bodyweight against the door.

He searched for more furniture to wedge the hatch. He fetched a sofa from the officers' quarters. He rolled it through the bridge.

'You okay?' called Jane, over her shoulder. 'Need any help?'

'I'm okay.'

He tipped the sofa over the railing. It hit the barricade with a crash. Brief respite from the pounding, then the impacts resumed.

Ivan descended the stairs. He put his ear to the hatch. Scuffling. Grunting.

He tried to reinforce the barricade, pile more furniture against the door.

'Got a moment?' he yelled. 'I think they're going to break through.'

Chairs shook and toppled. Ivan put his shoulder to the door. He strained to keep the hatch closed. He blinked sweat from his eyes.

Jane ran down the stairs and joined him at the barricade. She pushed against the door.

'This is no fucking good,' she said. 'Any more of those fire axes around? Maybe we can wedge this thing closed.'

'Don't know. Think I saw a toolbox in the purser's office.'

Jane ran up the stairs.

Ivan braced his back against the door. His boots slipped on the metal deck. The barricade slowly began to collapse.

The hatch was pushed ajar. Ivan snatched an extinguisher from the wall and directed a jet of foam through the gap. He used the empty extinguisher to pound at clawing, scrabbling fingers.

'I need some help here,' he shouted up the stairwell. 'Jane? Jane, you there? We're in some deep shit.'

Jane vaulted down the steps holding a claw hammer. She flailed at the squirming hand. The hammer sparked metal. She mashed fingers with heavy blows.

Jane and Ivan threw themselves against the steel door and tried to slam it closed. They heard bone crunch. They threw themselves at the door twice more. Blood spurt. The grasping hand fell to the deck, cut through at the wrist.

Jane cranked the hatch levers closed, and jammed them shut with the shaft of the hammer.

'Not on my bloody watch,' she muttered.

'Jesus,' said Ivan, looking down at the floor. The severed hand clenched and unclenched like an upturned crab. It tried to crawl. The Russian crossed himself. 'It's still alive.'

Punch passed a kitchen doorway. The Commodore Grill.

'We should keep moving,' said Ghost.

'Let me check it out. I need to see what we've got down here.'

Punch opened a freezer. Spoiled food. Green mould.

Ghost took a jar from a shelf.

'Jalapeños,' he said. 'We could sprinkle them on our cereal or something.'

A dry store. Bags of rice and dried pasta. Pallets of cans.

'Fucking mother lode,' said Punch. I bet there are kitchens like this all over the ship. Lots of little theme restaurants.'

'In a couple of days we can organise the men and do a systematic search. Take our pick. Fill some carts. But right now we need to get out of here.'

They turned to leave. A woman stood in the doorway. She wore a blue ball gown. Her eyes stared through a mask of metal spines.

'Back off, darling,' warned Punch.

She reached for him. He kicked her legs and she fell. He planted a boot on her chest to keep her down. He put the drill bit between her eyes and bored into her brain. He ground through bone. She arched her back then lay still.

'Holy mother of God,' he muttered, standing over the corpse. 'Let's go.'

They headed down the corridor.

A waitress slithered round the corner, dragging bloody, useless legs. Ghost hefted the axe, ready to strike a blow. A second infected crew member turned the corner, metal leaking from nose and ears. He was joined by a woman in jogging gear, arms fused to her sides. Ghost backed away.

'Getting crowded.'

More passengers, shuffling, limping, groping.

'Plan B,' said Punch.

They ran back to the engine room and sealed themselves inside. Fists thudded against the door. Ghost gripped his shotgun, clicked from Safety to Fire. Punch took out his radio.

'Jane, you there? We might have a little problem.'

*   *   *

Jane called the rig.

'*Hyperion* to Rampart, do you copy, over?'

'Rampart *here.*' Sian's voice.

'We've got control. We've got the basics. The propellers turn. We can steer left and right. We're heading your way. Ten knots. Slow, but making headway. I'll try to push it harder. Can you put up a flare? Something to guide us?'

'*Give me two minutes.*'

Jane stood on deck. The fog had cleared. She had found the captain's binoculars. She adjusted focus. She saw the red pin-prick of a distant flare.

She returned to the bridge. She nudged the joystick left. Brief rotation from the bow thrusters. She felt the massive vessel adjust course.

Ivan searched the officers' quarters for booze. He found a couple of miniatures, but couldn't find a full-size bottle.

One of the crew had left a humidor full of cigars and a heavy brass lighter on his desk. Cuban. Vaqueros Colorado Madura. Ivan filled his pockets. He didn't smoke, but he could trade when he got back to the rig. The Rampart crewmen liked cigars. Greedy for any little pleasure that would help them forget their predicament a while. Getting high was the new currency now that money was no good.

He heard an intermittent humming noise.

He stood in the corridor outside the crew cabins. More humming.

He approached the slide doors at the end of the passage. A bad smell like eggs, like rotting meat. He realised, with a wash of sickening fear, why the ship's systems had been off-line. The *Hyperion* crew wanted to seal infected passengers below deck. They had barricaded every door and sealed each stairwell. Then they shut off the power in case the shambling horde below figured out how to summon elevators.

A discreet ping. The doors began to slide open. Ivan backed away. He glimpsed an old lady melded to an electric wheelchair.

A crowd of infected passengers jostled for space around her. Bloody ball gowns and dinner suits. Stench of vomit and piss. Ivan turned and ran.

Jane steered the ship towards a winking red signal light, one of the aircraft warning strobes on top of a distillation tower.

She pictured the Rampart crew lining the refinery railings, applauding as the liner docked. She would play it cool and casual. '*Welcome aboard, boys.*' Bask in their new-found respect and admiration.

There was a button on the control panel. A trumpet icon. She hit the button and released the long, two-note bass boom of the ship's Tyfon horn.

Ivan ran through the door.

'The passengers. The fucks. They broke out. They're right here.' He grabbed Jane by the sleeve and pulled her towards an exterior door. 'We've got to go.'

'What about Punch and Ghost?'

'We have to get out of here.'

A group of infected crew were milling on the upper deck. Officers in dress uniform. They seized Ivan as he ran outside. He screamed. He fought. They fell on him and dragged him to the floor.

Jane swung the shotgun to her shoulder. She took aim at a bearded man with sunglasses fused to his face. The blast vaporised his head. The second shot caught two crewmen across the chest and hurled them backward.

A chef lunged for her. She shot him in the shoulder. His arm landed on a bench.

More passengers and crew climbed the steps from the lower deck. Jane backed on to the bridge.

Later, when they asked what happened to Ivan, she said, 'Swear to God, it was like they wanted to climb inside him. They stuck fingers in his eyes, his mouth. They bit off his fingers. They drove a fist into his stomach. They pretty much turned him inside out.'

Jane was trapped. Two shells left in the gun. She climbed over the captain's chair, shot out the window and squirmed outside. Jagged safety glass slit open her parka, spilling insulation foam.

She balanced on the sill. A ten-metre drop to the lower deck. She scrambled upward on to the roof of the bridge.

Jane paced the roof. Infected passengers reached up for her on all sides, hissing and clawing. She unzipped a box of shells from her backpack and reloaded the shotgun. She leaned against the radar mast and tried to breathe slowly. She took the radio from her pocket.

'Ghost? Punch? Can you hear me? I really need your help, folks.'

Sian stood on the helipad and flagged a searchlight back and forth. She was joined by the crew. They wanted to see the ship that would carry them to freedom.

They saw a gleam on the horizon like a low star. A quarter of an hour later they saw the running lights of a ship approaching fast. *Hyperion* lit bright and spectral. The great prow splintered ice. The horn blared. They cheered.

'It's massive,' said Nikki.

'There will be heaters,' said Sian. 'Imagine it. We will be warm. I've almost forgotten what it feels like.'

'It's a monster.'

'Look how quick it's moving,' said Sian. 'We'll be home in hours.'

'It's coming in pretty fast. Now would be a good time to hit the brakes.'

The ship didn't slow down. The crew stopped cheering, and backed away from the edge of the helipad.

The ship kept coming. They could hear it. The rumble of engines. The rush of water. The crack of splintering ice.

The ship slammed into the west corner of the rig. The impact bucked the refinery and knocked the crew from their feet. Sparks and shrieking metal as girders stressed and sheered. Thunder roar. One of the rig's great anchor cables broke free, wrenching away a chunk of superstructure.

Sian fell and broke her nose. She rolled on her back and lay stunned. She sneezed blood. A dream-image glimpsed through tears: the lights of the ship, the decks, portholes and festoons, passing like a carnival parade. A jagged gash was ripped in the side of the ship. Hull plates tore with an unearthly scream.

The damaged liner sped on, headed straight for the island.

The Wreck

Impact.

Ghost was thrown across the engine room. He grabbed a railing to stop himself falling against a massive, spinning propeller shaft.

He fell to the floor. An extractor fan broke loose from ductwork and hit the deck near his head. Tool lockers flew open. Punch curled foetal and covered his head as spanners skittered across the deck plates.

A final, cataclysmic concussion. The ship lurched. A section of walkway collapsed. An extinguisher burst, jetting the air with a blizzard of foam particles. Then the engine room was still.

Ghost sat up. He wiped foam from his face and hands. He spat foam from his mouth. The engine room was coated white like heavy snowfall.

'What did we hit?' asked Punch. 'Did we collide with an iceberg or something?'

'We've stopped. We're not moving. I think we ran aground.'

'Are you all right?'

'Banged my leg. I'm okay. You?'

'Fine.'

The propeller shafts were still spinning.

'Better kill the engines.'

The ship listed at a crazy angle. The engine room was a steep hill. Punch climbed the room and threw each breaker to Off. Engine noise slowly diminished and died. The four great propeller shafts gradually ceased to turn.

He left one of the disengaged turbines running.

'Better leave this baby ticking over,' said Ghost. 'It'll keep the lights on.'

'Where's the radio? Help me look. I think I dropped it.'

Ghost found the radio wedged behind the body of the dead engineer.

'Jane? Jane, can you hear me?'

No reply.

'Jane, do you copy, over?'

They sat for an hour. Ghost tried to raise Rampart every ten minutes.

'Do you think those things are still outside?' asked Punch.

'I expect so.'

Punch kicked the engineer.

'I killed a man,' said Punch. 'That's who I am now. A guy who kills people.'

'The world has changed. We better change with it.'

A scuffle and a thud. Punch climbed the gantry steps and put his ear to the door.

'What can you hear?' asked Ghost. 'Is someone outside?'

Punch mimed hush.

Three knocks.

'What do you reckon?' asked Punch. 'Open the door?'

Three more knocks.

'Pass me the gun,' said Punch. 'I'm going to open the door.'

Punch unlocked the hatch. He shouldered the shotgun and kicked the door open. Dr Rye stood with a bottle of Chivas Regal in her hand. 'Ready to go?' She lit a rag stuffed in the neck of the Chivas. She tossed the bottle at a gaggle of infected passengers massing at the end of the corridor. Burning booze splashed the walls and floor creating a barrier of flame. 'Let's not hang around.'

They hurried through the ship. The passageways and stair-wells listed at a nightmare angle.

'Okay,' said Rye. 'We'll need to cut through a couple of public spaces. We'll need to do it quickly and quietly. Way too many of these fuckers to fight off.'

They passed through the ship's library. Novels and magazines had fallen from the shelves when the ship ran aground. They kicked through mountains of paper.

'This is where we cut through the main lobby,' explained Rye. 'Could be tricky.'

They hurried along a balcony area overlooking the main lobby, the central communal area of the ship. Ghost stopped for a moment and looked over the balustrade.

Hundreds of infected passengers milling and moaning. Chaos and stench. Rich vacationers mutated to monstrous parodies of themselves. They stumbled over upturned tables and chairs. They rode escalators. They rode glass scenic elevators. They crawled up and down the great sweep of the staircase on hands and knees. They slid on scattered leaflets from the information desk. They tripped on glittering fragments of fallen chandelier.

'My God,' murmured Ghost.

Rye tugged his sleeve. 'Keep going.'

'How did you get here?' asked Ghost.

'I paddled a lifeboat from the rig,' said Rye. 'We'll use the zodiac to get back.'

'Did you find Jane?'

'I thought she was with you.'

Jane was hurled forward from the roof of the bridge at the moment of impact like a crash-test dummy propelled through a windscreen.

Mid-air. Body clenched for impact. 'It will be slow hell,' said a remote corner of her mind removed from the action. 'You'll hit the deck, and lie there, and think you are okay even though your back is broken. Then pain will build and build until it blots out the world.'

Her leg tangled in a decorative light-string hung at the prow. She dangled upside down for a moment, swung and spun, arms flailing, then the festoon snapped in a burst of sparks. She hit the deck, crunching bulb-glass beneath her. She got to her feet. Infected passengers would be on her any minute. She snatched up her shotgun and ran.

The Rampart zodiac was suspended from a couple of lifeboat cranes. Jane lowered the zodiac. It hit the ice. She slid down the crane-rope. She unhitched the rope and dragged the boat across the ice to the water's edge.

She had lost her radio. She huddled in her coat and waited to see if anyone else made it off *Hyperion*. Fifteen minutes later they approached across the snow. Ghost, Punch, Rye.

'I thought you must be dead,' Jane said.

'So what happened?'

'There were hundreds of them,' she mumbled. 'It was like they were hibernating down there in the dark.'

'Where's Ivan?' asked Ghost.

'They tore him apart.'

'Christ.'

'Let's get off this island,' said Jane. 'I don't even want to look at that fucking ship.'

They rode the zodiac to Rampart. They looked back.

The liner was beached three kilometres away, lights still blazing. The prow of the ship had lifted from the water. The hull plates were ripped open.

Nobody spoke.

Rye patched up Sian's face. Wiped blood from her nose and lashed a splint across the split skin.

'You'll be mouth-breathing for a while, but you should be okay.'

She gave Sian a couple of aspirin.

'Anyone else hurt?' asked Sian.

'Nail broke his arm.'

'Damn.'

'Fracture. No big deal.'

Jane sipped soup in the canteen. She warmed her hands round the mug. The remaining crew watched from the other side of the room.

'What do they want?' asked Jane. 'What do they want me to say?'

'I suppose they want to know if the ship still floats,' said Sian. Her nose was patched with tape. She sounded bunged up, like a heavy cold.

'How the hell would I know? Tell them to get off their arses and look. Do I have to do every little fucking thing?'

Jane locked herself in the toilet. She had filled her pockets with liquor miniatures during her brief exploration of *Hyperion*. She sat in the cubicle, balanced her flashlight on the toilet paper dispenser, and downed five shots of Jim Beam. She closed her eyes and waited for the rush.

Jane lay on her bunk. Two more shots of bourbon. She was numb, thoughtless. She hoped it would last.

There was a knock at the door.

'Ghost wants to fetch some stuff from the ship,' said Punch. 'There are things we could use.'

'Forget it. The place is a death trap.'

'Quick in and out, like a bank raid. Want to tag along?'

'I'm taking a holiday from the hero business.'

'Hope you don't mind if I borrow your gun.' Punch took the shotgun and shells from the table.

Jane rolled to face the wall.

Ghost and Punch rode the zodiac back to the island. They had lashed a long aluminium ladder across the boat. The ladder spread either side of the boat like steel wings.

Hyperion had run aground on the jagged rocks of the island's shore.

They carried the ladder to the ship's prow. They climbed into the ship through a gash in the side of the hull. Steel plates had been ripped away exposing a cross-section of rooms and stairs.

Ghost led Punch to a passageway near the bilge.

'There,' he said, pointing at the ceiling. A thick rope of cable lashed to the ductwork. 'Exactly what we need. Single core, high voltage. Big, juicy length of it. Perfect.'

He prised open a wall box with a screwdriver and threw an isolator switch.

'Perfect? We find an entire floating city, and all we can salvage is a bit of cable?'

'This is heat. This is light. This could get us through the winter. Remember: we're better off today than we were yesterday. Hold on to that thought.'

Punch closed a hatch at one end of the corridor and knotted it shut with a length of fire hose. He stood guard at the other end of the corridor with a pickle jar Molotov in his hand.

'Quick as you can,' he said. 'We don't want to attract a crowd.'

Ghost dragged a table from an office. He stood on it and got to work. He used a wrench to unbolt a socket joint in the cable. He dragged the table to the other end of the corridor and repeated the procedure.

A fat man in Bermuda shorts and a Hawaiian shirt turned the corner. He wore a sombrero. He had a camera round his neck. His legs were a tumorous mess of flesh-flaps and metal.

'We have our first customer,' said Punch. He took a Zippo from his pocket and lit the rag. The Molotov splashed burning kerosene across the corridor floor. The second Molotov smashed against the man's face and turned him to a pillar of flame. A guttural, inhuman howl. He collapsed and lay burning.

'See that?' said Punch. 'He won't lie still. He's dead but the metal keeps on trucking.'

He backed away from the burning man, repelled by the stench. He took another Molotov from his backpack.

'More on their way,' he warned. 'How's it going, Gee?'

'We're done.'

Ghost coiled the cable and slung it over his shoulder. Punch untied the fire hose and released the hatch. He allowed himself a backward glance. Monstrously deformed figures massing through flame and smoke. Punch threw his last Molotov and ran.

The alcohol buzz was starting to wane. Jane resolved to ask Ghost for a big bag of weed. So much easier to extinguish all thought and sleepwalk through the day.

She lay in the dark. The ceiling strip-light flickered to life then burned steadily. She shielded her eyes from the glare. Power had been restored.

She opened the door. There were lights in the corridor, lights in every room. She heard cheering from the canteen.

The crewmen stood beneath heating vents, faces turned upward, basking in a torrent of hot air like they were taking a shower. One of the men got the jukebox working. 'Sweet Home Alabama'. They would be toasting Ghost with fresh coffee when he returned from his work on C deck. Slapping his back, exchanging high fives. Jane didn't want to stick around and watch.

The power was back. Nikki ran across the pump hall to the storeroom. She flicked a switch. Brilliant arc-lights.

She circled the boat. It was her first chance to examine it in detail. The integrity of the welds. The tightness of the bolts. She kicked it. She slapped the hull.

She looped the hoist-chain over the prow and stern, and pressed Up. The winch began to wind and the chain pulled taut. The boat creaked and slowly lifted from the floor.

She hit a wall button. Warning beacons strobed yellow. The

hatch in the floor beneath the boat split open like the bomb bay of a B52. Typhoon ice particles. The silver sails wafted and billowed.

Nikki stood at the edge of the abyss and looked down into darkness and freezing wind. That was where she was headed. If she chose to sail home alone she would have to leave the light and warmth of the rig behind and immerse herself in perpetual night.

Flutter of excitement. All she had to do was press Down.

Jane sat on the edge of her bunk. Help someone, she told herself. When you are at your lowest ebb, feeling useless and ineffectual, reach out and help someone. Make yourself matter.

She headed for the submarine hangar.

Nail was lying on the deck. He was cushioned by his sleeping bag, luxuriating in a torrent of hot air from a wall-vent.

He had broken his right arm. A snapped broom handle for a splint. Ripped T-shirt for a bandage.

'Anything I can get you?' she asked. 'Do you want a drink? Something to eat?'

Nail slowly turned his head. He looked at her a long while like he was trying to remember her name.

'Jesus,' said Jane. 'Rye has you doped to the gills, doesn't she?'

He smiled and closed his eyes. Then he jolted awake and tried to sit up.

'Nikki,' he said.

'You want me to get her?'

'The lights are on.'

'Light and heat. That's right.'

'Power.'

'Yeah, power.'

'Nikki.'

'I can look for her, if you like.'

Nail tried to stand, but Jane gently pushed him back down.

'I don't know what Rye has given you, kid, but maybe you should just lie back and enjoy the ride.'

Ghost called a meeting in the canteen and laid out his plan. Nikki stood at the back of the room and listened.

Hyperion was partially beached. Spring would come, the ice would thaw, and the ship would float free. So the situation had yet to change. Conserve fuel. Conserve food. Ride out winter.

Ghost suggested the crew transfer from the refinery to *Hyperion*. Better accommodation. Easier to heat. All they had to do was disable the elevators and rebuild barricades to keep the rabid horde at bay. No reason it couldn't be done. The infected passengers were mindless, incapable of cunning or calculation. They could easily be suppressed.

'Think of the food,' said Ghost. 'Think of the booze.' He avoided Jane's eye, mildly ashamed to be luring the men to *Hyperion* with the promise of limitless alcohol.

Ghost took a vote. A fifty/fifty split. Arguments escalated towards fist fights. Half the guys said it was too dangerous to take a suite on the liner while ravening passengers massed the other side of the door. Half the guys said stateroom luxury was too good to miss.

Insults flew. Push-and-shove. The discussion looked like it would last long into the night so Nikki sneaked out of a side door.

She hurried to a lifeboat station. Red running-man signs all over the rig pointed the way. There were a cluster of rigid shell lifeboats at each corner of the refinery. Orange, fibre-glass cocoons the size of a bus. Room for thirty men. During the weekly fire drill crewmen were trained to strap themselves inside, seal the hatch, then pull a release handle. Explosive bolts would eject the lifeboat from a launch tube into the sea.

Nikki climbed inside the raft. She and Nail had raided the

lifeboats for equipment once before. She wanted stuff they left behind.

She dragged a case from beneath a bench seat. A flip-latch lid. Emergency gear: salt tablets, a manual bilge pump and a compact desalinator. She bagged them and ran to the C deck storeroom. She threw them into the boat.

She hurried to the food store. She upturned a wholesale box of dried noodles. Tins and cartons swept into the box. She ran to C deck and threw the box into the boat.

She levered floor plates. Bags of clothes, charts and flares hidden beside the pipes. She threw the bags into the boat.

She found clippers. She bent forward and shaved herself bald. Clumps of auburn hair fell to the deck.

Last look around. She took a crumpled sheet of paper from her pocket. Her checklist. Quick inventory: good to go.

She punched a green wall button with her fist. Trapdoors opened beneath the boat. A typhoon blast of freezing wind and ice particles.

The boat hung on a chain-hoist. Nikki pressed Down and jumped aboard the boat as it descended into the dark.

The boat touched down on the ice beneath the refinery. She unhooked the chains.

A couple of wheeled pallets roped to the underside of the yacht. The boat weighed the same as a van, but the ice was slick as glass.

Nikki buckled crampons to her boots and threw herself against the boat. Once the boat began to move it built momentum. She pushed the vessel, a step at a time, to the water's edge. She jumped aboard as brittle-crisp ice cracked beneath the weight of the boat and it settled into the sea. She pulled rope hand over hand and raised the sails.

Metallic motor noise. A flashlight beam suddenly trained in her face from above. Jane descending in the platform elevator. Nikki recoiled from the dazzling glare like she'd been slapped.

'Slinking away, is that the plan?' shouted Jane. The platform touched down.

'I didn't want to make a fuss.'

Nikki shielded her eyes and tried to squint beyond the blinding light. She tried to see if Jane were carrying a shotgun.

'I like what you did with your hair,' said Jane. 'You look like a boiled egg.'

Nikki didn't say anything. She waited to see what Jane would do.

'Here's the deal. You can take the boat. You can take the food. You can take whatever maritime charts you've stolen. But you have to take a radio, as well. You owe us that much. We need to hear how far you get. We need to hear what is waiting beyond the horizon.'

Nikki was hit on the chest by a big radio in a canvas bag. She instinctively caught the strap before the radio fell in the water.

'So how about it?'

'All right,' said Nikki. 'Call me any time you like. We'll chat, do lunch.'

'I'm serious. You were dying out there on the ice, remember? You were dead meat. We brought you back. We saved your life. You owe us a few minutes of your time.'

'Okay. Fuck it.'

'It'll be lonely out there. Few days alone in the dark. You might be grateful of a voice.'

The boat began to drift away from the ice.

Twenty metres. Thirty metres. Nikki moving beyond Jane's reach.

A hundred metres. Two hundred metres. Out of shotgun range.

Nikki was home free. Nail might commandeer the zodiac and try to chase her down, but he would struggle to find her. No running lamps. Too small for a radar fix.

Nikki looked back. Rampart dwindled behind her, a receding constellation of room lights. A massive, skeletal silhouette blotting out the stars.

Crackle as the craft bumped ice plates aside.

She turned her back on the refinery and looked towards the southern horizon, the point where a fabulous dust of the Milky Way met the impenetrable blackness of the sea. A heart-fluttering mix of excitement and fear. She locked the tiller in position with bungee line. She fitted a thermal mask to her face and pulled up her hood. She hunkered down in the cockpit ready for the long haul.

Nail lay in an opiate stupor. The world-obliterating white pain of his snapped ulna had been dulled to an ache by Demerol. He slipped in and out of consciousness for a couple of hours.

He woke. The drugs had worn off. The pain in his arm made his eyes water, made his teeth gnash.

He got to his feet and stumbled down cold corridors to the pump hall. He kicked the storeroom door wide. The floor hatch was open. The boat was gone.

'Fucking bitch,' he yelled.

Jane stood at the hatch controls. She pressed Close. The hydraulic rams retracted, pulling the floor hatch shut. It sealed with a heavy, metallic thud, cutting off wind noise.

'I don't know why you are acting all surprised and betrayed,' said Jane. 'She was aching to fuck you over. Anyone could see it. Personally, I would have hidden the fuse for the hatch controls. Replaced it with a dud. Make sure she couldn't take an unauthorised joyride while I wasn't around. You know, deep down, on a fundamental level, you are pretty stupid.'

'Fucking bitch,' murmured Nail.

Jane joined Sian on the floodlit helipad.

'Feeling a little under-appreciated?' asked Sian.

'Ghost did a fine job with the power.'

'It'll keep them happy for five minutes. Then it will dawn on them. They are still here. Still stuck. Still waiting for someone to get them home. They'll be knocking on your door soon enough.'

'And what do I tell them?'

'That we've got a ship. It's beached. It's got a big rip in the hull. But we'll get it moving, sooner or later.'

'I think the current occupants might object. Look over there, out on the island.' Moonlit figures gathered at the water's edge. 'They've come from the ship. A couple of weeks from now the ice-bridge will be complete. The sea from here to the island will be frozen solid. They'll be able to walk right to our door. You think things got better just because the lights are on? We are now officially under siege.'

The Specimen

'So are you back in hero mode?' asked Punch.

Jane was mopping her room. A water pipe had split, spraying water across her bed.

'I try to help people out, if I can. Mainly to kill time. If the TV actually worked I'm not sure I would give a shit.'

'You might want to check on Rye.'

'Any reason?'

'No. But it's that dog-whistle thing. Sometimes people don't have to say or do anything weird. They just sit there, quietly sipping tea, all the while putting out an ultrasonic scream like they are dying inside.'

'I'll swing by. Not much I can do until she asks for help.'

Nobody knew much about Rye. She stayed in her room most of the time. There was a photograph tacked above her bunk. A baby boy. The picture looked old. Plenty of creases, plenty of pin holes.

Jane sat in Rawlins's office and checked Rye's personnel file. She quit general practice and took a job on a rig three years later. No explanation for the three-year hiatus.

Jane headed for Rye's room. She would fake a migraine. Ask for painkillers.

The door was ajar. Rye sat on the bed. She had stripped down to underwear. She dug a knife into her thigh, scratched her name with the tip of the blade. She drew little beads of blood.

Jane coughed to announce her presence.

'Before you ask,' said Rye, 'no, I don't want to talk about it.'

The crew held a toga party. They turned up the heat until the accommodation block was sweltering hot.

Ghost led a raid on *Hyperion*. They battled their way to the Ocean Bar and loaded a cart with booze. Smash and grab. Jane told Ghost it was a stupid idea, risking his life for a few bottles.

'It's vital,' he said. 'If the guys don't let off some steam they'll go nuts.'

They dressed in bed sheets. They switched on the jukebox and selected Random Play. Punch was bartender. He mixed margaritas. Jane licked salt from the rim of her glass.

'Salut.'

Jane enjoyed the party. A few months ago, when she was super-obese, she would have stayed in her room. She couldn't wear a toga. The sheets weren't big enough.

Punch laid out canapés. Tube-cheese squeezed on to Ritz crackers. Sausage rolls.

A couple of guys took off their togas and danced in shorts.

Ghost passed round a couple of joints. He won a press-up contest with Gus and Mal.

Sian sat behind a table to stop guys staring at her legs.

Rye joined the party. She didn't wear a toga. She sat near the door and watched the action. She sipped tequila from a paper cup. Jane brought her a plate of food.

'Margarita?'

'I don't like the salt.'

'But you're holding up okay?'

'You know,' said Rye, 'everyone else on this rig may be desperate to explain themselves, to be understood, but I deal with my own shit.'

Rye crouched behind a snowdrift. She hunted by moonlight. She watched dim shadow-shapes of *Hyperion* passengers standing motionless on the ice. She used infrared binoculars. Distance-to-target calibrations, like a sniper-scope. The landscape in negative. Pale, luminescent figures on a black landscape. Body temperature was way down. The figures had barely any heat signature. Rye couldn't understand how they were still walking around. They should be frozen. They should be starved. There were a dozen different ways they should be dead.

She circled a crowd of passengers gathered at the waterline, mesmerised by the installation lights of the rig. She stalked a man in a dark suit who seemed to have strayed from the herd

She stepped from behind a snowdrift.

'Hey,' she called. 'Wanna buy a Rolex?'

The man turned. He took a couple of stumbling steps towards her, arms outstretched. She zapped him with the Taser. He fell in an epileptic spasm.

Rye threw a sleeping bag over the prostrate man and bound him with rope.

She gave the guy another jolt of current. She lashed him tight to a stepladder and dragged him to the zodiac.

She laid him in the boat. She pulled back the sleeping bag and shone a flashlight in the man's face. Metal erupting from flesh. A dog-collar. The man was a priest.

'What the fuck are you doing?' asked Jane. Rye had been spending a lot of time on C deck. Jane had tracked her to a vacant store-room.

'These freaks rule the world now. They are the dominant species. We better find out exactly what makes them tick.'

Four tables. Four passengers strapped down.

'There are dozens of them out there on the ice,' said Rye. She was wearing a lab coat, gloves and a heavy rubber apron. 'They've been there a while. Minus forty and they are walking around in ball gowns and tuxedos. The average guy would succumb to hypothermia in a couple of minutes. These folks have lasted days. Something pretty fundamental has happened to their metabolism.'

'You brought these fuckers on board without telling anyone? I'll help you put them over the side. We'll do it now, do it quick. If the guys in the canteen find out about this they'll break your fucking legs.'

'These creatures were adrift aboard *Hyperion* for weeks,' said Rye. 'No sign that they ate or drank. What the hell makes these things tick? Aren't you curious? Do they run on air, or what?'

'Damn. This guy's a priest.'

The priest's eyeballs were black. He stared up at her. He didn't blink.

A Bible on a nearby chair.

'It was in his pocket,' said Rye.

'King James. Good choice.'

An inscription on the flyleaf.

'David. Is that you? You used to be David.'

Jane recited the Lord's Prayer.

'Our Father, who art in heaven . . .'

The priest slowly lowered his head and closed his eyes.

'Doc, have you any idea how bad it smells down here? It smells like ammonia. My eyes are watering.'

'Let me show you something.'

Rye put on goggles and a mouth mask. She picked up a scalpel.

'Hey,' said Jane. 'This guy's still alive, all right? He's still breathing.'

Rye paid no attention. She stabbed Father David in the shoulder. She twisted the blade, dug it in.

'Whoa. Hold the fuck on.'

The priest lay, unconcerned, as the knife ground bone.

'Is he even alive?' asked Rye, talking to herself. 'Undead? Nosferatu? Is that what we are dealing with? I think he still has sensation. He can feel the knife. He just doesn't care.'

Rye twisted the knife some more.

'Less blood than I would expect,' she said. 'Look at his face. See his skin? Frost damage. His skin cells are turning to putty. He's slowly rotting. Those *Hyperion* passengers out on the ice aren't immortal. The cold is killing them sure enough. But it's taking a long while.'

Rye leaned over the priest's chest, leaving the scalpel imbedded in the man's shoulder.

'He seems to take a breath every couple of minutes. Can't get close enough to hear his heartbeat, but it must be way down. Basically, he's a vehicle. A chassis. A lump of meat steered left and right. Core body temperature doesn't seem to matter.'

She stood back and contemplated the priest.

'Is this what waits for us when we get home? Cities full of walking dead?'

Jane crossed the room. A table draped with a sheet.

'What's this?'

Rye pulled back the sheet.

'Fucking hell,' said Jane, covering her mouth.

A flayed body. Jane couldn't tell if it had been male or female. Skin and muscle stripped away. A skeletal frame of bone and sinew. The body was still strapped to the table. Hands grasped. It twisted and squirmed like it was trying to sit up.

'My God. How can it be alive?'

'He's dying,' said Rye. 'He was stumbling around out there dressed as a flamenco dancer. Blood loss and trauma are killing him as sure as they would a normal person. But it seems to be taking days. These filaments. This stuff embedded in gristle and bone. Definitely metal. It can be magnetised. But it seems to grow like hair. As far as I can tell it radiates from the central nervous system. All this stuff wrapped round his legs and arms can be traced back to his spine. And look at his head.'

Jane stood over the flayed man. The bloody skull-face watched her approach. Lipless jaws snapped and gnashed. Grinning, biting.

'More metal, see? Lots more, centred round the brain stem. Seems pretty obvious we are dealing with some kind of super-parasite. This isn't a man. This is a metal organism wearing a skin suit. Limited lifespan. Slowly kills the host. It's like ivy round a tree. God knows where it is from. Tough to kill. I gave one of them a dose of Librium. Should have been fatal. Didn't seem to bother him much. These things have the nervous system of a cockroach.'

Rye stood back and folded her arms.

'We have no alternative but to destroy the carrier. This is a terminal illness. Nobody will recover. That much is clear. Memories, personality. All gone. So we don't have to feel bad about killing them. It's pest control. It's not murder. Grenade, if you have one. Otherwise, a shot in the head will kill them stone dead. If you shoot them in the gut, if you blow off an arm or leg, they will keep trucking long enough to bite a chunk out of you. Headshot. Every time.'

'You're wrong,' said Jane. 'Something is left. Something remains.'

Jane returned to the priest. She opened the Bible.

'In the beginning was the word, and the word was with God, and God said: "Let there be light . . . "'

Father David thrashed and snarled, then slowly settled like he was soothed by a lullaby.

'See? He remembers.'

'You don't know for sure,' said Rye.

'No, I can tell. He remembers the words.'

'We have to find out everything we can about these creatures. We can't afford to be sentimental.'

Jane left. She came back with a shotgun. She put the barrel to the priest's head. He sniffed it.

'It's all right, Patrick.'

She blew his head off. Nothing above the neck but a flap of burning scalp. She shot the three remaining specimens. Lumps of brain tissue, flash-fried by gunpowder, lay on the floor and steamed.

'Clean up this shit and scrub the room down,' said Jane. She pressed the shotgun to the chest of Rye's lab coat. The hot barrel burned a scorch ring. 'You bring any more of these fucks aboard I will personally execute you on the spot. You think I'm kidding? Try me. Just fucking try me.'

Rye locked the door of her room. She sat on the bed. She shook a twist of foil from the battery compartment of her bedside clock. She tapped the powder into a spoon and cooked the mixture over a Zippo flame.

She shot up. She threw the hypo in the sink, lay back and relished the warm rush of well-being. A familiar sensation. She had taken the job on the rig to break an addiction to codeine. Seven years of general practice had passed in a blissed-out haze. It was a relief to give in to it once more. It felt like coming home.

Rye examined her left hand. The tip of her index finger was numb and starting to blacken. When did she become infected? Maybe it was out on the ice when she stunned the priest and tied him up. Maybe it was when she lashed him to the table.

She used a shoelace as a tourniquet. She stood at the sink with a pair of bolt cutters. She positioned the infected finger between the blades. This, she thought in a dreamy way, is going to hurt like a motherfucker.

Later, she sat in the canteen and watched scrolling interference on television. Punch asked if she was feeling okay.

'Fine,' she murmured, pushing her bandaged hand deeper into her coat pocket. 'Walking on sunshine.'

Diary of Dr Elizabeth Rye

Wednesday 28 October

I dressed and re-dressed my mutilated finger. I examined the wound every fifteen minutes. As far as I could tell from TV bulletins I saw in the canteen, there were no reported cases of recovery or remission. This illness is certain death. Yet I hoped for a reprieve. Perhaps I had a chance. Maybe I amputated the finger in time to halt the spread of the disease. Maybe I would be the first to get lucky and cure myself of infection.

Nothing for nine hours. Then the first glint of metal among the raw flesh. I probed the scabrous wound with tweezers. A metal spine growing out of bone. I jammed the stump of my finger between the bloody bolt cutters and cut it down to the knuckle. I bound the wound and passed out. When I woke, my entire hand had begun to necrotise.

Metal spines protrude from my palm like fine splinters. My hand feels heavy and numb, but otherwise I am in no discomfort. Codeine. Percodan. I'm so stoned I could walk through fire right now and not feel a thing. I keep my hand sheathed in a glove to avoid detection. I am, of course, infectious. If my illness were discovered I would be quarantined; however I prefer to die on my own terms.

The sea surrounding Rampart has started to freeze. The refinery will soon be joined to the island by an ice-bridge. The horde of infected *Hyperion* passengers crowding at the shoreline will be able to reach the rig. If they manage to board the refinery they will roam the passageways ravening for blood. I suspect they will leave me alone. They will take a sniff and decide I am one of their own. I will walk around unmolested while they rip the Rampart crew limb from limb.

This afternoon I helped Rajesh Ghosh and Reverend Blanc cut ladders and stairs from each refinery leg using oxyacetylene gear. The platform lift is now the only means of descending to the ice. *Hyperion* passengers may congregate beneath the refinery, hungry for fresh meat, but they will be unable to reach the crew.

I try to face death with stoic detachment but, let's face it, my state of Buddhistic serenity is the result of heavy doses of morphine rather than any hard-won wisdom. I shoot up every couple of hours. I have a shoe box full of used hypos hidden beneath my bunk. There aren't many syringes left. Enough to last the next few days. If, in months to come, the Rampart crew need to inject medication they will have to rinse and sterilise a used hypodermic. But that's their problem.

The sensation of snuggling warmth, the Wash I used to call it, feels like coming home. It took me years to quit. Resolution and relapse. I underwent a full year of detox to win back my licence to practise. I lost my house, my child, my job. I had to work at a supermarket. Swiping groceries sixty hours a week just to make the rent on a one-bedroom flat. It was a mercy I wasn't struck off altogether. But I suppose it doesn't matter now. Might as well enjoy the buzz.

During my time at Kings College I used to watch lung cancer patients in nightgowns and pyjamas wheel their drip-stands out of the hospital back entrance. They would congregate on a loading bay and savour a cigarette. Why quit? The worst had already happened. The damage was already done.

Last night I felt compelled to go outside, stand at a railing and face the island. Forty below, but I barely felt the cold. I stood there a long while and listened to the whispering voices in my head. Insinuating murmurs in my back-brain, faint like a weak radio signal, too faint to make out words. I have often suspected those infected with this disease share some kind of hive mind. These past few days I have often stood at the railing and watched infected *Hyperion* passengers mass at the shoreline. From what little I've seen they flock like birds. They move as a crowd. Each individual is slow and stupid, but when massed together they become a formidable tide.

A crate of booze has been left in the canteen. Vodka, tequila, cognac. Dregs left over from the riotous toga party, along with dried sausage rolls and crackers greased with cream cheese. Ghost gave a speech at the party. He thanked Jane for bringing *Hyperion* to the island. A transparent attempt to win back the approval of the crew. Jane seized a cruise liner, the most absurdly perfect transport we could hope to find, and managed to wreck it. I'm surprised they didn't build a gangplank and push her into the sea. Yet the crewmen seem strangely passive. The memory of their old lives has faded to such an extent they can't remember anything but the refinery. Nothing else seems real. They haunt the corridors like the sailors of the *Flying Dutchman*. They have each retreated into their own personal psychosis.

Mal often sits in front of the TV, watching static and tattooing the back of his hands. Jailhouse method. Biro ink pricked beneath the skin with a bent safety pin. He already had tattoos, but following an acid-burn from spilled caustic soda his knuckles spelt LOVE and HAT. He re-inked the letters and added spider-web decoration.

Gus has moved into the old gym. Camped among freezing treadmills and steppers. He has painted a bleak moonscape on the wall. He calls the place Tranquillity. He affects a posh accent and has begun to call himself the Duke of Amberley. It began as a joke, but he genuinely gets angry if he isn't addressed as Your Lordship. The crew seem happy to comply. There is a tacit understanding that they all need a holiday from sanity. I wish I could stick around and see how it plays out.

I suppose I shall endure this illness as long as I can, then jump in the sea. But what if I don't die? What if lack of oxygen and skull-crushing pressure don't kill me? I might find myself stumbling round the ocean floor in absolute darkness. My lungs would be full of water. I couldn't even scream.

I visited Nail in his room this evening. We made a trade. His arm looks better. I asked him about Nikki. No one has seen her for a while. He said I should go fuck myself.

Thursday 29 October

Jane knocked on my door this morning. I was still in bed. I hid my infected arm beneath the blanket then invited her inside.

She persists in her attempts to redeem me. I'm not quite sure what form this redemption is supposed to take. Maybe I should fall weeping and hug her knees. I like her. She's a sweet girl. Yet she is still young and naïve enough to believe people help one another. She has yet to look out of the window and realise the extent to which this great white nothing reflects our personal reality. We are all serving a life sentence. Trapped in the confines of our skull.

Jane and Ghost have concocted a plan. An ice shelf has spread from the island coast. It stretches towards the refinery. The sight of infected passengers jostling at the water's edge has banished all compassion and has convinced Jane to embark on an eradication programme. Ideally she and Ghost would like to move through *Hyperion* room by room systematically executing passengers, but they don't have enough ammunition. Instead they want to visit the old Russian bunker on the island. Ghost says there is equipment stored on the lower levels that may help exterminate a swathe of the infected. He refuses to be drawn further.

No one from the rig, as far as I know, has ever fully explored the bunker. It is a vast, multi-level catacomb intended to be a repository for nuclear waste. A relic of the militarised Arctic, the long cold war stand-off. Decades of spy plane over-flights, prowling submarines and incursion alerts.

Ghost undertook a brief expedition last year. He sprayed arrows on the walls so he could retrace his route to the entrance. He says he saw tiers of rooms that might have been intended for offices and dormitories. He says there is abandoned mining equipment parked in some of the deeper caverns. Rock drills as big as a house. Conveyors to carry rubble to the surface.

We leave the rig in two hours. We will ride the zodiac a kilometre north to avoid *Hyperion* passengers standing at the shore. We will travel across land to the bunker, lock the steel doors behind us and seal ourselves inside.

I once visited the Valley of the Kings. Part of my self-imposed detox programme. A cheap package holiday. Camels and sun cream. Escape my cravings, my fucked-up life. I signed up for a coach party. A day trip to explore the tombs of the Pharaohs.

There were no stairs. Each stone sarcophagus was slid underground down a steep ramp. Ghost tells me this bunker follows a similar design. Wide tunnels angled downward through Palaeocene sediment, rail tracks bolted to the concrete floor. Ghost speculates that the necropolis was built to hide more than submarine reactors. The place seems too elaborate, too deliberately labyrinthine, to be a simple storage space. Perhaps the Russians intended to store nuclear weapons down here. A way of subverting disarmament treaties. What better place to hide the distinctive radiation signature of nuclear warheads than next to a pile of fuel rods? Not that it matters any more. The Russians are dead. The Americans are dead. There's nobody left to care.

We are camping for the night on sub-level four. We have laid our sleeping bags on the concrete floor in the corner of a cavern. We are each quilted in survival gear. Dinner was chicken royale eaten from self-heating cans. I told them I wasn't hungry. They are both asleep now, so I have taken off my gloves to write this journal.

I am writing this by lamplight. Jane is lying on her back, mouth half open. Long plumes of steam-breath. The zip of her coat collar is partially undone. I can see the pulse in her neck. If I stare long and hard I feel a strange pull, a vampiric craving to bite and tear. A lust to penetrate and invade. I find myself leaning towards her, as if physically drawn. A sobering sensation. Until now I have thought of my illness as a personal tragedy. But I am starting to realise the extent to which I threaten the Rampart crew. If I return to the refinery and succumb to this disease, I might kill them all.

Jane looks almost gaunt. She was horribly obese and lethargic when we first met. A heart attack waiting to happen. She couldn't walk without hurting her knees. She sequestered herself in a distant accommodation block so we wouldn't be kept awake by her piggy snore. Now she seems fiercely alive. She'll be dead soon. They'll all be dead. But I suppose some people thrive in a crisis. They find their purpose. They say a happy childhood is a lousy preparation for life. Kids who spend their playground days fat, ginger or gay know the truth. The world has always been full of vicious predators. For plenty of people this carnage and savagery is business as usual.

Ghost led us to a stack of explosives hidden in a deep vault. C4 and thermite grenades. Apparently Jane and Punch discovered the munitions at a seismic research station some weeks ago. Rawlins ordered the explosives be stored in the bunker.

The packets of C4 look like bricks of clay wrapped in cellophane. They smell like petrol. Cable. Detonators. Battery-operated initiators. Ghost insists we each sleep cuddling a patty of frozen explosive in the hope our body heat will make it pliable. Tomorrow we blow some *Hyperion* passengers to hell.

Friday 30 October

We woke early, packed and stood at the bunker mouth. Arctic winter. Early morning, but it will be bright moonlight all day.

Ghost took one of the Skidoos and drove to the shore. Jane rode pillion. She balanced a holdall in her lap. I took binoculars to high ground.

He rode out on to the ice sheet that has extended from the island shoreline. He made a slow pass of passengers who stood mesmerised by the lights of the refinery. Jane unzipped the bag and unravelled detonator cord behind them. Fistfuls of explosives strung at four-metre intervals like a string of Christmas lights. Ghost brought the bike to a halt and they both crouched behind it for cover.

Ghost twisted wires to a hand-held initiator. He mouthed a three-count then clicked the trigger. The chain of high explosive blew, and threw a curtain of ice-dust into the air. No flame, no fireball. Just a fierce concussion. The sound of the explosion reached me a couple of seconds later. A sharp clap like thunder.

Four or five passengers were blown to pieces. Body parts littered the snow.

A web of jagged fissures split the ice. Slabs tipped and tilted. Figures toppled into dark water. No attempt to swim or struggle. They immediately sank. A couple of infected passengers stood at the centre of a detached ice floe and looked around, stupefied, as the current began to carry them south.

I could hear Ghost and Jane whoop and cheer. I'm not sure how many passengers they killed. Maybe twenty or thirty. Futile? People need to act, to feel in control of their fate. Jane and Ghost are intelligent people. I'm sure they are aware how little they achieved. Yet they fight, and I admire them for it.

I was supposed to meet Ghost and Jane at the zodiac, but instead I have returned to the bunker and locked myself inside.

Sian tried to contact me on the radio. She called over and over before I descended too deep for the signal to penetrate. 'Rampart *to Rye, do you copy, over?*' I suppose I should have told them not to look for me. I should have told them I was gone for good.

I'm reluctant to put down my pen. This is the end of my life. I don't want to sign off.

Sooner or later, Jane will search my room. She will find the remaining medical supplies laid out on my bed, with explanatory Post-it notes taped to each of them. I've left a simple medical encyclopaedia on my chair. *The A–Z of Family Health.* Dress a wound, deliver a baby or pull a tooth, then they will have to thumb through the index.

I've survived these past few years by ruthlessly suppressing all sentiment, declaring unending war on self-pity. Yet I can't help wishing I was leaving someone behind, someone who will miss me, someone who will remember my name. I haven't seen my son for years, and that is probably for the best. Easier all round if I stay out of his life. Easier if he thinks I'm dead in a ditch. Let him hate me. Hate is good. Hate is rocket fuel. It's a galvanising force. It will send him out into the world full of defiant energy. But right now I would give anything for a chance to say goodbye.

The infection has spread further up my arm. My thoughts are sometimes not my own. Shall I let myself be subsumed into this collective consciousness, or shall I kill myself? I shall either walk to the shore and jump into freezing water, or make my way to *Hyperion* and take my place among the colony. I have yet to decide.

I will leave my journal on the floor of this cavern in the hope that one day, when humanity is restored, it will be found.

My name was Elizabeth Rye.

The Body

Ghost took a team of men from the rig to secure the officers' quarters of *Hyperion*. He gave them each a fire axe.

Ghost passed round a bottle of Hennessey as they rode the zodiac to *Hyperion*.

'This could be messy,' he warned. 'Women, children. It's not going to be nice.'

They climbed aboard the ship and the slaughter began. They moved room to room. They swung and hacked. They wore masks and goggles to shield themselves from blood-spray.

They splashed kerosene at each intersection and drove back infected passengers with a barrier of flame.

They disabled the elevators and rebuilt the barricades. They booby-trapped the doors with thermite grenades.

They threw the bodies over the side of the ship, dropped them twenty metres on to the ice. They sponged blood from the walls and floor. They wore triple gloves and respirators to protect themselves from acrid bleach fumes.

Later, when they sat down to eat in the newly liberated officers' mess, they drank too much and laughed too loud. They were blooded. Each man had slashed and bludgeoned until their arms hurt. Ghost sat back and watched the men joke and sing. They were flushed with adrenalin. They had crossed a line. They were killers.

They transported their possessions from the rig and each took a stateroom with a double bed and en-suite bathroom, luxury they had never known aboard Rampart.

Each cabin had a wall-mounted plasma TV. The crew swapped DVDs. A bitter-sweet pastime. Each gangster flick and romantic comedy was a window on to a vanished world. Every glimpse of Manhattan, Los Angeles or London framed sunny streets that had since been transformed into a ravaged battlefield.

Ghost led a raid on the lower decks to check battery power. They took a detour to the Neptune Bar and filled a crate with Johnnie Walker Blue Label. The crew were drunk for a week.

Punch found a small galley and prepared food. He served breakfast each morning and a hot meal each night. He tried to impose a diurnal rhythm despite perpetual night.

They posted a patrol rota on the door of the bridge.

Punch on duty. He prowled the corridors with an axe. If he looked out of the portholes he could see infected passengers milling on the lower promenade decks. As he passed each barricade he could hear the scrabble and thump of passengers massed the other side of the bulkhead doors. The noise never ceased. Scratching and clawing, day and night.

'Breakout,' explained Ghost. 'We need a simple signal. If you see anything, if one of these freaks makes it up here from the lower decks, if they make it through the barricades, shout "Breakout". Everyone will pull on their boots, grab an axe and haul ass.'

Punch served dinner. He put on a show. He lit candles. He laid out silverware and linen napkins. He wore chef's starched whites. He found some dried mushrooms and made risotto.

The crew sat in a panelled dining room with galleons on the wall. They applauded as he lifted a cloche from each plate and uncorked wine.

Two empty seats. Jane had elected to stay aboard Rampart. Mal was patrolling the *Hyperion* barricades.

Punch took a seat at the table. He sat next to Sian. Nikki had sailed away on a raft. Rye was missing, probably suicide. Nobody missed them. But he was banging the only woman left aboard and was becoming aware of an undercurrent of jealousy.

'This is delicious,' said Ghost, pouring Chardonnay.

'Thanks.'

'Should have found some turkey, though.'

'Why's that?'

'Guess you haven't looked at a calendar lately.' He raised his glass. 'Merry Christmas.'

'You're shitting me.'

'So what do you think we should do when we get back home?' asked Ghost. 'Should we track down other survivors or hide ourselves away?'

Punch thought it over. The question had become a standard conversational gambit. Nobody wanted to discuss the past. They didn't want to think about family and friends dead and gone. By unspoken agreement they spoke only of the future. It became evening entertainment now the TV signal had died and DVDs provoked depression and heartache. Old-time storytelling. Campfire tales. Each crewman obliged to describe in baroque detail the life they would build when they got home.

Discussions like:

'What car will you drive when you get back to the world?'

'Lamborghini Countach. It's an antique heap of shit, but I glimpsed one in the street when I was a kid and I've wanted one ever since.'

'Better enjoy it while you can.'

'Why's that?'

'Couple of harsh winters. That's all it will take. Every road in the country will be cracked and rutted like a farm track. Land-Rover. It'll get you where you need to go.'

And:

'What kind of watch will you wear?'

'There used to be a posh jeweller in our high street. I saw it every day on my way to work. They had a bunch of Rolex watches laid

out on a blue velvet cushion. I used to tell myself: "One day, when I'm rich, I'll own one." A gold submariner the size of a dinner plate.'

'*So you'll smash a window and take a Rolex.*'

'*I'll take one for every day of the week.*'

'So you think there might be other survivors?' asked Punch.

'We can't be the last men on earth. I bet plenty of people are hidden in caves, or cellars, or remote farms. Some of them will want to reclaim the cities, I suppose. Reboot the world. Set it going, just the way it was. And some people will want to go all Amish. Create a simple, wholesome way of life. Me? I'm a log cabin kind of guy. I think I'll find a cottage in the Scottish Highlands. Somewhere wild and remote. Hunt and fish. Sit on a hill and count the clouds.'

'I'm torn,' said Punch. 'I'd be scared to live alone with all these infected fucks running around. I'd want to live in some kind of stockade. Safety in numbers. But on the other hand I don't want to find myself enslaved by some local tyrant. There will be no police, no law. Things will get feudal pretty quick.'

'Yeah.'

'Are you okay about Nikki?'

'What about her?'

'Jane said she took your boat.'

'I welded a couple of oil drums together,' said Ghost. 'She and Nail did most of the work. I doubt she'll make it home. And if she does? Well, good for her.'

'But it was your boat. Your idea.'

'Jane wants to get everyone home. I promised to help.'

Ghost gestured to an empty chair.

'Has anyone seen Mal?'

'No,' said Punch.

'It's eight o'clock. Who's taking over patrol?'

'Me,' said Gus.

'So where is Mal? He should have checked in half an hour ago.'

'Taking a shit. Changing his socks. Relax. He'll be here. He's not going to miss dinner.'

'I don't like it,' said Ghost. 'We put a man on guard and he goes AWOL.'

Ghost stood in the corridor.

'Mal? You out there?'

No reply.

Ghost stepped back inside the officers' mess.

'Everyone stay here, all right? Nobody go wandering off. Punch, get your gun.'

They searched Mal's cabin.

'Mal? Hello?'

They knocked on the bathroom door.

'Hello?'

Empty.

They searched the passageways and checked the barricades.

'Mal. Where are you?'

He wasn't on the bridge. He wasn't on deck. The zodiac still hung from a lifeboat crane. He hadn't gone back to the rig.

'Maybe he got drunk,' said Punch. 'Decided to go below deck on his own.'

'Why would he do that?'

'Bravado. He wanted something. Had a hankering for nachos or a cigar. Thought he could get it on his own. Outrun the freaks. Duck and swerve. Come back, brag, show off his trophy.'

'Yeah, that's the kind of idiotic thing he might do. I don't like it, though. Not knowing for sure.'

Sian found them on the bridge.

'There's something you should see.'

She led them to a door at the end of a corridor.

FÖRRÅD

A small storeroom. Toiletries and laundry.

A trickle of blood from beneath the door.

'Stand back,' said Ghost. He hefted the axe. He tested the door. Unlocked. He pushed it open with his foot.

'Hello? Mal?'

He reached round the doorframe and switched on the light. The trickle of blood snaked from behind a rack loaded with bed linen. Sheets, coverlets and pillow cases.

Mal lay dead on the floor. His eyes were open. His throat was cut. He held a knife in his hand.

'Blot some of that blood,' said Ghost. Punch threw down folded sheets to sop up the blood. 'Close the door. I want to take a long look around before anyone else comes in here.'

Jane jogged a circuit of C deck. There was light, but no heat. Many of the corridors had split open when D Module fell from the rig. Several passageways terminated in ragged metal and thin air. Jane enjoyed the sensation of cold. The rest of the crew had embraced the luxury of *Hyperion*, but Jane volunteered to stay behind in the steel austerity of Rampart and man the radio. She broadcast periodic maydays to the Arctic rim, and listened to the static of an empty waveband.

She and Ghost spoke, morning and evening, by radio. '*Take care, babycakes,*' he said, at the end of each call. She missed him.

Jane ran five kilometres, then stripped to her underwear and pumped iron in the corner of the deserted canteen. She used Nail's abandoned gym equipment. She was both repelled and attracted by Nail's pumped physique. Veins and striations. He was a human fortress. She envied his brute strength.

She played AC/DC on the jukebox as she hefted dumbbells. She played the music at full volume. 'Bad Boy Boogie' echoed down empty corridors.

Jane rested between each set of exercises by throwing a titanium shark knife at the canteen dartboard. The heavy blade thunked into cork, slowly ripping the board to pieces. Nail could hit a target at twenty metres. Jane trained herself to hit it at thirty.

Years ago, when the refinery was fully manned, the Starbucks coffee shop used to run a book exchange. The coffee shop was now a vacant retail unit with a couple of broken bar stools. Jane found a box of books among the litter, including thirty issues of *Combat Survival* magazine. Each issue contained carbine and pistol spec sheets. Back-page adverts for tactical holsters, mosquito nets and surplus Israeli gas masks.

She read about snake bites, reef knots and edible insects. She enjoyed the fantasy of desert sand and jungle heat. There were cut-and-keep plans for bear traps, squirrel snares and high-velocity slingshots. She made a mental note to search the boathouse for bungee line.

Jane made herself a sandwich. She sat in the observation bubble and read about bamboo jungle shelters. She learned the best way to cook a tarantula over a campfire. Ghost called her on the radio.

'*It looks like you'll be doing another funeral, I'm afraid.*'

'What do you mean?'

'*Mal didn't show up for dinner. I got worried. We went looking. We found him in a laundry cupboard. His throat was cut through.*'

'Do you think there is an infected passenger creeping round the crew quarters, hiding in the ducts? Someone you missed?'

'*We're doing a sweep. We're armed, moving in pairs. Nothing so far. The barricades are intact. None of the grenades has tripped. Besides, Mal was hidden in a cupboard. These diseased freaks maim and kill. They don't clean up afterwards.*'

'So what's the deal? What are we looking at?'

'*We found a kitchen knife with the body. He had it in his hand. Blood on the blade.*'

'Do you buy it? Did he kill himself? What's your instinct?'

'*Dead man holding a knife. Hard to argue it was anything but suicide. I guess I will have to tell the lads. It'll be bad for morale, but I can't lie to them.*'

'I suppose I'll have to give an address. God knows what I'll say. I barely knew the man.'

'*Another day, another shroud. Do you think there'll be any of us left by spring?*'

Punch and Ghost wrapped the body in a sheet. They dragged the corpse outside and laid it on a bench. Moans and snarls. Infected passengers watched from the promenade decks beneath them.

They searched Mal's pockets. A torch. A lighter. A packet of mints. No suicide note.

'Take his boots,' said Ghost. 'We don't need his coat, but we need snowboots.'

Punch inspected the neck wound with a flashlight.

'Cut through his windpipe. Cut down to vertebrae.'

'Did you speak to him much? Did he seem depressed?'

'Talk to Nail. Mal was his buddy.'

They bound the shrouded body and laid it in a lifeboat to chill.

Punch and Sian retired to their cabin. A four-room suite with a king-size bed, home entertainment system and kitchenette. The previous occupant must have been a senior member of the crew. Punch had cleaned out the man's possessions. He swept clothes, letters and photographs into a garbage bag. The guy was probably wandering mindless and mutilated below deck. Better not think too much about his fate.

Punch propped the door closed with a chair.

'Are you worried there might be an infected sailor slinking around?' asked Sian. She was running a bath.

'You saw the wound. It was a clean slice ear to ear. These rabid bastards bite. They like to rip and tear.'

'Maybe Mal couldn't stand the isolation. All that stuff going on back home. No daylight. I'm surprised more blokes haven't succumbed to depression.'

'His head was virtually severed.'

'What are you saying?'

'I'm not sure. Probably nothing. Despair can build into a type of mania, a type of super-strength. A person could do themselves a lot of damage if they put their mind to it.'

Punch stood in front of the bathroom mirror. He picked up a toothbrush and pretended to slit his throat.

'It could be done, I suppose. That kind of gash. A person could slice through their own jugular and windpipe if they did it hard and fast. They would have to be pretty determined. Only someone desperate to be dead could carry it through.'

'Murder? Is that what you are suggesting? A fight gone bad?'

'I don't know. From now on you better not walk around on your own if you can help it. And always carry a knife.'

Sian stripped and climbed into the bath. Punch kicked off his shoes and started to unbutton his shirt.

Sian had yet to comprehend that women had become a rare and valuable commodity. The years ahead were likely to be brutal and lawless. Punch used to be everyone's friend, but now he was envied and hated by the crewmen around him. If he wanted to possess Sian he would need to fight, and maybe kill, to keep her.

DSV

Ghost crossed to Rampart. The refinery was now joined to the island by a sheet of ice. He ran, swerved infected passengers, made it to the platform lift face steaming with sweat.

He and Jane sat in Rawlins's office.

The refinery was equipped with submerged cameras so the crew could monitor the integrity of the great floatation legs, and the status of the seabed pipeline and manifold.

They switched on a wall screen. They powered up the underwater floodlights and selected camera views. Pan and tilt.

The crumpled shell of D Module, lying on the silted moonscape of the ocean bed.

Jane selected a different camera position. Steel rope coiled on the seabed.

'That's all right,' said Ghost. 'The remaining tethers are intact. Pretty vicious riptides round here, but we'll hold firm.'

He swivelled a joystick. The camera angled upward. The floatation leg.

'What a fucking mess,' said Jane.

'A big dent, but no puncture,' said Ghost. 'Should keep us stable. Should keep us afloat.'

'We hope.'

'Your average liner is a series of hermetic compartments. Half the ship could flood and we would still be able to sail it home. Maybe we can get the mini-sub in the water. Take a look at the hull top-to-toe.'

*　　*　　*

Jane summoned Nail from *Hyperion*. They sat in the canteen.

'How's your arm?'

'Better.'

'You can work the mini-sub, yes? You and Gus. You can drive it, pilot it, whatever.'

'We used it to inspect the seabed pipeline.'

'How would you like to take a look at *Hyperion*'s hull? There's a hole in the plate. It's taken on water. It would be good to know the extent of the damage. There's no way we can check structural integrity from inside the vessel. Too much opposition. We need an under-sea survey.'

Nail rocked back in his chair. He had found some fancy clothes aboard *Hyperion*. He wore a black leather shirt. He wore a heavy gold bracelet and a Tag Heuer watch. He stank of booze.

'The sub hasn't been used for months. Strictly speaking, it should go back to shore for an overhaul.'

'I'm sure you want to get home as much as anyone. *Hyperion* is all we have left.'

'I'll mull it over.'

Deep Sea Vehicle *Mirabelle*.

Nail and Gus climbed through the roof hatch. Gus took the pilot's seat. Nail was co-pilot. They put on headsets.

They slapped rows of toggle switches and powered up the sub. Banks of instrumentation winked into life.

Gus took laminated sheets from a wall pocket. Pre-dive checks. Battery life. Ballast pressure. Air. Telemetry. Thrusters.

They packed sandwiches, mineral water and a piss bottle. They checked their escape suits.

They saw Jane through the cockpit bubble. She stood and waved. Nail tested the manipulator arms. He snapped the serrated titanium claws in front of her. She stood her ground.

'Reckon she and Ghost are actually fucking?' asked Gus.

'Not a pretty picture, is it?' said Nail.

Jane and Ghost spent a night in the observation bubble. They laid sleeping bags on the deck. They lay naked and looked at the stars.

'You think they can see us from here?' asked Jane.

'Who?'

'Guys on *Hyperion*. We'd better keep the lights off. They might have found binoculars.'

'Tempted to give them a flash.'

'You should stay here,' said Jane. 'I don't know why you hang out with those idiots on *Hyperion*. Brain-dead as the passengers. They haven't raised the average IQ a single point.'

'Shitty thing to say about Punch.'

'You know what I mean. You guys should come over here. You, Punch, Sian.'

'It would be a cosy little club, but if we let that kind of us-and-them situation develop things could get nasty pretty quick.'

'So you're going to leave me out here with Mal?'

'Lock a couple of doors if it creeps you out.'

Mal's body had been brought back to Rampart prior to burial at sea. The guys took a vote. The rig had been his home. It seemed appropriate to stand between the great floatation legs of the refinery and commit his body to the waves.

'Come back with me,' said Ghost. 'The staterooms are spectacular. The upper-echelon crew lived like kings.'

'And thousands of lunatics the other side of the door.'

'It kept me awake nights at first. But this is our life now. Europe is overrun. If we get back home we will have to spend the rest of our lives behind castle walls, one way or another. Might as well get used to the idea.'

'I can't help feeling it is a honey trap, a gilded cage. We'll fritter away our time. Get fat. Get drunk. Die out here at the edge of the world.'

Nail and Gus sat strapped in their seats as the DSV was lowered into the sea. Winch-judder made the flesh of their faces tremble. Nail hugged his bandaged arm.

Jolt and scrape as the submersible broke through the ice crust. Clunk of the winch release.

Nail and Gus unlatched their harnesses and sat forward.

Brief vent from the buoyancy tanks. Water bubbled past the portholes as the vehicle submerged.

Gus took control of the fly-by-wire control column and vectored forward and down.

'Kick in the arcs.'

Nail flipped a switch and the arc light array at the front of the vessel lit incandescent. Blackness beyond the portholes was replaced by swirling sediment, and air bubbles rippling like globules of mercury.

'Down fifty. Trim good. Forward point five.'

Gus checked an overhead screen. An acoustic beacon mapped their bearing from the rig.

Nail zipped his sweatshirt. He pulled on a woollen hat and fingerless gloves. Condensed breath trickled down the chilled metal of the pressure hull.

'Heading hold.'

The sub ran on auto-pilot.

Gus sipped water. Nail swigged from a hip flask.

'You've been hitting the sauce pretty hard these past few days,' said Gus. 'Better if you kept your head.'

Nail toasted him with the flask.

'L'chai-im'.

'Is it Mal?' asked Gus. 'Is that what's eating you up?'

'Fuck Mal.'

'Is it Nikki?'

'Just drive the fucking sub.'

'You're losing it. You're out of shape. Yeah, you broke your arm. But you're drunk all day, every day. The guys look up to you. They don't give a shit about Jane and her little gang. They're waiting for you to take a lead.'

'Fuck you,' said Nail. He took a long swig. 'Fuck the lot of you.'

They monitored the system screens. They didn't speak.

'Damn,' said Gus, breaking the silence. 'Take a look at this.'

A slow pass of D Module.

Buckled walls. Empty windows. The DSV thrusters stirred swirling debris.

'That's my old room,' said Gus. 'That one there.'

Nail took another swig. Gus looked at him in disgust.

'Jesus. Just sit back there, all right? Just keep out of the way.'

Jane and Ghost sat in Rawlins's office.

'Rampart to DSV, do you copy, over?'

'*Go ahead.*'

'How are you boys doing?'

'*Approaching* Hyperion. *We should reach it any minute.*'

'Can you give us a camera feed?'

'*Should be coming through now.*'

Jane switched on the desk screen. Blue murk. Darting particles of sediment. They sat back and waited for the sub to reach *Hyperion*.

'I'll give you another reason to move to the ship,' said Ghost.

'What's that?'

'The ice around Rampart has reached the island. Those fucks from *Hyperion* are right beneath the refinery. We can't zip back and forth between the rig and this ship without risking our necks. You're marooned.'

'All right. You sold me.'

Jane wanted to move in with Ghost, but she didn't want to seem too eager. She wanted to be wooed.

'*DSV to* Rampart.'

'Go ahead.'

'*Big sonar hit. Coming up on* Hyperion.'

Jane and Ghost leaned closer to the screen.

'Well, there it is,' said Ghost.

'Jesus.'

A massive, bronze propeller, as high as a house, emerged from the sediment fog.

The DSV passed the length of *Hyperion*'s keel. Gus and Nail looked through the overhead porthole. Nail sipped black coffee from a flask.

Riveted hull plates. Nail held up a video camera. Additional footage for review when they got back to Rampart.

Gus checked range estimation. The ping of the Sunwest sonar increased frequency until it became a steady tone. Collision warning.

'Here comes the rock wall.'

A jagged basalt cliff emerging from the gloom.

'Full stop.'

Gus brought the sub to a standstill.

'All right. Let's take a look.'

Gus re-angled the arc lights so they could check for damage below the waterline.

'There,' said Nail. 'A big split in the plates.'

Gus swivelled the thrusters and tilted the DSV to face the hull. Nail squirmed closer to the cockpit bubble and filmed the damage. Weld-seams had torn when *Hyperion* hit the refinery.

'Get us closer,' said Nail.

They approached the fissure. Plates peeled back like petals.

'Can we get more light in there?'

'Probably looks worse than it is,' said Gus. 'If this split ran the length of the ship we would be in trouble. Jane, are you getting this?'

'*Yeah, we see it. Looks like we lost a couple of compartments, but it's still sound. If we wait until the spring thaw, then throw the engines in reverse, it might float free.*'

'What's that?' said Nail, pressing closer to the glass.

'Where?'

'Right there.'

Gus re-angled the arc lights.

'Christ.'

Beyond the fissure, deep in the shadows of the flooded compartment, was a body. It floated, arms outstretched. A man in a boiler suit. Some kind of mechanic.

'Drag him out the way,' said Nail. 'Let's see how deep the damage runs. I'd like to check for structural issues.'

Gus shifted position and took hold of a joystick. He unfolded the starboard manipulator arm. The multi-jointed limb reached inside the hull. Titanium tweezer-claws swivelled and opened. Gus gripped the dead man's head and pulled him through the fissure.

Gus brought the mechanic closer to the cockpit window. The dead man's hair swirled in the current. His face was framed by steel fingers.

'He hasn't been dead long,' said Gus. 'I doubt he was killed when *Hyperion* ran aground. I bet he stumbled into the flooded compartment during the last couple of days.'

'No sign of infection.'

The dead man opened his eyes and stared directly at Nail. Jet-black eyeballs.

Gus pressed Close. The claws scissored shut. The mechanic's skull popped in a cloud of blood and brain tissue.

The Voyage

Nikki rode the swells. Seven days at sea. Seven days of perpetual starlit darkness. It was like sailing through space.

She had barely slept. Snatched moments of rest. She worried she would fall asleep at the tiller and quickly freeze.

The boat was frosted with ice. Fierce cold. Gentle waves. The weather had begun to turn. The brilliant dusting of stars was slowly eclipsed by cloud. Turbulence chasing her from the north, gaining fast. The boat was designed to survive a storm. As soon as bad weather hit, she could lower the sails and seal herself below deck. She would bob like a cork as the boat rode mountainous waves and troughs. If the bolts and welds held fast, she would survive.

She stood in the cockpit and ate dry cereal from the packet, washed down with sips of water. The rudder was locked in position with nylon cord.

A cold, blue haze began to lighten the southern sky. Somewhere, far over the horizon, it was daytime. Navigation was easy. No need for a compass. All she had to do was head for the light.

Nikki wore three fleece jackets and a foil blanket. Two weeks at sea. She stank. She couldn't wash herself or her clothes.

She rode the swells. Later, if the weather stayed calm, she would seal herself below and snatch an hour of sleep. The steel and aluminium hull of the boat had been lagged with polystyrene packing blocks to trap heat.

Grinding, growling plates of ice.

'*Nikki? Nikki, can you hear me?*' Jane's voice.

The radio was hung in a canvas bag beneath the hatch. Nikki spoke into a handset like a Bakelite telephone.

'How's it going, Jane?'

'*The crew transferred to* Hyperion. *I'm alone on the refinery.*'

'Nobody cares about your little gestures. Get over there and have a good time.'

'*Got a name for it yet?*'

'The boat? It's a pile of nuts and bolts. Things are what they are.'

'*A boat has to have a name.*'

'I don't want to find the poetry in my soul. I don't want to rediscover my lost humanity. I'm trying hard to keep things real, which is probably why I'm part way home and you're still trapped in that steel tomb.'

'*What will you do when you reach land? Have you thought about it?*'

'Survival. The sovereign state of me. It'll be bliss.'

'*How's the weather?*'

'Calm enough. The wind cuts like a knife. Seem to be making good time. Hard to judge speed, but the current is strong.'

'*Position?*'

'By my reckoning I'm north-west of Murmansk. The current should funnel me past Norway the next few days. I'll be out of radio contact long before then.'

'*Keep well. Keep lucky. I'll speak to you tomorrow.*'

Nikki slept in her bunk. The hull was packed with supplies. Boxes of food, bags of clothes. She had shoved them aside to create a tight coffin space in which she could stretch out in a sleeping bag. The aluminium roof of the hull was directly above her head. She lay in the dark and listened to her breath, loud and harsh in the confined space.

An impact. A metallic scrape against the side of the boat. A second impact. An iceberg? A whale?

She flipped open the hatch. There were strange shapes in the water, clustered boulders like drifting chunks of ice. She switched on her flashlight and scanned the surface of the ocean. The sea was full of floating cars. White Nissan Navaras. An undulating vista of gloss metal reflecting the moonlight. Some of the utility vehicles were upside down. Water washed over galvanised chassis and alloy wheels. A cargo ship must have spilled its load. Freight containers washed from the deck, smashed open as they hit the sea. The cars held enough trapped air to keep themselves afloat.

Each time the vehicles nudged the boat Nikki heard the shriek of abrading metal. She worried the repeated impact of the cars might rupture the hull. She spent an hour climbing back and forth along the length of the boat. Her boots slipped on slick metal. She strained to push cars away with her feet. She was tied to the mast by a short leash to make sure she could quickly get back on board if she fell into the sea.

Once she was free of the car-slick she sat with her back to the mast and caught her breath.

Survival.

Once it was all stripped away, her job, personal loyalties, her name and history, what was left? Just the fact that she was alive and aware, adrift on a vast ocean.

She tuned the radio.

'Hello? Hello? Hailing all vessels. Can anyone hear me?'

She heard a man's voice, a calm and measured murmur. She couldn't make out words. It was some kind of looped broadcast. It had faded in and out for days.

She looked to the horizon. The azure tint of distant daylight was mottled with heavy cloud. A storm heading her way.

Nikki stretched and composed herself, got ready to confront her next opponent like a boxer waiting for the round-one bell.

The Damned

Rye crossed the island, drawn by the lights of *Hyperion*. She wandered through the lower decks of the ship. The infection had spread down the entire right side of her body. Her flesh was blistered and scabrous. Metal filaments broke the skin of her right arm, her right leg and hip, and punctured her clothing. It didn't hurt. Her body was numb.

She was still Elizabeth Rye. Her mind was clear. She yearned for madness. She desperately wished her consciousness would fog and dissolve.

Rye had seen, during the dissections she performed aboard Rampart, how this strange parasite infiltrated the nervous system of its victims. She wondered why the same metallic strands had yet to invade her synapses, choking off memory and emotion. She wanted to be dumb and thoughtless. She expected her disintegrating body to pace the ship for weeks to come propelled by the strange organism, long after her own consciousness had vacated the shell. But it hadn't worked out that way. She was still present and aware.

Most of the passengers had gravitated to the vast lobby. Rye drifted through empty restaurants, a vacant cinema, a children's play area with ball-pit and slide.

She amused herself in the sports centre for a couple of hours. She played table tennis against a wall. Her mutated body retained good movement.

She shot hoops. She powered up the golf simulator and thwacked balls down a digital fairway.

She found a mini-nightclub. No music, but the glitter ball still revolved. She hopscotched across the dance floor. Each tile lit up as she stood on it.

She wondered where the other passengers had gone.

Rye sought out the medical bay. Maybe she could load a hypodermic with morphine and put herself to sleep like a sick dog. Mix it with bleach, oven cleaner. Press the plunger. Feel good. Press the plunger some more. Lie back and let corrosives melt her brain.

A friend from medical school got a job on a cruise ship. He had an easy time. He ate, flirted and swam. All he had to do was listen for coded Tannoy announcements. '*Dr Jones to the white courtesy phone,*' meant he should head to Medical. '*Dr Jones to the red courtesy phone,*' meant he should hurry to Medical to deal with an emergency. He dreaded the message '*Dr Rose please report to the Neptune Bar,*' because Rose was the code-word for a coronary. Most passengers were elderly. At least one heart attack per trip. Someone sprawled on a restaurant carpet turning blue. The ship's doctor would have to grab his resuscitation kit and haul ass.

Rye followed signs to Medical. Arrows and a little red cross.

Sjukhus

The infirmary had been ransacked. Instruments scattered across the floor. Bloody bed sheets bunched on the examination table. Blood sprayed up the wall. It looked as if an army surgical unit had treated hundreds of battlefield casualties then cleared out. The doctor aboard *Hyperion* had obviously done heroic work in his attempts to treat infected passengers before he too succumbed or was torn apart.

Rye felt hungry. She followed sombrero signs to the Tex Mex Grill. She wanted to crunch nachos.

She climbed stairs and walked down a passageway. Her path was blocked by a watertight door, one of the heavy steel hatches that had immediately dropped like a portcullis when *Hyperion* ran aground and took on water.

Rye put her ear to the hatch. She could hear faint music. 'Gimme Shelter'. Muffled voices. Men talking, laughing. The Rampart crew on the other side of the door. They must have taken over the Grill.

Rye was overcome by loneliness. She leaned against the wall and wept.

The casino. A plush, Monte Carlo gambling den. A couple of roulette wheels, a craps table and a bar.

A showgirl lay dead and rotting on the floor. Sequins and pink ostrich plumes. A pulped mess where her head used to be.

Rye stepped over the body and approached five men sitting round a blackjack table. They wore ripped and bloody dinner jackets. One man was so far gone he was virtually a pillar of dripping metal. He was fused rigid and would clearly never leave his chair again. The croupier was slumped like he had fallen asleep. His head had melted into the table. The other men retained movement in their arms. There were cards and chips scattered on the green baize. The least inhuman of the bunch, a passenger who still retained half a face, acted as dealer.

'Ah,' he said. 'Fresh blood.'

Rye took a seat at the table.

'Ready to lose your money?' asked the dealer, shuffling his cards.

'It's nice to hear another sane voice.'

'This thing, this contagion, seems to strike people different ways, as you have evidently discovered. Some people die outright. Not sure why. One bite and they keel over. Must be like a peanut allergy. But sometimes, if you're unlucky, it takes your body but not your mind. You're not one of the passengers, are you? I don't think I've seen you before.'

'I'm from an oil refinery near here.'

'The ship ran aground?'

'Yeah.'

'Do you know what is happening out there in the world?'

'No,' said Rye. 'Not a thing. You?'

'Nothing. Just rumours. We circled for weeks trying to find a port. Then there was an outbreak. It must have been with us all along. An infected crew member perhaps, hiding the disease from his colleagues. Who knows? Who cares? Here we are, waiting for the end to come. The cowards. The ones too chicken to slit our throats or leap into the sea. Doomed to live.' The dealer shuffled cards. 'Have you ever played blackjack?' he asked.

'It seems like a good time to learn.'

Rye saw men and women suffer and die during her time on a cancer ward. Most accepted the end of their lives with stoic resignation. Youngsters calmly faced death even though they had yet to live. Joked as they were wheeled into the operating theatre, joked as they got shot full of chemotherapy or blasted with radiation.

Rye knew she was a coward. She wanted to die, but it had to be quick and painless. She had seen scalpels scattered on the floor of the medical bay. She should have put a blade to her eye and punched it into her brain, but couldn't bring herself to do it. She wanted an easy exit. She wanted to slide into unbeing like she was drifting off to sleep.

Rye searched the ship for the means to kill herself.

She found shelves of barbecue equipment in a kitchen cupboard. She pictured *Hyperion* chefs organising a spit roast for the passengers. Handing roast pork baguettes to rich clientele as they stood in anoraks watching whales break water in the distance.

Rye toyed with the idea of releasing a propane valve then striking a match, but was too scared to go through with the plan. What if she didn't die? The fireball from a couple of tanks would quickly dissipate. She might sustain third-degree burns. Lie immobile in a delirium of pain. She knew, from her own experiments, that a person subject to advanced-stage infection was tough to kill. It might take her days to die.

She found some extension cable but the cord was too thick to make a noose. She wished she had a gun. If she had a pistol she could sit at a window, press the barrel to her temple, then distract herself by studying the view. She could try to name the constellations and, as she did so, casually switch off the world like it was a TV show that no longer held her interest.

A wasted life. Lousy doctor, lousy parent. Easy to blame the drugs, but her life was a downward spiral long before the first taste of codeine. A debilitating malaise that dogged her since childhood. Each day poisoned by a deep conviction that nothing was worthwhile. No matter where she went, or what she did, she could never quite bring herself to give a shit. But maybe there was something she could do. A final moment in which she could vindicate her life.

She, of all the Rampart crew, could pass through the liner with impunity. If the shambling mutants saw Jane or Ghost they would seize them and tear them apart. Yet when Rye walked by they seemed unaware of her existence. Rye could wave a hand in front of their faces, click fingers, push them around. They didn't react.

So maybe she should exploit her freedom to move around the ship and build a bomb. She had already found a cache of propane tanks. There must be reserves of diesel somewhere aboard. She still had a radio. She could warn the Rampart crew. Give them time to evacuate. Open the tanks, release the valves, flood the plant rooms with fuel then strike a match. There were a few *Hyperion* passengers out on the ice, but most were aboard the liner. She could incinerate them all. Fry the ship. Cleanse the island. And end her own life in an instant. An explosion of that magnitude would be instant extinction. The Rampart crew would watch from the rig. They would see the blast. They would appreciate the gesture. After all, *Hyperion* seemed beached for good. If it blew sky high, she would die a hero.

Woozy logic. A little voice warning that she wasn't thinking straight. She was spiralling into fantasy. She would get everyone killed.

Rye looked for the diesel tanks.

She found a multilingual brochure. '*Hyperion – Queen of the Seas*'. A fold-out floor plan. She headed for the Staff Only plant zones of the ship.

She saw a man sliding along a corridor wall. He was shirtless. His back was a mass of spines. The eartips of a stethoscope hung from his trouser pocket.

'Doc? Doctor? Can you hear me?'

No response.

'My name is Rye. I'm a doctor too. What's your name? Can you hear me? Can you tell me your name?'

The man slowly turned to face her.

'What's your name? Tell me your name.'

'Walczak. My name is Walczak.'

They sat in the stalls of the ship's cinema. A ripped screen framed by a proscenium arch.

'For a while I thought we had it contained,' he said. 'We locked infected passengers and crewmen in the clinic. We had them quarantined. But people didn't want to hand over their relatives. They didn't want to see them locked up with the screamers we had strapped to the beds. So they hid them in their cabins. Sons and daughters. Husbands and wives. Gave them aspirin, brought them meals, hoped they would get better. That's how the virus spread. We formed a posse. A couple of officers, a few crewmen. We knocked on doors. Took people by force. Plenty of anger, plenty of kicking and screaming.

'It was the same when it turned to war. Battles in the corridors, on the decks. Guys would confront a gang of infected people, all set to hack and burn, then realise their own wives and children were among the crowd. What would you do? Would you kill your children if it came down to it? I mean, do you have kids?'

'Yeah,' said Rye. 'I have a son.'

They walked to the Grand Lobby.

'This is where it kicked off,' said Walczak. 'This is where the carnage truly began. Everyone gathered for a banquet. Trying to forget their troubles. About thirty infected passengers broke out of the infirmary and headed this way. Blood everywhere. Stampede. It was mayhem. That was the point we lost control.'

Rye looked around. Upturned tables and chairs. Infected waitresses stumbled over broken crockery and flowers.

'Could you do me a favour?' asked Walczak.

'Sure,' said Rye.

He picked up a heavy statuette that had fallen from a wall niche. A dancing nymph.

'Kill me,' he said. 'Do it clean.'

He sat at a cocktail piano. He played 'I Get a Kick Out of You'. Rye stood behind him.

'You're pretty good,' said Rye.

'Yeah. Always wished I'd gone professional.'

Rye killed him halfway through the third verse.

She searched corridors surrounding the engine room. She opened every door marked with a red flame emblem. Paint. Lubricant. White spirit.

She found the fuel tanks. A long gantry overlooked vats of diesel and lightweight marine oil. She tried to spin stopcocks but couldn't get them to turn.

She descended steps to the tank hall floor. She hacked at the pipes with a wrench. A joint ruptured, a narrow copper coupling at the foot of a tank. Fuel glugged and splashed on to the deck plates. A slow leak, but if she returned in a couple of hours the floor would be awash with diesel.

'Codeine.' The dealer dealt two cards. Queen five.

Rye pushed the cards away. Fold.

'So what did you do? Write phantom prescriptions?'

'Yeah.'

'Sweet. Must be great to be a doctor. Kid in a candy store.'

'I lost a lot of years. I paid a heavy price.'

'Yeah. Well. Don't be too hard on yourself,' said the dealer. He took a silver cigarette case from his pocket, placed a cigarette carefully between his deformed lips, and lit it with a click of his Dunhill lighter. 'There's that line by Larkin. "All they might have done had they been loved." Every one of us could have ruled the world if we'd got up early and done the right thing. But we limp around dragging our personal damage like a tourist schlepping a heavy suitcase through an airport. Blame your genes, your parents, your school. Just a long chain of cause and effect. Life was mapped out long before you were born.'

'What is it about cards that makes people all priestly and sagacious?'

'It's like communion. Dishing out wafers. Dishing out fate. That's the beauty of blackjack. Blind chance. A reminder that you're not in control. You just sit back and watch the numbers dance.'

'You can pretend that you're not scared of dying. Personally, I'm terrified.'

'Anything is better than this.'

'Where's the fifth bloke?' Rye gestured to an empty seat. 'There were five of you. Now there are four.'

'Casper. A retired dentist. A pleasant man. A divorcé, looking for love. That's what he told me. Married thirty-five years. Wife took a bunch of cash and ran off with his brother. Didn't seem too bitter about it, though. We had a lot of time to talk it through, back in the days when he had a mouth.

'He finally went native. It happened yesterday evening. I saw it in his eyes. The moment the lights went out. He was looking at me. One minute he was Casper, next minute he wasn't. He became one of them. Mindless. Blank. Lucky bastard. All of us round this table praying for the same thing. That blessed day when it will all be over. I never imagined it would come to this. I never imagined I would hate to be alive.'

She heard a faint scuffing sound. The rasp of a chair nudged aside.

'That's him,' said the dealer. 'Casper. He's over there. He's lying by the wall. He moves, now and again.'

'What's he doing?'

'Migrating. Would you like to watch? Everyone joins the flock sooner or later.'

The dealer stood up. Half his face was rippled metal like melted candle wax. His cheek was smeared over his bow tie and lapel. The rest of him seemed untouched.

'Excuse me, ladies and gentlemen,' he said, addressing his fellow players. They were so far gone, so far mutated, they could barely turn their heads. Each face was a mask of blood and spines. Their eyes followed Rye and the dealer as they stood to leave. 'We'll be back in a few minutes.'

Casper slowly crawled towards the door. His legs appeared useless and his right arm was fused to his body. He dug fingernails into the plush carpet and hauled himself, little by little, through double doors into a service corridor. He slithered on cold linoleum. He seemed unaware that Rye and the dealer kept pace.

He slowly dragged himself along the corridor, hand slapping on the tiles. He reached a stairwell and began to squirm his way up the stairs.

'Where's he heading?' asked Rye.

'I'll show you.'

They left Casper behind them and climbed three flights of stairs. They found themselves standing at the back of a crowd.

Twenty or thirty passengers jostled in front of a locked door. They scratched and pawed at the metal.

'This is where they are drawn,' said the dealer. 'The barricades. We'll join them, when our time comes.' He guided her closer to the door. 'Just stand for a moment. Close your eyes. Can you feel it? Can you feel the pull?'

Rye closed her eyes. She felt it. A skin-prickle like heat. She turned her head, like she was turning her face to the sun.

'Yes, I can feel it.'

'Blood music. That's what I call it.'

She shouldered her way through the crowd and faced the locked door. She stroked the metal.

She could sense the crew of the refinery. She could smell them on the other side of the hatch. Rich and sweet. She began to salivate.

Fresh meat.

The Killer

Mal lay on the boathouse deck. His body had been stored in the unheated shed for a week. Too cold for decomposition. His shrouded corpse was completely frozen, rigid as a plank.

Jane used to live near the River Severn and had, on a couple of occasions, stood on the bank and blessed bloated cadavers as they were hauled from the water. The Severn Bridge was a popular venue for suicides. Corpses swollen with rot-gas frequently washed up on mudflats downstream. They were pecked by gulls until police frogmen dragged them to shore.

Mal would float south. He would probably wash up on the coast of Norway.

Jane decided to wrap a Ziploc bag beneath his shroud. She bagged his signet ring, his medallion and his passport. She wrote everything she knew about the man. Information from his personnel file. Home address, next of kin. It was a long shot. Even if his body washed up on a European beach there would be no one left alive to find him. But it seemed like the right thing to do. An attempt to preserve his identity as they dispatched him to the afterworld.

At some point during the funeral ceremony Jane would have to give an address. A summary of Mal's life. She would have to list his virtues, his enthusiasms, the struggles he faced and over-came. But she knew nothing about him at all.

Jane crossed the ice to *Hyperion*. She took a wide detour to avoid infected passengers that spilled from the rip in *Hyperion*'s side.

Mal's room.

The Magellan Suite. Red velvet and gilt fixtures. Lithographs of Napoleonic-era battleships. A senior officer's dress uniform hung in the wardrobe. Jane experienced a sudden rush of class hatred. She had been an underdog all her life. She instinctively identified with the ship's drone workers, east European immigrants who grovelled for tips. She wondered if junior members of the *Hyperion* crew, the cleaners, the waiters, the engine room staff, had been aware of the luxury enjoyed by the ship's officers. Probably not.

Mal's clothes lay in a heap by the bed. She prodded his long-johns with her boot.

Jane browsed the cupboards and shelves for any personal artefact that might give her an insight into the man's life. An open book, a stack of CDs, a family photograph. Something that might reveal who Mal had been.

Nothing. A couple of empty vodka bottles. Socks soaking in the bathroom sink. She wanted to believe everyone had value. Everyone had a rich internal life, everyone was a little universe. Not this guy. He was empty.

She had asked around. What was Mal actually like? What went on in his head? Nobody knew. He was Nail's shadow. Nail pulled deadlifts, and Mal pumped weights next to him. Nail watched TV, and Mal pulled up a chair.

Jane asked Nail for his opinion of the man. He shrugged.

'He didn't say a whole lot. I think he supported West Ham.'

She sat on the bath. She would have to talk to the other crewmen. Maybe Mal had confided his dreams, his great disappointments, to a friend during some late-night heart-to-heart.

There was something on the floor next to the toilet brush. A twist of foil dusted with brown powder. Jane held the crumpled foil in the palm of her hand and examined it from all angles.

Jane and Ghost took a suite near the bridge. Most nights they sat in silk bathrobes and watched a movie. They took turns to cook.

Jane felt self-conscious each time Ghost saw her naked. A life-time of fathood had left her with sagging skin. Ghost didn't seem to mind. He had a paunch and a hairy back.

'All the supermodels are dead, baby,' he told her. 'Let it go.'

'What do you make of this?' asked Jane.

Ghost paused *Annie Hall* and took the foil from her hand.

'Silver paper. What of it?'

'My old church. Holy Apostles. There were little scraps of foil in the porch each morning. They were left by junkies.'

'So where did you find this?'

'Mal. His old suite.'

'Some kind of drug deal gone bad, is that what you're saying? You think Mal got involved in a big argument. A trade. A dispute over money, or whatever counts for money these days. Maybe someone pulled a knife.'

'You used to sell weed, didn't you? Your little hydroponics lab.'

'I shared it around, swapped it for magazines and stuff. It was never an actual business.'

'Were you ever offered anything hard in exchange?'

'No, but it wouldn't surprise me if someone on board was dealing. It happens on a lot of offshore installations. A big bunch of guys, nowhere to go, nothing to do. If you smuggled a bag of pills or a brick of heroin on board you would find a ready market. Probably double your paycheque. Make everyone dance to your tune.'

Jane thought it over.

'Did Mal have a best friend? Anyone other than Nail?'

'No. Just the gym posse. Nail's little muscle cult. He barely spoke a word to anyone else. He was wallpaper. A complete blank.'

'Do you think they fell out? Him and Nail? What do you reckon? Could Nail slit a man's throat?'

'Yeah,' he said. 'He's got a mean streak. A wife-beater's rage. Could he kill a man in cold blood? I'm not sure. But would he lash out if someone pushed him hard enough? Yeah, I think he might.'

'Okay,' said Jane. 'I need to get it clear in my head. How does it fit together? What's the chronology?'

'Nikki took the boat. Nail's been simmering ever since. He got angry, argued with Mal. He lashed out. Plausible scenario.'

'He's been drunk for days. I thought he was pissed off at Nikki. Maybe it's guilt. Maybe it's Mal.'

Ghost thought it over.

'Punch cooked us all a meal. We sat in the officers' mess. I went looking and found the body.'

'So Mal may have been dead and hidden before you all sat down to eat.'

'Hard to credit,' said Ghost. 'Kill a guy then sit down for a plate of risotto? Talk and joke like nothing happened? If it's true, if this was murder, then we are dealing with a full-on psychopath.'

'We need proof. We need to know for sure.'

Next morning Jane and Ghost ran across the ice to Rampart and searched Nail's old room in the burned-out remains of D Module.

They shone flashlights over the scorched walls and ceiling. A grille had been removed from the mouth of a wall duct and positioned neatly on the sprung frame of the bed. The melted foam mattress had been laid in the corner.

'Someone was here,' said Ghost. 'They took something from the duct.'

'Mal or Nail?'

'Who knows? Maybe we're getting carried away. Maybe Mal cut his own throat, after all.'

Jane kicked through the planks and slats of a smashed cupboard. She sat on the bed. Frame-springs creaked and twanged.

Ghost sat on the burned chair and pulled Nail's personnel file from his shoulder bag.

'So what do you think we should do?' asked Ghost. 'Say we find a smoking gun. A bloody knife, a shoe box full of smack.

What then? Do we convene a jury? It's not like we can send him to jail. Take a vote? Hang the guy? He's still got friends. If we start throwing accusations around this could turn into civil war.'

'If we have been passing the time of day with a killer, we need to know about it. We can't let it go.'

'There is another option. Just so we understand the road we are heading down.'

'Let's hear it.'

'We're in charge. You and me. We didn't apply for the job, but we're holding the reins. If Nail is a problem, then it's down to us to deal.'

'Go on.'

'I'll take him on a trip inland. Find a pretext. Re-visit the capsule or something. I'd make sure he didn't come back. I'd tell everyone he fell down a crevasse.'

'No.'

'It's an option. That's all I'm saying.'

Ghost thumbed through the file. He held up a sheet of paper.

'Nigeria,' he said. 'Four years ago. He and Mal both worked for Chevron. I'm guessing that's where they met.'

Jane took a packet of beef jerky from her pocket.

'I don't know what I hoped to find,' she said. 'There's nothing here. I don't suppose we will ever know for sure.'

'Like I say, if Nail has been dealing, if he killed Mal in a fight, we aren't in much of a position to prove anything.'

'No.'

'So we might as well drop it.'

'Yeah.'

'Except for this.'

He held up a sheet of paper. A crude photocopy.

'Discharge papers. Private Edwin "Nail" Harper. Royal Engineers. He must have used it as a reference.' He handed the paper to Jane. 'Distinguishing features. Check it out.'

'I can barely read it.'

'Tattoos.'

'Second Battalion insignia right forearm. A lion on his back.'

'I helped him out of a wetsuit once,' said Ghost. 'He and some guys were inspecting the seabed pipeline. Testing the shut-off valve. I helped them decompress. He has a big cross on his back, and a wolf on his arm. No regimental insignia.'

'You're sure?'

'Pretty sure.'

'You're saying Nail Harper isn't Nail Harper?'

'Most of the guys on the rig were running from something. Maybe he, whoever he is, was running from the law. Trying to build a new life under a stolen identity.'

'So what happened to the real Nail Harper?'

'Dread to think.'

'You think we should challenge him?'

'He'll say he got the tattoo lasered off. Bad memories of Iraq, or some shit.'

'Christ,' said Jane.

'The sooner we cut him loose, the better.'

Nail's turn on patrol. Ghost kept him company. They walked the perimeter, the ring of barricades that kept the rabid population of *Hyperion* at bay.

They checked locks. They re-stacked furniture against each door. They stood on deck and watched mutant passengers mill on the tiered decks below them.

'They don't get any smarter,' said Ghost.

'You'd think they would rot,' said Nail. 'They can't keep going for ever. Sooner or later, they have to drop dead.'

Nail swigged from a hip flask.

'So how are you doing?' asked Ghost.

'All right.'

'You must be pretty cut up about Mal.'

'Fuck him. He was weak.'

'Any idea why he would want to kill himself?'

'Right now, every one of us has a dozen reasons to jump over the side.'

'He was your friend.'

'Nobody has friends. Not out here.'

Nail proffered his hip flask. Ghost took it and pretended to drink.

'Fancy a trip below deck?'

'What for?' asked Nail.

'The Neptune Bar. The guys want to hold a wake. We need to liberate a few supplies.'

'Yeah. Why not?'

Jane used a master key from the purser's office to let herself into Nail's cabin. She searched by torchlight. Ghost and Nail were out on deck. She didn't want Nail to see light at his cabin porthole.

'What exactly do you hope to find?' Ghost had asked.

'I don't know. Something incriminating. Some kind of contraband.'

Dumbbells. Empty bottles of Scotch. Five years of *Hustler*.

Jane tried to think like a junkie. Where would she hide her stash? Toilet cistern. Back of the washstand sink. Inside tubular, steel-frame furniture.

She checked beneath the bed with a Maglite pen torch. She tugged at the side panels of the bath. She pulled up carpet.

Nothing.

She headed for the door. She was reluctant to leave. Gut instinct told her there was something hidden in the room, something significant, but she didn't have time for a thorough search.

The crew took over the Tex Mex Grill. Ponchos hung on the wall, a plastic cactus stood by the door and a picture of Lee Van Cleef hung behind the bar.

Ghost and Nail had rescued three cases of Veuve Clicquot

from below deck. They filled buckets with ice chiselled from benches along the promenade, and set the champagne to chill.

'Have fun, boys,' said Ghost. His turn on patrol.

Gus put a CD player on the bar. Mal liked U2, so they played 'Joshua Tree'.

Gus muted the sound for a moment and stood on a chair. He proposed a toast.

'Mal. Here's to you, buddy. *Via con Dios.*'

They all drained their glasses except for Jane. She resolved to stay sober. She sat by a brass radiator. She stooped to pick up a fallen coaster and turned up the thermostat. She popped a fresh bottle and refilled glasses.

Nail took off his fleece. He stood on a table and clapped for silence. Another toast.

'Goodbye to a good man. Goodbye to our friend.'

Gus found bags of nachos in a back room. He filled bowls.

Jane stood next to Nail at the bar.

'You took off your bandages.'

'Guess I'm all better.'

'I spoke to Nikki on the radio,' said Jane. 'She says Hi.'

'Tell her to eat shit and die.'

'Did she leave a note?'

'Bitch stole my knife.'

The room was getting hot. Jane took off her fleece. She wore a black vest.

'Been working out?' asked Nail.

Jane pried the cap from a Corona.

'I took over your gym.'

'All right. Let's see what you've got.'

They cleared a table. The crew formed a circle. Nail pulled off his shirt. He sat and put his arm out ready to wrestle.

'Left hand, okay? I don't want to re-snap my wrist.'

Jane got into position and gripped his massive hand.

Gus counted them down: 'Three . . . two . . . one.'

Nail had a snarling wolf on his bicep. No regimental tattoo on his forearm. No lion on his back.

They wrestled. Nail nearly dislocated Jane's shoulder. He quickly pulled her arm over, but she kept her hand from touching the table. She fought and swore. She sweated and snarled. She refused to grant victory.

Later that night Jane cracked a fresh bottle of beer and stood at *Hyperion*'s prow.

She looked towards Rampart. A couple of standby floodlights still burned, even though no one was home.

Jane leaned over a prow railing and shone a flashlight downward. Half-frozen passengers stood far beneath her. She dropped her empty beer bottle. She watched it fall and smash on an infected passenger's head.

Someone behind her. Nail, with a bottle. He leaned over the railing. He took a swig of champagne and spat spray. He watched the droplets freeze as they fell, and scatter on the shoulders of passengers below like hail.

'Bored with singing?' he asked.

'Karaoke at a wake. Doesn't seem right.'

'Mal wouldn't care.'

'How are the crew getting on?' asked Jane, groping for something to say. 'How is morale? They don't confide in me much.'

'Pretty good. There are plenty of distractions aboard. Plenty of ways to waste time. We're all counting the days until March.'

'You're doing all right?'

'Fine.'

'Heard you were in the army.'

'Who told you that?' asked Nail.

'I don't recall. Just something I heard. So how was it?'

'Hot. Dull.'

'Why did you leave?'

'I'm not a follower. I don't like being told what to do.'

'Coming to the service tomorrow?'

'Dead is dead. Nothing we say or do will make a damn bit of difference.'

'Guilty as hell,' said Jane, when she got back to Ghost's room.

'You're sure?'

'He killed Mal. I'm certain. Don't know why it happened. Drug deal gone sour, argument over a chocolate bar, whatever. But he killed him. Bet my life on it.'

'You've got a shotgun. Maybe you should use it.'

'I couldn't do a thing like that. Yeah, we killed a bunch of infected. But we have to draw a line. I'm not a killer.'

'Of course you're a fucking killer. There is no higher authority any more. This is the way it is going to be. We have to sort this shit out ourselves.'

'Seriously? You'd do it? Pull the trigger on the guy? Take him out on the ice and shoot him in the back?'

'The man isn't stupid. If you're right, if he genuinely offed Mal, then he's a dangerous motherfucker. You know his big secret. He'll have sniffed it out in a second. Right now we're safe, but once we get back to the world it'll be a different story. He'll consider us a serious liability. We'd better watch our backs from now on. That's all I'm saying.'

Mal's funeral was scheduled for three in the afternoon. The crew gathered in the Rampart canteen. They kept it short, anxious to dispatch the man's body and quit the ice before *Hyperion* passengers surrounded them and attacked.

They trained floodlights on the ice between the refinery's cyclopean legs. The crew, those who knew and liked the man, descended from the rig. They stood over the shrouded body while Jane intoned the old words:

'Our days are like the grass; we flourish like a flower of the

249

field; when the wind goes over it, it is gone and its place will know it no more. But the merciful goodness of the Lord endures forever . . .'

Most of the guys didn't believe in God or heaven, but they liked the rhythm of elegiac prayers, the tone of resignation and acceptance.

They smashed a hole in the ice, then slid his body into the sea. The men watched Mal dragged away by the current. Every one of them thought the same thing. Is this how it will end? One by one pushed into the ocean and carried away by the tide. What would the last man do? That final, lone member of Rampart's crew about to succumb to starvation or infection? They would break a hole in the ice then say a prayer at the water's edge. Conduct their own funeral oration. Maybe sing a hymn. Then they would cross themselves, close their eyes and drop into the ocean.

The Voice

Nikki curled foetal and covered her head. Waves slammed into the boat. She had sealed herself below deck. She rode out a series of impacts like one car crash after another. She wrapped herself in a sleeping bag for extra protection. She lay in the dark. Every couple of minutes she felt the boat rise like it was about to take off, then dive into a deep trough. She sang to calm herself down, but couldn't hear her own voice above the white-noise roar of the maelstrom.

She was cramped. She could barely move. She had lowered the sail and rigging, folded the silver fabric, coiled the rope, and stowed them below deck.

The mast was still raised. A design fault. It was welded in place. It could not be lowered flat. A big steel spike raised skyward during a fierce lightning storm.

Nikki doubted she would feel a lightning bolt when it struck. Steel mast, aluminium hull. She would be microwaved in an instant. A cooked sailor, lying in her bunk, crisped and smoking, like a hunk of roast pork.

She lay waiting to see if the boat would shake itself to pieces. She waited to see if the bolts and welds would hold. She waited to see if she would live or die.

She wondered how long the storm would last. She checked the luminescent dial of her watch. Seven hours of wind and rain.

It felt like the waves were easing off. She switched on her flashlight. The cardboard storage boxes had split open. The interior of the cabin was a jumble of tins and cartons. Her sleeping bag was dusted with cornflakes.

She wriggled to the roof hatch. She reached for the deadbolt. She hesitated. This could be a big mistake. If the typhoon ripped the hatch from her hand the boat would quickly become inundated and sink. Yet the waves seemed to be diminishing. The boat was no longer hurled from side to side. Maybe the storm had passed.

Nikki released the deadbolt and lifted the hatch a fraction. Blast of frozen wind and salt spray.

Flash of lightning.

She let her eyes adjust. A seething ocean. Surging, frothing waves.

Second sheet of lightning.

Something up ahead. Something big, oncoming, eclipsing the stars.

'Holy fuck.'

A massive wave, high as an office block.

She slammed the hatch and hammered the deadbolts home. She threw herself on to the bunk and curled tight.

Building roar. The boat was rising, rising like an express elevator.

Brief moment of balance at the summit of the wave, like a rollercoaster about to plunge.

The boat pitched nose-first. Smash impact. Fast tumble. The boat flipped end over end. Nikki stayed foetal and protected her head as she was pelted with cans and cartons.

Deceleration. Slow spin, then calm and quiet.

She pushed boxes and bags aside and sat up. A trickling sensation down her neck. She took a pen torch from her pocket and switched it on. Blood on her neck. A cut beneath her right ear. Nothing serious.

She stretched. Her back was bruised. She sat in silence for a while, glad to be alive. She pressed a sock to her ear to sop blood.

Wind noise slowly began to ease.

A trickling sound. Nikki sat forward. Steady, constant drip-drip.

She kicked bags and boxes out of the way. A split in the hull. A cracked weld. A steady stream of seawater.

She stuffed a jacket against the crack and tried to stem the flow. Water sprayed her face.

She took Nail's dive knife from her pocket and tried to wedge fabric into the fissure with the tip of the blade. No good.

Water gathered at the bottom of the boat, covering her shoes. She threw open the roof hatch and bailed with a tin cup.

She tried to keep calm. If she allowed herself to panic, if she gave in to screaming terror, she would die.

Brainwave. She slapped a plastic plate over the leak and braced the plate tight in position with a ski pole. Fierce jets of water sprayed from behind the plate like sunrays. She hammered the pole into position. The leak slowed to a dribble, then stopped.

Knee-deep in freezing water. Bottles and bags floated around her. She bailed some more.

She woke, damp and shivering. She ached. She stretched.

She exhaled into a cupped hand. Her breath smelled like sewage. She found toothpaste among the clutter. She squeezed paste on to her finger and rubbed it over her teeth.

She took out the radio.

'Rampart, do you copy, over?'

It took an hour to raise a reply.

'*Rampart here.*'

A faint voice. A murmur through hiss and crackle.

'Jane? Is that you?'

'*How's it going, Nikki?*'

'The boat almost sank.'

'*Say again? The boat sank?*'

'There was a storm. I'm all right.'

'*What happened to the boat, Nikki? What went wrong?*'

'It was the welds. A big wave split the hull. If you build another boat, you'll have to make it stronger. The waves out here are like mountains.'

'*I'm losing you. You're passing out of range.*'

'I just wanted to say goodbye.'

'*Good luck, Nikki. God bless.*'

Nikki unrolled global maritime charts. Depth contours. Tides, wrecks and buoys. She had to be careful. The paper was wet and easy to rip.

She examined ocean currents. A map of the Arctic covered in swirling arrows. She was about to reach the Greenland Sea. She was caught in a current called the Beaufort Gyre. Part of a bigger system of circular currents that meshed like cogs and dictated transpolar drift. It would carry her south, then east to the Norwegian coast. But it might take weeks.

She was thirsty. She flipped open the hatch. She lowered the desalinator tube into the sea and cranked the handle. Fresh water dribbled from the output tube. She filled her canteen. It took an hour. Adrenalin was slowly ebbing away to be replaced by boredom and despair.

Nikki passed land. A serrated ridge on the pale horizon. A seagull wheeled high above the boat. She checked her map. She was passing the island of Longyearbyen. It was Norwegian territory. A barren rock. Russians used to mine coal. Whatever sparse population once scratched a living on the island had probably long since been evacuated, but there might be stores.

The sea surrounding Norwegian territory was supposed to be closed. AWACS planes were guiding a flotilla of gunboats. But she hadn't seen any planes and she hadn't seen any boats. She watched for the winking red strobes of high-altitude aircraft, but the skies were empty.

What would happen if she were confronted by a gunboat?

Would they tell her to turn round and head the other way? Would they take her prisoner? Drag her off to an internment camp? Most likely they would open up with a deck-mounted .50 cal and blow her from the water.

She found tins but the labels had come off. She shook them. A rattle. Chick peas. She couldn't find the tin opener. She stabbed at the tin with a nail file, but barely made a scratch.

She rationed her food. Three raisins for breakfast. A Ritz cracker with a scoop of peanut butter for dinner.

It took a long time to pump fresh water. A lot of muscle power. She filled a two-litre bottle. She allowed herself a swig every hour.

She drifted down the coast of Longyearbyen. Weak daylight. She found a pair of rubber-coated binoculars among the clutter below deck. She scanned the shore. Bleak volcanic crags. No birds, no grass, no life.

She looked south. A smudge against the sky. Was it a cloud or was it smoke?

The boat slowly rounded a headland. She saw the smouldering ruins of a wooden cabin. The roof had partially collapsed.

A fisherman's hut? Shelter built by whalers?

Nikki shouted towards the shore.

'Hello? Can anyone hear me?'

The boat drifted past the distant house.

'Hello? Is anyone there?'

Movement. A figure in the cabin doorway. Maybe someone scavenging supplies.

'Hey. Hey, over here.'

She waved her arms.

'Hey. Hello.'

The figure looked her way.

She took binoculars from a hook near the hatch. Focus, re-focus. Blood and metal. The guy had no jaw. His tongue flapped

255

loose. He was joined by two women. Their faces were a mess of spines. All three wore furs streaked in blood. They stood at the end of a wooden jetty, reaching for the distant boat with scabrous, clawing fingers.

Nikki let the current carry her south.

Morning. The southern sky was tinged azure.

Nikki saw a white dot on the horizon. A fragment of iceberg? A sail? The object grew closer. It was a fin. The tail of a plane. An Air France 747 floating low in the water.

Nikki drew alongside the massive passenger jet. She jumped on to the wing and slammed the barbed spike of the anchor into a riveted seam. She walked back and forth on the wing, boots crunching on the salt-crusted metal. She hadn't walked a single step for weeks. She spent each day crouched in the cockpit and, once a day, she crawled across the hull of the boat to check the mast and sail.

Nikki wiped a porthole with her sleeve. She saw, through the misted glass, rows of empty seats. She guessed the plane had been turned back from US airspace and run out of fuel halfway back to Europe. The aircraft ditched and the passengers used the evacuation slides as rafts. The last cabin staff to abandon the jet must have shut the hatch behind them out of domestic instinct. The plane was hermetically sealed, a steel bubble. It retained just enough air in its cargo hold, empty fuel tanks and passenger compartments to keep it above water. It would float for months, maybe years, riding out the squalls.

Nikki pushed the wing hatch with her shoulder. The rubber seals gave way with a squelch. The interior of the plane was lit by weak daylight shafting through the starboard portholes.

Economy class. Rows of empty seats. A tangle of oxygen masks hanging from the ceiling. Luggage was scattered in the aisles. No blood, no bodies.

Club and first class were both empty. Attaché cases and laptops had been left neatly on the seats as if the passengers would soon return and resume their journey.

The cockpit was empty. Banks of dead instrumentation and a view of empty ocean.

Nikki sought out the galley at the back of the plane. She hoped to find soft drinks, cartons of long-life milk and maybe biscuits.

She found cartons of orange juice in an overturned stewardess trolley. The cartons were frozen solid. She ripped away packaging. A yellow brick of juice. She smashed the brick in the galley basin and sucked shards as she explored the plane.

She noticed one of the toilets was engaged. She casually kicked the door, then jumped back when a voice said, *'Don't come in.'*

'Jesus,' said Nikki, addressing the bathroom door. 'How long have you been aboard?'

'Leave. Just leave.' A male voice.

'Look, there's no need to hide. There's just me. I'm on my own. Come on out.'

'The door's jammed. It's staying jammed. Don't come in.'

'Please. Come out.'

'No.'

'Look, this is stupid.'

'Fuck you.'

'The plane ditched. You know that, right? There's no one on board but you.'

'I'm not leaving.'

'You're in the middle of the fucking ocean. Everyone took to the rafts. You're alone. And this plane is barely afloat. If it takes on even a cupful of water it'll sink to the bottom and take you with it.'

'Just fuck off.'

'Well, shit. I'm not going to argue with you.'

Nikki found a pallet of bottled water in a galley locker. She stacked the bottles by the hatch.

She found a wash-bag and baby wipes among the scattered luggage and locked herself in a club-class lavatory. She stripped out of her hydro-suit and wiped herself down. She brushed her teeth and spat. She kept her lock-knife open on the edge of the basin in case her unseen companion decided to emerge from his den.

She found fresh clothes in a suitcase. Socks and underwear. She tried to repair her cracked and wrinkled hands with moisturiser.

She crouched on the wing and tried the radio. She hoped the metal plane would act as an antenna and boost the signal.

She couldn't raise Rampart. It was out of range, over the horizon and lost in perpetual night.

Nikki scanned the wavebands. A flickering LED. The radio was trying to lock on to a ghost signal.

'. . . *God's help . . . terrible deci . . . arkest day . . .*'

The voice died away.

Nikki loaded food and water on to the boat, then walked to the lavatory at the back of the plane. She knocked on the toilet door.

'This is your last chance. I'm leaving.'

'*Bye.*'

'Seriously. I'm heading south. You could join me. If you stay here you'll die.'

'*Then leave me. You can do that. You've done it before.*'

'Leave you?'

'*Yeah. Save your own ass. After all, everyone has a talent.*'

'Who are you?' demanded Nikki. 'What's your name?'

No reply.

'Alan? Is that you?'

Nikki kicked at the door. Four blows then the lock splintered. The cubicle was empty.

'Have I gone insane?' asked Nikki, interrogating her reflection. 'Is that the deal?'

'*Let's just say,*' said her dead boyfriend's voice, '*that your percep-
tions have undergone a radical adaptation.*'

Nikki enjoyed VIP luxury. She sat in a club seat. A porthole gave
her a view of open sea. She wrapped herself in airline blankets
and reclined. She clamped in-flight headphones to warm her ears.

'This place is a welcome piece of luck,' she murmured as she
snuggled down to sleep.

'*Yeah,*' said Alan. '*God crashed this plane just for you.*'

She pulled a TV from a slot in the arm of the chair. A little
screen on an armature. She jacked her headphones and selected
Brief Encounter from the menu. She dozed as the movie played.

'*You realise that screen is completely blank,*' said Alan. '*The plane
is dead. Nothing works.*'

'But I like the movie.'

'*Jesus. It's like that joke. My wife thinks she's a chicken. I'd take
her to the doctor, but we need the eggs.*'

'That's fucking ironic. My dead boyfriend posing as the voice
of sanity.'

'*You think you left me behind? You're stuck with me as long as
you live. Bonnie and Clyde. Sonny and Cher. I'll look after you,
until the end of your days.*'

'Could you get me back to Rampart?' asked Nikki. 'Could
you master the boat? The ropes, the sail? If I wanted to get back,
could you show me the way?'

'I can take you anywhere you need to go, Nikki.'

She sat cross-legged on the wing of the jet and ate crackers.

She saw a red glow on the skyline, a fine aurora. It was the
wrong time of day, the wrong point of the compass for sunset.

They must have nuked the cities. Ahead of her, beyond the
southern horizon, Europe was burning.

Army of the Damned

Self-awareness came and went like a weak radio signal. Stuttering, time-lapse moments of consciousness. It began in the main lobby. She was sipping Scotch. She hated Scotch ever since she vomited Macallan out of her nose during a college drinking game. She retched at the smell of it. A shot glass full of bile. But now she drank single malt like it was Coke. She couldn't taste it and it didn't make her drunk.

Three infected people in front of her. Two brass-buttoned waiters and an old lady welded to a walking frame.

Blackout.

Two naked old guys and a chef.

Blackout.

Two officers and a cleaner fused to a broom.

Rye smiled. It was like pulling the arm of a slot machine. Three different fruit, every time.

One moment Rye was sitting at the blackjack table, checking her cards, nudging chips with the rotted club that used to be her hand. Next moment she found herself standing in a deserted coffee bar staring out of a porthole at the stars. She wondered how much time had passed. The next instant she found herself standing in one of *Hyperion*'s little gift shops cramming fistfuls of shortbread into her mouth then spitting the biscuits because they tasted dry as dust. Time passed in a series of jumpcuts, each lucid moment met with anger and frustration. Why was she, among all the shambling, leprous passengers, one of the few cursed with long moments of wakefulness in which she experienced the full horror of her condition?

Rye checked the diesel tanks. She descended a ladder. Her boots splashed, ankle-deep. The floor of the fuel room was wet with octane. A flare would be enough, or a struck match.

She patted her pockets, tried to find a lighter. Next moment she couldn't remember who she was or why she was standing in a strange, wide room. She stood staring into space for hours, fuel slowly rising round her legs.

She found herself pounding a door. Infected passengers jostled around her, scraping and clawing at the metal.

She backed away from the crowd.

The hatch separated the Rampart crew from a savage horde that wanted to tear them apart.

Rye tried to drive the passengers back. She grabbed collars and pulled them away, but they immediately returned to punch and kick at the door. She blasted the crowd with a carbon extinguisher. Foam jetted over faces and bodies. The infected passengers were oblivious. They dripped white. Rye battered heads with the spent extinguisher. They shrugged off the blows.

Blackout.

Rye found herself among the group once more, hammering and scratching the metal.

Rye snapped alert. She found herself standing in front of a steel hatch, hand gripped around the release handle. She was alone. A remote lower deck.

DÖRR 26

She backed off. She had learned the layout of the ship from multilingual you-are-here wall charts mounted in each corridor to help passengers navigate their way from one theme-bar to another. Hatch 26 would lead to a passageway beneath the officers' quarters.

She rested her forehead against the cold metal and fought the overwhelming meat-lust that wanted to put her beyond the door and heading for the Rampart crew. She was lonely. She wanted to see Jane and Ghost once more. But she couldn't trust herself. She would seize them. She would rip and tear.

You should turn round, she told herself. Turn around and head the other way.

Rye cranked the handle and pulled the door ajar. She hesitated. The Rampart crew would have sought out every entrance to the officers' quarters. They would not have left the door undefended. They would have taken steps to protect themselves.

Rye squinted through the crack. She could see a red canister taped to the back of the hatch at eye level. A grenade, trip-wire pulled taut.

Rye squeezed her arm through the gap and gripped the grenade, careful not to dislodge the pin. She ripped the grenade free, snapping the thread. She examined the case. AH-M14 thermite grenade.

She put her eye to the gap and studied the barricade beyond the door. She could see a jumble of furniture. Desks and office chairs. A couple of filing cabinets. She could also see a couple of fine nylon threads, like wisps of cobweb. More grenades rigged around the doorway. If she opened the door wide she would have three seconds' grace before blowtorch heat seared flesh from her bones.

Rye sealed the hatch.

She wandered through the ship. She followed a draught of Arctic wind until she reached the gash ripped in *Hyperion*'s prow by the collision with the rig. An evacuation sign, a running man fleeing flames, pointed to where jagged, ice-dusted metal framed the night sky.

Rye stepped over buckled floor plates. She stood in the great wound and looked out at the stars, the sea, the lunar crags of the island.

There had been rumours. Months ago, Jane and Punch had returned to the rig from the island with crates. They had visited the site of a seismic research station and returned with some kind of munitions. The secret revealed: boxes of thermite grenades.

The grenades were not designed to explode and spit shrapnel like conventional anti-personnel ordnance. Once triggered, they burned at four thousand degrees for a full minute. The brief nova-heat could turn an engine block to a puddle of liquid metal in seconds. Arctic drill teams used them to melt quickly through permafrost.

Would it hurt if she lay down, pulled the pin and quickly wedged the grenade beneath her head like a pillow? Three, maybe four seconds of unimaginable pain as flesh crisped and flaked from her skull, then her brain would fizz and boil away. Her thoughts and memories would be vapour.

Do it, she told herself, for the sake of the Rampart crew. Do it for them.

The diesel tanks. A steady gush of fuel. Rye descended a ladder and waded knee-deep. She held the grenade. No more excuses. All she had to do was stand between the huge fuel tanks, wreathed in diesel vapour, and pull the pin. The blast would measure in megatons.

She hooked the grenade ring with her finger. What about the Rampart crew? She shook her head, tried to think straight. The guys were a couple of floors above her. If she detonated the grenade they would burn.

She looked down at the red cylinder in her hand. She was tired. She just wanted to sleep.

Rye woke. She lifted her head from a table. Green felt. *House must stand on 17.* She looked around. The casino. The blackjack table. The game.

'Welcome back,' said the dealer. He smiled with cracked and bloody lips. His face had begun to disintegrate. Skin hung in strips. 'I thought we'd lost you. Thought your lights were out for good. Well. Maybe tomorrow, if you're lucky. It surely won't be much longer.'

He skimmed a couple of playing cards across the table. Rye didn't bother reading her hand. She pushed a couple of chips towards the centre.

'Not going to check your cards?' he asked. 'Dancing to the music of chance?'

He drew seven. Bust.

Rye gestured to the empty seats around her.

'So the others all turned?'

'One by one. I'm glad for them, but I can't help asking, why not me? Why am I left behind?'

'The breaks.'

'Those fucking breaks. It's just you and me now. The living dead.'

'I feel like I've drawn the short straw all my life. Forgive the self-pity. I just want it to be done.'

'It'll happen, sister. Don't you worry.'

'I'm scared. I want to do something, take steps, if you know what I mean. But I have to admit, I'm scared.'

The dealer gestured to his legs. Rye craned to see beneath the table. Metal tendrils had burst from the dealer's shoes. They had punctured the carpet and fused with the deck plate beneath. It looked like he had taken root.

'Sadly, I'm not as mobile as I was. If I could get out of this chair I'd jump over the side.'

Rye took the grenade from her pocket and placed it on the table.

'I found this. I don't have the courage to use it.'

'Mind if I take it from you?'

'Be my guest.'

Rye slid the grenade across the table. The dealer examined it like a barstool drunk contemplating the bottom of his shot glass.

'Obliged to you.'

'Thank you for your company these past few days,' said Rye. 'It's been a comfort.'

'Good luck, Liz.'

Rye woke. She was sitting on a bed. Whose bed? She was in a third-class cabin. Cramped. Trashed by a previous occupant. Clothes and coins on the floor.

Blood on the bed sheets. Whose blood? Hers? The blood was black and old.

She stood up. A monster in the mirror. A face weeping metal. Eyes behind a mask of spines. She smashed the mirror with a grotesque club-hand.

Rye woke. Silver walls. She was standing in one of the walk-in freezers. A mouthful of rotten meat. A big slab of ribs, furred green, hung in front of her on a hook. Bite marks on the ribs. Rye spat half-chewed fat and splintered bone on to the floor. No substitute for fresh sinew, for sinking her teeth into warm flesh.

She turned to leave, but jerked to a stop. Her left hand was frozen to the wall. How long had she stood catatonic? Her clothes were stiff with ice. She tugged her hand away from the metal. Skin tore. No pain. A palm-print glued to the wall.

Rye woke. She found herself jostling with infected passengers. Stench and rot. A dozen monsters pounding at a door, scratching and hammering, trying to reach the meat. Hawaiian shirts and paper garlands. A night of limbo and piña coladas turned to hell.

Fingers raked the hatch metal. Broken nails and streaked blood.

The hatch was giving way. It was wedged shut by a barricade the other side of the door. Rye heard furniture start to shift.

Bodies hurled against the door. Chairs and tables began to subside.

Rye kicked legs. She tripped the passengers. She wanted to slow them down. She wished she had her radio. She could warn the Rampart crew of impending attack. They were about to be swamped. Cornered. Killed in their beds.

The door gave way and swung open. A collapsing mountain of furniture. Rye stepped back, waiting for grenades to detonate and consume the crowd in brilliant white fire.

Nothing.

Jane and Ghost were waiting on the other side of the door, shotguns raised like a firing squad. Twin muzzle flash. Explosive roar. Scrambled brain matter.

Jane stood hazed in gunsmoke. She slotted fresh shells and racked the slide. Efficient shots, point-blank to the face like a stone-cold killer.

'Hey,' shouted Rye. 'Hey, Jane.'

Jane saw her. No recognition. She raised her shotgun. Rye dived sideways to avoid the blast.

Jane and Ghost re-sealed the door. Rye lay among smouldering, headless bodies and listened as they rebuilt the barricade.

Rye's last moments of full consciousness, the last time she was truly herself, occurred deep in the heart of the ship. She was stumbling down a stairwell. She was not alone. She found herself leading a crowd of passengers in fancy dress.

On her left was a man in a dinner suit and pig mask. Spikes pierced the pig snout. The man could never remove the mask. He would spend the rest of his short life squinting through rubber eye-holes.

On her right was a man in a bunny costume, fur matted with blood.

The stairs led down into dark water. One of the hull plates had popped a seam below the waterline when *Hyperion* collided with the refinery. The ship was still seaworthy but a couple of mid-section compartments were flooded.

At the bottom of the stairwell, beneath the icy water, was a door that would lead to rooms directly below the officers' quarters. The door wouldn't be wedged shut and it wouldn't be strung with grenades. A blind spot. The Rampart crew wouldn't anticipate anyone would rise out of seawater.

Rye reached the point where water lapped the stairs. She kept walking. Knee-deep, waist-deep, chest-deep, and finally submerged.

Smothering silence. Green, sub-aqueous murk. Rye walked slowly like an astronaut. The cold should have killed her but she could barely feel it. She was breathing water, but it didn't seem to matter.

The bottom of the stairwell. A submerged electric wall lamp, sealed in a glass bubble, still burned bright. A sculpin swam past Rye's face and darted into a floor vent.

She found the hatch. She turned the handles and pulled it open. There must have been a cupboard of bathroom supplies nearby because the water around her was filled by a blizzard of dissolved toilet paper.

Rye walked through the doorway. She looked over her shoulder. The grotesque animal forms of her companions kept pace behind her. A clown with one arm. A ballet dancer, tights lumped and stretched by tumorous growth.

More stairs. Rye climbed upward, water cascading from her clothes as she broke the surface. Her companions followed, shaking water from their animal heads, stumbling under the weight of their sodden costumes.

Her thoughts cleared for a moment and she realised the terrible carnage she was about to unleash. The refinery crew were two decks above them, eating dinner, convinced they were safe behind barricades.

Rye reached in her pocket for the grenade, then remembered she had given it away. Maybe she should trigger the sprinkler system and raise the alarm. But a moment later she could no longer remember who she was, and why she was standing in a stairwell jostled by monsters in tattered carnival costume. She joined the herd and shambled up the stairs alongside her nightmare companions towards the Rampart crew, ready to rip and tear.

Part Three

Fallback

The Refuge

Nail and Gus were lost in the fog. Their flashlights lit snow and curling mist. Frozen beards. Clothes crusted with frost.

'We're lost.'

'We're not lost.'

Gus was badly burned. He leaned against Nail for support.

'Wait,' said Nail. 'Hold on.'

'What?'

Nail took a red bandana from his pocket and held it up like a wind sock.

'I think we're heading the right way. We just need to keep the wind behind us.'

'Then what? We're royally fucked.'

Nail's flashlight had started to fail.

'We have to keep moving. We have to find shelter.'

Hyperion had been overrun. Nail and Gus fled during the attack. They slid down knotted rope as the ship burned. Quickly rappelled down the smooth white hull to the ice. They didn't have coats. They each wore a T-shirt and fleece. They could survive maybe fifteen minutes before succumbing to the cold.

Gus sagged like he wanted to sit down.

'Keep moving,' commanded Nail, his voice flat and muffled by the fog. 'It can't be far.'

He was starting to shake.

They stumbled over snow and rock. Deep thuds behind them. Explosions aboard *Hyperion*.

Concrete jutted from the snow. The high arch of the bunker entrance.

'This is it,' said Nail. 'We made it.'

They reached the bunker door. An infected crewman stood sentry in front of the entrance. It looked like he had been there a while. Snow had collected on his head and shoulders. He was knee-deep, his uniform frosted white. He stood quite still, staring into the mist. He slowly came to life like a rusted robot. His clothes crackled with ice as he moved. He stumbled and reached for Nail and Gus. His face was frozen. His eyes couldn't turn in their sockets.

Nail kicked the crewman's legs from under him. He pushed the fallen man down the bunker steps with his foot. The body rolled into the fog.

Gus passed out. He fell against the door and slid to the ground. Nail tried to slap him awake but got no response. He checked for a pulse. Still alive.

Nail looked around. He glimpsed figures, grotesque silhouettes lurking in the fog.

'Gus. Wake up, man. We've got company. They sniffed us out.'

No response.

He checked the bunker doors. The padlock and chain were gone. He tried to pull the doors wide. They opened a few centimetres then jammed. They had been lashed shut from the inside with rope.

He searched Gus's pockets. He found a lock-knife. He flipped open the blade. He threw his flashlight into the mist to lure away the prowling figures that encircled them.

He worked by touch. He reached through the gap in the doorway and sawed at the rope.

'Gus? Still with me?'

No reply.

'Come on, dude. Don't check out on me now.'

He cut through the rope. He hauled open the door. He set his lighter to full-flame and dragged Gus into the bunker. A dark tunnel mouth.

He scanned shelves, picked through clutter. He found a lamp and switched it on. It was styled like a hurricane lamp, but had an LED bulb and a couple of Duracells.

He knotted the doors closed with scraps of rope.

He tried to wake Gus.

'Can you hear me? Can you hear what I'm saying? You have to focus, Gus. You have to listen to my voice. Shock and cold. Don't give in to it.'

Gus opened his eyes but couldn't focus. Semi-delirious.

Nail looked around. He had to create a fire or they were both dead.

Shelves against the tunnel wall loaded with Skidoo components. A few empty crates and fuel cans stacked by the wall. The snowmobiles themselves were under tarpaulin.

Nail swept the shelves clear and tipped them over. He stamped and smashed. He slopped a capful of petrol from a jerry can and set the shelves alight. He sat cross-legged in front of the fire and hugged Gus. He rubbed and slapped his companion until circulation returned.

'Christ,' murmured Gus. He struggled to sit up. He spat in the fire and watched spit fizzle.

'How are you feeling?' asked Nail.

'The pain comes and goes.'

Half Gus's face was scorched black. Cooked skin. Cracked and flaked. His hair was gone. His right shoulder was burned bare, scraps of polyester fleece fused to charred skin.

'Did you see Yakov?' asked Gus. 'Did you see him die?'

'Fucking horrible. Worst thing I ever saw in my life.'

'I didn't know a person could make that kind of noise. That's going to stay with me.'

The infected passengers had broken through the barricades at midnight. Somehow they circumvented locked doors, blocked corridors, and men on patrol. Hordes of them choking the passageways, some in fancy dress. Nail had been standing on the upper deck sharing a joint with Gus. They watched fog eclipse the moon and discussed girlfriends and heartbreak. If they'd been asleep in their cabins they would have been cornered, overwhelmed and ripped apart.

'We should go back,' Gus had said, as Nail pushed him across the *Hyperion* deck. The Rampart crew had prepared knotted ropes in case they needed to make a quick exit from the vessel. 'We should go back for the others.'

A burning passenger stumbled from a cabin doorway and gripped Gus in a bear hug. Gus screamed as his clothes caught alight. Nail kicked the passenger over a railing, then slapped Gus's fleece until the flames died out.

They glimpsed Yakov at the end of a companionway. He shouted and waved for help as he ran from monsters in party costume. He squealed like an abattoir pig as a Pierrot clown dragged him to the ground.

'Forget it,' said Nail. 'There's nothing we can do for him. We need to get the fuck out of here.'

They fled the ship. Grenades began to detonate with a concussive roar and set the ship ablaze. They were running across the ice when the fuel tanks blew. Heat washed over them. Smoking shrapnel peppered the snow.

'Do you think we are the only survivors?' asked Gus. 'Do you think anyone else made it off the ship? I didn't see any of the others. Jane and Ghost were in their room. Punch and Sian, too. We might be the only ones left. You and me.'

'I honestly have no idea.'

'But what if we are? What if it's just us?'

'Then we'll deal.'

'And even if they made it to the rig? No one knows we are here. How do we summon help?'

'You should rest. Seriously.'

'How long do you think that lantern will last?'

'Standard batteries. Four or five hours at the most. I'm going to leave you here for a little while, all right? I'm going to take a look around. Check out the tunnels. I need to find more wood.'

Nail walked into the tunnel holding a piece of blazing plank before him.

Echoing footfalls. Burning wood crackled and fizzed. The torch flame flickered. The tunnels whispered and sighed. There must be ventilation chimneys deep within the complex. How extensive was the tunnel network? Did it undermine the entire island?

He walked deeper down the sloping shaft. Black archways, sinister shapes. He wanted to explore but worried, if he strayed from the central passageway, he would quickly become lost. If his torch burned out, if a gust of wind extinguished the flame, he might have to make his way back to the surface by touch.

Vast cyclopean chambers. Ceilings so high weak torchlight couldn't penetrate shadow. The tunnel complex seemed built for some purpose other than nuclear storage. Too big, too elaborate to store fuel rods.

He stopped to catch his breath. Sudden, palpitating claustrophobia. Gut conviction that this ferro-concrete catacomb would be his grave. He was looking at the glistening, mildewed walls of his own coffin.

He wandered through caverns and halls. Incomplete galleries. Raw, unfinished bedrock. He was travelling downward through the strata, down through fossil layers. A coal-stripe of rainforest. Distant millennia compressed to a sliver of carbon crystal. The walls glittered with crushed shell and silica.

He once heard that a group of Soviet dissidents, exiled to work in a Siberian mine, discovered a mammoth preserved in ice. They cut strips and chewed it like jerky. It kept them alive.

*   *   *

Long corridors. Dormitories and offices. Desks and typewriters matted with stone dust. A military situation room frozen in time. Cold war Soviet maps. Portraits of Lenin. Rusted telex machines. Heavy dial phones.

Metal-frame furniture. Nothing to burn.

How much further should he explore? The plank was half burned down. He should head back.

He crouched and examined the tunnel floor. Fresh footprints in the dust. The grip-tread of his own heavy snowboots. And a second set of prints heading deeper into the tunnels.

He measured his foot against the print. Whoever had recently walked down this passageway wore small boots with chevron tread.

A white tiled chamber, dazzling after miles of drab concrete.

Nail knew he should turn back and head for the surface, but he was overcome by curiosity. This vast subterranean necropolis held secrets. He and Gus were in a hopeless situation, injured and marooned. Maybe if Nail pushed further, travelled deeper into the tunnel complex, he might unearth some kind of salvation.

Lockers, shower heads, a hatch in the floor.

Chemical warfare suits in the lockers. Rubber hoods with glass eye-holes.

The room was a decontamination suite. Soldiers could wash away radioactive fallout, unzip their suits, climb down the shaft and seal themselves inside the hermetic environment of Level Zero.

Nail approached the floor hatch. A hinged lid like the turret hatch of a tank. He heaved the door open. A gust of foetid air from far below ground. His torch fluttered and died.

Absolute dark. Nail fumbled in his pocket for his lighter. Three strikes. Sparks, then a steady flame. He re-lit the plank of wood.

He looked down the shaft beside him. Walls lit by flickering flame-light. For a moment, deep at the bottom of the shaft, he thought he glimpsed a figure looking up at him.

*　　　*　　　*

Nail returned to the bunker entrance an hour later. He carried a wooden chair over his shoulder. He smashed the chair and put the pieces on the fire.

Gus sat by the fire and rocked back and forth. The man was clearly in agony, sweating the pain minute by minute.

Nail chiselled ice from the wall with a spanner.

'Rub it on your burns. It'll help.'

'You found some wood.'

'There are some bunks down there. And some tables and chairs. Dormitories for the team that built the place. Enough wood to buy us some thinking time.'

'Nothing to eat, I bet.'

'I'll check the Skidoo panniers in a minute. I need to sit down a while. I'm exhausted.'

They dried their boots over the fire.

They heard a thud against the bunker door. Then another. Fists pounded. Fingers scratched.

'I truly don't get it,' said Gus. 'Can they smell us? Is that it? How do they know we are in here? Some kind of super-sense?'

'They can smell you all right. You stink like cooked bacon.'

They sat by the fire for an hour. A gentle draught drew wood-smoke down the tunnel like cigarette fumes sucked into a smoker's lungs. They listened to fists thump against the doors.

Gus watched the smoke.

'Are there vents down there? A second exit?'

'Fuck knows. It goes on for miles. A secret city. Some kind of major naval facility.'

'How many of them do you think are out there?' asked Gus.

'Two, I reckon. They're half frozen. We could get round them easily enough. If more show up I'll go out there and kill them. Thin out the herd. They're slow. They're stupid. I could do it. Wouldn't be a problem.'

'My face. Is it bad?'

'Yeah, it's pretty bad.'

'If I asked you to kill me, if it came down to it, would you help?'

Nail turned away.

A sudden flashback. The big argument. Mal shouting and cursing, jabbing his finger. A blur of steel as Nail lashed out. That shrill, bubbling squeal. That gush of arterial spray.

Nail hadn't slept for a month. Scared to close his eyes.

'Maybe it won't come to that.'

Nail pushed a couple more chair legs on to the fire.

'We have to get back to Rampart,' said Gus. 'That's our only chance. There will be food, heat and morphine. I'm in so much pain.'

'Let me think it over.'

A couple of nights earlier Nail had sat in the bridge of *Hyperion* unable to sleep. He sat in the captain's chair and looked at the stars. He was joined by Reverend Blanc. They made small talk. Little more than noise. But he could tell straight away she knew his big secret. She seemed too pleasant, too casual. Somehow she had figured out he killed Mal.

Maybe Jane and her friends were dead. Maybe they were ripped apart or died in the fire. But perhaps they escaped *Hyperion*. They might have taken refuge on Rampart armed with shotguns. Would Jane shoot on sight? What would he do, if their situation were reversed? *Sorry, guys. I thought she was one of those infected freaks.*

'I don't want to worry you,' said Gus quietly, 'but I've been watching the shadows behind you for a while and I swear there is someone standing against the far wall.'

Nail slowly turned around. The fire cast flickering shadows across the tunnel walls. He saw a figure in heavy snow gear half hidden in darkness.

Nail stood up.

'Hi,' he said. 'You're welcome to join us.'

No response.

He took a burning chair leg from the fire and approached the figure.

A Con Amalgam parka patched with duct tape.

'I'm Nail. Nail Harper.'

No reply.

'Hello? Can you hear me?'

He held up the chair leg so he could see the face beneath the hood. Chapped, peeling skin. Mad, staring eyes.

'Nikki. It's Nikki.'

The Plan

Jane and Ghost fled the island. Punch and Sian were close behind. They ran headlong. Jane was glad to trip over rocks. Rocks meant they were still close to shore. If they found themselves running through pristine snow it meant they had blundered inland and were running further and further from safety.

They scrambled down basalt boulders and ran out on to the frozen sea. They skidded and struggled to keep balance. The glow of the burning ship stained the ice blood red.

Jane had the only flashlight. They followed her lead.

'Keep together. Don't get separated.'

A succession of muffled thumps behind them. Floor by floor, room by room, *Hyperion* was blowing itself to bits. Grenades strapped to propane cylinders. Ghost's failsafe plan. If infected passengers broke through the barricades they would be incinerated. But localised detonations had run out of control. One by one the ship's fuel tanks exploded fore and aft, blasting holes in the hull, jetting flame through corridors and stairwells.

'We have to slow down,' shouted Jane. 'This is fresh ice. I don't want to break the crust and fall into the sea.'

They slowed from a run to a walk.

'Are you folks all right?' she asked. 'Everyone okay?'

She and Ghost had been in their room when the attack began. They were lying on the rug, listening to Johnny Cash and talking about the life they would build when they got home. They heard shouting. They heard a fight. '*Breakout.*' They had the presence of mind to grab polar coats and glacier boots.

The corridor outside their room was filled with bitter smoke. Thermite detonations nearby. They covered their mouths to mask acrid fumes. Burning paint. Melting metal.

They ran on deck. Fire from below. Windows blew out. A row of burning lifeboats. The zodiac was reduced to scraps of burning rubber hanging from a crane.

Punch and Sian had already retired to bed. They fled the ship wearing tracksuits and sneakers.

'We're fine,' said Sian, starting to shiver uncontrollably.

Jane switched off her flashlight. They stood in the dark.

'We have to get moving,' said Punch.

'Everyone keep calm,' said Jane.

'There.' A green, pulsing glow high above them in the fog. One of the aircraft warning strobes at the corner of the rig. 'The west leg,' she said. 'Come on.'

Jane helped Sian. Ghost helped Punch.

They hurried across the ice. They were beneath the refinery, heading for the south leg. They ran so long Jane wondered if they had missed their target and were fleeing blindly out into the Barents Sea.

'Do you think they are following us?' asked Punch.

'We've outrun them for now,' said Jane. 'But yeah, if we hang around long enough they'll catch up.'

The south leg. A Cyclopean cylinder of steel. Jane's flashlight played across a wall of metal studded with bolts and seams like the suture marks of an operation scar.

'Jane,' shouted Ghost.

She turned. A forklift truck drove straight at her. Pallet prongs slammed into the steel wall either side of her head. Wheels span on ice.

'What the fuck?'

An infected crewman part-melded to the controls.

Ghost grabbed the cab cage and kicked at the driver. Flesh tore. The crewman ripped away from the forklift and fell on the ice, steering wheel welded to his hands. Ghost stamped on the man's head until it burst.

'*Konecranes*. Not one of ours.'

'Must be from *Hyperion*. Most liners have a big marshalling area amidships. Side doors in the hull.'

'He just fell out and started driving around?'

'Sure. Why not?'

Punch and Sian hugged each other for warmth.

'Hold on, guys,' said Ghost. 'Nearly home.'

'I think the rope is round the side.'

They circled the leg and found a knotted rope dangling from the mist like a ladder to heaven. Jane seized the rope and climbed upwards into nothing. The platform lift was parked four metres above them. There was a brief silence, then a metallic grind as the lift descended to the ice. They climbed aboard. Jane hit Up.

'So fucking cold,' said Punch.

'Soon be warm,' said Ghost. 'A couple more minutes and we'll be inside.'

It wasn't until Sian collapsed they realised she had been stabbed in the side and her red tracksuit was crisp with frozen blood.

They carried Sian to the canteen. They laid her on a table. She tried to sit up. They pushed her down.

Jane ran to Rye's old room and swept medical supplies into a plastic bag. Bandages. Sterile dressings.

Jane examined the wound. Sian yelped and hit her. Punch held Sian's arms. She turned her head to avoid looking at the hole in her hip.

Jane wriggled on surgical gloves. She selected tweezers from an instrument pack. She sterilised the tweezers with a Zippo flame then dug into the wound. Sian writhed. Jane extracted a big, rusted woodscrew dripping gobbets of flesh.

'Any idea when it happened?' asked Jane.

'That last explosion as we reached the boat deck. I didn't feel it at the time. Too much going on.'

Jane swabbed the wound and taped a dressing in place.

'It should be okay, as long as you keep it clean. Let me rustle up some painkillers.' She dug in the bag.

'Did anyone see what happened to Gus?' asked Ghost.

'No,' said Jane.

'How about Nail? Did anyone see what happened to him?'

'No.'

'Yakov? How about Yakov?'

'Dead,' said Sian, struggling to sit up.

'Are you sure?'

'Punch and I ran from our room. He went back for his sneakers. I was alone on the upper deck. Just for a moment. Yakov was below me on the promenade. He was fighting off a guy in clown costume. Other passengers showed up. They had him cornered. I called to him. I leaned over the railing and held out my arm. I told him to jump for my hand. I don't know. I still think he could have made it. I could have hauled him up. He pulled the pin from a grenade with his teeth and held it beneath his chin. He looked up, looked me straight in the eye. I shouted. He just kept looking at me. I was the last thing he saw.'

'Jesus,' said Punch. 'I barely spoke a word to the man. He seemed nice, though. Quiet, but nice.'

'Bollocks,' said Jane. 'Don't give me that. He was one of Nail's muscle clones. None of you could stand the guy.'

'I asked him to sign his name on a couple of safety chits,' said Ghost. 'He put a cross. I don't think he could write at all.'

'How do you think they got in?' asked Punch. 'I swear those barricades were solid.'

'There were two waves,' said Jane. 'The first bunch, the bunch in fancy dress, they didn't trip any grenades. I heard screaming and shouting long before the first grenade blew. They must have found a way to circumvent the barricades. A back door. Something we missed. God knows how. I swear we had all the exits covered. But they just showed up in the corridors like they had been invited, like someone let them in. They second wave smashed their way inside. They crashed the party. They wanted some of the action, and that's when the fires began.'

'We should lower the platform lift,' said Punch. 'Some of the other guys might have survived.'

Jane checked her watch.

'It's been nearly two hours. If anyone stayed aboard *Hyperion*, hid or something, they burned. The ship was gutted, top to bottom. And if they made it over the side, they died of exposure. Face it. We are the only ones left.'

'Yeah.'

'And you know what? A little part of me is glad. Happy families. But look around. Whole lot of empty chairs. Whole lot of dead guys. Four of us left. Are we just going to sit around all nice and cosy and watch each other die?'

'It might be better if they didn't make it,' said Ghost. 'Nail. Better if he doesn't show up again.'

'Why's that?' asked Sian.

'I'm pretty sure he killed Mal.'

'You're kidding me.'

'There was some kind of argument, some kind of confrontation.'

'Jesus.'

'He might not even be Nail Harper. He might be using a stolen name.'

'Christ.'

'Nothing we could prove.'

'What happened? What was it all about?'

'There was some dealing going on. Murky shit. Even if he made it off *Hyperion*, he's too dangerous to allow back on the rig. I vote we pull up the drawbridge. Fuck him.'

284

'That's pretty harsh,' said Sian.

''Come on,' said Jane. 'Is there anyone in this room who isn't glad he's gone?'

Jane sealed the blast door that connected the accommodation block to the rest of the rig. She ripped the switch panel from the wall with a knife.

The rig was now a fortress. Accommodation Module A was their castle keep. Even if anyone managed to climb aboard Rampart they would freeze in unheated rooms and passageways.

'It's minus fifty out on the island,' said Ghost. 'Insane wind-chill. No one could survive more than a couple of minutes.'

'Let's be double-sure. Just for the next day or two, so we can sleep safe in our beds. Touch the wires and the door opens, all right? Otherwise it stays closed.'

'We should have stayed here all along. My idea to move to *Hyperion*.'

'It's all right.'

'It's not all right. People died.'

'I crashed the fucking ship into the island, so we've both got blood on our hands. But no more grenades, okay? No more booby traps. We've had enough excitement.'

'None left. We used them up.'

'The fire probably took care of most of them,' said Ghost. 'The infected. Everyone aboard the ship is toast. Couple of hundred left on the ice. They won't last. Nothing can survive that intense cold for long.'

'Great. But our ride home just went up in smoke.'

'I'm heading downstairs for a while,' said Ghost. 'I need a bit of quiet time.'

Jane returned to the canteen. She sipped tea.

'How's Ghost doing?' asked Punch.

'He'll get his shit together soon enough. He's a practical guy.

Not the kind to sit and mope. He wants to get out of here as much as any of us.'

'So what now?'

'We leave,' said Jane. 'We've wasted too much time pursuing abortive schemes. No more home-made rafts. No more sit-and-wait. We cook up a solid strategy right here, right now. Seriously. We've spent all our time reacting to events. Fuck that.'

'We should head for Canada,' said Punch. 'Fetch the snow-mobiles from the bunker. Load up and run for it before the sea melts. Yeah, I know. It's an old idea. You've heard it before. But I still say it's our best shot. It's mid-winter. The sea is cold as it is going to get. If we are going to travel, if we are going to make use of the ice, we'd better do it now.'

'We would never make it,' said Jane. 'Not all four of us. Too much kit to haul. Food, clothes, tents. Besides, what if the sea didn't completely freeze this winter? Global warming. I doubt we have a clear run to Canada, even now. We need to do better. We need a fighting chance.'

'So what's on your mind?'

'Get your coats. It's easier if I show you.'

Jane led Punch and Sian to a gantry overlooking the corner of the rig. Fog-shrouded walkways. Pipework and decking slick with ice.

They stood shivering in the darkness. Jane shone a heavy spotlight downward at one of the massive cables that anchored the refinery to the seabed.

'What if we detach the cables and float the refinery free?' said Jane. 'We already lost one of the cables when *Hyperion* collided with the refinery. Three left.'

'How do you plan on doing that?' asked Punch. 'Each weighs the same as a battleship. You need monster equipment to manip-ulate them.'

'There's no way on earth we could cut the cable. It would take an atom bomb. But look at the coupling. That's the weak point.

286

It's anchored by a four-tonne pin. If we could kick the pin out of its socket then the cable would drop and Rampart would drift free.'

'Be my guest.'

'That stuff from the seismic research station. The explosives. There should still be a bunch of C4 left, yes? Couple of cases at least. Ghost hid it in the bunker. We could pack a big wad of plastic round each pin and touch it off. Fire the pin clean out of the coupling. It would be our last roll of the dice, but worth a try.'

'Yeah. Fuck it. Let's go out with a bang.'

Jane went looking for Ghost. She found him on C deck, the lowest level of the accommodation block. Dark, low ceilings. Pipes and discarded tools. The kind of place a grease monkey like Ghost would instinctively make his den.

Ghost was stripped to the waist. He stood over a table. He was strapping a couple of SCUBA tanks together.

Jane kissed him between the shoulder blades. She put an arm round his waist.

'You okay?'

'Yeah,' he said. 'Just got a little frustrated at myself. I got seduced by *Hyperion*. The luxury. You were right all along. We should have stayed here. Kept focused.'

'I've got a plan. Fetch explosives from the bunker. Blow the lock-pins and release the tethers. Float our way out of here. What do you think?'

'I think you're stronger than me, and smarter than me, and if you want to give it a shot then I am along for the ride.'

'Cool.'

'So you want to head back to the island?'

'One last time.'

'Then I've got something that may help.' He shouldered the SCUBA tanks. 'Let's go up to the helipad. I want to show you something.'

*   *   *

The helipad. Big as a basketball court. A big red H lit by a ring of floodlights. Ghost wheeled an office chair to the centre of the H and draped a parka over it. He helped Jane strap the SCUBA tanks to her back. Thick hose led to a spray gun.

'Diesel pressurised with nitrogen,' said Ghost. 'Press that button on the barrel. That's a butane lighter from the kitchen. The igniter. Gives you a little nozzle flame. The big trigger releases fuel. Watch yourself, all right? Brace your legs, and don't pull the trigger unless you mean it.'

Jane stood twenty metres from the chair. She sparked the igniter. She adjusted her grip on the spray gun and pulled the trigger. A roaring, high-pressure jet of fuel-fire engulfed the office chair. Upholstery foam shrivelled and dripped. The plastic chair withered in a hurricane blast of flame.

Hunger

Nail and Gus sat by the fire.

'I feel like a caveman,' said Gus, prodding the embers.

'That's because we are living in a cave.'

'I could use a big juicy bison about now. What do you reckon? The infected. They hate fire, right? Maybe we could cook the virus out of them.'

'You want to eat a sailor?'

'Right now I'm prepared to give it a shot.'

'You are the sickest of fucks. So how are you feeling? Hunger aside?'

'Parched,' said Gus. 'It's fucking ridiculous. We can't even go outside to grab some snow.'

He stroked the remains of his beard. Weeping blisters. Scorched stubble clotted with pus.

'The burns feel like they are tightening up, you know? Like the skin is contracting. I'm frightened to move in case I split right open.'

'Maybe you should lie still a while.' Nail was preoccupied with his own misery. He was starting to sweat cold turkey. He didn't want to talk.

'The pain comes and goes. Ice helps.'

'Maybe we should grease you up. I think that's what you're supposed to do with bad burns. Seal the wound.'

'What's she doing?'

Nikki stood at the bunker entrance, ear to the door. She was mumbling to herself.

'Is she talking to them? Look at her. She speaks. She listens. She speaks again. She's holding a conversation.'

'Trying to work out how many of those infected fucks are out there waiting for us,' said Nail.

'Looks like she's having a nice long chat with them through the door. They act in concert sometimes. You've seen that, right? Watched them out on the ice? What if she can read their thoughts? What if some people can actually tune in?'

'Doubt it.'

'Where's her boat? If she made it back here she must have a boat.'

'Yeah.'

'She's insane, you know that, right? All that stuff last night. All that babble. Walking cities. Oceans of fire. She's lost it.'

'She sounds better this morning. She's actually making sense.'

'Do me a favour, all right?' said Gus. 'Don't leave me alone with her. Just don't leave me alone.'

'I'm going to get some wood. Take it easy.'

Nail stood up.

'Hey, Nikki,' he called. 'I'm going to fetch some more firewood. Care to join me?'

He led Nikki deep into the tunnels. They each held a piece of burning bed frame as a torch.

Damp concrete. Nail hadn't been outside for days. There would quickly come a time when he wouldn't want to leave. He would become habituated to the soothing silence of the passageways. A creature of the shadows.

'Better watch our step,' he said as they traversed damp, subterranean caverns. 'This place is only half built. They might have dug vertical shafts.'

'I think I might know this place better than you. These days I think of it as home.'

'What about food? What have you been eating this past couple of weeks?'

'Cans. I ate them all. None left.'

'So do you want to tell me about it?'

'Tell you what?' she asked.

'You took my boat. You sailed away. Now you are back, talking trippy bullshit about walking cities. Did you leave at all? Jane told us you sent radio messages. You went south, then sank. Was it all lies? Were you here all along?'

'It was a long journey. I passed Greenland. I nearly reached Norway. There were storms. I'm not entirely sure what happened. My memory plays tricks.'

'But why? Why come back? All that effort to get away, and you came back. If Europe has turned into some God-awful hell-world I need to know.'

'I saw cities on fire. And other stuff. I saw cities get up and walk. Strange creatures. Leviathans. It was madness. I knew it at the time. I knew it wasn't real.'

'But what will we find?' asked Nail. 'Your psychosis aside. If we actually make it back to Britain what will be waiting for us?'

'They nuked the cities. The armies. The governments. Scorched earth. Whatever else I dreamed, that much was real.'

'So if we head south we'll hit a radiation cloud. Is that why you came back?'

'I honestly don't know for sure. I was at sea, and then I was here. I can't explain it.'

'But where's the boat?'

'The hull was crushed by ice as I approached the island. It's at the bottom of the sea.'

'Shit.'

'Maybe I didn't come back at all. Maybe I'm dead. Maybe I'm a ghost.'

'You're sure they nuked the cities?'

'A cleansing fire.'

'I'm from Manchester. You know that, right?'

'Rubble. Plutonium dust. It'll be safe to go back and take a look in a half million years or so.'

'Fucking ironic. Jane and Ghost. Plotting how to get home, day and night. And it's all gone.'

'Are you going to tell them?' asked Nikki.

'We don't exactly get along.'

'My turn to wonder. Why are you and Gus skulking in this bunker when you could be back aboard Rampart? Did they run you off with a pitchfork?'

'Like I say. We don't get along.'

'Well, that's a shame. They've got drugs and dressings. Gus will die without them.'

'So why did you come back to this island? Okay: they nuked the cities. Plenty of other places you could have gone. Plenty of wilderness. Why here? This place is death.'

'I love it. I truly love it.'

'Queen of the Damned. Jesus. This gulag has driven you batshit.'

An air shaft. Nail looked up. Massive turbine blades dripped rust.

'I bet they were going to garrison whole armies down here.'

'This is my little camp,' said Nikki.

The installation manager's office. A leather chair and a desk. A faded Soviet flag and a little plaster bust of Lenin.

A mural. Farm workers driving tractors and combine harvesters across a golden field of wheat. They gazed towards Lenin, who stood on the horizon shooting rays like the rising sun.

Nail examined a photograph on the wall.

'Brezhnev. Early eighties.'

Scattered tins on the desk.

'Like I said. Ate them all, I'm afraid.'

Nail picked through wrappers and cans. He found a muesli bar.

'Hey,' said Nikki. 'How did I miss that?'

Nail split the bar in half.

'What about Gus?' asked Nikki. 'What about his share?'

Nail didn't reply. He crammed the bar in his mouth. He dropped crumbs. He picked them from the floor and ate them.

They found a couple of Russian Kraz trucks and a bulldozer parked in a cavern. The vehicles were slowly crumbling to rust. Nikki found a copy of *Hustler* in the cab. She tucked it into her coat pocket.

'Kindling?'

'Toilet paper.'

'Maybe there's some petrol in these tanks,' said Nail.

Nikki kicked a fuel tank bolted to the back of a cab. Dull gong. Empty.

'What about guns?' asked Nail. 'Find any weapons? Any old AKs lying around?'

'No. I looked. There's nothing.'

There was a leather jacket balled up on the bulldozer seat. Nikki checked the pockets.

'Give me your knife,' she said. She cut a small strip of leather and folded it into her mouth like a stick of gum. She cut a strip for Nail.

'Go ahead. Chew. It'll fool your stomach. Keep the hunger pangs at bay.'

'Not exactly a permanent solution.'

'It buys us time.'

They returned to the bunker entrance with armfuls of wood. They dumped the wood on the floor and fed the fire.

'Miss me?' asked Nail.

'Fuck you.' Gus smiled. He was shivering.

'Are you all right?'

'I need to get back to Rampart, otherwise I'm a dead man. They've got morphine. They've got antibiotics.'

Nail thought it over. Would Jane shoot him if he tried to board Rampart? Probably.

'Their medical supplies were pretty depleted,' said Nail. 'No guarantee they could help.'

'At least they've got hot food and water. I don't want to die on this concrete floor, stinking of my own shit. I want to be warm and clean. I want to die in a bed.'

Nikki dragged a snowmobile to the bunker door. She stood on the saddle and chipped away at ice accumulated at the top of the doorframe. She threw Nail and Gus a chunk of icicle to suck.

'So,' said Nail. 'Duke of Amberley. What was that all about?'

'Amberley. West Country. A cute village on the side of a hill. That's where I'll go when we get home.'

'Yeah?'

'Everyone has their heaven. Amberley is mine.'

'Right.'

'There's a house at the end of a long, country lane. I glimpsed it through trees. Ivy and Tudor beams. That's where I'll go.'

'But Duke?'

'Our old lives are gone. We can be whoever we like. A lord. A duke. A prince. Who is left to say No?'

Gus fell asleep an hour later.

Nail put more wood on the fire. He took the strip of chewed leather from his mouth and threw it into the flames. The leather crisped and curled. Nikki sat on the other side of the fire.

'Hell of a way to check out,' said Nail. 'Stuck down this hole, swigging our own piss.'

Nikki ignored him.

'So how about it?' asked Nail. 'Do you actually want to live? Do you actually want to get out of here? Or is this your new home? I know why I am hiding in this fucking mausoleum. But I don't fully understand why you came back to the island, and I don't understand why you are lurking down here instead of back aboard Rampart. You deserve desolation? You deserve hell? Is that honestly the reason?' She didn't reply.

'Canada,' said Nail. 'That's what I reckon. If a person took one of the snowmobiles they could get a long way before the fuel ran out. They would need stuff from Rampart, though. Food. Better clothes. You could tag along. Surely you don't want to stay here and starve?'

Nikki pushed more wood into the fire.

'I wish you could understand what we have here,' she said. 'Every one of you aboard Rampart was on the run, fleeing the world. Why are you all so anxious to get back home? It's all here. Everything we need. You just need to embrace the silence. Let it enter your head, fill your thoughts.'

'Everything we need? We're sitting here eating a leather jacket. You want to join those fucks out there? Get yourself bitten or something? Is that your big plan? Whatever. You can stay here if you like. Hang out with your invisible friend. But I want to live. I don't want to die in this sewer. I want to live.'

They sat in silence. Nail winced and clutched his stomach. Cramps. He stretched. Hunger had intensified from vague discomfort to an acute, stabbing pain. He hated himself for what he was about to do.

He struggled to his feet, careful not to look at Gus. He took a burning chair leg from the fire.

'I'm going for a walk,' he said. 'I'm going to look around for anything useful. I might be gone a while.'

Nikki nodded and smiled.

He headed into the darkness of the tunnel mouth leaving Nikki alone with Gus.

Nail returned an hour later. He sat by the campfire. He looked into the flames.

Nail was a murderer. He had stabbed Mal in the throat, then crouched over the dying man and begged forgiveness. He tried

295

to stem the flow, got sprayed as he tried to patch the slit jugular with bloody fingers.

Scrubbing in the shower. Blood on white porcelain. Scrubbing for hours.

Now this. Step by step into hell.

He gestured to Gus's immobile body.

'How's he doing?'

'Dead.'

'Yeah?'

'Yeah.'

'Well,' he heard himself say, 'then I suppose he won't mind.'

He sat and stared into the flames.

Nikki flicked open her knife, slit the fabric of Gus's trouser leg and cut strips of flesh from his thigh.

They roasted flesh over the campfire. Nail wept as he ate.

The Vault

'There's no reason all four of us should travel to the island,' said Jane. 'I'll take Punch for company.'

'I should go,' said Ghost. 'I know the bunker.'

'No point,' said Jane. 'My plan, my trip. Let me achieve something for once.'

Ghost drew a map.

'All right. The explosives are five levels down in a storage vault. You'll pass plenty of side tunnels. Ignore them. Stick to the main passageways. I spent two days down there exploring the bunker. Seemed like there was no end to the place.'

Jane folded the crude treasure map and tucked it in her pocket. They were sitting in the observation bubble. It was late January. A faint azure tint to the southern sky.

'Spring is coming,' said Ghost. 'We should have our first real sunrise in a couple of months.'

'*Hyperion* will float free. What little is left of it. Probably sink like a stone.'

'All those guys who died. None of it is down to you. They made their own luck.'

'How much explosive do you reckon we have stored in the bunker?'

'We used up the grenades. Used some C4 out on the ice, but there's still a bunch left. Couple of cases at least. Thirty or forty kilos. Enough to put an office block on the moon. You'll need a backpack.'

'I'll take the flamethrower as well.'

'I doubt you'll have much use for it. Most of the infected crowd from *Hyperion* fried aboard the ship. The rest seem to be succumbing to the cold. As long as you keep running, you should be okay. Once you reach the bunker you'll be home and dry.'

Jane and Punch dressed in the airlock. Ventile over-trousers. Heavy snowboots secured by ankle latches. Triple-seal parkas: zips, toggles, Velcro.

Jane shrugged on the flamethrower harness. Punch unsheathed the shotgun and chambered rounds.

They stood on the platform lift and descended the south leg of the refinery. They halted the elevator two metres from the surface and slid down a rope to the ice.

They walked across the frozen ocean.

'Ghost says avoid blue ice,' advised Jane. 'It's fresh. Looks pretty, but you could drop through it like a trapdoor. You won't get any warning.'

The sky was pale pink. They had a clear view of *Hyperion*. It was a scorched shell. The cabins were burned out. The decks were buckled and black. The funnels had collapsed.

She could smell it. Burned plastic. Cooked meat.

They could see a handful of infected passengers out on the ice. Black dots on the slopes of the island like sheep on a distant hillside.

'Let's make this a quick trip,' said Jane. 'Smash and grab. Hopefully, this will be the last time any of us leave the rig. The last time before home, anyway.'

A woman in a gold ball gown stood alone on the ice, slump-shouldered and forlorn. She saw Punch and Jane. She staggered forward, arms stretched towards them.

Jane checked the little blue igniter flame at the mouth of the flamethrower barrel.

'Let's see what this thing can do.'

Punch stood clear.

Jane braced her legs, took aim and pulled the trigger. She fired. An arc of burning fuel spat twenty metres. The woman was engulfed in fire. She stumbled. She fell to her knees. A second burst. Clothes and hair seared away by a typhoon of flame. She crawled on her hands. She fell forward and slowly melted into the ice.

They hurried across the frozen sea to the shore. They climbed on to the jetty and up concrete steps to the bunker entrance. Two infected crewmen were slumped in front of the bunker doors. Officers in brass-button dress uniform. Ice crackled as they struggled to their feet.

Punch kicked their legs from under them, and pulped their heads with the butt of his shotgun.

'The chain is gone,' said Jane. She tugged at the doors. 'They seem to be tied shut from the inside. Do you have a knife?'

Jane took off her glove, squirmed her fingers through the gap and sawed through the rope.

'Do you think someone made it off *Hyperion*?' asked Punch.

'Well, I can't picture any of those zombie fucks tying a reef knot.'

They entered the bunker. They swung the heavy doors shut and propped them closed with a snowmobile.

Punch examined the campfire. He kicked the burning planks. Burst of sparks.

'Fresh wood. Someone was here a moment ago.'

'There's a bone. A rib.'

Jane stood at the tunnel mouth and shouted into the darkness.

'Nail? Gus? Hello?'

'Must be Nail,' said Punch. 'Anyone else would come running.'

'Hello? Anyone?'

Jane released a puff of fire down the dark passageway, a rolling burst of flame. Brief glimpse of cracked concrete. Tunnel walls receded to vanishing point.

'Let's get what we came for,' she said.

Punch checked the map.

'Five levels down, then keep heading straight. Be all right as long as we don't deviate.'

'Don't creep,' said Jane. 'Let him hear us coming.'

They trudged down a passageway wide as a subway tunnel. Their flashlights lit damp concrete archways Bedrock ribbed with reinforced pillars.

'How much further?' asked Punch.

'Quite a way. Ghost hid the explosives in one of the deeper galleries. Can't find it by accident. You have to know where to look.'

They approached something blue on the tunnel floor. A snow-boot. Jane crouched and examined the shoe.

'Size ten. There's blood in it. Blood on the floor.'

Her flashlight lit a trail of drips.

They kept walking.

The tunnel terminated in a massive lead door. A skull etched above a cloverleaf radiation emblem.

Jane wiped away stone dust.

Фпасиость/*Danger*

Радиацига/*Radiation*

Beneath it, written in blood:

HELLBOUND

Jagged letters. Splatters and drips.

'This place stinks of madness,' said Punch.

Jane examined the blood. It was black. It crumbled and flaked to the touch. The letters had been daubed by a gloved hand.

'You know what?' she said. 'Whatever happened down here

simply isn't our problem. I'm just not interested. We get what we want then leave.'

The vault was big as a church nave. The walls and ceiling were lagged with lead plate. The chamber was built, Jane supposed, to house the decommissioned reactor core of a Soviet submarine or a nuclear ice-breaker. Relics of the Northern Fleet. The sleek hunter-killers that operated out of Archangel, prowling beneath the polar ice cap, waiting for their comms to flash red and chatter launch codes and target coordinates. The crusted, corroded reactor would be towed down the tunnel on a freight wagon and parked at the centre of the vault. The vault would be filled with salt and the doors sealed for a quarter of a million years.

The vault had been used as a temporary store for excavation equipment. There were picks and shovels, a jumble of hard-hats, and a couple of pneumatic drills propped against a wall. Hard to know why construction suddenly ceased. But the mining teams downed tools one day and didn't resume.

Tin mugs and plates. A broken welder's mask used as an ashtray. A bottle of Stolichnaya long since evaporated dry.

Punch pulled off his gauntlets and began to load his backpack. He pulled ammo boxes from the shelves. He flipped the latches and removed patties of explosive wrapped in brown paper.

Jane explored corner shadows. A scoop-digger with a broken track.

Something smelled bad. She lifted the edge of a tarpaulin. An emaciated hand. She pulled the tarpaulin aside.

'My God,' said Jane.

'What have you found?' Punch kept packing.

'A body.'

Jane crouched over the body. The corpse was jammed in the digger scoop. Thighs, calves and buttocks were gone. The upper arms, belly and chest had been flayed. Slow decay, despite the cold.

'Who is it?' asked Punch. 'Can you tell?'

Jane trained her flashlight on the bearded face. Sunken cheeks.

A rictus grin. Scraps of neck flesh. Fragments of a barbed tattoo.

'Gus. I think it's Gus. It looks like someone ate him.'

Punch stuffed a tin of detonators into the side pocket of his backpack.

'Ate him?'

'He's been butchered. Someone used a knife. Did a thorough job.'

'Let's get off this fucking island.'

'Punch,' shouted Jane. She trained her flashlight on the vault door. A figure in a red hooded parka was struggling to heave the door shut. 'Don't let him lock us in.'

Punch hurriedly shouldered his shotgun. He shot wide, and blew a crater in the lead wall. He fired again. The impact scoured a deep trench in the closing door. He threw the gun. It skittered across the concrete floor and jammed the vault door just as it closed.

He dived for the gun and grabbed the butt. He wrestled for the weapon with an unseen adversary. He pulled the trigger. Muzzle-flash. Blast like a thunderclap. A scream of rage.

'Punch, get out of the way,' shouted Jane.

Punch rolled clear. Jane fired the flamethrower. Screams. She ran across the room. Second burst. The walls and door dripped flame. Lead rivulets like lava. The chamber filled with smoke.

Jane kicked the door wide with her boot. A puff of fire from the flamethrower lit an empty tunnel. Scraps of smouldering fabric on the floor.

'Run, you fuck,' she shouted, her voice turned metallic by the tunnel walls. 'Keep running.'

Punch picked up his smouldering shotgun.

'Think it was Nail?' he asked.

'Who else would it be? Fetch the backpack. Let's go.'

They trudged upward, counting the levels. Jane turned round every few paces to check they weren't followed. Brief burst of flame at each junction. She inspected every crevice in case Nail was crouched waiting to launch a second ambush. He was injured but desperate enough to attack.

A distant wind-rush turned to an oceanic roar as they approached the bunker entrance. They leaned into the hurricane. The doors were open and a storm was raging outside. Jane's torch lit swarming snow particles.

'Where the hell did this come from?' Punch shouted to be heard over wind-roar.

'We can beat it.'

'Maybe we should wait.'

'No. Got your radio? Call Ghost. Tell him to switch the refinery floodlights on full and hit the foghorn every twenty seconds. That should guide us home safe and sound.'

They set off into the storm. They descended the concrete steps and walked out on to the frozen sea. They bent double against the gale. Snow furled around them like thick smoke. They couldn't see the floodlights of the rig, but they could feel the foghorn every twenty seconds, a deep rumbling throb that pulsed deeper than incessant wind noise.

Jane turned to Punch. She lifted her ski mask.

'We're making good time,' she reassured him. 'We should see the floodlights any second.'

An infected passenger stumbled out of the blizzard. A man in a blue tracksuit. Jane fired her flamethrower at close range.

The man was blown from his feet like he was hit by a fire hose. He skidded backward across the ice, burning, flames whipped by the wind. He tried to sit up. A second blast put him down for good.

A sudden blow to her back sent Jane sprawling, face down. She slid into the burning man. Her arm caught alight. She slapped to extinguish the flames.

She scrambled to her feet. Punch was gone. His shotgun and backpack lay on the ice.

She shouted into the squalling wind.

'Punch?'

She fired the flamethrower straight up. Flickering flame-light. She looked around.

'Punch? 'Where are you?'

She thought she heard Punch call her name. She ran in pursuit, ran headlong into the blizzard, but found nothing but darkness and driving snow. She wanted to search but was fighting hypothermia.

Jane headed for Rampart, a lone figure struggling through the storm.

The Bomb

Sian sat in Rawlins's office and hit the foghorn every twenty seconds. Massive funnels at each corner of the rig blasted a mournful, booming note. The funnels were surrounded by safety barriers and ear-guard warnings. A deep rumble resonated through the superstructure like an earth tremor.

Jane climbed into the platform lift. She dragged Punch's back-pack on to the deck. She pressed Up. She collapsed against the railing and sank to her knees. Movement out of the corner of her eye. An infected man in a white tuxedo had gripped the platform lift as it began its ascent and was hauling himself over the railing.

Jane aimed the flamethrower and pulled the trigger. Dribble of fuel. No fire. The wind was too strong. The igniter flame wouldn't spark.

She aimed Punch's shotgun. Click of an empty chamber.

She struggled to her feet and backed away from the advancing man, holding the shotgun by the barrel and swinging it like a club.

Ghost sat in the observation bubble and watched the storm. He listened to Mahler.

'*Hey, Gee.*' Sian's voice.

'Yeah?'

'*They're coming up in the platform lift.*'

* * *

Ghost waited in the south leg airlock. The airlock was a padded chamber lined with lockers and snow gear. A porthole in the door allowed Ghost to examine the underside of the refinery, the girders and pipework lashed by the gale. Floodlights strung beneath the rig glowed through the storm like a row of weak suns.

A yellow warning strobe above the airlock door began to revolve, accompanied by an insistent warning beep. The platform lift was active. Ghost watched through the porthole as the elevator cage drew level with the door. Two figures crusted in ice. One figure was wearing a tuxedo. He had a melted face.

Ghost grabbed a snowboot from the airlock floor. He hit Open and reeled from the sudden wind-blast. The lumbering mutant reached for Jane as she crouched exhausted and helpless on the platform deck. Ghost wore the snowboot on his hand like a boxing glove. He punched the infected man in the face. Repeated blows. He drove the man to the edge of the platform and kicked him over the railing. He threw the blood-spattered boot over the side.

He dragged Jane inside and hit Close. The door slid shut and the roar of the storm was silenced.

Jane shrugged off the flamethrower and slumped to her knees. Ghost pulled back her hood and tugged off her ski mask. Her skin was blue. Her eyelids drooped like she was half asleep.

'Jane,' shouted Ghost. 'Hey. Come on.' He gently slapped her face left and right. 'Come on, girl. Focus.'

She coughed back to life.

'Get the pack,' she said. 'It's out on the lift.'

Second blast of blizzard wind as Ghost retrieved the backpack. He emptied it on to the airlock floor. Explosives. Detonators. He examined the shoulder straps. They had been cut with a sharp blade.

Jane had dropped the shotgun. Quick inspection. Burned stock. Scorched metal. The gun beyond use.

He checked the breech. No shells. He sniffed the gun. Pepper smell of cordite. Recently fired.

Jane's eyes fluttered like she was struggling to stay awake.

'Jane? Can you hear me? Where the fuck is Punch?'

Ghost helped Jane to her room. He helped her strip and stood with her beneath the shower until she revived. She stood beneath a torrent of hot water and basked in the heat.

She got out, towelled and dressed.

'So we are down to three,' said Ghost.

'Nothing I could do,' said Jane. 'Nothing at all.'

'Nail?'

'He's turned that bunker into a fucking abattoir.'

'I hope he comes aboard. I really do. I'll make it slow. I'll make it last days.'

Jane took a mug of coffee to the observation bubble.

Sian was watching the blizzard scour the tanks and gantries of the refinery. She was weeping.

Jane put a hand on her shoulder.

'Easier if we just died,' said Sian. 'It would be better than this. A moment of fear, a moment of pain, then nothing. This is worse. This is slow torture.'

'Yeah.'

'Everyone I ever knew is dead. Family. Friends. But I had Punch. I was all right as long as I had Punch.'

'Yeah.'

'I've got nothing left. Absolutely nothing. Bit by bit it all got stripped away.' She gestured to the snowstorm. 'This place is hell. Barren. Sterile. It's like the universe has taken off its mask and we can see its true face.'

'Want to open a bottle of wine?' asked Jane, and immediately regretted the lame suggestion. Failing as a priest, failing as a friend. Absurd to think there was any consolation she could offer in the face of absolute despair, some combination of words that would make it all better.

She sat down.

A few nights ago, she and Ghost lay in bed and planned the future of the human race.

'If there are kids,' said Ghost, 'will you tell them about Jesus?'

'No,' said Jane. 'I'm happy to be the last Christian. If they come across a Bible I will tell them it's all fairy tales and nonsense.'

Jane put her arm round Sian's shoulder. They sat in the dark as the Arctic storm raged around them.

Jane visited Rawlins's office. She thumbed through the personnel files. Gary Punch. She snipped his picture from the front page of his file.

She took the picture to the improvised chapel she had established in one of the dormitory rooms. She taped the photograph to the memorial wall.

She sat and contemplated the mug shots.

Crew who left aboard oil supply vessel *Spirit of Endeavour:*

Rosie Smith.

Pete Baxter.

Ricki Coulby.

Edgar Bardock.

Frank Rawlins, first to succumb to the infection.

Dr Rye. Missing. Presumed suicide.

Ivan and Yakov. Both ripped apart aboard *Hyperion.*

Mal. Murdered.

Gus. Murdered and eaten.

Nail's picture lay on a chair. Jane didn't want to add him to the memorial wall. He didn't deserve it. No one would pray for him.

The canteen kitchen.

Sian sat morose on a bar stool while Ghost greased the

damaged shotgun. He reassembled the weapon. He racked the slide. The mechanism jammed. He threw the gun down on the kitchen counter.

'Fucked. And Punch took all the ammunition.'

Ghost took a cleaver from a drawer.

'Want to help me patrol?'

They walked the perimeter of the rig. Ghost brought the ruined shotgun. He swung it round his head and flung it far as he could. They watched it fall to the ice two hundred metres below.

They looked towards the island.

'Nail can't stay out there for ever,' said Ghost. 'Nothing for him in that bunker. We've got food, heat, everything he needs. Sooner or later he'll try to make it aboard. I reckon he'll try to climb an anchor cable. Doubt he could make it, but he'll give it a shot.'

'What about Punch?' asked Sian. Jane hadn't told her about the cannibalised remains they found in the bunker.

'I don't think he's coming back.'

Ghost decided to give her a task, something to keep her occupied.

'Do me a favour. Disable the platform lift. Take out a fuse or something.'

Sian headed for the airlock. She opened the exterior door and walked out on to the platform. She could see infected passengers milling on the ice far below her. She reached for the platform controls. She hesitated, then pressed Down.

The lift descended the south leg of the refinery.

Infected *Hyperion* passengers and crew looked up. They saw Sian descending to meet them, and stretched their arms to reach her.

She opened the railing gate and closed her eyes, ready to be torn apart.

The platform jolted to a halt. Sian fell to her knees. The lift rose. She looked up. Ghost high above her, leaning out of the airlock door.

He dragged Sian back inside the rig. He helped her to her feet.

'We'll pretend that didn't happen, all right?'

Jane sat with Ghost in the canteen. They emptied the backpack. They contemplated the stack of explosives and detonators on the table in front of them. Bricks of C4 wrapped in paper. *DEMO-LITION CHARGE M112 WITH TAGGANT.*

'Sian's probably right,' said Jane. 'We're kidding ourselves. We're not moving an inch. We are trapped here for ever. This place is our tomb.'

'I don't know about that.'

'This is the endgame. Nobody is coming to save us. We've got no ride home. If the cables don't drop, we're done.'

'My dad died of stomach cancer,' said Ghost. 'He had a car, an E-type Jag. He was restoring it in his garage. He worked hard even though he wouldn't get to drive it. I asked why he bothered. He said, "Never leave a job half done."'

'I'm so tired.'

'We've got a plan. We've got things we can do, moves we can make. Still plenty of fight left.'

'Yeah,' sighed Jane. 'I suppose. But that's the problem. I can cope with despair. But hope keeps fucking me up.'

Ghost stood and began to stack the explosives into three separate piles.

'Come on,' he said. 'Get the job done.'

Ghost refilled the flamethrower. He used a SCUBA compressor to pump the tanks with diesel, and pressurise them with nitrogen.

They went outside and thawed the couplings. Jane fired a jet of flame at each giant lock-pin. Ice liquefied and steamed, exposing metal.

Jane held the flashlight while Ghost rigged the explosives. He took off his gloves. He unwrapped C4. He slapped patties of explosive against the massive cable coupling, punched them with his fist, moulded them into a single tight mass. He pointed to a nearby wall.

'This is good. This should work well. We're boxed in. Nice, enclosed space. It should focus the concussion. Be a hell of a bang when it goes.'

He pressed blasting caps into the clay with his thumb before the explosive froze too hard to penetrate. They weatherproofed each charge with garbage bags.

'What do you want to use for detonation cord?' asked Jane.

'Strip some wire from a few extension leads. Nothing much to it. All we need is enough copper thread to carry a single six-volt pulse. Click. Bang.'

They returned to the canteen and spliced wire. Heaters. Dehumidifiers. Computers. Cases prised open with a screwdriver. Flex stripped, coiled and stacked on a Formica tabletop.

'We need about two hundred and fifty metres for each charge. We'll run the cord to a central point. We have to blow all three charges at once. If we blow the cables one at a time the last rope will take the full weight of the rig. It will be under so much tension we'll never get the pin to release.'

'Right.'

'No screw-ups. No breaks in the wire. We get one shot at this. No second go.'

The storm cleared. They slung cable over their shoulders and headed outside.

Jane helped Ghost run wire from each explosive charge. They spooled flex along the walkways and metal steps. They taped the wires to girders and railings. The wires converged at the pump house, a cabin that housed monitor equipment for the three great distillation tanks.

They smashed a window and fed the cables inside. Ghost webbed the remaining windows with duct tape. Proof against the blast. He laid three pairs of ear-defenders on a desk.

One last inspection to check the charges were properly rigged and the detonator wire unbroken.

'Beautiful sky,' said Jane. She pulled back her hood and craned to see a dusting of stars. A delicate pink twilight to the east.

She looked out over the refinery. A crystal palace. White-on-white. Frosted steel. Cross-beams and scaffold towers dripping ice. Snow-dusted storage tanks. Crane jibs heavy with icicles. Every north-facing surface caked and glazed.

'Reckon Nail is lurking round here?' asked Jane.

'Keep a lookout for prints,' said Ghost. 'I doubt he could make it up the anchor cables, but he's desperate enough to try.' He lifted his boot and pointed at the sole. 'Zigzag tread, all right? Anything else is him.'

Ghost struggled to unscrew the cap of his hip flask with a gloved hand. He swigged.

'Back in a moment, all right?'

Ghost had spent the last hour thinking it through. This was their last chance of escape. If the anchor cables failed to detach they would be permanently marooned at the top of the world. In a few weeks the food and fuel would run out and they would be forced to choose between a knife-slash to the throat or a long walk in the snow. He pictured his body on a high gantry facing the sea. A grinning corpse cradling a blade. Maybe Jane's mummified cadaver would be beside him, holding his skeletal hand.

He walked to the corner of the rig. He took a fist of explosive from his pocket. He had kept a small lump of C4. A vague plan. If the anchor cables failed to detach, he could prepare a small charge and tape it beneath a table in the canteen. Cook a meal. Invite Jane and Sian to sit for dinner. Make it quick and clean. End it all mid-conversation.

He told himself not to be so stupid. He had spent so long

facing down mortal terror he had made a fetish of death. He had been planning an elaborate demise instead of fighting to live.

He added the nub of explosive to the main charge.

Jane fetched the initiators from the canteen. A black plastic case. Three initiators sitting snug in a foam bed. Each initiator was a pistol-grip with a red Fire button on top.

Jane tested batteries in a Maglite, to make sure they held a charge.

She slotted batteries into the butt of each grip.

Jane looked for Sian.

'I think she went outside,' said Ghost.

Airlock 52. A winking red corridor light. An alert that the exterior door had been left open.

Jane put on her coat and stepped outside. She saw Sian standing at the end of a walkway. She was leaning over a railing, looking down at the ice far below.

Weeks ago, when Jane was fat and hopeless, she had leaned over a similar section of railing and willed herself to jump into the sea. She wondered if Sian was, at that moment, thinking of flinging herself from the refinery.

Sian leaned further forward.

'Hey,' said Jane, reaching for the only words that might cut through Sian's despair. 'Come on, girl. We need your help.'

They walked to the pump house. Ghost twisted wire round the terminals of each initiator.

'I taped up the windows,' he said. 'We should probably stand back from the glass. I'm not sure how big a bang this is going to be.'

They stood facing each other.

'Want to say a prayer?'

'No,' said Jane.

'Everybody ready?'

'Yeah.'

'Okay. Here we go. Three. Two. One.'

Countdown

Nikki pressed her ear to the bunker door. No wind noise.

She dug a crash helmet from a pile of snowmobile components heaped by the tunnel wall. She opened the bunker door. Two infected passengers stood with their backs to her, looking out to sea. She swung the helmet and smashed their skulls.

Nikki climbed crags. She crouched on high ground. She surveyed the refinery through binoculars. The fog had cleared. Rampart was lit by weak twilight, a dawn that would never break.

She adjusted focus.

'*You see?*' said the voice of Nikki's dead boyfriend. '*They've cut away the stairs and ladders. There is no way to get aboard.*'

'I could climb the cables.'

'*Too steep. Too smooth.*'

'I could fetch rope. I could grapple a railing.'

'*Too high. You would never manage the climb.*'

'There has to be a way.'

She switched to infrared. The frozen steel superstructure of the refinery betrayed no heat signature except for Accommodation Module A. The module glowed weak orange. Someone had switched on the heating.

She scanned walkways and gantries. A red dot. Zoom in. A glowing stick figure, walking slow, looking down as if they were following a trail.

'*Those bastards hold all the cards. They've got food, they've got heat and they've got guns.*'

'They are my responsibility. That's why I came back. I have to save them. I have to save them from themselves.'

Nikki was halfway back to the bunker when she heard the explosion. A deep, rumbling roar like thunder. She ran to the shoreline. Two of the refinery's great anchor cables were gone. The ice beneath the rig was shattered.

Nikki uncapped her binoculars. They were still set for infrared. The corner coupling burned crimson. Reset. Focus, re-focus. Mushroom clouds of smoke hanging over each coupling.

The third cable hung slack. A moment later the lock-pin broke loose of the coupling, and the cable dropped. It smashed through the ice crust and threw up a geyser of seawater.

'*Clever,*' said Alan. '*Can you see what they are trying to do?*'

'My God,' said Nikki. 'They want to float the rig free.'

'*Yes.*'

'Will it work?'

'*I doubt it.*'

'They keep trying. Despite it all, they never give up.'

'*They must never leave the island. You understand that, yes? They belong here with us.*'

Ghost replaced the platform lift fuse.

He and Jane rode the platform lift down to the ice. Jane walked out on to the polar crust. She circled the great wall of steel.

'Why the fuck is this thing not moving?'

'The rig is ice-locked,' said Ghost. 'We're stuck until the Arctic shelf melts and breaks up. We won't see our first full sunrise for three weeks. Then it will take another month or two for the ice to thaw and break up. Our food won't last that long.'

'How about thermite grenades? Any left? Any at all? They'd melt the ice in seconds.'

'No.'

316

'Explosives? Demolition charges from the bunker? Is there anything left? Anything at all?'

'No. Nothing.'

'Fuck. This thing weighs a million tonnes. Imagine the inertia. The momentum it would build up. If we could get it to shift a single centimetre it would keep going. It would be unstoppable. A juggernaut. It would plough through everything in its path.'

Jane sat on the platform lift. She pulled off a gauntlet and drew a smiley face on the frosted deck plate with her finger.

'If only there was some way we could give it a push.'

Ghost looked out across the ice to the white horizon.

'Got it,' he yelled. 'Come on.'

He ran to the lift and pressed Up. The platform juddered to life. It began to ascend.

'Do you have the combination to Rawlins's safe?' he asked.

'I found it in his address book.'

'Go to his office. Look in the safe. There should be a couple of red keys in a plastic box, okay? Bring them to the pump house.'

Jane found the pump house ankle-deep in scrunched paper. Ghost sat at a desk rifling through box files and binders. He leafed through sheet after sheet and threw them aside.

Jane picked up a fistful of paper. System flow charts. Input/output schematics. Reciprocating compressors. Heavy octane filtration.

'What are you looking for?'

'I did a little work in here a few months back. A guy showed me something. Trying to find the damn thing.'

'What does it look like?'

'It's a red sheet of paper.'

Jane leafed through files.

'Yeah, baby,' said Ghost, triumphantly waving a red laminated checklist.

She glimpsed DANGER in big letters at the top of the page.

'What the hell is that?'

Ghost didn't reply. He spun his chair across the room to the console, kicking box files aside.

The pump room windows had shattered when the demolitions charges blew. Ghost wiped snow and broken glass from the screens and consoles. He cranked isolator breakers to On. The pump consoles lit up and winked expectant green.

He jabbed the main touch-screen plan of the refinery and set each system flag from Off to amber Standby.

'Okay,' he said. 'The treaters are back on-line. The superheaters. The draw-pumps. Did you find the box?'

'Yeah.'

'There should be two keys inside.'

'Yeah.'

'And an envelope.'

Jane read out authorisation codes. Ghost typed. The screen in front of him flashed red.

The final code was Rawlins's employee number. Only he had sufficient high-level access to stop or re-start the refining process.

Jane read his employee number from an old payslip.

FAILSAFE WARNING
DO YOU WISH TO CONTINUE?

YES/NO

Ghost slotted keys into the main console.

'We need to turn both keys at the same time.'

'Are we launching a missile?' asked Jane.

'Remember Chernobyl? A couple of bored technicians nearly incinerated Europe. This is the biggest Merox treater in the world, give or take. Press the wrong button and we could pollute the entire western hemisphere.'

They turned the keys.

FULL SYSTEM PURGE IN PROGRESS

The screen began a ten-minute countdown.

'Why the countdown?' asked Jane.

'Because we are asking the refinery to do something epically stupid and it wants us to reconsider.'

Punch woke. He struggled to open his eyes. A cut in his forehead. Lashes glued shut by clotted blood.

Punch was bound hand and foot. His arms were tied behind his back by nylon cord. The cord cut his wrists like wire. He twisted his hands to restore circulation.

He lay on the floor of a bare room. The strip-light flickered. The walls were concrete. The ceiling was concrete. The floor was cold, green tiles. He guessed he was in the bunker.

He tried to roll. He tried to wriggle his hands free. He felt blood trickle into his palms.

The door opened. Small snowboots. Blue Ventile trousers. He lashed out with his legs. Someone kicked him in the face. He spat blood. He looked up. Nikki stood over him. She crouched and checked his cuffs.

'Where am I?'

'Where do you think you are?' asked Nikki, calm and pleasant.

'What the fuck is going on? Are you going to let me go, or what?'

'An exchange,' said Nikki. 'I'm going to trade you for food and fuel.'

'Food for what? Where are you heading?'

'I wouldn't worry too much about that.'

'Where's your boyfriend? Where's Nail?'

'He's around.'

'Cut me loose.'

'Not yet.'

'Go fuck yourself, Nikki.'

'You want to get out of here, don't you?'

'You're lying. Food and fuel. Bullshit. I don't know what you are planning, but it's not going to work.'

'Jane will need proof of life. Tell me something only Sian would know.'

'Help me up.'

'No.'

'Come on. I need a shit.'

'So shit.'

'I'm bleeding.'

'So bleed.'

'Go fuck yourself, Nikki. Seriously.'

Nikki left. The heavy door slammed. A key turned in a lock. Footsteps diminished down a passageway.

Punch squirmed across the floor to the wall. He tried to stand. Maybe he could ambush Nikki next time she walked through the door. Knock her out with a vicious headbutt. Get her on the floor and kneel on her throat. She would almost certainly have a knife in her pocket. He could free himself, and find his way back to Rampart.

He lost balance. He toppled to the floor. He hit his head and shoulder. He lay and stared at the wall. He felt hopeless and defeated.

Nikki returned an hour later. She crouched beside him. Punch didn't look up.

Proof of life.

'My favourite comic book character is John Constantine. When I was young I bought a trench-coat and smoked soft-pack Marlboros just so I could be like him.'

Nikki patted him on the shoulder. He heard the door close and a key turn in the lock.

*　　*　　*

Jane knocked on the door of Sian's room.

'Sian? Hello? Anyone home?'

No reply. Jane tried the door. It was unlocked. The room was dark, dimly lit by light spilling from the corridor. Sian was curled on her bunk staring at the wall. She was hugging her pillow.

'Sorry to intrude,' said Jane. 'Ghost said we should both come and see the fireworks.'

'What fireworks?'

Jane shrugged. 'Wouldn't say. He's acting all mysterious. Seems pretty excited though. May as well humour the man.'

Sian wearily sat up. She switched on her lamp and winced against the sudden glare. She laced her boots.

Jane wanted to make conversation. No point asking: Are you feeling all right? Are you doing okay? The best she could offer was companionship, small talk.

'We've still got a carton of *Hyperion* egg concentrate. Want a shitty omelette later?'

'I just want to be quiet for a while, Jane. I don't want much at all.'

Jane knew a little bit about loss. Not much. She hadn't wept at a graveside. But she had a boyfriend at university. Mark. He dumped her for a thinner girl. Dumped her by text. She had to watch them arm-in-arm round campus. Those first few days of heartbreak were hell. Jane walked around with a head full of black. Felt like she was drowning. She stood in the supermarket queue and tried to act casual, tried not to sob and scream. Friends told her the grief would slowly ebb. She would think about him a little less each day. But the knowledge that one day she would leaf through Mark's letters and feel nothing doubled her loss.

'We should head to the canteen later,' said Jane. 'I'll beat you at Monopoly.'

'I'll skip it.'

'No. You're going to play Monopoly. Then you are going to

watch me cook an omelette, and then you'll do the washing up, all right? You've got to keep on living.'

Ghost led them to C deck. He lifted a floor hatch.

SAFETY HARNESS TO BE WORN AT ALL TIMES

Blast of winds and ice particles.

They climbed down a ladder and found themselves standing on an inspection walkway slung beneath the rig. Miles of pipes and girders above their heads. Mesh beneath their feet, and a two-hundred-metre drop on to the ice.

Ghost checked his watch.

'Here it comes. Any second now.'

A shudder ran through the refinery, shaking loose icicles and slabs of snow. The pipes above their heads creaked and sang.

'The storage tanks are dry,' he explained. 'But there is plenty of octane-grade distillate in the pipework. I've reversed the injection pumps. The whole system is set to flush itself out.'

Liquid poured from a massive pipe mouth hung beneath the belly of the rig. The retracted seabed umbilicus. It looked like Rampart was taking a piss. A torrent of part-refined fuel. First a spattering stream, then a gush. Thousands of gallons of semi-purified petroleum poured in a thin cascade and splashed across the polar crust.

'Smell that?' said Ghost. 'Pure rocket fuel.' He took a flare pistol from his pocket and slotted a shell into the breech. 'This is going to be good.'

Nikki stood at the shoreline and watched the ocean burn. Flames danced spectral blue. The island was bathed in lavender light. The sea boiled with a gentle hiss, like a long exhalation.

She glimpsed the towers and girders of Rampart above great licks of fire. Melted ice fell from the superstructure in drips and slabs.

The refinery looked like Satan's citadel, a jagged fortress at the centre of hell.

Nikki dropped to her knees. She watched in awe. A giddy moment of heightened awareness. She felt like an astronaut fired at light-speed out of the solar system into uncharted space. Each day brought strange and wonderful vistas, stardust and nebulas, and took her a million miles further from home.

The fire quickly died down and the refinery was lost behind a wall of steam.

Nikki brushed away frozen tears with a gloved hand. She slowly climbed to her feet. She took out her radio.

'Rampart? Rampart, do you copy, over?'

Ghost opened the airlock door. He and Jane quickly pulled on thermal masks as the chamber filled with steam and smoke. They walked out on to the platform lift wreathed in fumes and vapour. They rode the elevator down to the ice.

The polar crust had melted and re-frozen. Their boots splashed in puddles of steaming water.

They looked up and inspected acres of smouldering cross-beams and pipes.

'Looks like the underside of the rig got pretty cooked,' said Ghost.

Petrified drips of steel hung from girders and ran down the blackened legs of the refinery like it was sweating metal.

'How thick is this fucking ice?' asked Jane, grinding her heel into the rippled surface. 'A mile deep? We're at the very edge of the Arctic Circle, the very edge of the polar field.' She stamped. 'This stuff is fresh. It should be wafer thin.'

'Most of the heat went up. It didn't penetrate.'

'I can't take this. Hope dashed every five minutes. It's killing me.'

They heard a metallic creak. They looked up.

'Cooling metal?' speculated Ghost.

'No. Something else.'

A low, mournful moan. A sudden tortured screech. A juddering rumble as the superstructure of the refinery began to flex. It sounded like whale song. A chorus of booms, whistles and shrieks.

'Holy shit,' murmured Jane. 'It's actually happening.'

The ice between their feet split. It sounded like gunfire. Seawater bubbled over their boots.

They ran from a fast-spreading web of cracks and fissures. Puffs of ice-dust. Frothing water. They struggled to keep their balance as they sprinted across a tilting, slow-shattering crust.

They threw themselves on to the platform lift. The ice around them had broken into plates. The plates began to buckle and grind.

Tremors ran through the refinery. They gripped the platform railing for support.

'Feel that?' said Ghost. 'We're actually moving.'

Ghost headed for the canteen. Weeks ago, he rescued a bottle of champagne from *Hyperion* and set it to chill in a refrigerator hidden behind big blocks of cheese.

'I know Sian is hurting. But I want to celebrate. Maybe that's selfish. Plenty of people have died. But we made it. We're going to live.'

Jane searched for Sian.

Sian wasn't in her cabin.

Jane checked the observation bubble. No one around.

She stood at the window and watched the burned-out wreck of *Hyperion* slowly recede. The current was carrying the refinery south at a brisk walking pace. It was gouging through the ice at six or seven kilometres an hour.

Jane switched on the short-wave radio and turned up the volume. Hiss of static. She sat back and put her feet on the mixing desk.

The rig was moving south. They would pass through shipping lanes and European territorial waters. Maybe she should resume broadcasting a mayday message. Or maybe she should just monitor the airwaves. They had no idea what kind of world they would find when they reached home.

Jane became aware of a faint voice from a console speaker.

'Rampart, do you copy, over?'

She sat forward.

'Kasker Rampart, do you copy, over?'

She grasped the mike. 'Nikki? Nikki, is that you?'

'Hello, Jane. How have you been?'

Jane ran down the stairs two steps at a time. She sprinted down corridors.

She kicked open the kitchen door. She vaulted a counter, scattering pots and mixing pans. She skidded to a halt. She fumbled for keys and unlocked a freezer.

They had been using the freezer as a gun safe.

She checked the breech of the remaining shotgun.

Empty.

She checked ammunition boxes.

Empty.

'Fuck.'

She threw the empty boxes across the room.

She took out her radio.

'Ghost? Ghost, do you copy?'

No reply.

'What's going on?' asked Sian. She sat on a counter in the corner of the kitchen, swinging her legs and eating yogurt.

'I need Ghost. Where is he?'

'No idea.'

Jane slapped the yogurt from her hand and pulled her upright.

'Come with me. Right now.'

They ran down a corridor.

'Let me ask you something,' said Jane. 'I need you to think hard. Punch liked comic books, right? Graphic novels. Did he ever mention his favourite character?'

'No. Not that I remember.'

'Constantine? Did he ever mention John Constantine?'

'Actually, yeah. Some sort of gumshoe tough-guy. He battled demons. There's a poster in his room. Punch bought a trench-coat so he could dress like him. Why do you ask?'

They reached an airlock. Jane grabbed clothing from a rack. Heavy over-trousers. She buckled crampons to the soles of her boots. She zipped an Arctic parka.

'Punch is alive,' said Jane. 'Nikki and Nail have him hostage on the island.'

'Nikki?'

'She's back. Don't ask me how.'

Jane found a toolbox. She slipped a big claw hammer into her coat pocket. She buttoned a diver's knife into the utility pocket of her trousers.

Sian helped Jane shoulder the flamethrower and buckle it to her back.

'He's alive?' asked Sian. 'You're sure?'

'He's out there, and I'm going to bring him back.'

'My God.'

Jane buckled gauntlets.

'We should search for Ghost,' said Sian.

'No time.'

'What does Nikki want?'

'She wants to swap him for food.'

'Give it to her.'

'We don't have time to play games. She's a nut. Unbalanced. She has some kind of sick agenda I bet even she doesn't fully understand. I'm going to find her and I'm going to kill her.'

Jane opened a locker full of fire-fighting equipment and took an axe.

'I'm coming with you,' said Sian.

'No. I need you to lower me on to the ice.'

They heaved open the outer door of the airlock.

They ran across the deck.

'You can operate the freight crane, right?' asked Jane.

'Ivan showed me the controls during the fire.'

'You can raise and lower the hook, right? That's all I need.'

'Yeah. I think so.'

'The refinery is ripping a channel south. There is nothing beneath us but seawater and broken ice. The platform lift is no good. It'll drop me in the ocean. If you lower me in front of the rig I'll have eight or nine seconds to get clear before it runs me down.'

'How will you get back on board?'

'Catch up with the rig. Stand in front of it. You can lift me off the ice with the crane hook before I get squashed like a bug.'

'Bloody risky. It would be a split-second thing.'

They climbed a ladder to the crane platform. The cab hung over the edge of the refinery. There was a window in the floor. They could see the ice two hundred metres below. Sian swivelled the jib with a joystick. The half-tonne hook swung like a pendulum.

'Like I said. Up and down. That's all I need. Just raise and lower the hook.'

'See that?' Sian pointed south. Waves in the far distance. 'Open sea. We lost the zodiac when *Hyperion* caught fire. Once we pass out of the ice-field you won't be able to get back on board. You'll be marooned.'

'Yeah.'

Sian unbuckled her Casio watch and strapped it round the wrist of Jane's gauntlet.

'Find him, all right? Find him and bring him back.' She set the stopwatch. 'Sixty minutes. That's your turn-around time. Sixty minutes from now you head back to the refinery no matter what, okay?'

327

She pressed Start.

59:59

The seconds ticked down.

Part Four

Endgame

The Final Hour

Jane jogged across the ice towards the island. She clumped in heavy boots. Crampon teeth bit into ice. Diesel sloshed in the SCUBA tanks strapped to her back.

She climbed the rocky shoreline. Gauntlet hands searched out niches and outcrops. She scrambled over the jumble of basalt boulders and hauled herself up on to the snow plateau of the island plain.

She headed for the burned-out hulk of the ship.

The blackened hull of the superliner was split in two. The interior of the ship was exposed like a picture book cut-away diagram. Bilge and plant equipment near the keel, then ascending layers of opulence. A dance floor, glitter ball swinging in the breeze. Padded treatment recliners hanging over a steel precipice. Charred staterooms.

The multiple blasts that ripped the ship apart had ejected debris across the snow. Twisted hull plates like jagged petals. Giant worm-lengths of air-con ducts.

Jane walked among cabin refuse. Cupboards, chairs and lamps. It was like someone set up home on the ice.

Jane stood in the shadow of the ship and looked up at the exposed rooms and stairways. Ragged bed sheets wafted in the breeze. Flakes of ash drifted from the wreck like black snow.

Quick inspection of the broken hulk. Nikki might anticipate a raiding party might come calling. She might vacate the bunker. Hide herself aboard *Hyperion*.

A hand gripped Jane's ankle. She looked down. An infected

passenger half buried in snow. Jane pulled herself free. The frozen figure tried to stand. Legs missing from below the knee. She stamped on his head with a crampon boot. Skull-burst. Snow stained red.

The snow beside her bulged and split, and a second frosted figure struggled to its feet. The creature stumbled like a drunk. Jane kicked him over. He lay on his back, still struggling to walk like a toppled automaton.

Snow cracked and crumbled. A dozen passengers sitting up, struggling from the ice. Jane triggered the flamethrower. Slow pass, back and forth. Burning figures thrashed in the snow.

One last glance at *Hyperion*. The ship was too trashed, too burned-out to provide refuge. Nikki must still be in the bunker.

Jane jogged away from the ship, skirting spastic, flailing bodies. She swerved beds, wardrobes and chairs.

Sian climbed down from the crane and ran to the deck railing. Binoculars. She followed a thin, hairline track across the ice. A channel dug by Jane's crampons as she headed back to the island.

She took out her radio.

'Ghost? Ghost, do you copy? Come on, Gee. Where are you?'

She searched the rig. She ran room to room. She found Ghost in the canteen cold store. He had uncorked a bottle. He poured frothing champagne into a paper cup. She stood panting in the doorway.

'Well. On our way home,' he said. He held out a cup. 'You're probably not in a mood to celebrate. It's good champagne, though.'

'Where's your radio?'

'Why would I need to carry it? We're out of here.'

'Jane is heading back to the island. She's gone to find Punch.'

Sian and Ghost ran down the corridor. Ghost struggled to zip his coat.

'Why the fuck didn't you come and get me?'

'We couldn't find you. There wasn't time to wait.'

'How long has she been gone?'

'About ten minutes. She made it to the island. I lost sight of her once she reached the coast.'

'I'm going after her.'

'She said no. She said you would want to follow her, and she said no. She reckoned it would be easier on her own.'

'Fuck it. I'm going anyway.'

They ran across the deck. Ghost pulled on gauntlets. Sian handed him an axe.

'I'm not staying here alone.'

'We need someone to stay behind and operate the crane. You want to help? You want to be crucial? Stay in that cab. Watch for our flare, and be ready to lift us off the ice.'

Sian rotated the crane jib towards a gantry. Ghost stood on the walkway. He embraced the half-tonne hook as it swung towards him. He stepped on to the hook and wrapped an arm around the chain. He gave a thumbs up. Sian swung him over the railing. He looked down. Two-hundred-metre drop on to the ice. He gripped the chain hard.

Sian lowered the hook.

Rampart was ripping a gouge in the polar crust half a kilo-metre wide. The pristine snow field already scarred by a long wake of bubbling seawater and bobbing ice plates. The forward legs of the rig shunted a continual avalanche of ice-rubble ahead of them. Ghost would be lowered in front of churning snow and ice-boulders. He estimated he would have less than ten seconds to run clear or be pulverised and submerged.

The moment the hook touched down and dragged on the ice Ghost stepped clear and started to run. He fell. He had forgotten to buckle crampon teeth to his boots. He slipped and skidded as he tried to run clear of the advancing refinery. It was a waking nightmare. Trying to sprint, trying to cover ground, sliding on glass. He was eclipsed by shadow as the rig bore down on him. The roar of shattering ice was deafening. You've made a simple, stupid mistake, he thought, and it's going to kill you.

Moment of decision. Should he turn back and try to reach the hook? Or keep running and try to reach Jane?

He ran towards the island.

The ice beneath him began to crack and buckle. He hopscotched across tilting, bobbing plates. He threw himself clear of the approaching avalanche. He rolled and watched the massive gantries and girders of the refinery pass by high above him. A dream image. Towers and crenellations. A floating sky city.

He got to his feet and faced the island. He picked up his axe. He took two paces then the ice beneath him cracked and broke. He slid waist-deep into Arctic water. Sudden, heart-stopping cold. He scrabbled at the snow. Gauntlets grasped and raked, clawed for some kind of purchase.

Instinct saved him. The axe lay beside him. He reached, stretched until his fingertips snagged the shaft. He slammed the axe into the ice and hauled himself out of the sea. He lay shivering like an epileptic seizure.

He got to his feet. He still faced a choice. He could run to the island and try to help Jane. Hope vigorous movement would warm him up. Or he could radio Sian and get her to haul him back to the warmth and safety of Rampart.

'Get the job done,' he murmured.

He decided to head for the island. He couldn't pull the axe free so he left it behind.

Despite his predicament, despite his viciously tight bonds, Punch fell asleep. One moment he was leaning with his back to the cell wall, trying to stay awake, stay alert. Next moment he was sunk in dark dreams in which he screamed and squirmed as he was slowly crushed by strange machines.

He was jolted awake. Footsteps. Key turn. Nikki opened the

door, grabbed him by the ankle and dragged him into the corridor. She hauled him down a tiled passageway.

Green walls. Flickering strip-lights.

'What the fuck are you doing?'

No reply. She didn't even look him in the eye.

The passage met a wide, ribbed tunnel, big enough for a subway train.

She tied him to a wall girder. She left a lamp burning on the tunnel floor. She left.

A man lay tied to the opposite wall of the tunnel. He was dressed in polar survival gear and bound hand and foot. Nail. Bruised face. Split lip. His right sleeve was ripped and bloody. White nylon stuffing spilled from the quilted fabric. A wound caused, Punch guessed, when he and Nail fought for possession of a shotgun.

Nail was lashed to the girder by rope tied round his chest. Punch couldn't tell if he was dead or alive.

Punch looked around. Raw rock buttressed by girders. At a guess, some kind of excavation tunnel. The bunker was half-built. Plenty of wide access passageways throughout the complex to get mine machinery below ground.

'Hey. Hey, Nail.'

No reply.

Punch squinted into darkness. Something round in the shadows, like a giant cannonball. An open hatch. The capsule. Soviet space debris. Fell to earth miles away. How did it get here? Did *Hyperion* passengers retrieve the object? Drag it across the ice? Could the mindless mutants be guided and controlled?

He whistled.

'Hey. Nail.'

Nothing.

Why leave them by the capsule? Did Nikki expect something to crawl out and feed? Ghost said he tossed a thermite grenade into the capsule interior. Nothing could have survived.

'Hey,' shouted Punch. 'Nail. Nail, you fuck.'

Nail slowly looked up. Exhausted, frightened eyes.

'What's going on?' asked Punch. 'What does she want?'

Nail looked him over, but didn't reply. His hands were bound in front of him, rather than behind his back.

He spat a fifty kopeck coin into his palm and started to sharpen it against the tunnel floor. There was a deep scratch in the concrete. He had been sharpening the coin for a while. Maybe he hid it in his mouth each time Nikki passed by.

'So what's the deal?' asked Punch. 'Is she going to eat us or what?'

Nail didn't reply. He continued to sharpen the coin.

'Guess it didn't work out. You and her.'

Nail tested the edge of the sharpened coin. He put the coin between his teeth and tried to tear open his wrist, quickly drew his arm back and forth across the crude blade.

'Dude, what the fuck are you doing?' demanded Punch.

Nail drew blood but couldn't reach an artery. Either the coin was too blunt or he didn't have the courage to kill himself. He let the coin drop to the ground. He leaned his forehead against the wall and sobbed.

'Talk to me,' said Punch. 'Say something, you dumb fuck. What the hell is going on? Has she got us lined up for dinner? Is that it?'

'Worse. Way worse.'

'Like what? What's on her mind?'

'I knew she was nuts. Talking to herself. But I had no idea. She's pure darkness. She's sicker, way sicker than those infected fucks. She's a black hole. Total anti-matter.'

'Is she infected? Does she have this disease?'

'No.'

'But they are here, aren't they?'

'She's got an army out there in the tunnels. I've heard them. I've seen them.'

'Get your shit together, Nail. How sharp is that coin? Can it cut rope?'

'No.'

'Throw it over here. I want to try, anyway.'

Nail threw the coin. It chimed and skittered across the tunnel floor. Punch hooked the coin with his boot and kicked it towards his hands. He fumbled with his fingers. He tried to saw the rope binding his wrists. Nail watched.

'So what's your name?' asked Punch. 'Your real name? It's not Nail. I know that much.'

'What does it matter?'

'I'm curious.'

'Dave. My name is David.'

'Why change it?'

'You never wanted to reboot your life? Start again from scratch?'

'Every hour of every day. Changing my name wouldn't help, though. So who was the real Nail Harper? What happened to him?'

'I honestly don't think that's any of your business.'

'What kind of army are we talking about? What's out there?'

'Passengers and crew from *Hyperion*. They follow Nikki. I don't know why.'

'What does she want from me? What is her plan?'

'You're bait. She wants to lure your friends from Rampart. Jane will come running to your rescue. Ghost will come too. Sian will tag along.'

'But what does Nikki want? Where is all this leading?'

'She wants to keep you all here. She says this is our new home.'

Punch sawed at the rope.

'You know what?' he said. 'Everyone gets tested. You never see it coming. But sooner or later the moment arrives and you have to account for yourself. Snivel like a bitch if you like, but I'm getting out of here.'

*   *   *

337

Ghost reached the island shore. Boulders and scree. He climbed fast as he could, trying to generate metabolic heat. He was slowly succumbing to hypothermia. Creeping numbness. Limbs weak and starting to stiffen.

He reached the bunker.

'Jane?' he called into the dark tunnel entrance. 'Jane, it's me.'

He took a flashlight from his pocket. Water behind the lens. Useless. He threw it aside.

The campfire was cold and dead. He piled more wood and slopped petrol from a jerry can. His hands shook. He poured too much gasoline. He struck a match anyway, and shielded his face from the flame-ball. Fire scorched the tunnel roof.

Ghost tried his radio. Waterlogged. Dead. He threw it aside.

He closed the bunker doors.

He didn't have time to dry his clothes. He poured water from his boots then held them directly in the flames. Water fizzed, boiled and steamed. He wrung his coat, balled it and held it in the fire until it smoked.

He dressed.

Ghost took a burning stick from the fire, held it above his head and set off down the dark tunnel mouth.

Sian left the cab to fetch a flask of coffee. Kill time, she told herself. Do something ordinary. Kid yourself everything is fine.

She boiled a kettle in the canteen kitchen. Silent corridors. Empty rooms. What if Jane and Ghost didn't make it back? Drifting for thousands of miles in the dark and derelict refinery. She was terrified of isolation.

She returned to the cab, unscrewed the Thermos and poured coffee. She let the metal mug warm her hands. The windows steamed up. She wiped away condensation. The island was receding. The wreck of *Hyperion* was a distant, ragged silhouette against the Arctic twilight.

She put her cup on the cab floor and uncapped binoculars. She looked south. She could clearly see the edge of the ice-field. The point where snow gave way to heavy black waves.

She estimated Jane, Ghost and Punch had less than three hours to make it back to Rampart before the refinery reached open sea and they were left behind.

Sian took out her radio.

'Rampart to Jane, can you hear me, over? Jane, do you copy?'

Static.

'Jane? Ghost? Can you hear me?'

Jane stood at the open doors of the bunker.

A weak voice: *'Jane, do you copy? Jane, do you copy, over?'*

Jane took out her radio.

'Sian? Sian, can you hear me?'

Nothing but feedback. Weak LED. Dying batteries.

The campfire was lit. She crouched and examined sticks of burning furniture. A recent fire. Someone was here moments ago.

She examined a discarded flashlight. It belonged to Ghost. Weeks ago, she had watched him bind it with duct tape to seal a crack in the case.

Ghost had travelled from the rig. He must have headed straight for the bunker and reached it ahead of her.

'Ghost?'

No reply.

Jane aimed her flamethrower down the dark tunnel. Flame-roar. She glimpsed concrete walls receding deep underground.

Jane checked her watch.

41:54

She shone her flashlight on the tunnel floor. Scuffed boot-prints led into shadows.

She hitched the flamethrower, gripped her flashlight and followed the footprints downward into the dark

The Pit

The damp tunnel floor betrayed the thick tread of snowboots. Jane crouched. Multiple tracks. Big prints, old and new, and a set of smaller feet. Probably Nikki.

Jane followed the tracks, flamethrower primed. She triggered puffs of fire at each junction.

The slope-shaft led downward into bedrock. The air got colder. The walls sparkled with pyrite and silica.

Silent passageways and galleries. She paused every couple of minutes and listened to hear if she was being followed. No sound but distant tunnel drips, her breathing, the gentle hiss of the flamethrower igniter flame.

She leaned against the tunnel wall. A sudden wave of heart-hammering fear. Her legs felt weak. Every instinct told her to turn and run back to the refinery. Rampart was floating away, and she was about to be left behind. It wasn't too late. She could still make it home.

She closed her eyes for a moment. Giddy with adrenalin. Memories came, vivid and immediate like a fever dream.

'Courage, like all personality traits, is essentially a habit,' explained Jane's old English teacher. Mr Stratford. Young, anxious to think himself inspirational. It was Jane's turn to read a poem at assembly. Byron. She would have to stand in front of the entire school. Stand at a lectern during chapel. She was terrified. 'If you act brave every day, adopt a confident posture, adopt a confident tone, eventually it becomes innate,' explained

Mr Wilson. 'Yes, it's phoney. Utterly bogus pretence. But if you fake any trait long enough it becomes an essential part of you, like your fingerprint. So there's no point telling yourself not to be scared. You can't control your thoughts and emotions. But you can control your actions. In the end, we are the sum of what we do.'

Jane had spent the past few months trying to save the crew of Rampart. And here she was. Transformed. Lean. Super-weapon strapped to her back. A stranger to herself.

Jane kept walking.

She used to read books of Chinese philosophy. Bushido. The Samurai code. Her young, fat days were dominated by fear. She was terrified of school, scared to walk round town on a busy day. 'Fat bitch.' 'Porker.' 'Cow.' The world was a war zone. It took warrior courage to leave the front door.

Samurai soldiers called themselves dead men. They tied their hair in a ponytail before each battle to make it easy for their enemies to lift their severed heads as a trophy. A warrior with no regard for his own life, who flew into battle powered by careless, suicidal rage, was unbeatable. Negative courage. Give up on yourself, and you have nothing left to fear. You become invincible.

The shaft took her further below ground. She felt wind on her face. Maybe there were other routes to the surface. Airshafts and ancillary exits. Ghost said there was an old airstrip nearby with an Antonov cargo plane turning to rust. Maybe there was a connecting passageway.

A figure stood in the dark up ahead. A man standing sentinel in the middle of the tunnel. Jane wondered how long he had been alone in the dark.

She waited for him to make a move. He remained still.

She crept closer. She shone a flashlight in his face. Officer uniform. Brass buttons, epaulettes, anchor insignia.

Jet-black eyes.

The figure slowly inclined his head to look directly at Jane. He screamed. A long, unearthly howl. Mouthful of metal spines.

The scream seemed to last minutes, seemed like it would never end. Jane sparked the flamethrower and blew the man off his feet and down the tunnel.

She stepped over the burning figure.

A shriek from deep within the tunnels. Something, down in the depths of the bunker, was answering the sailor's call.

The tunnels played strange music. Gentle, fluted breaths that rose and fell as she passed through passageways and galleries.

A vertical shaft to the surface. Ventilation. A massive air-con turbine in the tunnel roof. Rusted blades.

Snow had tumbled down the shaft. A high mound of ice blocked Jane's path.

Sustained blast from the flamethrower. Ice shrivelled, lique-fied, steamed.

She found a sailor sitting against the tunnel wall. Jane trained her flashlight on his face. Beard. Striped naval tunic. He was weak and emaciated. Metal leaked from his ears. His eyes glowed red like a cat lit by headlights. He hissed.

Jane pushed him over and stamped on his head.

She headed downward, deeper into the fossil layers. Her flash-light lit glittering mineral veins. Cambrian, pre-Cambrian. That dark and distant epoch when Arctica was raging volcanism.

She checked her watch. How far had Rampart drifted from the island? It might already be four or five kilometres offshore. Might be fifteen or twenty kilometres distant by the time she reached the surface. She could make it, though. She could sprint across the ice. She had stamina.

Sudden flashback. A cross-country run. Bleak fields. Lumbering along an endless, rural lane. Sweating, sobbing with exhaustion. Long since left behind.

Miss Gibson, the PE teacher, leaning on a farm gate.

'Come on, stinky. Make an effort.'

Storage vaults. Lead doors high as an aircraft hangar.

One of the doors was ajar. No time to explore. But if the vaults hid infected passengers from *Hyperion* she might find her route back to the surface cut off.

She stood in the giant doorway and shone her flashlight into the darkness.

A wall of black. A massive propeller. The tail section of an Akula Class nuclear sub. Black, anechoic hull plates. Rudders. Stern planes. Jagged metal where the tail had been plasma-cut from the main hull.

The reactor had evidently been dredged from the ocean bed. Barnacled and streaked with sediment.

Hard to comprehend the vast scale of the wreckage.

What was the radiation count in the vault? Rust pools on the chamber floor. The interment was incomplete. The wreckage should be buried in salt and sealed in lead. Instead, the reactor chamber was exposed to open air.

She hurried onward.

School days.

The chapel. Jane walking up the aisle, trying not to waddle, trying not to shake. She stood at the lectern. She looked at the blazered congregation. Rose, the gum-smacking class bitch, sitting in the back pew with her smirking, sneering gang.

Jane took paper from her pocket and unfolded the poem. She cleared her throat, blushed as the cough was amplified throughout the chapel.

She adjusted the mike position.

She stared, mesmerised, into the foam bulb of the microphone.

She froze. She couldn't speak. And she knew, in a giddy rush of heightened awareness, that she would relive this memory her entire life. The sounds, the textures. The shame would be seared into her like the pavement burn-shadow of a Hiroshima pedestrian.

She stared at the mike. She could see, in the periphery of her vision, ranks of schoolgirls staring at her. They started to fidget. They started to giggle.

Wherever she went, whatever she did, part of her would be trapped in this moment. A fat girl, clutching the lectern, paralysed with fear.

Jane's flashlight started to fail.

She hurried down tunnels shored with steel props. She passed evidence of interrupted excavation. Uncleared rubble. Discarded tools. Dormant diggers.

She saw something move in the darkness up ahead. A white figure stepped away from the tunnel wall.

'Hello?' called Jane. 'Are you on your own, or did you come with friends?'

The spectral figure didn't move.

Jane rested her flashlight on a ledge. She triggered the igniter flame. Quiet hiss of gas. She strode forward.

'All right then, babycakes,' she muttered to herself. 'Let's dance.'

The man shuffled towards her. A chef. He had bottles and jars taped to his chest like he was wearing some kind of suicide vest.

The chef tore a pickle jar from his chest and smashed it on his forehead. Kerosene. Jane backed away. He held a lighter in his left hand. He struck it. Jane ran. The blast threw her down the tunnel. Big dent in the SCUBA tanks. She got to her feet and retrieved her torch. The tunnel was blocked by a wall of fire.

Jane covered her face and ran through the blaze. Her boots caught alight. She stamped out the flames.

Ignition. Motor roar, amplified by the tunnel walls. Dazzling headbeams.

Jane shielded her eyes. Gear change. Escalating roar. Headbeams approaching.

Jane squinted into the glare. The serrated teeth of a digger scoop heading her way. She hugged the left tunnel wall. The digger drove straight at her. She dived clear at the last moment. The scoop dug into the tunnel wall, bringing down rock.

She glimpsed heavy caterpillar tread, and a hunched, misshapen figure in the yellow cab.

The digger backed up. Jane hugged the right tunnel wall. The digger drove at her. Dumb enough to fall for the same trick.

Jane dived clear. The scoop dug into the tunnel wall. Rockfall. The digger pinned by boulders, engine house partially crushed.

Jane got a good look at the driver. Two dinner-suited passengers fused together like Siamese twins. The digger tried to reverse. The damaged engine coughed and revved. Gouts of smoke from the exhaust. Caterpillar tread ground and span.

Jane fried the cab. The twin drivers were consumed in a typhoon of flame.

The jet of flame stuttered and died. Jane took off the SCUBA tanks and shook them. Empty. She left the spent flamethrower by the burning digger.

White tiles. Shower heads.

Some kind of decontamination area.

Lockers. Rubber radiation suits hung on pegs like human skin left to tan. Ghoulish, skull-eyed gas hoods.

The passage led to a bare chamber. Bloody letters:

WELCOME HOME, JANE

Dried blood drips. Black flakes.

Nikki knew she was coming. The guys in the tunnels, the men melded to the digger, had just been entertainment. Nikki knew Jane would make it to Level Zero, and prepared a welcome.

Jane heard a scratching sound behind her. Another fuel-soaked crewman trying to spark a Zippo. She snatched the claw hammer from her pocket and shattered his head. She crouched over his body. She ripped a kerosene bottle from his chest and slipped it into her coat pocket.

White tiles. Shower heads.

The school changing rooms. Hiss of water. Thick steam. Five girls jeering, chanting, screaming. '*Stinky bitch. Stinky bitch.*' Pelting their victim with soap. A small, Asian girl cowering fully clothed in the corner of the communal shower. Jane among her tormentors. '*Stinky bitch.*' A shameful memory. A reminder that Jane wasn't always a righteous victim. Sometimes cowardice made her join the herd.

There was a steel lid in the floor like the turret hatch of a tank.

She heaved the hatch aside. A deep, vertical shaft. Flickering light at the bottom.

She checked her watch.

17:25

'You're nothing special,' she told herself. 'You're not a hero. You've been a coward and a victim all your life. But plenty of others would turn and run right now. The girls who made your schooldays hell. That jeering, hateful crowd that drove you to the ends of the earth. None of them would have the courage to walk into this bunker and battle their way to the lowest levels.'

We are what we do.

She could be riding Rampart home. Instead she walked into hell to rescue a friend.

She climbed into the shaft and gripped the wall-rungs. She recited Byron as she began to descend.

> *I had a dream which was not all a dream.*
> *The bright sun was extinguish'd, and the stars*
> *Did wander darkling in the eternal space.*
> *And men forgot their passions in the dread*
> *Of this desolation; and all hearts*
> *Were chill'd into a selfish prayer for light.*

The Hive

Approaching footsteps. Dancing flashlight beam.

Nikki grasped Nail by the ankle and dragged him down the tunnel. She was half Nail's body weight, but possessed a maniac's super-strength. He sobbed and begged. His fingers raked concrete. Punch could hear Nail pleading as he was dragged away down the corridor. Echoing screams.

Punch adjusted his grip on the sharpened coin. He cut as fast as he could. The cord binding his wrists had started to fray.

Nikki returned and untied him from the girder. She dragged him down the tunnel. He didn't scream. Whatever horror Nikki planned for him, he resolved his last words would be 'Fuck you.'

There was an office chair in the middle of the tunnel. Nikki tied him to the chair and pushed him down the tunnel.

'Where are we going?' demanded Punch.

'To meet the family.'

Nikki kicked open double doors and propelled Punch into some kind of operations centre.

The room was rippled with liquid metal like melted candle wax. *Hyperion* passengers were melded to the walls and ceiling like flies trapped in a web.

Hyperion crewmen stood sentry round the walls. Drones. Worker bees. Officers in brass-button uniform. Deckhands in striped tunics.

A figure at the centre of the room. A body lying in state. A Russian cosmonaut in a scorched pressure suit, part cooked by thermite but still intact. Canvas hanging in charred strips, under-suit ribbed with cooling tubes. The helmet visor was raised. Metal tendrils snaked from inside the enamel helmet, hung from the table, wound across the floor and fused with the wall.

Nikki parked Punch at the back of the room. He craned to see past Nail. A figure tied to a chair.

Ghost.

They both leaned forward so they could talk. Nail sat between them, sobbing.

'How the hell did you get here, Gee?'

'I came across the ice,' said Ghost. 'I came to help Jane. They caught me in the tunnels. Two of them. Thought they would kill me for sure, but they dragged me down here. It was like they had orders.'

'Are you okay? Are you infected?'

'I'm all right.'

A wall screen pulsed static. A figure was fused to the screen.

'Who's that?'

'I think it's Rye,' said Ghost. 'What's left of her.'

'Thought she was long dead.'

'She was on *Hyperion* all the time we were living it up. She was down below with the passengers. Guess she survived the fire.'

Nail kept sobbing.

'Nail. Hey, Nail.'

Nail didn't look up.

'Forget him,' said Ghost. 'He's lost it.'

'Have you got your knife?'

'She took it.'

'I can't get my hands free.'

'Jane is around here some place,' said Ghost. 'The best we can do is stall for time.'

*   *   *

Jane checked her watch. The final seconds.

00:00

Turn-around time. If she wanted to save her own skin, she should forget Punch and head for Rampart before it drifted beyond reach. Take a guaranteed ride back home.

She unbuckled the watch and threw it away. Fuck it.

Jane stood at the end of a corridor. She guessed the lower levels of the nuclear waste repository hid some kind of doomsday, continuation-of-government facility built during the cold war. A minor synapse of the Soviet command structure. Perhaps regional control for the submarine fleet.

She passed a communal shower.

She passed a powerhouse. Three rusted diesel generators. The generators appeared dead. She laid a hand on the metal housing. Cold. No vibration. Output dials smashed, needles at zero. So why were the lights on? The ceiling strip-lights pulsed like a slow heartbeat. She wondered if something had infiltrated the ducts and conduits. Perhaps the bunker itself was somehow alive and sentient.

She glanced into a side office. A pin-board map faded sepia. Canada, Norway and Alaska, the rest of the Arctic Circle. The stand-off zone. The theatre of war. Chart coordinates of the Soviet armada, the bomber fleet, patrolling the frontier, waiting for the order to attack.

An infected crewman from *Hyperion* stood in the corner of the room beneath a mildewed portrait of Lenin straddling the Arctic Ocean like a colossus. The semi-decomposed figure stood sentry like he was waiting for instructions.

Scattered equipment on the floor. New stuff. Tin mugs. Balled socks. Russian *Playboy*. Jane kicked through the litter. She kept her eyes on the infected crewman in case he made a move. He remained still, lit by intermittent, flickering light.

Jane thought about the infected crewmen she encountered in

the upper levels of the complex. They wouldn't have the intelligence or dexterity to improvise a suicide vest. Something was manipulating them, using them as a defence perimeter. Nikki? Had she got them trained like dogs? Sit, heel, beg.

Jane quietly backed out of the room. The rotted sentinel watched her leave but made no move to follow.

Something was aware Jane had entered the lowest levels of the bunker and was content to let her walk deeper into the subterranean complex.

Nikki wandered around the ops centre, hands in her pockets, casual confidence, like she ran the place. No sign of infection.

'What's the deal, Nikki?' demanded Ghost. 'Are we lunch, or what?'

Nikki turned to face him. Mild surprise, like she had forgotten he was there.

'Believe it or not,' she said, 'I'm doing my best to help you.'

She was mild, good-humoured, utterly insane.

'That's nice.'

'Jane will be here any minute,' said Nikki, glancing at a *Hyperion* officer as if she expected him to provide confirmation. 'I'm anxious to speak to her.'

'We blew the anchor cables, Nikki. Rampart is floating free. It's caught in the current. It's heading south. We can all go home. You can come too. But we have to leave right now. We don't have time to fuck around. It's drifting out of range.'

Nikki shook her head and smiled.

'They bombed the cities. Nuked them. I saw it myself, when I sailed south. I saw the sky lit up. I saw the world on fire. There's nothing beyond the horizon, Rajesh. Europe has been wiped clean. America too, as far as I know. We are the last people on earth, and this is our home.'

'You can't be sure.'

'Embrace it. It's evolution. We are the next stage, the next level. Open your eyes. We are on the cusp of something wonderful.'

Nikki took gloves from her pocket and pulled them on. She stood over the dead cosmonaut. She reached inside the helmet and snapped a rivulet of metal. She examined it.

'So who do you think he was? What happened up there?'

She stood in front of Ghost.

'What do you think it is?' she asked, holding the sliver in front of Ghost's face.

He shied away from the gleaming splinter.

'Where does it come from? Is it man-made? Nanobots run wild? Maybe it's not from earth at all. Maybe it came from somewhere else.' She gestured to *Hyperion* passengers fused to the wall. 'Do you think they finally understand? Once you surrender to it, once the transformation takes hold, do you think it all becomes clear? What it's like on the other side? Aren't you curious to find out?'

'No.'

'How can you not want to know? This is the dominant life form on the planet now.'

'Doesn't mean shit. It's a virus. Bacteria. It can kill, but I don't hold it in high esteem.'

'This is very different.'

'These *Hyperion* guys. They follow you like a puppy dog. How does that work?'

Nikki took a radio from her pocket. A Rampart walkie-talkie. She switched it on. A strange, tocking signal. Nikki held the radio to the dead cosmonaut's helmet. The signal got louder, more insistent, then dissolved to feedback.

'They sing to each other. Some kind of high-frequency chatter. They merge their thoughts.'

'I don't see much thought going on.'

Nikki stood behind Nail. She slapped a hand on his bald scalp and pulled back his head. He yelped in pain. She dropped the sliver of metal into his mouth then clamped his jaw closed. He gnashed his teeth. He bucked and thrashed in his chair. He arched his back. She held him a full minute, then released her grip. He spat the metal shard on to the floor.

'You fuck,' he sobbed. 'You fucking fuck.' He retched. He spat. Pathetic attempt to purge infection from his mouth.

Nikki grabbed a swivel chair and positioned it in front of Ghost.

'His name isn't Nail Harper, you know that, right? He's David Tuddenham. A fuck-up. Petty thief. Petty everything. But now all that hurt, all that damage, will evaporate. A lifetime of failure will just melt away.'

'You're nuts,' said Ghost. 'You are one hundred per cent, grade-A batshit.'

'Think,' said Nikki. She got up, and paced up and down like she was lecturing a class. 'Just take a moment and think. This situation, this new state of being, it's weird, but is it necessarily bad? This could be a wonderful opportunity to become something new. That's good, right? Most people spend their whole lives wishing they could be different.'

'You were a student in Brighton, is that right? Brighton University?'

'Sure.'

'What did you study?'

'Biogeography,' said Nikki. 'Ocean science. Ecosystems.'

'Did you enjoy it?'

'Of course. That's why I did it.'

'Think back. Remember. What did you enjoy?'

'Nightlife. Alan and I had a flat on the seafront. It was heaven.'

'Do you remember your first day at university? The day you first arrived. Do you remember how you felt?'

'My parents dropped me with suitcases. I was excited to leave home. Nervous I wouldn't make friends.'

'That girl. The person you used to be. Can you remember her? Can you bring her back just for a moment? What would she say if she saw you now?'

Nikki snapped another nugget of metal from inside the cosmonaut's enamel helmet. She looked at it a long while.

'I'm so sick of being me.'

'I can help you, Nikki. There's a way back from all this.'

'The burden of selfhood,' she sighed. 'Life-long anguish. Straining to support an elaborate artifice every waking moment. Trying to maintain our bullshit personas. Haircuts, clothes. Making our big fucking statements to an indifferent world. We drink, we smoke, we squander fortunes on DVDs, anything to escape ourselves for a few blessed minutes.'

'You don't have to turn Martian just to feel better. That's like shooting yourself in the brain to cure a headache.'

Nikki closed her eyes, placed the globule of metal on her tongue and swallowed. She smiled.

She stood over Nail. She bent and kissed him.

She resumed her seat in front of Ghost.

'I'm so sorry, Nikki.'

'I wanted to kill you. I was going to kill you all. I hated you so damn much. I don't know why. But I want you to join us. I'm not going to force you. Nail? He's a child. I had to decide on his behalf. But I want you folks to volunteer.'

Jane walked through a series of plant rooms. Most of the ceiling lights were smashed. She wanted to save her flashlight batteries. She struck a flare. It burned fierce purple.

Ventilation flues. Dehumidification filters.

The air conditioning was shot. The plenum fans that should have pushed air through the complex were rusted and still. Yet, when she took off a glove and put a hand to the wall-vent, she could feel a breath of wind.

She found the canteen. Metal tables and chairs. A communist mural of heroic agricultural workers holding sickles and scythes, gazing towards a golden dawn.

She got tired of searching.

'Punch,' she shouted. 'Where are you, dude?'

Jane stepped into the corridor. She was faced by a dozen *Hyperion* passengers. They stood the length of the passageway, lit by flickering strip-light.

Jane backed away from the stink of piss and rotting flesh. A dozen ravaged faces. A dozen pairs of jet-black eyes. She expected the foul creatures to attack. They stood quite still, as if awaiting instructions.

They shrank back into darkened doorways. A clear invitation for Jane to proceed.

Nikki approached the situation board, a flickering, back-lit map of the western hemisphere. A figure was fused to the glass by metal filaments.

'She's here,' murmured Rye, slowly lifting her head. Metal tendrils from her eye sockets. She was plugged in to the walls, plugged in to the collective conscious, monitoring the inhabitants of the bunker with strange new senses. 'She's outside the door.'

Nikki turned to face the entrance.

Jane looked around the ops centre. Ghost, Punch and Nail lashed to chairs. Bodies melded to the walls and ceiling. Jane looked up. An old woman spread-eagled on the ceiling directly above her head. The woman gently squirmed, like she was trying to work out how she came to be pinned to the roof.

Nikki at the centre of it all, hands in her pockets, smiling a welcoming smile.

Jane glanced at Ghost and Punch. Quick inspection for injury or infection.

'Good to see you, Jane,' said Ghost.

'You guys all right?'

'Punch is all right. I'm fine. Don't think Nail will be coming home.'

Nail sobbed. The big man snivelled and drooled snot.

'I'm so glad you came,' said Nikki.

'That's sweet.'

Jane edged around the room. She held the flare like she was warding off a vampire. Spitting, fizzing purple flame. Wax dripped over her gloved hand.

She dug in her pocket with her left hand and took out her lock-knife. She flicked open the blade with her thumb and handed it to Ghost. He cut his wrists free then released his ankles. He quickly shook and stretched to restore circulation.

'I want to talk to you,' said Nikki. 'Just talk.'

'Sure,' said Jane, super-calm, placating a lunatic. 'Fire away.'

'I want you to stay with us. Europe is a radioactive cinder. There's nothing for you back home. Just death and ruins. But there's a place for you here, a place to belong. Call Sian. She can stay too.'

'Sure she'll appreciate the sentiment.'

Ghost cut Punch free and helped him to his feet. He dropped the knife in Nail's lap.

'Hey. Nail. Do yourself a favour. Slit your throat while you have the chance.'

'Look around you, Nikki,' said Jane. 'Take a moment and look. Why would anyone spend a single second in this fucking abattoir? There are some diesel drums in the plant room. Seriously. Torch the place.'

Nail cut himself lose. He moved on Nikki, gripping the lock-knife like he was ready to shiv her in the gut. She stepped back. Two rotting *Hyperion* officers shuffled forward to block his path. Nail ran from the room.

Jane, Ghost and Punch edged towards the door.

'Why be scared?' asked Nikki. 'What do you have to lose? Your body will change, but so what? It's not like any of us danced for the Royal Ballet. You've been fat all your life. You got thin, but you still bear the marks of obesity. Wide bones. Splayed feet. What's so great about being you? What are you holding out for? I'm trying to help. I'm trying to do the biggest favour of your life.'

Nikki stepped forward, arms outstretched in a pleading gesture.

'Join us. Join us, Jane.'

Jane threw the hammer. A spinning blur. The hammer smacked Nikki's forehead. She was knocked from her feet.

The phalanx of *Hyperion* crewmen began to shuffle forward, antibodies preparing to repel an intruder.

Jane took the jar of kerosene from her pocket and dashed it on the floor. She threw the flare and shielded her face from the eruption of flame.

She tossed Ghost her radio.

'Run,' she said. 'I'll be right behind you.'

Ghost grabbed an extinguisher from the wall, like he was ready to stand and fight.

'Don't be a fucking idiot,' said Jane. 'Take Punch. Get a head start. Go on. Run.'

She picked up an office chair and held it, ready to fend off attack.

Nikki got to her feet, hand pressed to her bleeding forehead. Hammer imprint between her eyes.

Nikki examined the blood in her palm. Woozy smile. She faced Jane through a wall of fire, watched her back towards the doorway.

'I know you better than anyone, Jane. I can see through you like a fucking X-ray. You hate yourself, every molecule. I know what that's like. You've been lonely your whole life. Every waking moment screaming out for some kind of contact, some kind of warmth. But you're not alone. That bleak, psychic terrain. I'm right there with you. I'm your soulmate, Jane. Yin-yang. You and me. Not those guys.'

'See you in the next life, Nikki.'

'Wait. Listen to me. There's no shame in wanting to belong. You and the rest of the human race. Everyone desperate to escape the confines of their skull, cramming themselves into cinemas, football stadiums, church pews, all yearning for some kind of collective experience. It's a life sentence, Jane. A life in solitary. But we don't have to be out in the cold any more. This is our chance. We can come home. You think it's all back in Europe. Contentment. But you've been living that way for years. Tell me I'm wrong. Dreaming happiness is somewhere else, somewhere over the horizon. But you're home, Jane. It's right here. Everything we ever wanted. We can finally belong.'

'You know what?' said Jane. 'You're wrong. I like being me.'

She turned and ran.

'You'll be alone,' shouted Nikki. 'You'll be alone your whole damn life.'

The Race

Punch climbed the ladder. He left the light and warmth of Level Zero and ascended to the freezing dark of the main tunnels. He struggled to grip the rungs. His wrists and ankles were bleeding.

'Are you all right?' called Ghost from the top of the shaft.

'Grinning from ear to fucking ear.'

Ghost hauled Punch from the shaft. He helped Punch to his feet.

'Can you walk?'

'Yeah.'

'Can you run?'

'I'll try.'

Ghost struck a flare.

'If we don't make it to Rampart before it reaches open sea we are dead men.'

Punch put his arm round Ghost's waist. They hurried down the tunnel. A steady slope to the surface.

They glimpsed a *Hyperion* passenger standing in an alcove. Fancy dress. A guy in a dinner suit and bull mask. The emaciated creature watched them pass. It slowly turned its head like a CCTV camera recording their progress.

'Is it following us?' asked Punch as he limped along.

Ghost looked over his shoulder. 'No. It's just standing there.'

'Christ, I can't wait to be out of this place. I just want to breathe clean air.'

'Damn right,' said Ghost.

They kept jogging.

'You know what?' said Punch.

Ghost was about to reply when Nail lunged from the shadows and knocked them to the ground. He sat on Ghost's chest and squeezed his throat.

Nail's lips were bruised and swollen. He looked like he was wearing black lipstick. He sank his teeth into Ghost's cheek and tore away a flap of flesh. Ghost yelled in pain. He jammed the flare into Nail's eye socket. Nail screamed. He threw himself clear and ran.

'Are you all right?' asked Punch.

'He got me,' said Ghost, trying to staunch the flow of blood. 'Fucker got me.'

'You'll be all right.'

'He got me. I'm fucked.'

'You don't know that.'

'Don't touch me. Don't get blood on you.'

'We'll get you back to Rampart. We'll patch you up.'

Punch hauled Ghost to his feet.

'Put your arm round my shoulder.'

Punch helped Ghost stumble towards the bunker exit.

'We should wait for Jane,' said Ghost.

'She's buying us time. Let's not waste it.'

They reached the mouth of the bunker. Ghost slumped against the wall. Punch pulled the tarpaulin from a snowmobile. He sat on the bike, turned the ignition and gunned the engine.

'Jane?' Ghost shouted into the tunnel. 'Jane? Are you coming?'

'She'll take the other bike,' said Punch. 'Come on. Let's not add to her problems.'

Ghost struggled to mount the bike. He rode pillion.

It was dark outside. They couldn't see further than the head-beam of the Skidoo. The bike bucked and swerved over jagged rock. They cruised the rocky shoreline and looked for a route on to the ice.

'There.' Ghost pointed. A path led down to the frozen sea. Punch swung the bike down the steep ramp and drove on to the ice.

'Hold on,' shouted Punch. He revved and headed south at full speed.

Ghost let the wind freeze his face. The bite wound stopped bleeding and soon he could feel no pain.

'I can't see the rig,' shouted Punch over his shoulder.

Ghost fumbled for his radio.

'Sian,' he shouted, struggling to be heard over wind noise. 'Hit the floodlights.'

Sian sat in the darkened cab. Night had fallen. She knew she should switch on the refinery floodlights but delayed the moment. She didn't want to see the approaching ocean. Some time in the next hour Rampart would break from the ice-field and float into open sea. From that moment she would be irrevocably alone. Adrift for weeks, possibly months. If she passed land she would have to row ashore in a lifeboat and explore the ruins of Europe on her own.

Her radio crackled. A voice. She couldn't make out words. Just a brief snatch of wind noise. Jane, Ghost and Punch must be trying to make it back to the rig.

She ran from the cab to a switch room on deck. She threw breakers. The Rampart superstructure suddenly lit celestial white by halogen floodlights.

Sian returned to the cab. The ice in front of the refinery was lit by arc lights. She could see the Arctic Ocean up ahead.

A snowmobile raced across the polar crust and pulled up in front of the refinery. Sian wiped condensation to get a better view. Two figures climbed from the bike, both wearing blue Rampart-issue survival coats. Two of her friends had made it back to the rig.

A sudden pang of guilt: if she could make a deal with Fate, she would happily trade Jane or Ghost to get Punch back alive.

*   *   *

The refinery ploughed through the Arctic crust with a roar like steady thunder. Each of the massive buoyant legs bulldozed a mountain of ice rubble before it.

Punch and Ghost faced the approaching avalanche and waited for Sian to lower the hook.

'We'll have to grab the chain at the same time,' said Punch, shouting to be heard over the rumble of shattering ice.

'I'm not coming with you,' said Ghost. He backed away. 'It's been a privilege. I always liked you, Punch. Always thought you were one of the good guys.'

'What are you doing?'

'Look after Sian. Enjoy each other. Find a decent place and build a life.' Ghost turned and ran.

Punch called after him.

'Ghost. Come on, Gee, we need you, man.'

Punch wanted to run after Ghost, but the refinery was nearly upon him. The crane hook descended out of blinding arc light.

'Ghost,' he called, one last time, but he knew he couldn't be heard over the jet-roar of ripping ice.

Punch was so close to the shattering crust he had to shield his eyes from snow and sea-spray. He saw the snowmobile smashed flat by a slab of ice. He stepped aboard the massive hook and hugged the chain.

Punch gave a signal-wave. He was slowly lifted upward and enveloped in light.

Ghost watched Rampart pass by and float away. A steel city heading south.

He thought about Punch and Sian safe aboard the rig.

He realised all he was about to lose. He wouldn't laugh, sip coffee or feel rain on his face ever again.

He took a long, shuddering breath.

We've all got it coming, he reminded himself.

He turned his back on the heat and light of the refinery. He walked north across the frozen sea. He pulled back his hood so he could look at the stars.

Departure

Jane ran through the bunker. She found a discarded flare smouldering on the tunnel floor. She couldn't be far behind Ghost and Punch.

She reached the bunker entrance. One of the snowmobiles was gone. She pulled the tarpaulin from the second Skidoo and straddled the bike. She reached for the ignition. An empty slot. Nikki or Nail must have the key. I'm going to die, she thought, just because some fool put the key in their pocket instead of leaving it in the ignition.

She stood at the bunker entrance and looked south. She saw a gleam in the far distance like a bright star. The arc lights of the refinery. She tried to judge distance. Rampart was over fifteen kilometres away.

She climbed down the rocky shoreline to the frozen sea. She checked her crampons were securely buckled to her boots. She threw away her flashlight.

'All right,' she muttered. 'You can do this.'

She ran, quickly accelerating from a trot to a sprint, and headed for the distant light.

She ran in total darkness, eyes fixed on the beacon lights of the rig. Pretend you are jogging a circuit of C deck, she told herself. Stay calm. Control your breathing. Get into a rhythm.

She muttered the lyrics of 'All Along the Watchtower' as she ran.

She drew closer to the rig. She saw shattering ice. Sweet relief. The refinery had yet to reach the ocean.

Jane looked beyond Rampart. The moon reflected in rippling water. The refinery had reached the edge of the polar ice-field and was about to break into open sea.

Jane ran alongside the rig. She passed the south legs. She sprinted in front of the refinery and collapsed, crippled by exhaustion, on the narrow strip of ice that separated Rampart from the ocean.

Jane dug in her pockets. She pulled out a couple of flares.

She stood, lit the flares and waved them back and forth above her head. She squinted into dazzling arc light. If Sian had left the cab, if she didn't see Jane standing ahead of the refinery, Jane would be crushed and submerged.

Jane let the flares fall at her feet. She stood, blinded by searchlights, deafened by the roar as the oncoming refinery punched through the polar crust. She closed her eyes. She was enveloped in ice-dust and sea-spray.

Sian sat in the crane cab. Punch crouched beside her.

'There,' shouted Punch. He scrubbed away condensation. They saw a solitary figure standing on the ice. Jane. Two purple flares burning at her feet. 'Drop the hook.'

Jane opened her eyes. The massive steel hook descended out of dazzling light. She stepped forward to meet it.

Jane was hit by a snowmobile and sent spinning across the ice. She sat up. She wondered if her hip were broken. She looked around. The snowmobile skidded to a halt and turned. The bike from the bunker. Nail must have had the key.

Jane struggled to her feet. She unzipped her parka. Nail drove at her. She jumped to one side and threw her coat beneath the bike. The caterpillar tread chewed her coat and jammed. The bike flipped. Nail was thrown across the ice. He got to his feet.

They both ran for the hook. Jane got there first. She grabbed the chain. Nail seized her throat and they fell to the ground. He sat on Jane's chest and began to throttle. His lips were black and turning to metal. His right eye socket was burned out.

Contest of strength. Jane pushed his face away with a gloved hand. She gripped his leg, tried to tip him from her chest.

Something in the utility pocket of his trousers. Jane's knife.

She pressed fingers into his remaining eye. He roared in pain. He gripped her right arm and tried to snap it. She had the knife in her left hand. She flicked open the blade and stabbed him in the belly.

Nail convulsed. She threw him aside. She looked up. Sian had raised the hook. It hung fifty metres above their heads.

Nail lay on his back. He saw the hook high above him and realised what was about to happen. He screamed. His cry merged with the roar of breaking ice.

Sian hit Release. Gears disengaged. The chain spun free.

Jane rolled clear as the half-tonne hook slammed down like a fist. It punched clean through the ice leaving nothing of Nail but a fine pink blood-mist.

Sian engaged the gears and raised the chain. The hook rose from the depths, splitting ice, dripping seawater. Jane stepped on to the hook, and was lifted upward into the light.

Sian lowered Jane on to a walkway. Jane stepped from the hook. She stumbled and fell.

Sian and Punch climbed from the cab and ran to her. They helped her up.

'Are you all right?' asked Punch.

'I hurt my hip,' said Jane. 'I think I'm okay.' She looked around. 'Where's Ghost?'

Jane stood at the north railing and watched the Arctic ice slowly recede. A bleak landscape lit spectral white by moonlight.

Jane spoke into her radio.

'Ghost? Can you hear me?'

'*Jane? Where are you?*' A weak signal. Ghost, somewhere out on the ice, alone in the dark.

'I made it. I'm on the rig.'

'*You're all right?*'

'We're fine.'

'*Look after those kids, yeah? That's your mission. Keep them safe. Get them home.*'

'We're leaving now. We've cleared the ice. The current is taking us south. I'm so sorry, Gee. There's nothing I can do.'

'*These past few weeks. You and me. I wouldn't have missed them for the world.*'

'I love you, Rajesh.'

Ghost's reply was lost in white-noise crackle as his radio passed out of range.

Jane saw the pin-prick of a distress flare fired in the far distance. The star-shell burned intense red for a full minute then died away. Ghost's final salute.

Jane lay on her bunk and cried. Always dealt the losing hand.

You'll be alone. You'll be alone your whole damn life.

Maybe she made the wrong choice. Maybe she should have joined Nikki's weird commune. Become a member of the herd. Or maybe her old, fat self had been right all along. Why live? Why struggle? Why not jump from the refinery and end it all?

She stared at the ceiling and tried to think of a reason to keep breathing.

Keep them safe. Get them home.

Jane got up. She wiped her eyes and blew her nose. She showered and found fresh clothes. She limped to the canteen. She looked for Punch and Sian. She saw them through a porthole. They were standing on the helipad. She joined them outside.

Punch had a black box in his hand. He examined the gauge.

'Geiger counter,' he explained. 'They used to locate blockages in the treater by flushing isotopes through the pipes.'

'What's the reading?'

'Eighty. Standard background. I'll take a fresh reading every day. Not there's much we can do if we hit a radiation hot-spot. It's not like we can turn round and head the other way.'

'How's the fuel holding out?'

'We should be able to keep the lights on for a few weeks.'

'Food?'

'Some. Not much.'

'We'll make it,' said Jane. 'It'll be tough, but we'll make it.'

Jane made her way to the observation bubble. She settled herself in a chair and massaged her injured leg.

She powered up the radio and scanned the wavebands. Nothing but the pops and whistles of unmanned transmission equipment, military and civilian, singing to the ionosphere.

'*This is a test of the Emergency Broadcast System. The broadcasters of your area in voluntary cooperation with federal, state and local authorities have developed this system to keep you informed in the event of an emergency. If this had been an actual emergency the Attention Signal you just heard would have been followed by official information, news or instructions. This concludes the test of the Emergency Broadcast System.*'

Jane picked up the microphone.

'This is Kasker Rampart hailing any vessel, over.'

No reply.

'Mayday, mayday. This is Kasker Rampart. Can anyone hear me, over?'

No reply.

'Mayday, mayday. This is Jane Blanc aboard Con Amalgam refinery Kasker Rampart. Is anyone out there?'

Ghost

Midnight at the top of the world. Darkness. Lethal cold.

The Aurora Borealis. A flickering ion stream washes across the polar sky. Iridescent colour. Dancing emerald fire.

Rajesh Ghosh sits at the centre of the snow plain. A speck in vast white nothing. He is the last human north of the Arctic Circle now that cities lie in ruin, mankind has been swept away, and a strange new intelligence rules the earth.

He kneels on the ice, hands in his lap. He has taken off his coat and gloves. He sits in T-shirt and shorts. He will never move again.

His flesh has hardened to rock. His skin is frosted with snow crystals. His eyes have turned to glass. He is looking up. A white statue, smiling at the stars.

If you liked *Outpost*, you'll enjoy

The first Jack Nightingale supernatural thriller

STEPHEN LEATHER

Nightfall

'You're going to hell, Jack Nightingale':

They are words that ended his career as a police negotiator. Now Jack's a struggling private detective – and the chilling words come back to haunt him.

Nightingale's life is turned upside down the day that he inherits a mansion with a priceless library; it comes from a man who claims to be his father, and it comes with a warning. That Nightingale's soul was sold at birth and a devil will come to claim it on his thirty-third birthday – just three weeks away.

Jack doesn't believe in Hell, probably doesn't believe in Heaven either. But when people close to him start to die horrible, he is led to the inescapable conclusion that real evil may be at work. And that if he doesn't find a way out he'll be damned in hell for eternity.

'A great thriller with a devilish twist' James Herbert

Out now

Read on for a chilling extract . . .

HODDER

I

Jack Nightingale didn't intend to kill anyone when he woke up on that chilly November morning. He shaved, showered and dressed, made himself coffee and a bacon sandwich, and at no point did he even contemplate the taking of a human life, even though he had spent the last five years training to do just that. As a serving member of the Metropolitan Police's elite CO19 armed-response unit he was more than capable of putting a bullet in a man's head or chest if it was necessary and provided he had been given the necessary authorisation by a senior officer.

His mobile phone rang just as he was pouring the coffee from his cafetiere. It was the Co-ordinator of the Metropolitan Police's negotiating team. 'Jack, I've just had a call from the Duty Officer at Fulham. They have a person in crisis down at Chelsea Harbour. Can you get there?'

'No problem,' said Nightingale. After two courses at the Met's Bramshill Officer Training College he was now one of several dozen officers qualified to talk to hostage-takers and potential suicides in addition to his regular duties.

'I'm told it's a jumper on a ledge but that's all I have. I'm trying to get back up for you but we've got four guys tied up with a domestic in Brixton.'

'Give me the address,' said Nightingale, reaching for a pen.

He ate his bacon sandwich as he drove his MGB Roadster to Chelsea Harbour. During the three years he had worked as a negotiator he had been called to more than forty attempted suicides but on only three occasions had he seen someone take their own life. In his experience, people either wanted to kill themselves or they wanted to talk. They rarely wanted to do both. Suicide was a relatively easy matter. You climbed to the top of a high building or a bridge and you jumped. Or you swallowed a lot of tablets. Or you tied a rope around your neck and stepped off a chair. Or you took a razor blade and made deep cuts in your wrist or throat. If you were lucky enough to have a gun you put it in your mouth or against your temple and pulled the trigger. What you didn't do if you really wanted to kill yourself was say you were going to do it, then wait for a trained police negotiator to arrive. People who did that usually just wanted someone to listen to their problems and reassure them that their lives were worth living. Once they'd got whatever was worrying them off their chests they came off the ledge, or put down the gun or lowered the knife, and everyone cheered, patted Nightingale on the back and told him 'job well done'.

When he reached the address that the Duty Officer had given him, his way was blocked by a police car and two Community Support Officers in police-type uniforms and yellow fluorescent jackets. One pointed the way Nightingale had come and told him to turn around, in a tone that suggested his motivation for becoming a CSO had more to do with wielding power than helping his fellow citizens. Nightingale wound down the window and showed them his warrant card. 'Inspector Nightingale,' he said. 'I'm the negotiator.'

'Sorry, sir,' said the CSO, suddenly all sweetness and light. He gestured at a parked ambulance. 'You can leave your car there, I'll keep an eye on it.' He and his colleague moved aside to allow Nightingale to drive through. He pulled up behind the ambulance and climbed out, stretching and yawning.

If you'd asked Nightingale what he was expecting that chilly November morning, he'd probably have shrugged carelessly and said that jumpers tended to be either men the worse for drink, women the worse for anti-depressants or druggies the worse for their Class-A drug of choice, generally cocaine or amphetamines. Nightingale's drug of choice while working was nicotine so he lit himself a Marlboro and blew smoke at the cloudless sky.

A uniformed inspector hurried over, holding a transceiver. 'I'm glad it's you, Jack,' he said.

'And I'm glad it's you.' He'd known Colin Duggan for almost a decade. He was old school – a good reliable thief-taker who, like Nightingale, was a smoker. He offered him a Marlboro and lit it for him, even though smoking in uniform was a disciplinary offence.

'It's a kid, Jack,' said Duggan, scratching his fleshy neck.

'Gang-banger? Drug deal gone wrong?' Nightingale inhaled and held the smoke deep in his lungs.

'A kid kid,' said Duggan. 'Nine-year-old girl.'

Nightingale frowned as he blew a tight plume of smoke. Nine-year-old girls didn't kill themselves. They played with their PlayStations or Wiis, or they went rollerblading, and sometimes they were kidnapped and raped by paedophiles, but they never, ever killed themselves.

Duggan pointed up at a luxury tower block overlooking the Thames. 'Her name's Sophie, she's locked herself on the thirteenth-floor balcony and she's sitting there talking to her doll.'

'Where are the parents?' said Nightingale. There was a cold feeling of dread in the pit of his stomach.

'Father's at work, mother's shopping. She was left in the care of the au pair.' Duggan waved his cigarette at an anorexic blonde who was sitting on a bench, sobbing, as a uniformed WPC tried to comfort her. 'Polish girl. She was ironing, then saw Sophie on the balcony. She banged on the window but Sophie had locked it from the outside.'

'And what makes her think Sophie wants to jump?'

'She's talking to her doll, won't look at anyone. We sent up two WPCs but she won't talk to them.'

'You're supposed to wait for me, Colin,' said Nightingale. He dropped his cigarette onto the ground and crushed it with his heel. 'Amateurs only complicate matters, you know that.'

'She's a kid on a balcony,' said Duggan. 'We couldn't just wait.'

'You're sure she's a potential jumper?'

'She's sitting on the edge, Jack. A gust of wind and she could blow right off. We're trying to get an airbag brought out but no one seems to know where to find one.'

'How close can I get to her?'

'You could talk to her through the balcony window.'

Nightingale shook his head. 'I need to see her face, to watch how she reacts. And I don't want to be shouting.'

'Then there are two possibilities,' said Duggan. 'She's too high to use a ladder, so we can either lower you from the roof or we can get you into the flat next door.'

'Lower me?'

'We can put you in a harness and the Fire Brigade boys will drop you down.'

'And I talk to her hanging from a string like a bloody puppet? Come on, Colin, I'm a negotiator, not a bloody marionette.'

'The other balcony it is, then,' said Duggan. He flicked away his butt. 'Let's get to it.' He waved over a uniformed constable and told him to escort Nightingale up to the thirteenth floor. 'Except it isn't the thirteenth, it's the fourteenth,' said Duggan.

'What?'

'It's a superstitious thing. Don't ask me why. It is the thirteenth floor, but the lift says fourteen. It goes from twelve to fourteen. No thirteen.'

'That's ridiculous,' said Nightingale.

'Tell the developer, not me,' said Duggan. 'Besides, you're talking to the wrong person. You won't catch me walking under a ladder or breaking a mirror. I can understand people not wanting to live on the thirteenth floor.' He grinned at Nightingale. 'Break a leg, yeah?'

'Yeah,' said Nightingale. He nodded at the constable, a lanky specimen whose uniform seemed a couple of sizes too small for him. 'Lead on, Macduff.'

The constable frowned. 'My name's not Macduff,' he said.

Nightingale patted him on the back. 'Let's go,' he said. 'But first I want a word with the au pair.'

The two men went to the sobbing woman, who was still being comforted by the WPC. At least fifty people had gathered to stare up at the little girl. There were pensioners, huddled together like penguins on an ice floe, mothers with toddlers in pushchairs, teenagers chewing gum and sniggering, a girl in Goth clothing with a collie that grinned at Nightingale as he walked by, workmen in overalls, and a group of waitresses from a nearby pizza restaurant.

'Why aren't you up there, getting her down?' shouted a bald man, holding a metal tool box. He pointed at Nightingale and the young constable. 'You should do something instead of pissing about down here.'

'Can't you Taser him?' asked Nightingale.

'We're not issued with Tasers, sir,' said the constable.

'Use your truncheon, then.'

'We're not . . .' He grimaced as he realised that Nightingale was joking.

They reached the au pair, who was blowing her nose into a large white handkerchief. Nightingale acknowledged the WPC. 'I'm the negotiator,' he said.

'Yes, sir,' she said.

Nightingale smiled at the au pair. 'Hi, what's your name?' he asked.

'Inga.' The girl sniffed, dabbing her eyes with the handkerchief. 'Are you a policeman?'

'I'm Jack Nightingale,' he said, showing her his warrant card. 'I'm the one who's going to talk to Sophie.'

'Am I in trouble?'

'No, of course you're not,' said Nightingale. 'You did the right thing, calling the police.'

'Her parents will kill me,' said the au pair.

'They won't,' said Nightingale.

'They'll send me back to Poland.'

'They can't do that – Poland's in the EU. You have every right to be here.'

'They'll send me to prison, I know they will.'

Nightingale's heart hardened. The au pair seemed more concerned about her own future than about what was happening thirteen storeys up. 'They won't,' he said. 'Tell me, Inga, why isn't Sophie at school today?'

'She said she had a stomach-ache. She didn't feel well. Her mother said she could stay at home.'

'Her mother's shopping?'

The au pair nodded. 'I phoned her and she's coming back now. Her father's mobile phone is switched off so I left a message on his voicemail.'

'Where does he work?'

'In Canary Wharf.' Still sniffing, she took a wallet out of the back pocket of her jeans and fished out a business card. She gave it to Nightingale. 'This is him.'

Nightingale looked at it. Simon Underwood was a vice president at a large American bank. 'Inga, has Sophie done anything like this before?'

The au pair shook her head fiercely. 'Never. She's a quiet child. As good as gold.'

'Tell me what happened. How did she come to be on the balcony?'

'I don't know,' said the au pair. 'I was ironing. She was watching a Hannah Montana DVD but when I looked up she was on the balcony and she'd locked the door.'

'You can lock it from the outside?'

'There's only one key and she had it. I shouted at her to

378

open the door but it was like she couldn't hear me. I banged on the window but she didn't look at me. That was when I called the police.'

'And she wasn't sad this morning? Or angry? Upset by something or somebody?'

'She was quiet,' said the au pair, 'but she's always quiet.'

'You didn't argue with her about anything?'

The au pair's eyes flashed. 'You're going to blame me, aren't you? You're going to send me to prison?' she wailed.

'No one's blaming you, Inga.'

The au pair buried her face in her handkerchief and sobbed.

'Let's go,' Nightingale said to the constable.

'What will you do?' the officer asked, as they walked past the crowd of onlookers.

'Talk to her. See if I can find out what's troubling her, see what it is she wants.'

'She wants something?'

'They always want something. If they didn't they'd just go ahead and do it. The key is to find out what it is they want.'

'Wankers!' shouted the bald man with the tool box.

Nightingale stopped and glared at him. 'What's your problem, pal?'

'My problem is that there's a little girl up there and you tossers aren't doing anything about it.'

'And what exactly are you doing? Gawping in case she takes a dive off the balcony? Is that what you want? You want to see her slap into the ground, do you? You want to hear her bones break and her skull smash and see her blood splatter over the concrete? Because that's the only reason you could have for standing there. You're sure as hell not helping by shouting abuse and making a tit of yourself. I'm here to help, you're here on the off-chance that you might see a child die so I'd say that makes you the tosser. I'm going up there now to see how I can help her, and if you're still here when I get down I'll shove your tools so far up your arse that you'll be coughing up spanners for months. Are we clear, *tosser*?'

The bald man's face reddened. Nightingale sneered at him and made for the entrance. The constable hurried after him.

The reception area was plush with overstuffed sofas and a large coffee-table covered with glossy magazines. A doorman in a green uniform was talking to two PCs. 'Where are the stairs?' asked Nightingale.

The doorman pointed to three lift doors. 'The lifts are there, sir,' he said.

'I need the stairs,' said Nightingale.

'It's thirteen floors, sir,' said the constable at his side.

'I know it's thirteen floors, Macduff,' said Nightingale. He jerked his chin at the doorman. 'Stairs?'

The doorman pointed to the left. 'Around the side there, sir,' he said.

Nightingale hurried towards them, followed by the constable. He pushed through the doors and started up, taking the steps two at a time. The number of each floor was painted on the white wall in green, and by the time they'd reached the tenth floor both men were panting like dogs. 'Why can't we use the lift, sir?' gasped the constable. 'Is it procedure with jumpers?'

'It's because I hate lifts,' said Nightingale.

'Claustrophobia?'

'Nothing to do with confined spaces,' said Nightingale. 'I just don't like dangling over nothing.'

'So it's fear of heights?'

'It's fear of lifts,' said Nightingale. 'I'm fine with heights. As you're about to find out.'

They reached the twelfth floor. The policeman had taken off his helmet and unbuttoned his tunic. Nightingale's overcoat was draped over his shoulder.

They reached the thirteenth floor, though the number stencilled on the wall was '14'. Nightingale pulled open the door and went into the corridor. 'What number is her flat?' he asked.

'Fourteen C,' said the constable. 'We can get into Fourteen D. A Mr and Mrs Wilson live there and they've agreed to give us access.'

'Okay, when we get in there, keep the Wilsons away from the balcony. The girl mustn't see them and she sure as hell mustn't see you. Nothing personal, but the uniform could spook her.'

'Got you,' said the policeman.

'You'll be just fine, Macduff,' said Nightingale. He knocked on the door of Fourteen D. It was opened by a man in his early sixties, grey-haired and slightly stooped. Nightingale flashed his warrant card. 'Mr Wilson, I'm Jack Nightingale. I gather you're happy for me to go out on your balcony.'

'I wouldn't exactly say that I was happy, but we need to get that little girl back inside.'

He opened the door wide and Nightingale walked in with the constable. The man's wife was sitting on a flower-print sofa, her hands in her lap. She was also grey-haired, and when she stood up to greet Nightingale he saw that she had the same curved spine. 'Please don't get up, Mrs Wilson,' he said.

'What's going to happen?' she said anxiously. Like her husband she was well-spoken, with an accent that would have done credit to a Radio 4 announcer. They were good, middle-class people, the sort who would rarely cross paths with a policeman – Nightingale sensed their unease at having him and the constable in their home.

'I'm just going to talk to her, Mrs Wilson, that's all.'

'Would you like a cup of tea?' she asked.

Nightingale smiled. More often than not as a member of CO19 he was treated with contempt, if not open hostility, and the Wilsons were a breath of fresh air. 'You could certainly put the kettle on, Wilson' he said. 'Now, do you know Sophie?'

'We say hello to her, but she's a shy little thing, wouldn't say boo to a goose.'

'A happy girl?'

'I wouldn't say so,' said Mrs Wilson.

'She cries sometimes,' said her husband quietly. 'At night.'

'What sort of crying?' asked Nightingale. 'Screaming?'

'Sobbing,' said Mr Wilson. 'Her bedroom's next to our bathroom, and sometimes when I'm getting ready for bed I can hear her.'

'We've both heard her,' added Mrs Wilson. Her husband walked over to her and put his arm around her.

For a brief moment Nightingale flashed back to his own parents. His father had been equally protective of his mother, never scared to hold her hand in public or to demonstrate his affection in other ways. In his last memory of them they were standing at the door of their house in Manchester, his arm around her shoulders, as they waved him off to start his second year at university. His mother had looked up at Nightingale's father with the same adoration he saw now in Mrs Wilson's eyes.

'Any idea why she'd be unhappy?' Nightingale asked. 'Did you see her with her parents?'

'Rarely,' said Mr Wilson. 'They've been here – what, five years?' he asked his wife.

'Six,' she said.

'Six years, and I can count on the fingers of one hand the number of times I've seen Sophie with her mother or father. It's always an au pair, and they seem to change them every six months or so.' He looked at his wife and she nodded almost imperceptibly. 'One doesn't like to talk out of school but they don't seem the most attentive of parents.'

'I understand,' Nightingale said. He took his lighter and cigarettes from the pocket of his overcoat and gave it to the constable. 'Why don't you take a seat while I go out and talk to her?' he said to the Wilsons.

Mr Wilson helped his wife onto the sofa while Nightingale went to the glass door that led on to the balcony. It was actually a terrace, with terracotta tiles and space for a small circular white metal table, four chairs and several pots of flowering shrubs, and was surrounded by a waist-high wall.

The door slid to the side and Nightingale could hear traffic in the distance and the crackle of police radios. He stepped out slowly, then looked to the right.

The little girl was sitting on the wall of the balcony next door. She was holding a Barbie doll and seemed to be whispering to it. She was wearing a white sweatshirt with a blue cotton skirt and silver trainers with blue stars on them. She had porcelain-white skin and shoulder-length blonde hair that she'd tucked behind her ears.

There was a gap of about six feet between the terrace where he was and the one where she was sitting. Nightingale figured that he could just about jump across but only as a last resort. He walked slowly to the side of the terrace and stood next to a tall, thin conifer in a concrete pot. In the distance he could see the river Thames and far off to his left the London Eye. The child didn't seem to have noticed him, but Nightingale knew she must have heard the door slide open. 'Hi,' he said.

Sophie looked at him but didn't say anything. Nightingale stared out over the Thames as he slid a cigarette between his lips and flicked his lighter.

'Cigarettes are bad for you,' said Sophie.

'I know,' said Nightingale. He lit it and inhaled deeply.

'You can get cancer,' said Sophie.

Nightingale tilted his head back and blew two perfect smoke-rings. 'I know that too,' he said.

'How do you do that?' she asked.

'Do what?'

'Blow those rings.'

Nightingale shrugged. 'You just blow and stick your tongue out a bit,' he said. He grinned amiably and held out the cigarette. 'Do you want to try?'

She shook her head solemnly. 'I'm a child and children can't smoke, and even if I could smoke I wouldn't because it gives you cancer.'

Nightingale took another drag on the cigarette. 'It's a beautiful day, isn't it?' he said, his eyes on the river again.

'Who are you?' Sophie asked.

'My name's Jack.'

'Like *Jack and the Beanstalk*?'

'Yeah, but I don't have my beanstalk with me today. I had to use the stairs.'

'Why didn't you use the lift?'

'I don't like lifts.'

Sophie put the doll to her ear and frowned as if she was listening intently. Then she nodded. 'Jessica doesn't like lifts, either.'

'Nice name – Jessica.'

'Jessica Lovely – that's her full name. What's your full name?'

'Nightingale. Jack Nightingale.'

'Like the bird?'

'That's right. Like the bird.'

'I wish I was a bird.' She cuddled the doll as she stared across the river with unseeing eyes.

'I wish I could fly.'

Nightingale blew two more smoke-rings. This time they held together for less than a second before the wind whipped them apart. 'It's not so much fun, being a bird. They can't watch TV, they can't play video games or play with dolls, and they have to eat off the floor.'

Below a siren kicked into life, and Sophie flinched as if she'd been struck. 'It's okay,' said Nightingale. 'It's a fire engine.'

'I thought it was the police.'

'The police siren sounds different.' Nightingale made the

384

woo-woo-woo sound, and Sophie giggled. He leaned against the terrace wall. He had set his phone to vibrate and felt it judder in his inside pocket. He took it out and peered at the screen. It was Robbie Hoyle, one of his negotiator colleagues. He'd known Hoyle for more than a decade. He was an inspector with the Territorial Support Group, the force's heavy mob who went in with riot shields, truncheons and Tasers when necessary. Hoyle was a big man, well over six feet tall with the build of a rugby player, but he had a soft voice and was one of the Met's most able negotiators. 'Sorry, Sophie, I'm going to have to take this,' he said. He pressed the green button. 'Hi, Robbie.'

'I've just arrived, do you want me up there?'

'I'm not sure that's a good idea,' said Nightingale. Whenever possible the negotiators preferred to act in teams of three, one doing the talking, another listening and the third gathering intelligence, but Nightingale figured that too many men on the balcony would only spook the little girl.

'How's it going?' asked Hoyle.

'Calm,' said Nightingale. 'I'll get back to you, okay? Try to get rid of the onlookers, but softly-softly.' He ended the call and put the phone away.

'You're a policeman, aren't you?' said Sophie.

Nightingale smiled. 'How did you know?'

Sophie pointed down at Colin Duggan, who was staring up at them, shielding his eyes from the sun with a hand. Robbie Hoyle was standing next to him. 'That policeman there spoke to you when you got out of your car.'

'You saw me arrive, yeah?'

'I like sports cars,' she said. 'It's an MGB.'

'That's right,' said Nightingale, 'an old one. How old are you?'

'Nine,' she said.

'Well my car's twenty-six years old. How about that?'

'That's old,' she said. 'Very old.'

'There's another thing birds can't do,' said Nightingale. 'When

385

was the last time you saw a bird driving a car? They can't do it. No hands.'

Sophie pressed the doll to her ear as if she was listening to it, then took it away and looked at Nightingale. 'Am I in trouble?' she said.

'No, Sophie. We just want to be sure you're okay.'

Sophie shuddered, as if icy water had trickled down her spine.

'The girl who looks after you, what's her name?' asked Nightingale.

'Inga. She's from Poland.'

'She's worried about you.'

'She's stupid.'

'Why do you say that?'

'She can't even use the microwave properly.'

'I have trouble getting my video recorder to work,' Nightingale told her.

'Videoplus,' said Sophie.

'What?'

'Videoplus. You just put in the number from the newspaper. The machine does it for you. Everyone knows that.'

'I didn't.' A gust blew across from the river and Sophie put a hand on her skirt to stop it billowing up. Nightingale caught a glimpse of a dark bruise above her knee. 'What happened to your leg?' he asked.

'Nothing,' she said quickly.

Too quickly, Nightingale noticed. He blew smoke and avoided looking at her. 'Why didn't you go to school today?'

'Mummy said I didn't have to.'

'Are you poorly?'

'Not really.' She bit her lower lip and cuddled her doll. 'I *am* in trouble, aren't I?'

'No, you're not,' said Nightingale. He made the sign of the cross over his heart. 'Cross my heart you're not.'

Sophie forced a smile. 'Do you have children?'

Nightingale dropped the butt of his cigarette and ground it with his heel. 'I'm not married.'

'You don't have to be married to have children.' Tears ran down her cheeks.

'What's wrong, Sophie?'

'Nothing.' She sniffed and wiped her eyes on her doll.

'Sophie, let's go inside. It's cold out here.'

She sniffed again but didn't look at him. Nightingale started to pull himself up onto the wall but his foot scraped against the concrete and she flinched. 'Don't come near me,' she said.

'I just wanted to sit like you,' said Nightingale. 'I'm tired of standing.'

She glared at him. 'You were going to jump over,' she said. 'You were going to try to grab me.'

'I wasn't, I swear,' lied Nightingale. He sat down, swinging his legs as if he didn't have a care in the world but his heart was pounding. 'Sophie, whatever's wrong, maybe I can help you.'

'No one can help me.'

'I can try.'

'He said I mustn't tell anyone.'

'Why? Why can't you tell anyone?'

'He said they'd take me away. Put me in a home.'

'Your father?'

Sophie pressed her doll to her face. 'He said they'd blame me. He said they'd take me away and make me live in a home and that everyone would say it was my fault.'

The wind whipped up her skirt again. The bruise was a good six inches long. 'Did he do that?' said Nightingale.

Sophie pushed her skirt down and nodded.

'Let's go inside, Sophie – we can talk to your mummy.'

Sophie closed her eyes. 'She already knows.'

Nightingale's stomach lurched. His hands were palm down on the wall, his fingers gripping the concrete, but he felt as if something was pushing the small of his back. 'I can help you, Sophie. Just come inside and we'll talk about it. I can help you, honestly I can. Cross my heart.'

'You can't help me,' she said, her voice a monotone. 'No one can.' She lifted her doll, kissed the top of its head, and slid off the balcony without a sound.

Horrified, Nightingale thrust himself forward and reached out with his right hand even though he knew there was nothing he could do. 'Sophie!' he screamed. Her golden hair was whipping in the wind as she dropped straight down, still hugging the doll. 'Sophie!' He closed his eyes at the last second but he couldn't blot out the sound she made as she hit the ground, a dull, wet thud as if a wall had been slapped with a wet blanket.

Nightingale slid down the wall. He lit a cigarette with trembling hands and smoked it as he crouched there, his back against the concrete, his legs drawn up against his stomach.

The uniformed constable who had escorted him up the stairs appeared at the balcony door. 'Are you okay, sir?'

Nightingale ignored him.

'Sir, are you okay?' The constable's radio crackled and a female voice asked him for a situation report.

Nightingale stood up and pushed him out of the way.

'Sir, your coat!' the constable called after him.

The elderly couple were standing in the middle of the living room, holding each other. They looked at Nightingale expectantly but he said nothing as he rushed past them. He took the stairs three at a time, his fingers brushing the handrail as he hurtled down, his footsteps echoing off the concrete walls.

There were two paramedics and half a dozen uniformed officers in the reception area, all talking into their radios. Duggan was there and opened his mouth to speak, but Nightingale silenced him with a pointed finger and walked past.

Two female paramedics were crouched over the little girl's body. The younger of them was crying. Four firemen in bulky fluorescent jackets were standing behind the paramedics. One was wiping tears from his eyes with the back of a glove. Nightingale knew there was nothing anyone could do. No one survived a fall from thirteen floors. As he turned away he saw blood glistening around the body.

Hoyle was standing next to a PC, frowning as he spoke into his mobile. He put it away as Nightingale came up to him. 'Superintendent Chalmers wants you in his office, Jack,' he said. 'Now.'

Nightingale said nothing. He brushed past Hoyle and headed for his MGB.

'Now, Jack. He wants to see you now.'

'I'm busy,' said Nightingale.

'He'll want you to see the shrink, too,' said Hoyle, hurrying after him. It was standard procedure after a death.

'I don't need to see the shrink,' said Nightingale.

Hoyle put a hand on Nightingale's shoulder. 'It wasn't your fault, Jack. It's natural to feel guilty, to feel that you've failed.'

Nightingale glared at him. 'Don't try to empathise with me and don't sympathise. I don't need it, Robbie.'

'And what do I tell Chalmers?'

'Tell him whatever you want,' said Nightingale, twisting out of Hoyle's grip. He climbed into the MGB and drove off.